SUNSET AT NOON

The fourth King James of Scotland never lacked women to love him or men to die for him. His enigmatic figure moves across history in a blaze of colour, yet in death's shadow. Music, the roar of cannon, the clash of armour, the thunder of galloping hooves, are all about him. Yet at the core of the enigma is a strange silence. King in his teens, this Renaissance ruler was the darling of his people, yet believed the guilt for his father's death to lie darkly on his soul. To many women he was a tempestuous lover, to the Tudor princess, that child wife whom he never loved, he showed the rarest compassion, but it was to Margaret Drummond, it seems, that he gave his heart. Would he have made her his Queen? After Margaret's tragic death there is a reckless discordant gaiety about James not out of keeping with a man with a secret grief, as he gropes his way through the untimely darkness which had come down on his fairest hopes towards the sunset splendour of Flodden Field.

SUNSET
AT
NOON

Jane Oliver

COLLINS
ST JAMES'S PLACE, LONDON
1955

63944

PRINTED IN GREAT BRITAIN

COLLINS CLEAR-TYPE PRESS: LONDON AND GLASGOW

For

DR. & MRS. HERBERT GRAY

with much affection

*The sun shall be turned into darkness
and the moon into blood . . .*

ACTS 2: 20

PREFACE

ACCOUNT books, once the bane of overworked clerks, survive to be the candles of the chronicler. Letters may lie, diaries be written with a sly glance towards posterity, but the volumes of the four-hundred-year-old Accounts of the Lord High Treasurer of Scotland, published at the beginning of this century under the direction of the Depute Clerk Register of Scotland, bear the most faithful witness that I know. Here are the precious common-places, the undramatic, everyday gettings and spendings, of which, whether we like it or not, life in any century is so largely composed that the volumes which record them also illuminate character and motive, rescuing from the limbo of legend traditions which now seem too fantastic to be true.

Did King James IV wear an iron belt as a penance for the part he played in the events leading to his father's death? Tradition says yes, but debunking modernity says no. The Accounts not only put the facts beyond dispute, but cast in the process new light on a generation which swung between almost incredible extremes of superstition and indulgence. The King's iron belt is explicitly mentioned, not once, but twice, in the Accounts. And the legend that he wore it next his body is further confirmed by the entry, against the 26th of January, 1506, of worsted for use with it, no doubt at a time when it had caused chafing of the skin. Two and a half years later, in June, 1508, George Bell, lorimer, charges twenty-three shillings for making the King another iron belt, together with further items which prevent us from determining the cost of each. As James was then thirty-five, the implication that a slight increase in girth made a new belt necessary is tempting. It also suggests, perhaps, that he wore a hinged iron band, rather than a chain, to which links could have been added as required.

No expenditure, fortunately, seems to have been too trivial for the Treasurer to record. Specially interesting are the entries of the King's casual kindnesses to all sorts of people. Old wives brought him presents of butter, eggs or strawberries, a poor child took him by the hand, a crooked vicar sang to him, and each was rewarded. Light is also thrown on customs now forgotten which were once part of daily life. When James distracted attention from the choir's singing by tramping into church with chiming spurs, he paid 'spur silver' to the choristers. 'Bridle silver' was given to the men who brought him horses. Any servant injured in his service was cared for, and farmers were compensated for damage done by the royal huntsmen to standing crops.

Here also is the diverse tale of the ladies who held a place in the King's affections, the children to whom he was devoted, the names of his jesters, the expenses of his wedding, the fee he gave to the barber-surgeon for allowing him to extract teeth, the sums spent on the nostalgic search for the mysterious Fifth Essence and the Philosopher's Stone. Did he, who was so often called fickle, indeed remember Margaret Drummond to the day of his death? Did he allow the ladies in attendance on his English bride to shear him like Samson on the morning after his wedding? What did he eat? What were his hobbies? How much did he spend at cards?

The answers are all there. The very fabric of a century may be unfolded from the Lord High Treasurer's safe-keeping like some gorgeous tapestry. Armoured knights and distracting ladies move among chanting monks, thrifty merchants and sturdy vagabonds about the medieval scene along dusty bridle-paths winding through a landscape garnished with forests and castles and waterfalls, against a sky of madonna blue, across which the winds shepherd a flock of fleece-white clouds.

King James was a sufficiently gifted linguist to delight the Spanish Ambassador, Don Pedro de Ayala, who loved Scotland so well that he was recalled to Spain. For their Spanish Majesties, Ferdinand and Isabella, had already promised the Infanta Catherine to King Henry for his son Arthur, in the fateful marriage which was to have such unexpected consequences. From Don Pedro we learn that James spoke 'Latin, very well, French, German, Flemish, Italian and Spanish.' He also spoke Gaelic, or as Don Pedro put it, ' the language of the savages who live in some parts of Scotland and on the islands.'

At his Court, therefore, several languages seem still to have been spoken, though Scots was becoming the accepted tongue of the gentle and simple, as its use in official records, such as the Accounts, definitely shows. James, who was a linguist and probably proud of it, no doubt welcomed the chance of displaying his skill. So I have used a uniform English, enriched by occasional Scottish idiom, for the conversation of the King and his immediate circle, and reserved the Scots tongue for other ranks, in an attempt to show that though those in Court circles knew and spoke Scots, they also used such languages as French, Latin or Gaelic, in a pastiche which it would be almost impossible for me to convey or anyone to understand. Those who used Scots all the time have been allowed to do so.

My gratitude for all sorts of advice and help is due to more people than I know how to thank. As ever, I owe much to Dr. Agnes Mure Mackenzie that no mere mention of her books can convey. Still more I appreciate the patience and pungency of her correspondence, in which not only her great knowledge, but her greater love of our dramatic past seem almost to leap from the page. But since this book went to press the news of her sudden death has saddened, it seems, all Scotland. I also acknowledge with gratitude the kindness of Miss J. S. Lindsay in checking my rendering of some of James's correspondence in Latin; and of Rouge Dragon Pursuivant for supplying me with heraldic details of Margaret Tudor's wedding procession, also for showing me the sword and dagger of Spanish workmanship, displayed in the College of Arms, which expert opinion, I was delighted to learn, now regards as of too late a date to have been taken from James's body. (My contention being that the King's body was never, in fact, found, and that it was the remains of one of his bodyguard, wearing the royal device, which was taken south by the victors after Flodden, leaving those of James and the men who had died for him to lie only Heaven now knows where.)

I also have to thank Lord Elibank, C.M.G., D.S.O., Miss Marion Lochhead, Dr. C. A. Malcolm, of the Signet Library, Mrs. M. V. Murdoch, Miss Isobel Rae, Professor Sayles and Dr.

Douglas Simpson of the University of Aberdeen for the loan of important books and for much helpful information, also the staff of the London Library for all their work in tracing and dispatching the many volumes I required. I also owe a unique debt to Mrs. E. D. Lukens, for criticism illuminated by the rarest understanding, and the care which has never once failed through‑ out the arduous business of preparing a long and practically illegible typescript for the publisher.

PART ONE

1480-1488

CHAPTER ONE

THE lean man in the greasy black habit assessed the mood of his audience with an unobtrusive, expert glance, then rolled his eyes upwards, shuddering into rigidity as the liverishly tinged crescents grew almost semi-lunar in the shadow of the hood he had drawn forward to hide his clerical tonsure. The recently consecrated Archbishop of St. Andrews, himself a distinguished amateur of astrology, was known to tolerate the allied arts. But other churchmen were not so well disposed towards the exhibitions of sorcery from which quite a useful sum never found its way into the Priory's coffers. It was, on the whole, safer to remain anonymous.

Moreover, the King, as his employer had warned him, was no fool, to be satisfied with such mountebank tricks as would have disposed of a pack-load of love-philtres to the lads and lasses at a May Day fair. He must do better than that. If his performance were inadequate he would be returned to the menial duties from which his necromancies had rescued him.

He did his best, therefore, his teeth locked in a sensational rigor, body arched and limbs rigid, a little froth spilling from the corners of his greyish lips. His breathing rattled in his throat and his limbs jerked like those of a puppet on strings. Covering his face with his hands, he seemed to shut out a vision so terrible that a groan shuddered upwards, as if from the depths of his bowels.

The King, sombrely intent, leant forward, his slight limbs huddled in the heavy robe he had drawn about him against the winter chill of the secluded chamber under the battlements of the castle set high on Stirling's rock. Such seclusion pleased him, sensitively aware as he was of his own shortcomings. For he, the third James Stewart to rule Scotland, lacked both the physical beauty and triumphant health which had done so much to endear his forebears to their people. In his late twenties now, he remained punily unathletic, regrettably clumsy, in spite of all his in-

structors' efforts, with sword and spear, even timidly awkward
with the horses he had ridden since childhood.

Had he been base-born, they would have made a clerk of
him, and in the cloisters he would have fared well enough, for
his intelligence was keen as the lance-points of those who run a
course *à l'outrance*. But in fifteenth-century Scotland a king must
have other qualities if he were to hold the respect of the arrogant,
easily angered, hard-riding and shrewd-striking men he ruled.
Over-sensitive, as he was over-intelligent, the King guessed at the
patronage in their smiles when he ventured to join them at their
pastimes, the sly winks exchanged when he made shift to couch
a lance in the lists, their irritable tolerance of his bungling when
his horse swerved unbidden or his hawk took another man's
prey.

He made too much of it, as thin-skinned people do. Had he
persisted, they would have admired his courage and tried to show
him their skill. With a sense of humour, he might have mocked
his clumsiness and so defeated the loneliness it brought upon him.
But humour he lacked utterly, and though he was not without
courage, it was of another kind. So he withdrew from the company of those he could not rival. Then, because loneliness
dismayed him, he chose baser-born associates: some were
gifted in the arts, others masters of various crafts, others again
adept only in the use of flattery. More darkly still, the eager
curiosity of his race, which had so far found its fulfilment in
adventurous exploits, knightly extravagance, or in the love of
women, turned inwards to seek fulfilment in practices which at
their most innocent must impoverish him; and at the other
extreme might threaten his very soul. In his avid search for
knowledge which might bring power, for wealth which offered
security, for companionship which promised consolation, he was
ready to reach far into the darkness of forbidden things, beyond
the pale set by Holy Church for the safeguarding of those in her
care.

So now he listened, huddled in his furred robe, to the mouth-
ings of the creature who had been brought to him as one who had
come to terms with the unseen. It was dark as well as cold in the
comfortless chamber, for the brazier's glowing coals had been

daunted by the secret powders flung upon them, from which
coloured smoke had now risen to hover in strange forms that
might well possess a lurid life of their own, malevolently over-
shadowing the sterterously breathing man who sprawled obscurely
below. The scene had a subtle horror, a suggestion of nameless
evil, for the hovering shapes of vapour seemed to have appeared
in response to the suffumigation rather than to have been caused
by it. And though the concentric circles chalked on the flags from
which the rushes had been swept aside bore in every arc of their
circumference the terrible names of God, the watchers were aware
of a vile stench which was said to indicate the approach of lost
creatures from the Pit, avid for sustenance offered by men reckless
of their salvation, made desperate by the assured damnation of
their own souls.

The suspense mounted. Incautiously, it seemed, the sorcerer
had overstepped the limits of the protective circles, and now
writhed as if invisible hordes plucked at his limbs, seared his
flesh with sulphurous breath, sought to gouge out his very eyes.
The King still watched, unstirring, but among the others consternation grew as the drama proceeded, for the supernatural had
approached them more nearly than they had either expected or
desired.

They were an oddly assorted company for a King's companions. None was nobly born. Schevez, Archbishop and
astrologer, had climbed almost from the gutter to the highest
position in the Scottish Church by working on the King's avidity
for occult knowledge, ridding himself of his venerable predecessor
by the useful charge of heresy. Cochrane was an architect, whose
resourcefulness had produced the sorcerer as an expedient to
alienate the King from his nobler subjects, above all from his own
kin. He had ability in his proper sphere. It was his tragedy that
ambition had raised him above it. Rogers, the musician, shared a
genuine love of his art with the King for whom that love was to
prove disastrous. Each of the other parasites had a certain skill,
but they were greedy rather than bold, so that, as they watched
the conjuration, sweat trickled towards their eyes and tremors
ran coldly down their spines.

It was impossible to tell, in the choking dimness, what the

King himself thought. It would still have been hard to say, even had the light been stronger. For he had learned to conceal his feelings since the sultry August morning, soon after his ninth birthday, on which he had been called to become the nominal ruler of Scotland. When the great brazen cannon, once the pride of his grandfather at the siege of Roxburgh, had burst and killed his father at the very same spot twenty-four years later, the shocking thing had seemed like a blow from heaven beneath which his father had died and he himself must cower. Outwardly at least, he was obedient. But inwardly, from the first, he had rebelled. He had never wished to be a King; his heart's desire lay not with the brawling, vigorous, bawdy men of action, but with the intellectual minority whom the rest of his subjects despised. A King under compulsion, he was prouder to call himself a philosopher. Those who shared his interests were less his subjects than his friends. To them he could turn for sympathy, understanding, even love, as he believed. At their desire for power he did not guess.

But the sorcerer now began to mumble more coherently, and the unobtrusive addition of a few drops of viscous liquid produced from the smouldering coals a greenish glare which illuminated the sweat-streaked pallor of the faces of his audience, before the deft change of phials suffused them in a lurid glow.

"I see . . . I see . . . I see . . ."

He covered his face with his hands, and the folds of his drab habit were agitated as if by the transit of forms invisible. The horrified watchers were aware of an icy draught, which seemed to indicate the passage of creatures who never hoped to see the light of heaven. It was, in fact, caused by the surreptitious opening of a door behind the folds of the heavy arras which hung, weighted by the dust of years, from the high tenterhooks, as a small boy, who had been exploring the by-ways of the castle, now came unawares upon the infernal conclave. James, Duke of Rothesay, the King's eldest son, flattened himself against the rough stones of the four-foot thick wall, too startled to make his escape by the stairs up which he had just come, though his half-numb fingers scrabbled for the bolts and contrived to open the door again so that the draught whirled once more up the stone

spiral. The heavy hangings billowed away from it, then were
sucked back as he let it close. It was fortunate that the men about
the brazier were too engrossed to notice the bulge which revealed
his slight figure as the hangings swung back against the wall.
Scared men can be hasty with their daggers. But no head turned,
and after a little while young James discovered a convenient hole
in the arras, and put an inquisitive eye to it, holding his nose
against the tickling danger of a sneeze.

Among the coils of stinking, livid vapour the sorcerer still
crouched. One shaking index finger pointed to a horror that the
others could not see, the progress of which he seemed to trace on
the unburdened air.

"I see . . . a lion devoured . . . by his own whelps. . . ."

A lion. . . . The company was instantly alert, accustomed as
they were to interpreting verbal descriptions in pictorial terms, to
see an armed knight coupled with the device he bore on his shield.
A lion . . . the unqualified term was not precise enough. Lions
rampant, lions combatant, blood-red gules or raven sable; the
device was borne by too many noble Scottish houses for the
listeners to glean much from the hint wrung from the dwellers
in the nether world; even, perhaps, from the prince of the powers
of the air.

The sorcerer's hands were now grappling with those of an
unseen adversary who appeared to be strangling him. Gasping,
the listeners imagined the figure of a monstrous fiend among
the billowing wreaths of stinking smoke, now sulphurous and
yellowish, which stifled them till they seemed to feel hellish hands
fumbling at their own throats.

"I see a King . . ."

Ah, that made it all clear. The lion rampant, gules, was the
emblem of the King of Scots. The King . . . the King was
threatened. Heads turned, with intake of breath, towards the
motionless figure in their midst. Alone among them all, the King
himself gave no sign that he had heard.

"A King . . . is in danger from his near kindred. . . ." gasped
the sorcerer. Then, his message given, his symbolism made clear,
he crumpled, seemed to fold in upon himself like a sawdust-
stuffed toy, then collapsed into a stupor of exhaustion which was

quite evidently genuine. No one paid any attention to him now. He was left to lie there, like a puppet indeed, whose performance is at an end, while the spectators clustered round Cochrane and the King.

King James had gone very pale, his sallow skin yellower than ever as the blood drained from it. His eyes, darkly encircled, seemed enormous. As he threw aside the heavy robe which had suddenly become oppressive, he stood before them in doublet and hose, spindle-shanked, his knees sagging a little, his fingers fumbling uncertainly at his lips. To find that his cherished science had so betrayed him by threatening his own death was as disillusioning as to have his hand bitten by a faithful dog. Abruptly he turned away, preparing to leave the chamber without another glance at smoking brazier or exhausted sorcerer.

" I'll have no more of it." He spoke like an outraged child. " Ill-omened prating——"

Cochrane, tall, handsome and confident, thrust an arm under the King's, crooking it about his patron's thin elbow. His voice was resonant, rallying.

" My lord, ill omens can serve us well enough. It is better to be warned than to run, witless, into the danger they ward off. Are you so sure of your kinsmen's loyalty that you can afford to ignore what the spirits have said of them? "

The King's teeth, dirling in his head, were not to be silenced. He thrust his fist against them and spoke defiantly: " I have many kinsmen . . . they cannot all desire my death. . . ."

Cochrane smiled. " The spirits indicated your near kinsmen, my lord. They spoke also of a lion that his whelps devoured——"

" A likely thing——"

" By whelps," said Cochrane hastily, " it seems, my lord, that full-grown creatures must be intended though younger than yourself. Brothers, maybe——"

The King drew in a quick breath. He saw them as Cochrane spoke, his two younger brothers, who surpassed him in all but years, either of whom would have worn the crown of Scotland with so much grace. Albany . . . Mar . . .

" No," he said sharply. Fair, knightly, extolled, all those things which he was not, they were still his brothers. They had been children by one hearth, shared the same bed. . . . He could think no such ill of them. . . .

"My lord Archbishop . . ." Piteously, the King implored consolation from the representative of Holy Church. Archbishop Schevez pursed his lips and frowned. He had given his approval of the sorcerer's invitation, but he had, in fact, a poor opinion of the scallywag. Given a little time, and a few of the inducements which inquisitors found so helpful, he fancied he could persuade Cochrane's cat's-paw to name the sum he had been offered for this evening's performance. But he did not say so. His own elevation to his high office had been in the face of too much aristocratic opposition for him to defend the established order of nobility against other adventurers. He temporised, therefore, running his tongue over his full lips, as he chose his words.

"My lord the King, we have witnessed a strange conflict. It may be that the message wrung from the infernal powers by that fellow yonder "—he jerked his head towards the prostrate figure —" is not in all respects accurate. It is notorious that fallen spirits speak the truth only when it is less profitable to lie——"

"Then it is not so? My brothers——"

The Archbishop shook his head portentously. "On your brothers' state of mind, my lord, I should not care to venture. Within a tissue of falsehood, there is often a grain of truth, which must be purged from the baser elements as we purge the metals in our crucibles. It is no light task to distinguish the truth hidden among so many errors in the human heart, my lord. He who undertakes to do so must be equipped with the virtues of——"

But the King was in no mood for a pious dissertation. Already distraught by the suggestion of disloyalty among his kinsmen, the Archbishop's ponderous evasions merely worked on his anxiety like a ferment. But Cochrane, the boldest of the favourites whose continued prosperity depended on the King's alienation from those closest to the throne, watched the progress of his scheme with his head slightly on one side, as an artist views the progress of work with which he is not displeased.

"There . . . is also my son," said the King abruptly. "My brothers make much of him. If they are indeed against me . . . then he too . . ."

The sudden convulsion of the arras might well have betrayed the outraged small boy behind it. But the attention of those in the smoke-wreathed chamber was concentrated now on the King. The Archbishop bowed in silence, and the movements of his hands, like those of Pilate, refused further part in the affair. But while he did not confirm, neither did he deny the possibility which had been suggested to the King's anxious mind.

" The lion devoured by its whelps. . . ." murmured the King. He beat his head with his fists, as if to beat the thought from his brain. " Surely . . . it could not be. . . ." His voice implored the denial which those who surrounded him were not prepared to give. If the great nobles had their way, Cochrane and the others knew well, it would be bundle and go for the lot of them. It was expedient, therefore, that the King should lose faith in his kinsmen, for fear his kinsmen should be too successful in influencing him against his friends.

" Surely it could not be. . . ." said the King again. His voice was anguished, pleading against the evidence, as he supposed, of the unseen.

" Could it not, my lord? " Cochrane pondered. " Is it not natural for such a handsome head as that of my lord of Albany to consider that a crown would become it well? Have you not yourself seen him accept the applause of the crowd after the jousting as if he were King of more than the lists that day? "

" He has skill in such matters and I have not," the King muttered unhappily. But he remembered well how it had irked him to have to take his place among the spectators in the tapestry-decked stands, while his two younger brothers clashed in their armour past the lines of delighted ladies, laughing in the shadow of their raised visors at the shower of favours and rosebuds which greeted them as they jogged by.

" My lord of Mar, it is said, has tried his skill in other matters. Magic has been his latest study. . . ."

The King forced a laugh. " My brother of Mar is but a lad barely out of his teens. If he consults magicians for love-philtres and forgets to tell his confessor, who shall blame him overmuch? " He spoke anxiously, for he, the ungainly, bashful eldest brother, had a protective devotion for a brilliant lad who was deft where he was clumsy, bold where he was timid, admired where he was, as he well knew, pitied for his ineptitude in all spectacular things.

" It is not a question of love-philtres, my lord," murmured Cochrane, shaking his head.

" Of what, then? " asked the King.

Cochrane sighed. " Of darker things, I fear. What would you say to stories of waxen images, carefully fashioned, so that there can be no mistake? If further proof were needed, such images, my lord, are sworn to wear a crown. Spells of power draw the spirit from the victim as he sleeps into the image which is set to dwindle before a fire, or pierced with sharp points till life forsakes the man it stands for."

" It is all fancy," said the King desperately.

" Is it all fancy, my lord, that you have drooped lately with great weariness, so that you have found it hard to keep your thoughts even on those studies of design and music which were once your delight? Is it not true that you have refused to take your turn with Torphichen at sword-play more than once of late, though formerly such skill as he could teach you was your heart's desire? "

" I have been weary, yes," the King admitted. " But the burden of government lies heavily on me. There is much to be arranged as regards the English alliances. My brother Albany's own English marriage is in question as soon as the present affair may be annulled——"

" As to that, my lord, I understand that my lord of Albany is on excellent terms with England. On such terms, perhaps, as one King is with another——"

" I will not believe it," King James groaned.

" Very properly, my lord. Yet it may be that the spirits see further into such dark matters than we do."

" It is true," the King whispered, " that sometimes I feel the very life within me drain away as if the physician had opened a vein and afterwards forgotten to bind it up again. Life seems too burdensome to be endured. As if I——"

" My lord," Cochrane murmured in extreme concern, " so, so precisely, a man speaks and feels when the image which represents his spirit is wasting before a slow fire. We know not how these things may be contrived, we can but recognise their working. Believe me, you are in the gravest danger. . . ."

The King's eyes widened. " Can it be that a man's soul may be reft from him as slyly as the meat is sucked from an egg-shell by a wanton lad? "

Raising his eyebrows, Cochrane turned to the Archbishop.

" No doubt, by those that have the skill," the Archbishop said.

The King took his head in his hands. It was true that he felt ill, lifeless, drained of vitality as if of blood. He pushed his knuckles against his eyes, trying to rid his mind of the persistent picture of an ungainly wax image, long-necked, spindle-shanked, wearing a royal crown, which slowly began to lose shape, to blur, to run together as great tears of wax bled from the shrunken limbs.

" Such skill must be derived from the aid of creatures of the devil. . . ."

The Archbishop, who had been watching the King intently, his expression calculating and withdrawn, now spoke with the authority of his office.

" Creatures of the devil indeed, whose purpose is our damnation."

" I take it, my lord, the King," Cochrane wheedled, " that you will at least investigate the reports we have so strangely gained? If they prove to have substance——"

" I do not care to owe my safety to creatures of the Pit, whose business, as the Archbishop himself has just declared, is our damnation," said the King.

The Archbishop shook his head judicially. " My lord the King, I did not say that such revelations as we have just witnessed came from the creatures of the Pit. The evocation of the spirits was most properly conducted, and the intermediary appropriately protected. I said, if you will permit me to remind you, that if any man sought your destruction by means of images pierced or molten to the accompaniment of spells, such power could not be derived from above, but from below."

" If then, my lord of Mar——" said Cochrane quickly.

But the King had risen, fists clenched, his body trembling. For a moment he seemed almost prepared to strike the man who had presumed too much on his influence and tried to work too fast. Then he let his hands fall to his sides, shrugging himself away from the persuasion of that pleasant, warning voice.

" I will hear no more against my lords of Albany and Mar," he said peevishly. " I thank you for the diversion you have arranged for us. We have been well entertained, have we not, my lord Archbishop? "

In silence the Archbishop inclined his head.

" You have a gifted fellow there," the high voice trailed on, " but I wish to see no more of him. At least . . . not at this time. My lord Archbishop, I will now go with you to the chapel to hear the office said. . . ."

The Archbishop bowed approval. He and the King left the chamber together, while Cochrane, grinning at the group of his associates, took the opportunity of rousing the prostrate sorcerer with a kick.

" Away with you. We wish to hear no more of your groaning."

The sharp-faced monk scrambled to his feet, deferential but persistent. " And my fee, sirs? I was promised three angels for my pains. I did well enough, you'll grant? The powers of the air were stubborn, I went in fear of my life because of their displeasure. . . ."

" Bah! " said Cochrane, tweaking the coins from the embroidered pouch which hung at his belt with his dagger, " spare us your patter, fool. Take these and hold your tongue. I may need you again."

" The lord Archbishop was not displeased? You will speak for me if need be? "

" I care not what anathemas he may thunder at you," Cochrane said carelessly. " His coming was no affair of mine. The King brought him."

" If the Prior were to hear . . ."

" Bread and water for a week would harm you little. Get out of my sight."

As the fellow shambled away, the others more deliberately prepared to follow him, questioning Cochrane eagerly. Did he think they had achieved anything with the King?

Cochrane shrugged. " I cannot say. If I know anything of

him he will pretend to disbelieve all he has heard. But the memory will work in him like the yeast in a goodwife's dough. Later, we shall see. For the present, nothing is to be gained by persuading him further. That you can see for yourselves."

"If he should tell my lord of Albany of this, naming us for bringing the sorcerer to speak against him——"

"He will not. He will brood," said Cochrane confidently. "You know the secret habit of his mind. And who are you to say the sorcerer but did our bidding when he spoke against my lords of Albany and Mar? What do you know of the workings of the unseen world? Would it be so strange if he had caught a glimpse of things hid from us? My lord of Albany may well have dealings with the King of England, who is perhaps ready to see him in his brother's place. More ready, it may be, to see dissension in Scotland. And no doubt my lord of Mar seeks the aid of magic arts to rid him of the King who curbs his pleasures. If so, is it not as well the King should know?"

"It seems likely to make little odds whether he knows or not. He has refused to believe it," said Torphichen, the master of arms, gloomily.

Cochrane grinned. "You are all too rash. You seek to have men move as fast as the spirits that that stinking fellow from the Priory kitchen conjured out of the smoke. Wait and see what comes of it. Seeds must be sown. And whether the soil be a garden's earth, a woman's womb, or a King's brain, none will bring forth its fruit overnight. Come back to my lodgings. The cask of claret I ordered from the shippers of Leith has had time to settle now."

Still talking, he led them away. The chamber, dimmed by the last wreaths of smoke from the brazier in which the fire had died to a few embers, was apparently empty. But the agitation of the arras indicated a struggle behind it, from which a red-headed small boy of about seven, dressed in cobwebbed crimson velvet, presently emerged, his face daubed with dirt as he violently rubbed his itching nose, ready to bolt behind the arras again if his father and his friends returned. But only a page, a few months older than himself, came in whistling. At the sight of the dishevelled small boy he paused, hands on hips and grinning broadly, then bowed low with the wariness of one who knew that any suggestion of mockery might not be well received.

" So this is where you are, my lord James. The ladies of the Queen your mother's household are skirling upstairs and down seeking you."

" Let them skirl," said young James vaguely. He had other matters on his mind. Still bemused by all he had heard, understanding little, he was yet aware that danger and disaster threatened his young uncles of Albany and Mar. Anxiously he sought, frowning, for some way in which that horrible, shaking creature who rolled about on the ground could have been mistaken. Then his face cleared. The man had spoken of a lion. . . . Why should that lion have been his father? Was there not a real lion in the castle, kept behind bars, both as a strange beast and as the emblem of the Scottish crown? Perhaps . . . perhaps already it had been set on by its whelps. If so . . . If so his father need not be angered and his uncles of Albany and Mar would be safe.

" Whither now? " the page demanded, as young James hurried towards the stairhead. It was no light matter, to be put in charge of the prince, he grumbled, as the younger boy's voice floated faintly, incomprehensibly, up to him, defiant in its irrational hope.

" I am . . . going to see if the lion's whelps are devouring it in the den below. . . ."

" What whelps? " the page called after him. " It is an old and mangy beast that has been caged alone for years. . . ."

But James had no wish to hear. Thrusting his fingers into his ears, he pounded on.

CHAPTER TWO

THE little pony, its head held by a stable lad, stood stock-still, dozing in the warm sunshine, while young James sauntered towards it, outwardly nonchalant, but with his heart leaping so wildly within him that he fancied unless he kept his teeth clenched it would shoot out of his mouth. For among the casually chatting nobles assembled in the Castle yard to watch him set out for his riding lesson lounged his uncles of Albany and Mar, whose approval meant more to him than the applause of any others on earth, or the prospect, occasionally held out to him by his confessor, of a place among the blessed in heaven.

James broke into a run as he neared the drowsy pony, clutched saddle and mane, jolted his feet together, then sprang, as he had seen his uncles do, straight from the ground, without putting foot to stirrup, into the saddle. . . . For a breathless instant he gloried in his triumph, heard the startled laughter, the crackle of clapping hands, from the spectators by the gateway, then realised that he had brought an unexpected crisis upon himself. For the pony, roused by his sudden arrival, flung up its head, wrenching it free from the stable lad, and bolted at full gallop across the courtyard with the reins flying.

There was nothing that the terrified spectators dared do. Had they run out, they would have risked alarming the pony more, and a shy might have sent the little boy flying. Alexander of Albany checked his brother of Mar as he started forward.

" Wait——"

" If the beast trips over the reins James will be thrown," said the young Earl of Mar anxiously.

" Nothing of the sort," said Albany with confidence. " See how he reaches for the reins with one hand while he grips the mane with the other. The child has the way of it——"

" He might have broken his neck," sighed Mar, still too badly scared for his young nephew's safety to admire the way he balanced on the pony's back like a little cat, clawing for the reins while the startled beast curvetted and pranced. But Alexander, setting his hands on his hips, threw back his head and roared with laughter. Himself a dare-devil whom danger intoxicated, the sight of his young nephew's escapade delighted him.

" Who would have thought that that poor stick our brother ever sired him? " Alexander murmured behind his hand. " By all the saints in heaven he is more like a child of mine."

Mar chuckled, as he watched James straighten himself in the

saddle, the reins clutched in his free hand; then, crimson-faced
and with his red-gold hair flying, he kicked the pony slyly with his
unspurred heels, so that they whirled again round the courtyard
at a gallop.

"The young devil," Albany laughed. "Did you see that,
John?"

John, Earl of Mar, nodded, watching young James grin as he
came round again, cheerfully acknowledging the applause of the
little crowd which had gathered to see him. When he reined
back at last, his uncles, as he had hoped, came towards him
smiling.

"Well done, moppet," said Alexander. "We shall make a
horseman of you yet, I believe."

"You scared me half out of my wits," said the Earl of Mar.

James looked at them worshipfully as they stood by his pony's
side, their fair heads bare, the grace of their long limbs evident
in every careless movement, their blue eyes meeting his with
comradely affection. They were his pattern of all knightly valour
and beauty. To them, rather than to his father, he looked for an
example of all right conduct. From them he would accept praise
or blame with equal homage. With the sun and the stars about
them, they bestrode the mountains. When their actions were
strange it was but because he had lost sight of them among the
clouds.

Albany waved aside the Master of Horse who was waiting to
escort the King's son. "I will teach him myself," he said. "I
could scarcely hope for a better pupil. John, you and I will give
the lad the beginnings of his knightly instruction. Bring me a
wooden lance and a light shield," he commanded. And an
esquire ran.

Rigid with delight, James listened passionately to every word,
as his glorious uncle showed him how the shield slung on the left
arm must cover the heart, while the left hand grasped the reins
and the right hand couched the spear along the forearm, steadying
it between arm and side. When they brought the mimic weapons
he grasped them deftly, and Albany's sandy brows rose as James
took up his position without an instant's fumbling.

"Who has taught you before?"

" No man, Uncle."

" Strange. You sit there as to the manner born."

" He must have watched the jousting, brother," said the Earl of Mar.

" No, sir. My father forbade it," said James.

The two young men made briefly expressive sounds. " Did he indeed? Why so? " Albany demanded.

" He said I must first gain book-learning. . . ."

John of Mar grinned. " He would make a clerk of you, eh? And what do you say to that? "

" I like book-learning well enough," said James, " but I would sooner learn the things that you and my uncle of Albany can teach."

" I fear," said Alexander, " that I have not much book-learning. That "—he shrugged his indifference—" I am content to leave to the clerks. But I have some skill in knightly things. So also has your uncle of Mar. That we can teach, since you would gladly learn."

" Indeed I would," said James eagerly.

" Then we will teach you what we know. John, take shield and spear and run a course in sport. Now, lad, remember. Never strike a man's horse, nor yet his thigh or groin. Aim, for a while, at the centre of his shield. Later we can consider the blow to the helm which is the most worshipful. But since it is the hardest——"

" Let me essay it, then, Uncle," James begged.

Albany laughed. " Why, popinjay, do you think you have so much skill? "

" No, Uncle," said James meekly, yet with a hint of mischief in his wide eyes, " but if it is the hardest blow of all, must I not essay it most often? "

Albany brought his own hand down on his nephew's knee. " My lad, you have the makings of as wily a bishop as ever out-faced the devil or argued with a King. And yet, you will aim lower for a while, if only because I say so. You understand? "

" Yes, Uncle."

" And will obey? "

" Yes, Uncle," James said sadly.

" That is as well. Since my brother wears no helm I have no

wish to see you gouge out one of his eyes to demonstrate your dexterity. You have shown enough prowess already, nephew."

But his voice was kinder than his words. Meeting his eyes, James grinned, and set his pony prancing with shrewd little digs at its flanks. The desire to show his uncles how well he could control the beast was not only the child's habitual desire to show off before his elders. It was the beginnings of that romantic worship of the knightly ideal, to be offered in all circumstances and at his own utmost peril, which was to be one of his ruling passions all his life long.

So the lesson proceeded, with Albany always at the boy's side to check his grip on shield or sword, to show the guiding pressure of his knee, the swing of the body which reinforced the coercion of the reins, so that he might turn his pony here and there at will. James found it easy to learn from Albany, though he did not know it was because his uncle was so deeply versed in what he taught that the knowledge seemed to spill from him, till his very presence offered a sort of contagion which worked more subtly on the spirit than the shrewdest instruction on the mind.

If Albany was forceful, Mar was gay. The very fact of being alive seemed to intoxicate him so that he laughed all the time, at himself, at his companions, at James, yet not hurtfully, for there was no malice in him. Nor need he envy any man, for he and his brother Albany were by far the most brilliant figures at Court. Among those who watched the pleasant picture of the two gallant young princes instructing the little boy, not a few murmured to each other that either of the young men would make a fine figure of a King. Finer, perhaps, than the King fate had given them already.

Or so the King himself fancied, as he looked out of an upper window upon the scene between his brothers and his son. He did not fail to notice the worshipful attention with which young James followed every word, every gesture of his instructors. When he made a mistake, now and then, Mar would parody his clumsiness, so that the little boy doubled himself over his saddle-bow and the sound of his helpless laughter floated upwards. It was a pleasant scene, except to the man who watched it from the window.

" A lion shall be devoured by his whelps. . . . A King is in danger from his near kindred. . . ." The words rang hollow in his memory, as if rising from the mouth of an open grave. He had tried to push them aside, to forget, to make friends with the younger brothers who were so much more popular than himself. Yet every so often, whispers reached him. Albany, who was Governor of Berwick, besides holding the Border Earldom of March, and being, as Warden, responsible for the eastern part of the frontier with England, had no small opinion of himself, it seemed. In fact, his dealings with England were less those of a Warden than of a ruler. Or so they said. Cochrane and others lost no chance of saying it, again and again.

Looking down from the window at the laughing group in the sunlit courtyard, the King was wrung with the pains of anger, malice and all uncharitableness as he remembered the sorcerer's warning. Then turning away, he tried to obliterate the memory by engrossing himself in the composition of music for the choristers of his beloved Chapel Royal. But every now and then his brooding habit reasserted itself, spreading contagion into every part of his nature as the anger and fear festered within him. Each day found the conviction of his brothers' treachery more deeply established, till suddenly, as weak men act, after long hesitation, he ceased to be particular as to the truth of the original tale, and sent for the officer of the guard.

" Take a sufficient force," he said abruptly, " and arrest my lords of Albany and Mar."

" My lord the King! " gasped the startled man before him. " On what charge? "

" For my lord of Albany, on the charge of treasonable dealings with the King of England. For my lord of Mar "—the voice shook in spite of himself, for he had loved his younger brother— " the charge of using subtleties to bring about my death."

" Sir! "

" Do as I bid you." The King's voice rose almost to a scream. As he spoke he seemed to see, not the astounded officer, but that waxen image, pierced through and through with vicious bodkins, its limbs twisting and shrinking in the searing heat of the fire. . . . Such an image had been found in Mar's lodgings . . . they said.

Things like that were easy to say, easier to believe, when fear and envy had inflamed a man beyond the point at which his reason could check and steady his judgment. It would not be a popular decision, but the King did not care. Treason and witchcraft were the sort of things that came of too much popularity. Given so much power, men greedily sought more. For his own safety, and the safety of the country that his brother would be ready to sell to England, he must stand by the order he had just given.

Yet afterwards, pacing about his chamber as he brooded over the imprisonment of his brothers, and the stammering, incoherent protests with which his young son had received the news, the King was bewildered and sad. Even the performance of his new composition by the musicians who were almost always able to lighten the darkness which came down so often on his anxious soul, could offer, for once, no comfort. Though he was surrounded as usual by his chosen friends he had never felt so terrifyingly alone.

The young Earls, naturally, raged against their brother. John of Mar, unable to obtain an interview with him, or to make any impression on the defences of the grim fortress of Edinburgh, fretted himself literally into a fever. Albany, more fortunate, escaped from Craigmillar and took ship to France, leaving the governor and his subordinate dead as well as drunk in the cell from which he had let himself down by the rope sent by his friends in the cask of wine with which he had besotted his gaolers.

So much young James gathered from the rumours which hissed about the Court. His father shut himself away with his unpopular associates, refusing to see either the Queen or his son, guessing that the little boy's purpose in seeking an interview would be to plead for his uncles' release. And beyond that, who knew? Was he not the lion's whelp? But Cochrane, a man who laid plans for all contingencies, tried to make friends with his patron's son. He waylaid James as he was vainly seeking admission to the King's privy chamber.

" My lord James, I fear the King cannot see you. He is occupied with affairs of state."

" He cannot always be so occupied. I pray you, persuade him to see me," James implored.

" Can I not be of service? " Cochrane wheedled, smiling
blandly. " I may not know the answer to the questions you have
to ask. But I can seek such information gladly."

" I thank you. No," said James. He swung round to trudge
unhappily away, increasing his pace as he found Cochrane, big
and heavily jocular, still sauntering beside him.

" I have not seen you exercising in the tilting yard of late,
my lord of Rothesay."

" No," said James sullenly. " I—I do not care to ride."

" Why not, my lord? "

James hunched his shoulders and made no reply. He did
not mean to explain to this wheedling fellow that it hurt him too
much to remember that his uncle of Albany was no longer at
hand to show him how to couch a lance, nor his gay uncle of Mar
to ride threateningly down upon him, mocking the thunder of
his charge with a broad grin. If they might not now use the tilting
yard, he himself would ride there no more.

" Surely, my lord, now that you have begun to learn to joust
you need all the practice you can have," said Cochrane. " I will
myself be your instructor——"

" No," said James furiously. Then, unable to check himself
longer, he whirled, fists clenched, upon the big, floridly handsome
man. " But tell me, is it true that my uncle of Albany has
escaped? "

" It is," Cochrane agreed. " And so given us proof of his
guilt. If he were innocent, would he have fled to France? "

" At least he will be safe there," James said gleefully. " And
my uncle of Mar? "

" Ah, now I must disappoint you," said Cochrane smoothly.
" My lord of Mar fretted himself into a fever, as you may have
heard——"

" I have. What then? "

" The King, your father, in his brotherly love, gave orders
that the Earl should be removed to the house of a physician in
the Canongate, where he might be more carefully treated. And
there——"

" Go on." James stamped his foot in sudden panic at the
meaning pause.

Looking gravely down at the furious small boy, Cochrane proceeded deliberately. " Because of his delirium, he was bled, as the physicians directed. His arm was afterwards bandaged. But while he was still in the warm bath which had also been prescribed he tore the bandage from it, and by some sad mishap the bleeding was not detected in time to save his life."

" You mean——" said young James shrilly, " that—he is —dead? "

" I fear so, my lord of Rothesay."

James glared up at him, trembling with rage because he could not keep the tears from filling his eyes at a time when he would have given everything he possessed to be able to outface the hateful man with all the dry-eyed wrath he felt. But at the thought of his dearly loved uncle, all his gaiety quenched, the blood drained out of him, done to death so that he would never joke again, the tears came flooding. They spilled down his cheeks and his mouth shook so that when at last he could control his voice enough to speak, it broke ignobly on a sob.

" You—you have—murdered him! "

Cochrane forced an unconvincing laugh at the sight of his small fury. " Scarcely, my lord James," he explained carefully. " Bleeding is a most excellent remedy, and had it not been for the violence of the young man's disposition, which made him recklessly tear off the bandage . . ."

But James did not wait to hear more. Sobbing, he rushed wildly away, blundering through doorways and along passages, upstairs and down, without any clear idea of where he was going, provided it took him away from the big blond man who had told him that his uncle of Mar was dead and his uncle of Albany gone.

CHAPTER THREE

THE Queen, peering fretfully at the embroidery, over which, in spite of her ill health, she still spent so many hours, was startled when James plunged between the ladies seated about her, to throw himself at her feet, his arms clasping her knees, his desperate weeping suddenly loud in the quiet room.

Scared and whispering, the ladies bunched together like a flock of sheep, while the Queen, her hand to her heart, half-turned towards the doorway, as if awaiting those in pursuit. But James had not been followed. As the flustered circle re-formed, retrieving scattered silks, they all relaxed again, relieved that it seemed no more than some childish crisis which had brought James for sanctuary. His Danish-born mother stooped over him, vaguely, helplessly, with such crooning endearments as she would have used to comfort the little Marquis of Ormond, now gaping at his brother, or the baby, wakened by the flurry, who was wailing so disconsolately in his cradle that she could hardly distinguish her eldest son's broken phrases from the noise her youngest made.

When at last she understood, she was appalled. Long ago her husband had made it clear enough, before she had been many months in Scotland, that he preferred the society of intimates of his choice before that of either his wife or his nobler subjects. But she would never have believed that Cochrane's influence would have succeeded in turning him against his own brothers. She knew enough of his strong family feeling to be amazed.

Now, Heaven knew what might follow. If her husband could be turned against his brother, might he not also be turned against his sons? She herself had become accustomed to his indifference. It was at least an excuse for her to withdraw from the life of the Court and rest a little. Rest . . . it was all she longed for. Ever since the birth of her last child everything seemed too much trouble. Even her embroidery needle wearied her thin hand.

Her legs felt numb, and her mind with them. So many things about her marriage which had caused her distress and pain at first scarcely seemed to matter any more. All she wanted was to be left in peace.

So now, as she stroked and patted James's hair, her thoughts fluttered here and there like hens with an owl overhead. She saw the imprisonment of her husband's brothers less as a danger to national unity than as something which threatened her own peace, that blessed peace which came between the bouts of pain over which the physicians shook their heads and prescribed disgusting remedies which only made her vomit. Peace—if they would only all leave her in peace.

But her ladies had caught phrases here and there in the midst of James's frantic sobbing. Whispering together, their consternation increased as the picture of recent events took shape. Speculating, guessing, weaving fantastic fabrics out of the possibilities of things to come, they moved before James's grief-blurred eyes like vivid, wind-shaken flowers.

" Oh, Madam . . . the King's own brother——"

" The Duke of Albany has escaped to France. Will the French King make war on us? "

" The Earl of Mar has been murdered. . . . Then none of us are safe! "

" Madam, you can guess who is at the back of this. . . ."

" How can the King endure the fellow? "

" They say that he has bewitched our Sovereign lord's wits."

" Indeed, would our lord otherwise have shown such cruel indifference to our sweet lady? "

" What will become of the blessed children? "

" Be quiet, all of you," implored the Queen, as she raised trembling hands to her ears. " I dare say this will have shown the King that he has listened to the wrong advice. His brother's death must have shocked him as sorely as it has dismayed us. James, my sweeting, dry your eyes and be comforted. Surely the King, your father, will not be long deceived by wicked counsellors."

" Be comforted . . . be comforted. . . ."

The murmured solicitude of her attendant ladies rose about him, subtly soothing as the crooning of the pigeons in the crow-stepped dovecot beyond the tilting yard on a summer afternoon.

James was only seven, and exhausted with unhappiness. He allowed the indignant kisses and protestations of his mother and her ladies to blur the edge of his amazement and grief. Perhaps his father would indeed be reconciled to his uncle of Albany. His mother gave him enough money to provide a trental of masses for the soul of his uncle of Mar, and somebody produced a box of sugar comfits lately brought from the East by that daring sailor, Sir Andrew Wood. They fussed over him, bathing his eyes with sweetly scented water to take away the ache of tears, patting him like a favourite puppy, giving him cushions to sit on and tucking him up by his mother's side till at last he fell asleep, half-persuaded that somehow or other, all that was amiss would be mended, and the King's rightful advisers soon dismiss the jumped-up fellows who had done so much harm.

But the jumped-up fellows were not to be so easily dislodged. Cochrane strutted about the Court, complacently aware of his supreme importance and gratified by the success of his action against those who might have challenged it. And the King, as if to underline that success, actually went so far as to give Cochrane his dead brother's earldom of Mar, with all its revenues, to the horror of many people who had not formerly believed the young man's death to be anything but the tragic accident it appeared.

But now, anything seemed possible. Cochrane, who had already enriched himself handsomely, was now using his influence with the King to urge the further folly of debasing the coinage with a fresh issue of adulterated silver coins.

" Gladly would I stuff thae Cochrane placks down his greedy maw," said one merchant to another. " What is to come of a man's self-respect when others ring the coins he offers on their counters and grin at the sound of them? "

" They say my lord of Albany has besought the King of France to send an army that will hale yon fellow Cochrane frae the King's Councils by the hair of the head."

" I've heard tell that my lord of Albany will come to terms with the King of England if France fails him——"

" Never! Would he do that? "

" Ye could scarcely wonder. The man's been sorely wronged. I doubt he'll not be particular where he seeks vengeance."

" Mercy on us, would he march with the English across his own Border? And him still a Warden, since the King will not declare him forfeit! "

" Them that's seen him say that now he cares not what he does."

" Is he out, think ye, for the crown? "

" Some think he'd become it better than the puir miserly creature that wears it now."

So the rumours flitted to and fro about the market-places up and down Scotland during the two years that followed the King's estrangement from his brothers. Sober men discounted most of them, including the possibility that, whether the earlier accusation of treachery were true or false, the treatment he had received had now driven the Duke of Albany to treachery indeed. But, as occasionally happens, the current rumours were less startling than the facts, and the excesses attributed to the outraged Duke of Albany were not, even at their most speculative, altogether wide of the mark.

For the most part such rumours passed over young James's head, since he was now occupied with the arduous business of equipping himself for the grown-up world. Rising nine, he had been taken from the comfortable pampering of his mother and her ladies, and deprived of his pleasant superiority over his two small brothers. Instead he was attended by governors and tutors, in an establishment which, though nominally his, seemed more a place of incarceration than of residence. James, confronted with compulsory education, made the best of it. He was far too intelligent to dislike learning, and startled his teachers by the progress he made with the languages of those Frenchmen, Italians and Spaniards sent to instruct him. But the graver pedagogues complained that he amused himself by picking up a variety of pungent expressions from the varlets who served the foreign gentlemen, for the purpose of startling the solemn scholars who came to teach him the Latin tongue.

James was also learning other things. He had begun to notice, with some gratification, that a number of eminent people were beginning to take some trouble to please him, though he did not yet altogether know why. It was equally evident, though less pleasing, that others were increasingly antagonistic. That formidable veteran, Archibald, Earl of Argyll, one of the commissioners who had negotiated with the King of Engand for James's betrothal to the little Lady Cecilia when both were scarcely out of their cradles, treated him, for instance, with elaborate courtesy, but the Earls of Athol and Buchan, his great-uncles, were contrastingly curt. Most of the northern lords, as King's men, followed Athol and Buchan's lead, but others began to ingratiate themselves with James, some with obvious clumsiness, but others with a sincerer kindness which promised future loyalty.

So, under pressure of the progressive alienation between father and son, the Scottish nobility began tentatively to divide into those who stood for the King, right or wrong, because of his kingship, and others whose intention, so far, was only to see the King put right. But it was inevitable that those of the second party should seek the favour of the King's son. For if the King could not be righted, his son might have to replace him sooner than the natural course of things decreed. James was not easily impressed by flattery, for he had a child's mistrust of fair words with a leaden ring. But he liked his elders to be courteous, like old Campbell of Argyll, and did not care for those who were casual or sarcastic like his great-uncles. About others, such as the big, fiery Earl of Angus, he was not sure. For Angus was too much occupied with his own projects, both personal and dynastic, to have much time for a small boy not yet in his teens.

One evening, however, he was startled into awareness of James. Waiting with the rest for dinner in the great hall at Stirling where the King's Court was then resident, James accidentally overheard something the Earl was saying to a friend and broke into the conversation without ceremony.

" My lord of Angus, do you know indeed that my uncle of Albany has left France for England? "

The Earl looked down at the boy from his great height, disconcerted as if a lamb had bitten him. He was also annoyed to know that all those within ten yards must have heard the question and were awaiting his answer. He glared down at James, who, surprised by the sensation he had created, tried to explain.

" My lord, I only ask because I hope he will come and see me soon. I—I have wearied—tell him so, I beg you—since he went away."

" I doubt," said the Earl of Angus gruffly, " that he will not come to Scotland yet awhile."

" Why not, my lord? "

" Because the King, your father, has not been kind to him."

" Is the English King kinder? "

" He might be. At a price," said Angus, with a grin which James could not understand. For only a few men in Scotland, Angus among them, knew of the secret treaty which the exiled Albany had outrageously consented to sign, and by which he had recently bound himself to do homage for all Scotland if King Edward would help him to become its King. Angus was also aware that Albany had undertaken, for good measure, to break Scotland's alliance with France, to surrender Berwick, Liddesdale, Eskdale, Annandale and Lochmaben into English hands, and to marry the very little Princess Cecilia who was still nominally betrothed to his nephew James.

" And a stiff price, too, as some might think," Angus added, winking over James's head at Lord Gray who stood behind him. " Well, there's much to be said for a change of riders, if the horse is restive."

James bit his lip. He was aware of being mocked, he suspected that the Earl of Angus revered neither his father, the King, nor his uncle of Albany, and anger made his heart race as he glared up at the great, complacent hulk of a fighter.

" I do not understand you, my lord."

The big Earl guffawed. " And a good thing too, my lad."

At this point James allowed his attention to be distracted. Patrick Hepburn had recently succeeded his grandfather as Lord Hailes, and James admired him most earnestly for his wild way with a horse, a spear or a sword, as well as for the conspiratorial skill with which he included James in such expeditions as he could by any means find an excuse to claim as part of his education. With him now were the young Master of Lennox, and Alexander

Gordon, Master of Huntly, both of whom believed in getting as much amusement as possible out of the Court formalities by which some of their elders set such store. Huntly's especial butt was the staid Earl Marischal, whose fondness for prolonged dissertation, just as the trumpets were about to summon them to take their seats at table, was a constant trial to the hungrier young men at Court.

" Heaven save us," young Gordon murmured, with a mocking grimace of agony, " there goes old Hearken and Take Heed once more. We shall get no food till nightfall."

James, who had not heard the nickname before, giggled explosively as the Earl prefaced his discourse with the usual admonition. Heads turned in the direction of the small boy, now trying to stifle his laughter with the cushion Darnley, Master of Lennox, had snatched up from a window-seat. Some frowned, but others smiled. Since the King, as usual, was closeted with his creatures in the solar, and would not join the company for dinner in the hall, it was as well, perhaps, that his son showed a more convivial disposition, even if he lacked respect for elder noblemen.

For national affairs, still beyond James's understanding, were moving rapidly towards a crisis, as the odd conversation between the Earl of Angus and Lord Gray had indicated. Cochrane had that day taken pleasure in informing the King that his brother of Albany had succeeded in persuading Edward, King of England, to take up his cause. Richard, Duke of Gloucester, had been ordered to invade Scotland in support of the Duke of Albany's claim to Scotland's crown.

Shaken as he was by the news, the King summoned all his liege subjects on the Boroughmoor outside Edinburgh with the gloomy satisfaction of a man whose foreboding of disaster has been fulfilled, though he was wholeheartedly averse from the personal necessity of riding southwards at the head of his armed forces, on which Cochrane, to his dismay, seemed set. But most of his subjects were quite prepared to enjoy the warlike expedition, especially James, included by the resourceful Sir Patrick, who had begged a holiday for him on the plea that, as his father's heir, it was his duty to ride with those who defended his father's honour, though his father, it seemed, cared little whether his honour were defended or not.

Huddled on the quiet horse which he managed so badly, the King of Scots looked wretchedly about him, as they moved off. Prised away from the peaceful seclusion in which he sought to spend his days, he had been clamped into unfamiliar armour which chafed or pinched him at half a dozen places, and sent clanging southwards, to face the unpleasant prospect of a personal brawl with the English under the Duke of Gloucester—a man of scholarship and distinction on an ignoble errand—and his brother Albany, who must undoubtedly have taken leave of his wits, since he had apparently described himself as Alexander, King of Scots.

It was so unnecessary. Surely Cochrane could have dealt with it and let him stay at home? It was, at midsummer, 1482, sufficiently hot to make the thought of riding across the treeless hills in full armour unendurable to any reasonable man. The only consolation, the King thought peevishly, was that his friends at least rode with him. He had insisted on that, though most of them were as disinclined to violence as himself. But why should he suffer while they sat at ease? So, creaking and grumbling, they bestrode their nags behind him, a sorry, unsoldierly group of intellectuals, with gowns tucked up and shoulders hunched as the jolting shook them. Only Cochrane, Earl of Mar, and Master of the Artillery, did his patron credit as he pranced beside him, plumed and surcoated, gorgeously flaunting the gold chain and jewelled hunting-horn which had been the King's gifts. Cochrane had an air, a presence, the King thought, which all these arrogant lords, biting their nails as usual in the background, might well envy. He bore himself as a King's chief counsellor should, while the others, who were his humbler friends, pressed closer in the great man's shadow.

" That fellow! " said James furiously as he caught sight of Cochrane at his father's side. " Why should he have the place which is mine by right? "

" Do not fear, my lord James," said Sir Patrick Hepburn as the cavalcade began to wind up the track which led to Soutra Edge. " He will not hold it long."

He held it as far as Lauder, a little township on the south side of Soutra Edge where the host halted for the night. It had not been an easy journey. The long, slow climb had wearied the horses, and the heat and the weight of their armour had tried the men who rode them. Tempers had grown short, as the Scottish lords watched the little group of unsoldierly men riding about the King.

" Master of Artillery, the fellow Cochrane may call himself," someone grumbled. " But he cares little whether the cannon win over the edge or sink in the bog below."

Certainly Cochrane was paying little attention to the progress of the half-dozen lumbering bronze cannon, each drawn by a straining team of oxen, which brought up the rear of the long procession. He pranced still beside the King, on a magnificent charger, another royal gift, not knowing, or not caring that hatred surrounded him like the summer flies against which he flicked a hastily snatched stem of the bracken while his horse toiled through it, belly-deep. His very nonchalance, as he beat off the droning hordes of insects, increased the exasperation of those who watched, and in their exasperation the heat and persistence of the flies seemed harder to endure, working up in their turn the slow smoulder of hatred to such a pitch that the slightest additional pretext was liable to touch off a conflagration. So the unwary Cochrane rode regardless of the mutterings of his enemies from which he might have taken warning as from the premonitory rolling of a thunderstorm.

Young James caught snatches of talk as he pushed his sturdy little pony on to keep up with the bigger horses, riding first with one group and now with another, talking of his new hawk to the Master of Huntly and the litter of puppies in the Castle stables at Stirling to Sir Patrick Hepburn. But he found his friends unexpectedly absent-minded. They scarcely seemed to hear what he had to say. Even the Master, whose interest in hawks was extreme, merely nodded when James spoke of his and craned his neck to hear what the Earl of Angus was saying to the Earl of Lennox.

James found this most perplexing. He had been enjoying it all very much, for he had managed to convince himself that when his uncle of Albany saw their army he would prudently decide to

be friends with the Scots again instead of with the King of
England. "Old Hearken and Take Heed," the Earl Marischal,
had said as much to his father before they started. James had
heard him. So of course it would be all right.

It was difficult to say afterwards just when the midsummer
dreaming turned into nightmare. In later years, James refused
to think of it, pushing the whole thing violently out of his mind
by day, though he never knew when the horror was going to wake
him at night in a trembling sweat, or suddenly come down like a
black wall between him and the waking world, so that he must
once again do penance for the part he had played in setting the
wheels of tragedy turning, as he believed they had first turned
that day.

But as they rode into Lauder the changing mood of those about
him was beyond his ken. He watched the servants setting up the
King's pavilion, a splendid affair of red and yellow silk, then
turned to go with his own friends. But Sir Patrick shook his
head. James, it seemed, must leave them to their conference in
Lauder Kirk while he supped with his father and his father's
associates.

" May I not come with you? " James begged. " I hate being
with those men. They talk about things I do not understand——"

" This evening, my lord James," said Sir Patrick, with an odd
smile, " we must do the same. The Earl of Angus has summoned
us——"

" And he does not want me? "

" Not now. But afterwards, we will return——"

" Be sure you do. And soon. You must do something to make
up for leaving me with those men who mince and strum and
chatter. Ugh, I hate them, and Cochrane most of all."

" Leave that to us, my lord James. We will deal with them."

How soon, and how dramatically that promise was to be
fulfilled, neither James nor Sir Patrick, who had merely said the
first thing that came into his head to soothe the boy, could have
known. The climax came, as such things do, before it was
expected. Had Cochrane not happened to hear some hint of where
the Council, from which he had been excluded, was being held,
had he not boldly interrupted it on the instant that the Earl of

Angus had capped Lord Gray's story of the cat, the mice and the
bell with the boast which was to earn him a nickname for the rest
of his days, nothing, just then, might have come of all their anger
and talk.

But as it was, the storm broke with a violence which re-shaped
many destinies as abruptly as a sudden cloudburst changes the
face of a country-side. Having bound the incredulous Cochrane,
the confederates left the Kirk to collect his associates from the
King's tent. To young James, the strangest thing about it all was
the speed of what happened next. One moment he was lounging
in a corner of his father's pavilion, tossing dice against himself,
while his father and his friends murmured over their wine at the
trestle table, and Rogers the musician idly strummed the lute
which lay across his kness. The next, it seemed, the group around
his father had been broken up and the King's friends hustled
away. It was all over almost between yawns.

For as James opened his mouth the tent flap was wrenched
aside by men still in their armour. Angus came first, then
Lennox, Huntly, Crawford, and Sir Patrick Hepburn. There
were others, but those at least James had time to recognise before
they wrenched the astounded men to their feet, hauling them
across the overturned benches and out of the tent. Despairingly,
they shrieked aloud to the King to save them.

" Are you drunk or demented, my lords? " their patron
protested. " Release these men at once."

" We are sober and in earnest, my lord the King," said Angus
briefly. " It grieves us to disobey."

" They are my friends——"

" They are no friends to Scotland. They shall all hang.
Now."

Breathless, forgotten in his corner, James surveyed the chaos
of overturned furniture, the shrieking, terrified captives, and
purposeful intruders. One only, John Ramsay, the young Earl
of Bothwell, a clerkly lad a few years older than himself, clung
round his master's knees so that he could not be plucked away
without risking injury to the King. Since this was no part of
their plan, they spared him and lived to regret it.

Most of the rest of the outrageous affair remained a mere blur in James's memory, achieving precision only in the occasional nightmares from which, on his knees, he prayed to be delivered. But every so often, do what he would, his memory recalled the scene, shadowy as moonlit tapestry on a sleepless night of storm. Long afterwards, King of a country which was coming to play an increasingly important part in the affairs of Christendom; corresponding with the Emperor, the rulers of France and Scandinavia, arbiter of the affairs of Gueldres, consulted by King Henry of England, placated by the Pope, James would suddenly become again the boy of nine whose stomach heaved at the pendulum-swing of the inert figures below the arch of Lauder Bridge. Cochrane's head would once more loll sideways on his broken neck, its protruding eyes bloodshot, mocking them all, it seemed, with out-thrust, swollen tongue across which a fly walked horribly, though corpse and bluebottle had been dust on the March winds for twenty years.

They had made the King watch the execution of his favourites. He stood, white and silent, by the bridge, his desolation reproaching James more subtly than any protest could have done. Stung by compunction, he broke away from the avenging nobles, and ran impulsively towards his father. With outstretched hands he offered love and loyalty to the man he scarcely knew, because it was intolerable to see him so forlorn. But the King merely looked at him with pale distaste. Then, moving like a sleep-walker, he turned away.

CHAPTER FOUR

PATRICK HEPBURN came presently upon James as he stood staring, and led the white-faced boy away from the riverside. " I have killed too many men in fair fight to think twice of it," he admitted; " but such a sight as that might well turn a stronger stomach than yours."

James nodded, not daring to unclamp his teeth for fear Patrick would hear them dirling in his head.

D

" Wine," said Patrick cheerfully, " will wash the memory away. Come to my tent."

Others, it seemed, had also felt the same need. Even the recent executioners stood about between the ranked pavilions, talking loudly as they drank, while pages scurried about with flagons, inquisitive and alert. Silence brooded over the men's quarters about the camp-fires which had begun to glow in the failing light, periodically eclipsed by the movement of shadowy figures, as the latest rumours were borne to and fro.

For the news of what had befallen Cochrane and his confederates had spread throughout the camp almost before the victims ceased to jerk among the echoes under the mossy arch. Rough justice was well enough, some said, but the violence might not end there. Others wondered uneasily if any harm had come to the King. Would they still march against the English or had they come so far only to turn homewards, without the plunder which they had been promised? Low whistles summoned the importantly strutting pages to give what news they could as they came and went among their masters, but though the lads talked willingly, their news was but a garnished hotch-potch of half-heard sentences.

" The King is sick. . . ."

" No, he is well enough. . . . He has commanded the loyal lords to string up those responsible beside their victims. . . ."

" Angus has taken the King prisoner. . . ."

" The King is guarded by my lords of Athol and Buchan. . . ."

" He is to be handed over to the English, by command of my lord of Angus. . . ."

" We are to march into England. . . ."

" We shall go home in the morning. . . ."

Gentle or simple, they talked half the night. For Angus had indeed suggested to the lords in conference that they might as well rid themselves of the King, besides those he had favoured, by handing him over to the Duke of Gloucester and receiving his brother Albany as King in his stead. It could all be arranged most comfortably, he argued. As King Alexander, the Earl of Albany would be much the better bargain, since he had already reached an understanding with the English. Why not take the

chance of ridding themselves of a poor scarecrow who thought of
nothing but his clerkly maunderings? Thus Angus argued, with
the impatience of a man reluctant to let outworn ideals interfere
with an advantageous new allegiance. Counting on the gratitude
of his peers for his disposal of the detested favourites, he pushed
his advantage too far, and bit unexpectedly on the unyielding
substance of loyalty with the shock of a man encountering a fruit-
stone in what seemed pulp.

"An understanding with the English? How is that known
to you?"

"Have you also made terms with our enemies?"

"Are we to take whatever King the English choose to thrust
upon us?" growled the Earl of Lennox.

Angus, looking from one to another, shrugged his broad
shoulders contemptuously. "Heaven save me from such a
thankless lot," he said. "Have I not relieved you of those irksome
fellows?"

"Aye, but we have not asked you to relieve us of our King,"
the Earl of Crawford pointed out.

"Nor to go behind our backs to make terms with the enemy
on our very border," Lennox added.

"What was it worth to you, Archibald Bell-the-Cat?"
Patrick Hepburn asked bluntly.

"I will ram that infamous question down your throat with
my dagger's point," Angus roared, surging forward.

"It is a question we must needs all ask, my lord of Angus,"
said the Earl of Lennox, calmly barring his way. "The truth is
not to be pushed out of sight because it does not please you."

Finding himself, disconcertingly, alone, Angus prepared to
shift his ground. He peered at them, darkly grouped against
the afterglow in the western sky, grumbling that they were fools
to reject the best chance of setting the country on its feet they had
ever been offered. But if they would have none of it they must
go their own way. He had done his best and got no thanks for it.
He would trouble himself no further. Shouting for his page to
bring a torch, he swung off towards his tent.

They were shaken by the thought that if Angus had been in
touch with the English leaders others might also have been ap-

proached. Uncomfortably, they glanced at each other. Was this man false? Was that man true? They were in no shape, they realised, to meet the enemy who had so undermined their unity, for the only thing on which they were now agreed was the impossibility of surrendering the King. Better to withdraw, with the King their prisoner, than attempt to encounter their enemies with a front so shaken. Given time, some peaceful solution might be found. Athol and Buchan would see to their kinsman's safety. And the Castle of Edinburgh was the safest place they knew.

Angus, who was not prepared to make open cause against his countrymen, heard their decision with indifference. Since he was willing to sit on the fence as long as need be, he agreed without demur to strike camp and withdraw with the rest. But he was already discussing future possibilities with such men as he knew to be well disposed towards Albany as the army trailed back over Soutra Edge.

Young James, shaken and scared, rode north in silence, his gaiety eclipsed, as it was to be at intervals, all his life, by a mystery of darkness. For, somehow, things had gone wrong and he feared that his own incautious words bore their share of blame for it. Though the detested Cochrane was no longer at his father's side, his father had looked at him with such evident hostility that he dared not approach. Instead, as they set off, James saw his formidable great-uncles, Athol and Buchan, close in to ride one on either side of the forlorn figure of the King.

The retreat itself puzzled him, since he had been excluded from their councils. "What has become of the English? Did we not set out to fight them?" he demanded. "Have they run away?"

They grinned at him. But some looked shamefaced and others uncertain. "It seems somewhat as if we were doing the running," said Sir Patrick, his white teeth gleaming between his dark moustache and beard.

"But why?" asked James.

"Before a goodman sets out to beat the robbers from his door, he must make sure that no one is planning to let them in by the window," Sir Patrick said.

"Would any man admit our enemies?"

Sir Patrick sighed. " It seems so, my lord James."

" What must we do then? "

" First return to set our house in order," said Sir Patrick, with his crooked grin.

" Will my uncle of Albany come and help us? "

" It is uncertain whether he will come, and still more uncertain whether he will help," said Sir Patrick.

" But surely he will help," said James in astonishment. " Do you not know my uncle? With sword and spear I swear he has no equal," he added earnestly. " I pray you, send for him——"

" My lord James, if the decision rested with me, indeed I would," Sir Patrick said. But his voice for once had the tone of someone humouring a small boy whose prattle he endures, without giving it too close attention. And James recognised the indulgence only too well. He dug his heels into his pony's flanks and urged it forward, reflecting that it was the only living creature he seemed to be able to influence at all.

Subsequent events were sheer bewilderment. James caught distracting snatches of conversation which first suggested that his father, though he was the King, was the prisoner of his own subjects, guarded by the Earls of Athol and Buchan in the Castle of Edinburgh, while the English army, led by Richard, Duke of Gloucester, slowly advanced across Lothian, and the Scottish lords, agreed at least upon the necessity of halting them, assembled at Haddington to bar their way.

Then came talk of mediation between the royal brothers, and afterwards the first word of his Uncle Albany's return. For it seemed that the Scottish Bishops had persuaded him to rejoin his countrymen after all, and his first flamboyant action was to rescue his brother, the King, from the Castle with the help of the loyal citizens of Edinburgh. And then, all of a sudden, the English were on their way south again, and James was summoned to the banquet in the great hall of the Castle with which his father proposed to celebrate his reconciliation with the prodigal.

That assembly was a strange sight for a child. The hall of the Castle was thronged by his father's greatest subjects in their brightest, richest clothing, so that the drab stone walls, hastily

draped with mildewed tapestries shaken out of the chests where
they had lain for years because the King entertained so seldom,
formed a sombre background for a medley of velvets and satins,
furs, jewels and costly brocades, the blue and yellow and crimson
and purple and green of the men's doublets, furred gowns, and
parti-coloured hose rivalling the glories of the women's sweeping
skirts and steeple head-dresses from which gauzy veils floated above
their bare shoulders as they moved.

But the strangeness was not only in the unaccustomed
splendour of the entertainment. Far stranger was the unreality
which hung about those attending it. Men looked askance even
while they toasted each other, for though the King set the example
as he sat beside his brother, dipping his thin fingers daintily into
the dish they shared, the gaiety had a hollow ring about it. Fear
and mistrust peered through the conviviality as the dark stone
peered through the threadbare tapestry.

James walked doggedly towards the high table, scarcely aware
of the curtsys of the ladies who smiled so archly as they made
way for the small boy whose eyes were only on his father and his
uncle, puzzled by the unconvincing display of brotherly affection,
as Albany slapped his knees, laughing uproariously at some joke,
while the King, watching him, thinly smiled.

Pausing in front of them, James swept off his plumed bonnet,
as he had been taught, and knelt before his father. Bowing his
head, he waited confidently for Albany's expected greeting. For
surely his uncle would be glad to see him again? But the deep,
slightly nasal drawl scarcely paused. It seemed that Albany had
been well pleased by what he saw in the south, and he hoped
his brother would consider installing the latest English improve-
ments.

"Glass for the windows, my lord, is something they make
better in Edward's kingdom. I have a fancy for being able to see
through it. Here in Scotland, we might as well be under the
sea."

"It is not good. But to change it would cost a great deal,"
said the King nervously.

"I do not think so. We must look into it. Why, how do you,
nephew, these days? My faith, but he has grown, brother, this

lad of yours," chuckled Albany. "To keep him clothed will cost
more than a few panes of glass needed to lighten the darkness of
your palaces."

The King nodded gloomily. His eyes were devoid of expression,
dead as pebbles from a dried-up river-bed as he looked at his son.
They chilled James as he recognised with a shock that both his
father and his beloved uncle had forgotten him. For his father's
cold eyes looked over his head, and the Duke of Albany had
turned away, smiling over his shoulder at the lady who sat on his
right hand.

Incredulous and hurt, James found tears pricking his eyelids
as he rose from his knee and swung round, careless of where he
went, anxious only to plunge through the surrounding crowd and
escape from the hall.

But the little drama, though he had not guessed it, had been
watched by a score of those closely interested in the relationship
between the King and his son, and the rebuff James had received
had been resented by the women whose high head-dresses tilted
as they whispered together.

" For shame to treat the bairn so churlishly. . . ."

" His own son. . . ."

" He is too fair and forward . . . his father fears him. . . ."

" My lord James, will you not drink with us? . . ."

" Here is a place. . . ."

" No—here. . . ."

" This bench is cushioned. . . ."

" Sit on my knee, dear lad. It is a better cushion. . . ."

James blinked at them, beginning to smile uncertainly as their
sympathy swept round him, soft as swansdown. The white hands
of ladies, gently patting, were like kittens' paws. Their perfume
made him think of flower gardens, their arms were kind, their
breath spicy with mulled wine, as their cheeks touched his, their
bright lips brushed his forehead.

He felt dizzy with the sweetness of it all. His mother, her
ladies, his nurse, had petted and spoiled him often enough. But
this was different. This roused strange new feelings within him,
made him want to possess, to dominate, instead of passively
receiving their caresses like a child. He gulped down the wine

they offered, and looked from one smiling face to another, while
the men, watching in the background, grinned.

"It will not be long before that lad asks more of a woman than
kisses and comfits," someone murmured.

"Who will have his first favours, think you? Will you wager?"

"Save us, he is not yet in his teens!"

"Yet I can tell a lusty young cock when I see one, I swear."

The voices criss-crossed over his head, while the caresses and
the perfumes, the strong, spiced wine, and the increasing warmth
of the crowded hall, made James's senses swim. He was glad to
relax on the wide, motherly lap of the elderly lady who knew how
sleepy he suddenly felt. Finger to lip, she shook her head at the
others, while from the high tables, the Duke of Albany, concealing
a yawn, took note of the commotion his young nephew seemed to
have caused. For the first time, frowning, he saw the boy as a
potential rival. It would be tiresome if, having hoodwinked his
brother sufficiently to advance his own purpose, he had still to
deal with a faction which remained loyal to his brother's son.

For loyalty was a faculty about which the Duke of Albany felt
a vast indifference. It pleased him to accept the assistance, even
the devotion of those who freely offered it. But afterwards it also
pleased him to go his way, unhampered by the burden of gratitude,
or the thought of offering assistance in his turn. He had long ago
taken his brother's measure as a poor-spirited creature good only
for fleecing. So now he accepted the title of Lieutenant of the
Realm of Scotland, just as if Lord Gray and the Earl of Angus
were not already jogging through the wild weather with which
1483 began, to meet Edward, King of England, and renew the
secret treaty concocted at Fotheringay the summer before.

It was easy enough to justify the treachery to himself. His
brother, who had suspected him unjustly, should now expiate that
injustice in very truth. The King had brought his misfortunes on
himself, argued Albany, between exhibitions of brotherly love.
He also boasted, rather too often and somewhat too loudly, for
those who surrounded the King were not all either knaves or
boors. When the rumours of his machinations first reached
William Elphinstone, Bishop-elect of Aberdeen, he was in no
doubt of the need for action. Sadly, for he had hoped much from

the reconciliation between the brothers, he prepared to hale the
King from the new fool's paradise in which he had taken refuge
almost as soon as the old one had been sent tumbling about his
ears.

In his early fifties, the Bishop's commanding presence, when
he rode about Edinburgh, attracted the attention which his plain-
dark riding-clothes sought to avoid. Hooded and furred less
richly than many a thrifty merchant, his escort merely a groom
mounted like himself on an undistinguished nag, it should have
been possible to mistake him for an ordinary citizen on his way
to market, but such an error would be unlikely after a close
encounter with the Bishop. There was something about the lean,
humorous, and extremely intellectual face which checked the
superficial judgment, and made even the thoughtless look again
at the man who had returned from ten years' study of canon law
in Paris to become first Rector of the University founded at
Glasgow in mid-century, and afterwards Episcopal Judge of
Lothian.

Perhaps the discerning might first have been struck by the
severity of an expression unmarred by the anxiety to serve both
God and mammon which made a battlefield of so many faces, so
that greed strove with piety and humility was ousted by the
love of power. The Bishop's vocation had left him with so few
illusions about humanity that his sincere conviction of heaven's
care for its salvation constantly caused him awe and amazement.
And being a logician as well as a priest, it was clear to him
accordingly that his own gifts would best be employed in humble
obedience, seeking by heaven's grace to feed his Master's lambs.
And so, thus dedicated to seeking the greater glory of God, he was
without anxiety for his own.

But as he dismounted in the Castle courtyard about which the
searing March wind was driving wisps of straw and feathers from
the kitchen quarters where the scullions were plucking fowls for
the royal table, the Bishop was reluctant to seek the audience for
which he had come. He had seen enough of the King, both in
connection with the diplomatic missions he had undertaken for
him, and the more personal matters discussed in his capacity of
spiritual adviser, to know that this disillusionment would strike

the younger man hard. Compassionate as well as courageous, the
Bishop disliked the necessity for striking such a blow.

There was, however, no alternative. For Albany's guilt was
not in doubt. The Bishop himself had heard him speak in such
terms of his agreement with the King of England that he quite
evidently believed it would be as easy to shake his brother from
his throne as a rotten apple from a tree. Such confidence,
indicating that Albany's plans were well matured, hinted too
strongly at the danger of delay. So the Bishop, gathering his cloak
about him, went sadly in search of the King, suddenly aware that
the chill of the March morning seemed to search flesh and blood,
reaching towards men's very bones. The soldiers on duty, the
gentlemen-in-waiting, even the scampering pages, kept warmer
by constant calls to bring fresh logs for their masters' fires, were
short-tempered and blue-nosed. And the King himself, closeted in
a small, arras-hung chamber stiflingly warmed by a high-piled
fire, peered out, the Bishop fancied, from the midst of his furs as
a hedgehog from a drift of autumn leaves.

" Well, my lord Bishop, this is dire weather for a man to be
abroad. In your place I would have remained by my own
fireside."

" I doubt it, my lord the King," said the Bishop gravely. " In
my place, I should like to think you would have also set forth, as
I did, out of my humble duty and regard for your greater safety."

The King's narrow face seemed to sharpen. " My safety? Is
it endangered? "

" I fear so, my lord the King."

" Then sit down, my lord Bishop, and tell me as much as I
must know. Other men might perhaps plague me with uncertainties. But you would not? " he questioned plaintively.

" I would not have come, my lord," said the Bishop briefly,
" had I not with my own ears, heard your brother, my lord of
Albany, boast of the new agreement with the King of England
by which he hopes to obtain your throne."

The King shrank within his furs as the hedgehog might have
shrunk back under the leaves at the prod of a cudgel. When he
spoke at last, his voice was a mere thread of sound.

" Oh, my lord," he said wearily, " surely that is all past?

We knew of such an agreement, but since he returned to his allegiance the Duke has promised to abandon all such vain schemes——"

" So he promised indeed. But it seems he has failed to keep his promise. Others, on whose word you can rely, but yesterday heard him boast of his plans. I can bring them here to bear witness of what I say. . . ."

" No need, no need," said the King forlornly. " Since I take your word, my lord Bishop, for those things which concern my soul's salvation, I see no need to doubt it on the lesser affairs. Yet my brother has seemed so fond and spoken so fair——"

" I know it, my lord the King. But I have heard him, in his cups, speak otherwise——"

" In his cups? " Eagerly the King grasped at the straw of consolation. " It may be no more than a drunken man's boasting——"

" In vino veritas," murmured the Bishop, with a grim smile. " I have also taken care to verify the statements made with the actions of those known to be his associates. There is reason to suppose that others are involved——"

" Others? " Wildly the King peered about him, as if assassins lurked in each fold of the arras that swung to and fro as a searching draught swept under the heavy door. " You know their names? "

The Bishop bowed. " It has not been difficult to discover them. My lord of Albany, it seems, has been so confident of success that he has attempted no concealment."

" Then—what must I do? "

" You must punish them as they deserve, my lord the King."

" Not with death—my own brother——"

" With forfeiture and banishment at least."

" That, perhaps——"

" Without doubt, I fear, my lord."

" I had hoped—we could have shamed him into repentance."

" My lord," said the Bishop dryly, " it is my duty as a churchman to remind you that all things are possible with God. But as a student of humanity I am bound to add that the conversion of my lord of Albany seems one of the less likely."

" My lord Bishop——"

Tears stood in the King's eyes, checked his uncertain voice. He shook his head, clenching and unclencing the long-fingered, womanish hands which were so much defter on the strings of his beloved lute than clasped about the hilts of the great two-handed swords which other men brandished and he could scarcely lift.

"—if I must confront my brother with his treason, you will support me? "

" I will, my lord the King."

" Then—let him be summoned. If it needs to be done, I shall have no peace till it is done with. . . ."

The Duke of Albany, when challenged, made no attempt to deny his association with King Edward of England. Nor did he make any secret of the fact that the Earl of Angus, even the Earls of Athol and Buchan, and their kinsman, the Bishop of Moray, had been parties to it. His very effrontery shook the King's resolution, as he had reckoned that it would. Bishop Elphinstone contrived to persuade the King that Albany must not retain the office of Lieutenant, but he and his associates, though banished from Court, were still allowed to retain their titles and lands.

Albany, helpless with laughter at the sorrowful leniency of his brother's reproof, merely went on with his plans by preparing to hand over Dunbar to his English allies. What would have come of his collaboration no one could tell, since in April, King Edward of England died, and before the summer was over, Richard of Gloucester had made himself King in his stead. To Albany, this was a catastrophe, for Richard's position was much too uncertain to risk war with Scotland, so that when Albany invited him to endorse the treaty of Fotheringay, he refused, and Albany was left to face the indignation of the Scottish people, to whom his negotiations were now revealed. He took refuge, at first in England, from the sentence of forfeiture passed by the Three Estates, and then, after Bishop Elphinstone had secured a renewal of the Anglo-Scottish truce, and his final abortive attempt to lead a raiding force across the Border had failed, he returned to France in disgust. But his reception there, perhaps to his disappointment, did nothing to impair the Franco-Scottish alliance which had been cordially confirmed on the accession of Charles VIII.

In Scotland, the arrival of the French ambassador, that famous hero of chivalry, Bernard Stewart d'Aubigny, was celebrated with tournaments which bored the King as excessively as they enthralled his eldest son. For James, liberated from his studies to attend them, hung over the gorgeously decorated rail of the royal stand for hour after hour, watching every encounter with the passionate eagerness which was in such contrast to his father's indifference that the gallant French ambassador, somewhat piqued by the Scottish King's yawns, made a special point of saluting his hero-worshipper as well as his host, as he clattered past the stand on his way to unhorse yet another assailant. His elaborate reverence made the boy flush with pleasure, and Bishop Elphinstone smile.

" We have seen some fine jousting, my lord. Never, I think, have we been better entertained."

" Indeed? "

" I shared your distress, my lord, that our lady the Queen was unable to be present."

" The Queen? She is always in poor health nowadays."

" Can the physicians still discover nothing to dispel the ill humour which troubles her? "

" It seems not," said the King indifferently.

" The Prince, at least, was well pleased."

" He should have been at his studies." The King's voice was peevishly sharp.

" Do you not think, sir, that it is as well he should now be by your side on such occasions? The French ambassador was much gratified——"

" So I saw."

" The Prince is a fine lad. I hear from his instructors that he promises exceptionally in all respects——"

" So did my brother——"

" Your son, my lord the King, is very different."

" Is he, my lord Bishop? "

The King glanced at his spiritual adviser with suddenly narrowed eyes, then began to fumble among the papers on the table before him with nervous, uncertain hands.

" My lord, what reason have you to doubt it? " said Bishop

Elphinstone. Here, in this furtive, dark suspicion, this hostility between father and son, fresh trouble undoubtedly lurked, and he must bring all his influence to bear against it. But the King shrugged narrow shoulders, pursed obstinate lips, and said nothing. He had no intention of mentioning the sorcerer's fearful words. The Bishop, he well knew, would not tolerate such things. But had they not been proved true already, as far as his brother was concerned? Was it not all the more likely that they would also be true of his son?

"Reason? I have my own reasons," he said at last.

"But, my lord," Elphinstone protested, "you will surely not let it be seen by the people that you are also at odds with your son? What could be more unwise?"

"To dote on a thankless child would show more unwisdom," mumbled the King. "I am coming to realise that his younger brother shows by far the fairer promise——"

"My lord, the Marquis of Ormond is but a child——"

"Better a child that can be guided than the aptest lad who is set on running astray."

"My lord, you have seen him so little," pleaded the Bishop. "Surely you who have been so tender towards an erring brother, will not be harsh against a high-spirited son?"

"High-spirited is one word. Rebellious might be another," the King persisted, with all the dogged obstinacy of weakness. Recognising it, the Bishop sighed. Strange, how much harder it sometimes was to deal with weakness than with strength.

"At least I beg you, my lord, to do nothing in haste which will show that the Prince is in disfavour. That would tell sorely against the English royal marriage which has been arranged for him——"

"English marriage! I put no faith in an English marriage," said the King peevishly. "Was James not betrothed in his cradle to the Lady Cecilia? Yet nothing came of it. Now he has been betrothed to King Richard's niece. But who is to say this scheme will fare better? It will go the way the other went, I swear."

"As to that," said the Bishop, with a wry smile, "I own I should not care to take a wager, my lord, even were I not a churchman, who is forbidden to meddle with such things. The throne of England does not seem one on which men sit long these days."

"Heaven knows why any man should wish to," mumbled the King, "since of all seats known to man a throne is the most comfortless."

"Yet you would not willingly surrender your own, my lord?"

"Such is man's perversity that I would not," the King agreed, with a bleak smile.

CHAPTER FIVE

"YET another King of England, my lord Bishop?" James, glad of the diversion, grinned triumphantly at the interruption of his studies as his meek tutor rose and bowed to Bishop Elphinstone. He spread his fingers and ticked off a name on each. "King Edward, King Edward, King Richard, King Henry. Who comes next? My lord, are all the tales I hear true?"

Bishop Elphinstone shook his head. "I know neither what the truth may be nor what tales you have heard, my lord James. Only that both King Edward's young sons died, poor babes, in the Tower. Now King Richard is dead also, on Bosworth Field, and King Henry reigns in his stead."

"Poor Edward! He was no more than a midsummer King," James said. "But young Richard of York was much of an age with me. I wish he had not died. We might have been companions. If King Richard, their uncle, did not want them, why did he not send them to me? I would have received them gladly. It is wearisome to study always alone, and my own brothers are but bairns. Now Richard and I——"

"My lord James, what have you heard concerning the death of these poor children?" asked Bishop Elphinstone.

James frowned. "Many things, my lord, and all at odds with each other. Some said that it was the fever, caught from the dank vapours of the Tower. Others . . . spoke of misadventure. But most of murder. King Richard himself, some named. . . ."

" Inevitably," the Bishop agreed. " Yet nothing is certainly known," he went on, talking half to himself. " England has passed through a time of terror in which every man's hand was turned against his neighbour and no man knew whom he dared trust. Now that King Henry is to marry Elizabeth of York he has declared her legitimate. And if she, then her brothers also. Aye, there's the sting. For they, if they live, must then both have a better right to the throne of England than he. So to him, more than any other, their death is welcome. It may well be . . . that Tyrell acted on the King's orders," the Bishop murmured. " If King Henry is to remain——"

James giggled. " If he does not, my lord, the throne of England will be like the vantage point from which the children push each other in their play." He began to chant, drumming the rhythm with his fists on the table-top. " ' I am the King in his Castle. . . . And you but a dirty rascal. . . .' "

Bishop Elphinstone raised a slender hand to hide a smile. " Indeed, my lord James, that is true enough."

" When I am King," James said, " I will look well about me lest others seek to push me from my throne."

" When you are King . . ." murmured the Bishop. " That will not be for a long time. You are barely thirteen . . .".

" My lord Bishop, I am all but fourteen," said James promptly. " And many people have told me that I may be King sooner than I expect. . . ."

" Have they, indeed? " said the Bishop. " They spoke in jest, no doubt."

James shook his head till the heavy auburn hair which fell to his collar swung with his vehemence. " Forgive me, my lord Bishop, but it did not seem so."

" Have many said this? " the Bishop probed. His face was troubled, for James's innocent boasting confirmed his own secret fears.

" Many and often," James declared. " They say my father craves the honour but neglects the duties of kingship, that he hoards his wealth and shuts himself away——"

" Since your lady mother died it may be that he is sorrowful——"

" He cared little for my mother, my lord," said James candidly, " and he cares less for me."

" My lord James," said Bishop Elphinstone, " that is an ill thing to say——"

" It is also the truth," said James, flushing. " For years now he has scarcely spoken to me. He makes much of that brat, my brother of Ormond. But ever since the day——"

" What day, my lord James? "

But James shook his head and closed his lips firmly, knuckling his eyes as if to scrub from his memory all traces of the strange scene he had glimpsed through the stinking smoke that bellied out above the sorcerer's brazier. The lion . . . who was to be devoured by his own whelps . . . the King in danger from his near kindred. . . .

" The day he came to believe that I sought to do him harm," he said warily. " Ever since he has wished himself rid of me as he ridded himself of my uncles of Albany and Mar."

" My lord James," said Bishop Elphinstone, " I am persuaded that the King, your father, has no such intention. Who has suggested such a monstrous thing? "

" My friends," said James, with a vague sweeping gesture which suggested familiarity with the waves of the sea or the moods of the wind.

" They are poor friends who seek to stir up such differences between father and son," the Bishop said sternly.

" They meant no such harm, I am sure," James said defensively.

" Who meant no harm? "

" Why, the great lords of Angus and Argyll, besides lords Hailes and Home and Lyle and many others—they have all declared themselves to be my very good friends, my lord Bishop. They have been kinder to me than my father, at least," he added defiantly.

Bishop Elphinstone laid a hand over the fist James clenched on the table. He knew well that he, unlike his father, was not to be cowed by terror; on the contrary, he detected in him already a passionate purpose which could carry him and the country he ruled either to triumph or disaster, according to the way in which

E

it was employed. Here was a boy who could never be driven, and only led, if at all, by those he trusted and loved.

"You have a right to your friends, lad," he said gently. "And I would ask you to count me among their number, except only as such friendship may be directed against my lord the King. I am not to be persuaded into one of two rival factions which must tear Scotland apart. My first duties are to our Lord and His blessed Mother and to Holy Church. By their command I seek to offer what counsel I may to the King who, under God, reigns over us. If you were to be King, my lord James, you would find that I offered such counsel also to you, striving to speak truth whether you found it pleasing or otherwise."

James gave him a sudden, candid grin. "My lord Bishop, that I already know. And I am glad of it. When I seek to ford a stream in flood a rock is more welcome than a quicksand. When I am King I will often seek your counsel."

"But will you receive it now?" the Bishop asked.

More doubtfully, James nodded.

"Then do not allow yourself to be flattered by those who seek to use you for their own ends by turning you against your father."

"I knew you would say that," James sighed. "And—and I promise I will do nothing to harm my father unless he first seeks to harm me."

"That I am sure he will not do," said Bishop Elphinstone.

"Will he not? I would not be too sure."

The Bishop sighed. With the boy in this wilful mood, little could be done. The situation was as full of explosive possibilities as a keg of the new-fangled gunpowder which the knights had mocked at as a magician's trickery when it first set the great stone cannon-balls roaring from the mouths of the monstrous bombards that many men feared to approach. But the new weapons had made headway in spite of their mockery. Now they seemed likely to change the whole face of war, perhaps to put an end to it, since against them the heaviest plate and the staunchest castle walls were vain.

As he made his way back to the courtyard where his horse and groom waited, the Bishop considered the possibility that this latest product of men's evil genius might come to serve heaven instead of hell. For surely, once all Christendom knew that war was no longer a question of brave men confronting each other with spear or sword, weapons dependent on their personal courage and skill, face to face with their enemies, no rational being would persist in a conflict which offered so little scope for knightly skill?

Who would contemplate butchering alien men, women and children, wrecking city and castle, knowing that the same treatment would be inevitably meted out to their own? And yet, the perversity of mankind being what it was, were there any real grounds for hope that the threat of consequences would turn man from the error of his ways? Had all the terrors of rack and red-hot pincers, even the culminating horror of faggots and the stake, produced the change of heart for which the Inquisitors had hoped? Would men ever learn that Satan could not be employed to cast out Satan? For every heretic who had recanted in terror, had not another died in defiance? Bishop Elphinstone, rejecting as a logician the wastefulness of such failure, also recoiled as a merciful man from the infliction of so much pain. Yet, unless Holy Church were to admit herself, unthinkably, to be mistaken, what else could she do but seek to rescue the impenitent by the ordeal of earthly fire from the fires of eternity? So warfare, as it became yet more terrible, offered yet another challenge to those who preached the peace of Christ.

War against infidels, as the Holy Father had indicated, was not only permissible, but beneficial to those who earned remission of sins by taking part in it. But war between Christian princes, still more between the subjects of the same Christian prince, was a very different matter, which he must do everything in his power to prevent. It would be a terrible thing if the infection of civil war from which England had suffered so sorely should spread north across the Border. Had Scotland not yet borne enough? Her agriculture, devastated for so long, her trade and commerce, her coinage, shipping and fisheries, had only begun slowly to swing back towards prosperity during a century of queasy truce with a disunited England. It would be catastrophic if the breach between the Scottish King and his eldest son were allowed to plunge Scotland into the senseless sort of conflict in which the new promise of prosperity must be utterly lost.

The Bishop did what he could, counselling moderation on the King, urging Parliament to undertake legislation to preserve peace, seeking to anticipate and eliminate any pretext which might convert the smoulder of conflicting resentments into a blaze. Given time, he believed that it might all die down, for though the King lacked the open-handed charm which had made the earlier Stewarts so much loved, he was willing enough to accept advice if such acceptance seemed likely to mean that he would be left in peace. The trouble was, as Bishop Elphinstone recognised only too well, that many people in Scotland as elsewhere preferred war, even civil war, if it offered them the chance of personal aggrandise-ment, while James's eager ambition and tumultuous self-will made him dangerously vulnerable to the intoxicant flattery that the disaffected offered.

And yet the new King of England, Henry VII, was well enough disposed towards Scotland. His people were heartily sick of civil war, he himself did not fancy foreign adventure, and he wished to consolidate his position at home. His envoys, therefore, presently came with pacific suggestions of English betrothals for Prince James and his young brother, the Marquis of Ormond, and the matter was going forward pleasantly when the Scottish King, with one of his flashes of perversity, refused to consider the proposals further unless they were coupled with the restoration of Berwick, recently captured by the Duke of Gloucester. Its loss irked him the more since the treachery of his brother Albany had brought it about. His insistence checked the cordiality of the negotiations, but was popular in Scotland, where the loss of Berwick rankled still.

Less popular was his apparently trifling decision to annex the Priory of Coldingham to the Chapel Royal at Stirling, where he needed extra revenue to defray the expenses of his new choir. The King's love of music, which had prompted him to show too much favour to musicians in the past, now caused trouble again by infuriating the Border families of Hepburn and Home, who con-sidered the Priory their traditional concern. It seemed too trivial a matter to cause more than a few grumbles. In fact, it was the one spark necessary to touch off the explosion. Early in 1488, the resentment of the nobles concerned broke out into such violent wrath that even the King was roused to lively awareness of his danger. Floundering uncertainly among the problems of what looked like incipient rebellion, he sent for Elphinstone, whose loyalty had never been in doubt.

" My lord Bishop, is it possible that this affair of a few singing men and boys can have influenced all the south of Scotland against me? "

" Perhaps not, my lord the King. Yet from one cause or another, it seems that all the south is in arms."

The King took his head in his hands and groaned. ". I have summoned Angus. But he will not come. Argyll, too, is with them. My lord Bishop, I am like a man standing in the midst of a quaking bog. What shall I do? "

" Make sure of the custody of the Prince immediately," said Bishop Elphinstone. " That, at all costs, you must have. Where is he now? "

" At Stirling, with his tutors."

" Shaw of Fintry is Stirling's governor. Can you trust him? "

" I believe so."

" Instruct him, then, to hold fast. Send him reinforcements in all haste. Deprive Argyll of his office. We can scarcely permit the Lord High Chancellor to march with the rebels," said the Bishop dryly.

" Yet I must have a Chancellor. I—I shall appoint you, my lord Bishop."

" I will serve you whether I hold office or not, as well you know, my lord the King," said Bishop Elphinstone. " I suggest also that you leave Edinburgh."

" Leave Edinburgh? Where shall I find a fortress of such strength? "

" The fortress matters less, my lord, than the spirit of those who surround you," said Bishop Elphinstone. " The northern lords are loyal. I will send a messenger in haste to Sir Andrew Wood, whose ships are lying at Leith. You can rely on him to ferry you across the Forth. An envoy, too, should go to England."

" Must I proclaim to the world that my own nobles are in arms against me? " the King groaned.

" King Henry will receive such news with more sympathy

than surprise," said the Bishop. "The situation has been a commonplace south of the Border for these many years."

"At least I shall leave my treasure here in Edinburgh for safe keeping."

"Do so, my lord. But make all haste, I pray you," urged the Bishop. "Command a troop of horsemen to escort you to Leith. The reports which have reached me indicate that those in arms had hoped to take you by surprise. If you are captured——"

"That, by heaven, I will not be, my lord Bishop," said the King. "I have not forgotten Lauder Bridge."

As it happened, he barely escaped. Bishop Elphinstone had not exaggerated. The Homes and Hepburns, Angus and his adherents, Argyll and his, had already raised most of Scotland south of the Forth, and the King only just reached Leith before the rebels. As the horses of his escort clattered over the cobbles of the harbour, the hoofbeats of those in pursuit of them rang like an echo.

Sir Andrew Wood, stocky, bronzed and loyally indignant, received the King and gave immediate orders. The little ship cast off in such haste that the King's personal luggage was forgotten on the quayside. Across the widening gap of heaving, greenish water, the King watched his pursuers pounce on it.

"I am sorry, my lord," said Sir Andrew. "But had I waited for your gear they would have captured the lot of us. I have but a dozen mariners aboard. You will do better across the Forth."

"But—but to oppose their King in arms—it is monstrous——" the King stuttered.

"It is that," Sir Andrew agreed, stroking his chin as he watched the harbour of Leith dwindle into the eastern haar. A strong force seemed already to be making its way towards Edinburgh. Dust clouds in the distance indicated the approach of others. How serious the situation might be he did not know, since his task had merely been to secure the safety of the King's person, on the urgent request of Bishop Elphinstone, now Chancellor of Scotland.

"But it is no more than an affair of a few discontented Border lairds. The country will not support them against me," the King declared.

" I can promise at least that I will not, my lord the King," said Sir Andrew Wood.

Once across the Forth, the King raised Fife, then rode to Aberdeen, where in the Bishop's palace the northern leaders joined him; Athol and Huntly, Errol, Ruthven and lesser folk. They, too, took it for granted that the rebellion was a trumpery affair. But when leading the contingent south again the King was greeted at Perth by news that struck him as coldly as if the dead hand of fate had closed about his heart.

" My lord, the insurgents have made for Stirling——"

" What folly! They cannot hope to take such a fortress——"

" But they have been admitted, my lord. Shaw of Fintry has permitted Prince James to join the rebels and he has now placed himself at their head."

The King threw up a hand as if to ward off a blow. He heard the buzz of incredulous comment as if from a great distance. Nearer and more dreadful were the remembered words of the sorcerer who had warned him, years ago, of this very thing. "A lion . . . devoured by its whelps . . . a King in danger from his near kindred. . . ."

They did what they could to comfort him.

" My lord the King," said the Earl of Crawford, " Prince James is but a lad. This is a midsummer prank. When we have settled with those who have misled him, you shall skelp more sense into him yourself."

" No doubt they compelled him to ride with them," someone else suggested.

" We must not be too harsh," said the Earl of Errol.

" At a conference, the matter may yet be peaceably settled," Huntly declared.

For a time it looked as if the optimists were right. At Blackness the forces met, Huntly and Errol secured a nominal pacification by which the rebellion was to be forgiven, the King's safety guaranteed, a council of the ablest lords and churchmen formed for his guidance.

Young James, at the first sounds of the returning envoys, ran out of the pavilion which had been pitched for him under the same Lion standard as that which flew outside his father's tent

in the opposing camp. " What is the news, my lord of Angus? "
he demanded impatiently.

The Earl of Angus, ponderous in his armour, descended
laboriously from his horse and stooped so that his esquire could
undo his helmet, booming at James from within.

" They received us," he said, " like a company of ill-behaved
children. We were scolded and given our instructions. We are
expected to go meekly home."

" Indeed, my lord," said James indignantly, " I hope you
said we would do no such thing? "

Angus's tawny head and scarlet face emerged as his esquire
detached the helmet and dragged it off. He looked down,
grinning, at James.

" You will not obey? "

" Not if I bide alone," said James. " Has my father not set
me aside and given all his favours to my brothers? I will show
him that some think better of me than that."

" Well crowed, young cockerel," Angus guffawed. " You are
a lad after my very heart. You shall bide. And not alone."

James frowned, wincing as a huge hand gripped his shoulder.
He liked the Earl of Angus and his patronage less and less.

" Do not fear, my lord James," said Patrick Hepburn. " You
shall see them run before you yet, if you will have a little patience."

Patience. James thrust the unwelcome word aside like a
persistent fly. It was a quality which was to elude him his whole
life long, his lack of it determining at last the manner and the hour
of his death. Yet unlike the cold faults which made his father
mistrusted, the fire and zeal which blazed the more fiercely in
James for want of all restraint made him the more beloved. For
men turn to a fiery spirit as they turn to a fire in the winter's
darkening. Throughout his life James never went short of men
—or women, for that matter—who would gladly die for him
because of his blazing vitality from which their own zeal caught
fire.

Those who had been glad to adopt a lad barely fifteen more as
a mascot than as a leader of their rebellion, welcomed that impatience now. Pacification offered too poor a prospect. They had
not left their homes and ridden half across Scotland merely to

return, not a penny the better off, by the way they had come. If nothing was to be gained from the King, many were beginning to mutter, better be rid of him. Let him abdicate. His son would know how to reward his friends.

The insurgents remained in arms, therefore, with James enjoying the excitement, unconcerned with the graver issues, innocently believing that these men were altruistic enough to undertake such a campaign for his sake. Their purpose, as far as he could tell, was to make his father come to terms and recognise him as his heir. Between one encounter and another, they hunted, enjoyed a few days' hawking, jousted to pass the time before they took the field against the King again. But beneath the smooth surface of their gallant show the purpose which had been clear from the beginning only in the minds of a few, was now, as it received the consideration of others, progressing secretly, as moles tunnel below the gay inconsequence of meadow flowers, though James was aware only of a masquerade by means of which he and his father would presently be reconciled.

In this expectation, however, he was mistaken. The spectacle of his son among the rebels merely offered confirmation of suspicion which hearsay had begun, and closed the King's heart against his eldest son for ever. In a gesture of despairing defiance, the King made his second son Ormond, a little boy still in his nurse's care, Duke of Ross, and his loyal servant, the Earl of Crawford, Duke of Montrose. Casting concealment aside, he also sent out urgent appeals for help to Henry of England as well as to the King of France and the Pope in Rome. But since their help could not reach him in time, no choice remained now but to pursue the dreadful farce to its end. Wretchedly, the King gave the order to advance against the insurgents, unhappily aware that the last wry quirk to the affair was its setting. For they were within a few miles of the scene of his ancestor's greatest triumph on the field of Bannockburn.

Those surrounding the King did their utmost to rouse him from his black mood of brooding, for fear of its effect on the men they led. The King himself, smiling forlornly, did his best to strike a warlike attitude as they girt him with the sword of his great ancestor. Lord Lindsay, too good a horseman himself to

guess at the danger of his gift, also insisted on giving him his own
horse, a superb and spirited grey.

"My lord the King, he is the fastest in all Scotland. No
enemy can hope to escape you when you ride him in pursuit."

Too sick at heart to care whether he rode against his son on
Lord Lindsay's great grey stallion or the sorriest nag from a gipsy
encampment, the King tried to force some enthusiasm into his
thanks. And presently they hoisted him across the beast, inert
within his armour as a sack of meal, King Robert's great sword
hanging by his side, his head aching from the clamour of the
trumpet calls.

To young James it was still make-believe, a joyous tourney
which would enable him to show his father that he was a man
to make terms with, not a child to thrust aside. He enjoyed
himself, therefore, as he galloped about, knowing that he sat his
horse well and managed his weapons with dexterity. He had
given imperious orders that his father was not to be hurt. But
though these had been received with deference, quite a number
of people guessed that the real leaders of the expedition would
prefer them to be ignored.

The King, pacing sombrely forward on the great grey horse,
flinched at the clash of arms as the vanguards of the opposing
forces met. The pace of those about him quickened. He urged the
grey stallion to a trot, though in his agony of mind the nervous
tightening of his grip on the reins contradicted the sharp authority
of his spurs. Unaccustomed to such confusion in his rider, excited
by the clamour of battle about him, the big grey began to plunge,
and the King's efforts to control it only made it more confused,
till the climax came as Bruce's sword caught it on its sensitive
flank, from which the gorgeously embroidered caparison, caught
on a thorn bush, had been torn away. The flailing sword, the
clutching hands, the pricking spurs, were all too much. The big
grey took the bit between its teeth and bolted madly from the
field of battle, with its rider bumping and the sword flailing on
its back.

Some of the King's enemies caught sight of him as he rode,
apparently in headlong flight. Swinging their horses out of the
general hubbub, they pounded down the slope towards the

Bannock burn in furious pursuit. But Lord Lindsay had not exaggerated when he praised his horse's turn of speed. The King still clung to the reins, and though his lean thighs were so numb that they could no longer grip the saddle, he might have escaped them altogether, had the goodwife from Beaton's Mill not chosen to go to the burn for water as the grey stallion thundered towards the ford.

At the fearsome sight she dropped her pitcher and fled. The grey, alarmed by the crash, shied so violently that his inexpert rider went headlong, to slam heavily on the cobbles of the crossing and lie still.

The miller and his wife did what they could. As they carried him indoors he recovered consciousness sufficiently to murmur words they could scarcely hear.

" He is asking for a priest," the miller whispered to his wife.

" Aye, sir. We'll seek one," she soothed the groaning man. " Are ye sair stricken? What'll be your name? "

They had loosed his helmet now. His face was ghastly as he lay on the miller's pallet, one cheek smeared with the blood that had spurted from his nose.

" I—I was your King—this morning. . . ." he said faintly. " So . . ."

His words sent the goodwife screeching out, her apron to her eyes, as three of his out-distanced pursuers came pounding to the ford.

" A priest—send a priest, sirs—for my lord the King," she cried.

At her words they drew rein so abruptly that one of the horses slid on its haunches almost to her side. Its rider swung himself from the saddle, his voice hollow from within his helm.

" I am a priest, goodwife. Take me to the King."

Doubting nothing, because she knew so little, she led him into the dim room where the King lay. The stranger knelt beside the pallet, and spoke, his face still unseen.

" Are you so sore stricken, my lord? "

" It may be," said the King faintly, " that I am less stricken than—at first I supposed. But for my comfort—let a priest shrive me."

The stranger's movement was too quick for the simple folk of the mill to follow, much less to prevent. For before they could guess at anything amiss, the man who called himself a priest had drawn a dagger and thrust it into the sick man's throat.

" Let this blade shrive ye," they heard him say. Then, as the blood spurted from the severed artery, he was up and away.

They brought the news to Angus. During a lull in the battle, James was gaily describing the panic of a group of camp followers that he had ridden down. His flushed face shone in an infernal halo of flies which he fanned away with a glove, and it was some time before he noticed that his listeners, as they caught snatches of the messenger's story, had lost interest in his own. One by one they turned away, whispering to each other, so that James was isolated in the last instants of his make-believe as Angus stepped forward. In a loud voice he proclaimed without preamble:

" The King is dead. . . ."

Then, swinging about with a sudden clash of plate armour in a melodramatic, deliberately mocking reverence, he knelt at James's feet.

" Long live the King! "

PART TWO

1488 - 1498

CHAPTER SIX

"**B**LACK velvet for his coronation? 'Tis unchancy," whispered the old wives. For word of the hasty preparations being made to crown one King almost before they had buried another had got about, as the Master of the Wardrobe instructed the grooms of the chamber, and was overheard by the keeper of the napery, who let it reach the ushers of the hall door, till finally the yeomen of the kitchen, the apothecary's lads and the hangers-on about the great courtyard of Stirling Castle sent it far and wide. " 'Tis a terrible thing. Whose choice is it, think you? The Council or the King? "

" 'Tis the King's own command, they say. He has heart for naught else. . . ."

" Yet he rode back from Sauchie as gay as a cockerel that's won his first main."

" Aye, just like a bairn. Play-acting, it would all seem, at first. . . ."

And play-acting it had seemed indeed till the morning James rode to the Abbey of Cambuskenneth where his father's body was lying in state before the High Altar. The makeshift Council had been glad to let him go. They were wrangling fiercely about the probable extent of the late King's wealth, and the choice of a deputation to go to Edinburgh and claim his coffers from the Castle there. So James, when advised of the propriety of visiting the Abbey, took half a dozen men-at-arms, and left them to kick their heels outside. It was between offices when he reached Cambus Kenneth Abbey, and all the play-acting pandemonium of the last few days, the trampling and shouting, the pealing of trumpets, the chime of bridle-bits and the clash of plate armour fell back on the impact of an utter stillness, broken only by the distant patter of prayer, and the sharp sound of his spurs on the flags, as he walked alone up the shadowy nave to where his father's body lay, already embalmed, his face drained of blood till it was waxen as the tall candles which stood like angelic witnesses about the catafalque.

Awestruck, James looked on a mysterious alienation. For death's touch had erased all the peevish inadequacy of the man who had exasperated so many people because he was both obstinate and afraid. In his place lay a pale stranger, marbled in serenity, as if his journey had already taken him far beyond both obstinacy and terror, from whose face every line of petulance and irascibility had disappeared.

Crossing himself, James knelt, and the unpausing prayer of the watchers in their dark habits passed over him as leaves rustle from autumnal trees on a night of frost; the tick-tap of their beads touching his awareness as lightly as leafless branches on a window-pane. Then a candle guttered, a draught from a distant opening door sent a wave of incense towards him, and in a moment everything was changed. He was back behind the arras, half-stifled by the dust of years, his nose pinched between finger and thumb to check a threatening sneeze, his eyes to a hole through which he could see the smoke-hazed chamber in which his father listened, his face almost as waxen-pale as it was now, to the gasping of the sorcerer kneeling among drifting vapours, his arm extended as as if to indicate a horror of which he alone was aware.

" I . . . see . . . I see . . . a lion . . . devoured . . . by his whelps. . . . A King . . . in danger from his . . . near . . . kindred. . . ."

The words loomed over James with such a weight of memory that he was borne down by it, to crouch, head in hands, on the unrelenting stones. The knowledge of the part he himself had played in bringing the prophecy to pass was like stone also, stone descending, stone crushing, stone of the upper millstone upon the nether millstone, grinding out the reproaches which pulverised his soul. With a frenzied effort he scrambled to his feet, and fled without a backward glance at the white terror of that deathly accusing face, running without purpose, drawn only by the faint light from the candles in a side-chapel, there falling again on his knees before the crowned statue of the Queen of Heaven, as he had blundered once before towards the shelter of maternal arms.

Until that moment James had not been able to weep for his father's death. But now the tears broke from him in a sudden

spate of sorrow, less for the father he had never understood, than
for the fatherhood he himself had longed for during the years
when he had overheard so many gibes at his father's oddity, seen
so many men grin and wink at his eccentric friends. So, without
knowing it, he first wept for himself, then for his mother, at
whose loneliness he had guessed, as children guess these things.
And then he wept for the violence and waste and cruelty of the
way it had all ended, for the remembered horror of the line of
corpses bobbing against the arch of Lauder Bridge, for the ravaged
sorrow of his father's face as he stood by the riverside. Last of all,
seeing now the pawn's part he had played in the final tragedy, he
wept in terror for the millstone weight pressing on his soul, groping
in an utter darkness of loneliness and fear from which he was
unexpectedly recalled by the touch of a hand on his shoulder.

Raising his head from the flagstones which his tears had
darkened, James peered under swollen lids at a small, thin man
in the drab habit of the Friars Observant, whose face had the
illuminated expression of one who looks less at the world about
him than through it to another beyond.

"My son," said the friar softly, "may God in His mercy
comfort you. What is the cause of your distress?"

"Father . . . I have sinned . . . against heaven. . . ."

"Then make your confession, my son."

James blundered through the story of the last few weeks. The
Franciscan was already familiar with it, for his monastery lay in
the hunting forest of Glenartney, nearby, and fugitives from the
late King's broken army had appalled the community with the
news of their defeat and their leader's death, though he had not
at first recognised his penitent as the King's son who had so
dreadfully inherited his throne.

The priest, who was afterwards to be James's confessor, sat
long silent, as the weight of his new responsibility bowed him
down. For he had fled from the cares of the world only to be
pursued by them in the person of his young King. At last he said:

"None of us, my son, can tell to what dire precipice our sins
will suddenly lead us. It is a well-known device of our eternal
enemy to make the way so smooth and innocently bordered that
when the steep place is reached we are over the edge as we stoop

F

to pluck one more flower. You know how grievously you sinned in taking part against your father? "

" I do."

" Yet how long will you remember? "

" I—surely I could never forget? "

" It is easier to forget than you think, my son. You have made yourself a King, and I lay upon you as your penance the task of ruling Scotland greatly."

" Father, I will seek to obey."

" But I charge you also to remember all your life long the manner in which you came to your kingdom." The small friar looked at James with piercing kindness. " Wear the memory as a fetter, night and day. . . ."

" Father, I will. And to ensure it I—I will wear a fetter indeed. . . ."

" I spoke only of fettering the spirit, my son. But if it assists you to fetter the body, so be it," he added, with a smile. For he had already guessed at the romantic temper of the young man who would worship more devoutly for personifying the Mother of God as the Queen of his heart, and the saints as his brothers in arms.

" I will have such a chain made by the armourer. . . . I will be crowned in sorrow."

Above his bent head the Franciscan nodded understandingly. The boy at his feet was so evidently a creature of extremes. He could be captured by fantasy where reason would leave him indifferent, though his acute intelligence was something he would always seek to overleap rather than defy. As he began the words of absolution, the boy's taut poise relaxed. But when he returned to the waiting men-at-arms they thought him fey with grief. And his first command was for mourning at his coronation.

" Black velvet? 'Tis more like a funeral," the common people were still saying as they made their way towards Scone.

" A funeral? And well it might be. Is not the King his father scarcely cold in his grave? "

" No blame to the lad that's King now."

"Is it no'? Did he no' lead them that drove his father to his death? "

" The lad was ill-advised. Some folk should hae kennt better. . . ."

" Shame on the bairn that listened. . . ."

" Whit's dune's dune wi'. . . ."

" Aye, gie the lad his chance. . . ."

" Whit chance did his father hae? "

The sound of their voices was like the fretting of an angry sea about the ancient walls of the Abbey of Scone on that June morning. Inside, preparations were complete. Archbishop Schevez, that same fishy-faced astrologer-physician to whom the dead King had looked for comfort in vain, waited complacently with his assisting bishops and clergy, while outside the Abbey the horsemen escorting the great lords came clashing up to clear a path into the Abbey for their masters. But after each contingent had passed in, the crowds surged forward again, peering, whispering, shaking their heads.

" All in black. Whoever saw sic' a thing? 'Tis ill-omened, if ever onything was. . . ."

" Whit way will it end, a reign that's gotten sic' a drumly start? "

" D'ye ken that folk say the Archbishop spends mair time spiering after yon Philosopher's Stane than ever he spends on his knees? "

" The Philosopher's Stane? Whit's yon? "

" Tuts, I dinna ken. But they're aye after it, the clerkly bodies. I've heard tell it turns a' things intae gowd. A daftlike occupation, wad ye not think, for them that's sworn to poverty? "

" Gie's a haud on't. I've mair stanes on ma land than I ken whit to dae wi'——"

" Wheesht, here comes him they ca' Archibald Bell-the-Cat. Eh, but my lord Angus is weel pleased wi' hissel' nowadays."

Angus cantered slowly by at the head of his men, controlling his magnificent horse almost effortlessly, it seemed, raising a cloud of dust which slowly settled on the doubtful, inquisitive faces and drab clothes of the people who had scattered obediently at the shouts of his escort, and closed in as quickly behind them. He was pleased, and with reason, at the way things were going. His assumption of the office of James's guardian had been unchallenged, though it practically amounted to that of Regent so long as he retained his influence over the boy and prevented others from acquiring it. Sombre and superb in black satin, he dismounted at the doorway and waited while his page carefully laid a furred cloak on his shoulders and followed him within.

" Yon's Patrick Hepburn, Earl of Bothwell, forsooth, as he is now. Master o' the King's Household, Keeper o' Edinburgh Castle, Warden o' the Marches, dear kens what besides."

Patrick Hepburn clattered up more sedately. Beside him, looking paler for his black clothes, rode a thin boy of twelve, who ducked his chin to avoid the glances of the inquisitive crowd.

" That'll be the King's brither, the Duke of Ross, puir bairn. The wee yin'll no be here, likely."

" Aye, but he is. Yonder, wi' Lord Home . . ."

" Here comes Argyll, him that's Chancellor again."

They were only to be glimpsed now through a veil of dust, churned by the hasty hooves of many horses. Alexander, Lord Home, had annexed the custody of James's youngest brother, that little Earl of Mar who was to flit like a shadow across the margin of Scottish affairs; Lord Lyle was now Justiciar; Sir William Knollis, Lord High Treasurer. With them came the representatives of most of the great houses of Scotland, though now and again the names of significant absentees were caught up by the crowd, passing along the restive ranks, as summer lightning, heralding a storm, flickers along the threatening darkness of a bank of cloud.

Inside the Abbey James was preparing, with nervous resolution, to play the chief part in the ceremony which seemed such a strange contradiction in terms, as the rejoicing colours of tabard and banner, ermine, miniver, and cloth of gold; the crown, orb and sceptre, the wand and great sword of State which spoke of triumph and rejoicing, were contradicted by the unrelieved black worn by his officers of State, the eight young noblemen who were the henchmen of his personal bodyguard, and by the congregation. Even now, strengthened by his confessor's advice, purged and cleansed by his own penitence, James felt the people's doubts strike up at him like the clammy fingers of a rolling fog, as he slowly ascended the steps of the throne.

Archbishop Schevez, guessing the boy's instant of hesitation, moved forward, as if to frustrate the possibility that he might, seized with panic, try to run away. James winced at the grip of those fingers, cold through the black velvet of his sleeve, and freed his arm unobtrusively as he turned to confront the blur of faces which swam up at him as if out of dark water. For a moment the sight checked the breath in his throat, shocking him into unreality. Then as the Archbishop's voice creaked into the opening phrases of the ceremony in which he had been so carefully rehearsed, his body and soul came together again.

The ancient ritual of rejoicing, now set so strangely in a scene of sorrow, followed its perversely appointed course. The great officers of State, bearing the Honours of Scotland, took their tone from the Archbishop, whose portentous solemnity was for some reason contradicted rather than enhanced by an occasional tear.

But only Angus allowed his impatience to appear, as the proceedings continued, through his attention to his duties, as a spur might irrelevantly poke out below the furred border of a rich gown. He was frankly irritated by the Archbishop's snuffling and droning. The sooner the business were over and they could get on to the necessary legislation the better. A good deal more dissatisfaction had been caused by the business at Sauchieburn than he had expected. The former King, as dry a stick as a man ever snapped across his knee, might well make more trouble dead than he had done in his lifetime. He hoped that Patrick Hepburn could be relied on to keep a firm grip on the boy for whom his elder brother had nearly been disinherited. No dissatisfied party must gain a hold on the Duke of Ross. Or the little Earl of Mar either.

But the children were biddable enough, even terrorised as they sagged wearily by the side of their governors, borne down by the heavy, sombre clothing with which they were laden, stifling in the close-packed crowd, their high, shaken voices contrasting forlornly with the gruff tones of their elders as they stumbled forward at last to kneel at James's feet and babble their nervous, uncomprehending homage.

And James himself was now so weary that the reiteration of the same pledge broke over him in meaningless waves of sound

that threatened to sweep him from his place; their impact
almost as tangible as the surge of an east coast sea.

"By the eternal and almighty God . . ."

". . . almighty God who liveth . . ."

". . . liveth and reigneth for ever . . ."

". . . for ever, I become your liege man . . ."

". . . I become your liege man, and truth and faith . . ."

". . . truth and faith shall bear unto you . . ."

". . . shall bear unto you, and live and die with you. . . ."

The scintillation of many jewels passing in and out of the
beam of sunlight towards the cushion at his feet on which prelates
and noblemen knelt in turn, dazzled him, the heat and glare, the
pealing trumpets and the weight of the robes he bore made his
head ache, and he was confused by the stare of many eyes. Eyes
. . . he was surrounded by them, pierced by them, impaled like
a poor fowl on a spit. Whenever for a moment James closed his
own eyes, the eyes of all those who surrounded him stabbed at
him still. . . .

Ironic and speculative, under thick sandy brows; those were
the eyes of the Earl of Angus, standing close, prompting, guiding
him with patronising, half-contemptuous authority. Authority
. . . James did not care for that. . . . Cold eyes, grey and close-set;
that was Argyll, his Chancellor. Gay and reckless, set among
laughter-creases under black brows: it was a relief to know that
Patrick Hepburn was close at hand, with Lord Home, the Lord
Chamberlain, and his grandson, Alexander, the royal cup-bearer.
The Master of Home, not many years older than himself, contrived to give James an occasional conspiratorial grin, quickly
checked as the greenish, fishy eyes of the Archbishop of St.
Andrews slowly swivelled along the line of noblemen approaching
the throne.

Fishy eyes, James thought, as he laid his hands over those of
the next nobleman who had creaked down on his knees at his
feet. Why had churchmen such fishy eyes? Was it their habit
of eating so much fish that gave many of them a look of the fat
carp that swam sluggishly about in monastic fishponds till the
lay brothers whipped them out on fast days? He began to amuse
himself by looking along the line of churchmen and picturing

them as fish. The fat ones were salmon or carp, the thin ones
herrings, the acolytes sprats. Pleased with his fancy, he found it
checked by eyes which were unexpectedly unfish-like, as he
encountered the compassionate gaze of William Elphinstone,
Bishop of Aberdeen. Here at least was a prelate who was strong
and kind and comforting. From time to time, as the ceremony
approached its conclusion, James found himself looking round the
hall for the reassurance of the Bishop's steady eyes, for now that
he was weary, he was once more afraid of the changed face of
his world. At first it had been pleasant to ride the tidal wave,
as it were, in triumph, till it bore him on its crest to the highest
position in the land. When he had promised the friar who
had heard his confession in Cambuskenneth Abbey to take as his
penance the task of ruling Scotland greatly, it had seemed a
simple thing. But now that he bore the crown and sceptre which
were the visible symbols of that promise, its magnitude daunted
him.

The trumpet calls . . . the acclamation. . . . Waves of noise
thundered about him till he had to clench his fists to prevent
himself from stuffing his fingers in his ears. And then, at last, it
was over. They had taken his hands and were helping him to rise,
to come down from his throne. They were going to present him
to the common people outside the Abbey. Like one who faces an
ultimate ordeal, James nerved himself to endure yet another burst
of sound.

But only silence greeted him. The people of Scotland, as
represented by the crowd which had been eddying about the
Abbey since before the coronation service began, surveyed their
new King and those who had crowned him with brooding uncertainty. At last someone in the distance began a ragged half-
hostile clamour, which was taken up here and there, subsided,
picked up again, then died away.

It was a new experience for James. The men constantly about
him had all profited by the rising which had ended so tragically
at Sauchieburn. From them he had been given the version of the
affair that had been most expedient for him to hear. They
maintained that they had rebelled against his father's mis-
government, demanded his abdication because only thus could

the country be saved from those who were destroying it. His
father's death had been an unhappy accident which no one
deplored more than those whose rebellion had caused it. Had
they not shown their grief by the funereal trappings of the
coronation?

But now James faced the silent, uneasy crowd of common
people who had gained nothing from the change of rulers. Nor
had they heard the carefully edited version of the affair. They
knew only that the King had been done to death and those
responsible for it were also responsible for the coronation of his
son. Murder. . . . The ominous word hovered still on the air.
Doubts began to flock about him, settling in his mind like a flock
of carrion crows.

And doubt, in major matters, was a bewilderingly new sensation. James had been instructed in the Christian faith as became
the heir to the throne. He could not know that the richly
romanticised version which the medieval priesthood approved
had been devised by the class-conscious nobility of Christendom,
for whom the original revelation of the Fatherhood of God and
the brotherhood of mankind, made long ago in Galilee, would
have had less than no appeal.

All imaginative excesses in worship were permitted, therefore,
except those which threatened the authority or diminished the
wealth of the Church. Wise in their generation, churchmen
encouraged such virtues as might be suitably personified by
those of gentle birth. The knight who cantered in his jangling
plate armour was habitually shriven before battle, whether his
cause were just or not, and the lady who posed among her maids
at her devotions for the admiration of her tenantry might afterwards cut a servant's cheek open with her bunch of keys for the
theft of a sugared comfit.

The lower classes, though not likely to be interestingly virtuous,
might become the objects of the virtue of their betters. Here and
there, defying the profitable delusions fostered by their pastors, a
few men and women of compassionate genius outraged public
opinion by venerating the fortitude of those who wore the rags
of poverty or the hideous disguise of disease. But most were
content to interpret their religion in terms of the chivalric

romances which described the search less for holiness than for a
Holy Grail to be actually perceived by the earthly eyes of the
deserving. And the Gospels were kissed more often than they
were ever read.

Like most of his contemporaries, James accepted what appealed
to him; the blessings, the music, the processions, the gorgeous
festivals, and left disputation to the theologians. He was as awed
as any by the wonder-working relics which were so valuable to
the communities which possessed such bait for the simple-hearted.
For pilgrims, they knew, would journey across the country for the
privilege of believing that they had kissed St. Thomas's little
finger, and contribute handsomely in consequence to the funds
of the church which guarded it.

James had often shared the excitement of a great congregation at the carefully contrived phenomena associated with the
images of the blessed saints. Because he was intelligent, he would
not have been deceived by statues which nodded, tears that
flowed, or blood which oozed from ancient wounds had he not
earnestly desired the faith which he had been taught to associate
with such deceptions.

So now he was disconcerted by the converse spectacle of a
crowd sullen with doubt and anger, hostile and unbelieving. As
he took his seat under the cloth of State hung behind the chief
place at the high table, the memory troubled him still.

"Why so glum, my lord James?" Patrick Hepburn leant
forward to demand as he sat silent, while the roar of talk about
him rose like a solid wall of sound.

James looked at the Master of his Household with a rueful
smile. "I know not, Patrick. Except that I wonder why the
common folk outside the Abbey looked at me so unlovingly. Was
it—because they held me guilty—of my father's death?" He
jerked out the question, as he might have wrenched a festering
barb from his flesh. But it was too late. The poison of that guilt
was in his bloodstream. Patrick's hearty guffaw of laughter could
not cauterise it, though it could subdue its manifestations for a
while.

"Never think of it, my lord James," he said robustly. "It
was a mishap, no wish of yours."

"Who killed him, Patrick?" James asked suddenly.

"Believe me, I do not know," Patrick Hepburn turned his shoulder to those seated beyond him and spoke for James alone. "I wish I did. It has stirred the common people more than I would have believed. I am not one of those who fit the dead out with a halo as soon as the earth is stamped down over them," he said candidly. "Your father, may God rest his soul, never, while he lived, won much affection from his people. Why then should there be so much indignation at the manner of his death?"

"Someone shouted murder at me from the crowd," said James shakily.

"They have shouted after me too," Patrick Hepburn admitted frankly. "It is past my comprehension. We maintained your father was no longer fit to govern. Therefore, because he would not yield, we took up arms against him. In the battle, it so came about that he was slain. Such things happen in battles, and though men may grieve, they do not raise this outcry of murder. What does it matter to the common people? They will go hungry, seek food, make love, give birth and die, though another James rules over them, just as they always did."

"I do not like it," James said unhappily.

"It will pass, my lord," said Patrick Hepburn. He snapped his fingers. "Drink, and forget it. Nothing they say can harm you. We will see to that."

"But . . . if it be true . . ."

"Truth is a double-edged blade, my lord. It goes ill for those who grasp it. The well-advised take it by the hilt, which is well guarded by reservations, so that they may use the blade on those who oppose them. But this is sour talk for festivities. Drink, my lord. Your cup-bearer has been waiting so long that the pattern of the rushes must be printed on his knee."

So James drank and let the memory of the hostile crowd fade as his mood changed under the influence of food and wine and music, swinging as usual from one extreme to its opposite, till his gaiety matched that of any member of his Court as the boards were cleared and the fiddlers began to saw out dance tunes in their gallery overhead.

But the members of his Council were well aware of the continuing hostility in certain quarters, as they gathered round James, less like the obedient subjects who had paid homage at Scone than the testy governors of an inattentive pupil who has yet much to learn.

"My lord . . . I submit the names of grooms for your chamber. . . ."

"My lord, I have here an account of the Comptroller's expenses. . . ."

"A number of the gentlemen of Perth are without and seeking audience. . . ."

James stretched his arms above his head and yawned till his jaw cracked. "Alas, my lords," he cried despairingly, "you deave me with more duties than I can endure. Is the King of Scots never to have time for idleness and laughter again?"

"Mirth is the luxury of lesser men, my lord," the Earl of Argyll reproved him. "I beg you will give your attention to the urgent matters in hand."

James rolled his eyes upward, looked despairingly about him, and wished that Patrick Hepburn, who was at least of his way of thinking as regarded the necessity for mirth, had not been absent on urgent business concerning the defence of the Border Marches. He craved for amusement as a bored child craves for sweets. And since a state visit from an elderly kinsman could not be considered spectacularly lively, his need of diversion could be measured by the eagerness with which he presently learned of the prospect of the arrival from Denmark of his great-uncle, that fantastic old reprobate, Junker Gerhard.

CHAPTER SEVEN

WHEN the news came, early in August, that the Danish ships had appeared off the coast at Leith, James leapt at the chance of greeting his mother's legendary kinsman as a kennelled pup leaps at an opening door.

"I can attend to no more business," he told his Council. "I

must set out at once if I am to reach the harbour in time to greet Junker Gerhard."

" It might well be more in keeping with the dignity of the King of Scots, my lord, if you were to permit the Danish embassy to wait on your pleasure at Linlithgow," said the Earl of Argyll.

" And lose a chance of seeing the Danish ships? I shall send for Sir Andrew Wood——"

" Sir Andrew has not yet made his submission, my lord," Argyll pointed out.

" Because he is a great sailor," said James rebelliously, " I shall send for him, my lords, all the same."

As they arrived at Leith, James took deep breaths of delight as the tang of the snell wind excited him. The Danish ships were becalmed some distance off shore, but the battered little ship made fast by the quayside was flying the Scottish saltire. " What vessel is that? " he demanded.

" *The Flower*, my lord," someone said.

" *The Flower?* . . . Is Sir Andrew Wood aboard? "

" Shall I discover, my lord? " squeaked an officious page.

James nodded, ignoring the glum looks about him. " If you find Sir Andrew," he added defiantly, " bring him here to me."

Exasperated, the members of the Council who had ridden to Leith with James turned their attention to the Danish ships now hoisting sail to take advantage of the slight breeze, so that the return of the page with the stocky sailor who held his head so proudly, took them all by surprise.

" Sir Andrew Wood, my lord," said the page reverently.

James took one look at the man who confronted him with such a candid air of resentful sorrow, then stepped forward with outstretched hand. The charm that few men were to be able to resist was no calculated thing with James. When he behaved as though he liked people it was because, in fact, he did. The admiration which now lit his eyes was not conveniently assumed. For James was never able either to dissemble or to lie.

" Sir Andrew, I am glad to find you here," he said. " I shall have need of you."

" Sir," said Sir Andrew frankly, " these gentlemen will tell you, if I do not, that I was your father's man, not yours, in the recent troubles."

" I am happy to think," said James, " that my father was so well served. I could not look for fairer loyalty. And so I trust you will also serve me."

Sir Andrew Wood's face, so deeply tanned in its grizzle of whiskers that it seemed like a chestnut in sheep's wool, creased with a sudden grin. He took James's hand in both his own, and knelt laboriously.

" My lord," he said gruffly, " you may be assured I will."

James looked over his shoulder at the Danish ships, now slowly approaching. " They will not reach the shore yet awhile? "

" I think not, my lord."

" Then there will be time for you to show me *The Flower*," said James delightedly. " My lords, I believe it will be more in keeping with the dignity of the King of Scots to receive Junker Gerhard aboard a Scottish ship instead of awaiting him on the cobblestones."

" My lord, that will do very well," agreed the Earl of Angus, to whom the thought of standing about awaiting other people's pleasure never made any appeal.

Junker Gerhard was a great florid, golden giant of a man, obese as a barrel, with a wheezing bellow of a voice and a harsh cackling laugh which was as startling as most things about the uncle of the King of Denmark. He greeted James, characteristically, with a low bow which dismissed the formalities and left him free to express his genuine cordiality with embracing arms and a wide grin which showed irregular, blackish teeth, between the magnificent thicket of golden moustache and beard.

" Heaven be praised, nephew," said Junker Gerhard, "that you take more after your mother than your poor father, God rest his soul. Aye, bless me, Denmark will have cause to be proud of that marriage yet. And how does it please you to be a King? " the big Dane demanded, still crushing James's hands between his and surveying his great-nephew with his leonine head on one side.

" It is somewhat tedious at times," James admitted, wincing slightly as he extricated his hands from that heroic clasp.

Junker Gerhard tilted his beard towards the circling seagulls

and let out a caw of laughter as discordant as theirs. " Tedious?
I believe you," he said, glancing round the disapproving circle
of silent noblemen. " We must see what we can do about that."
He leant forward, laying a finger along his nose in a gesture of
knowing intimacy. " When we have done our duty towards these
gentlemen," he confided in a whisper which was borne far on the
gusty wind, " we must find ourselves some amusement, you and
I."

James, restraining the desire to giggle at the sight of the
affronted faces about him, replied gravely, " Indeed, Uncle,
nothing would please me more."

" We will speak of this again, nephew," Junker Gerhard
confided with a vast wink. " Meanwhile——"

" My lord the King will no doubt wish to know what arrangements have been made for his guest's reception," the Comptroller
of the Household said suavely when the introductions had been
made. " I have arranged a lodging for him at the house of Peter
the Fowler here at Leith, since he will wish to be near his ships
and merchandise while his business is being done——"

Junker Gerhard, who had expected to make an indefinite stay
at the Palace of Linlithgow, ruefully perceived that his reputation
had preceded him. He shrugged. " I shall do well enough there,
no doubt."

" But you will spare the time, Uncle, from your business to
dine with me at the Palace? "

" Nephew, I most surely will," Junker Gerhard said.

Polite discouragement bounced off the bulky Dane as hail-
stones bounce off plate armour. He presented himself at the
Palace of Linlithgow just as the silver trumpets summoned James's
household to dinner in the great hall, and in spite of the muttered
comments of those about him, James made it clear that he was
delighted to see him.

" Make way there," he commanded, gesturing the courtiers
aside. " Uncle, you shall sit at my right hand."

Junker Gerhard made himself quite at home at the high
table, pushing out his elbows and letting the grease drip negligently
from his golden moustache as he swept meat and gravy and great
gobblets of fat into his cavernous mouth on the blade of his knife.

James, who had inherited moderation in such matters from his father, observed his heroic capacity for food and drink with awe, and his uncle, who was also insatiably inquisitive, occasionally paused in his operations with knife and trencher to make inquiries with such a warmth of interest that they were hard to resent.

" You are well served here, nephew? " Junker Gerhard's little bright blue eyes, under the jutting thatch of fierce blond brows, glanced up and down the hall, comparing the decorous procession of carvers, cup-bearers and stewards who waited on the King at the high table on its raised dais, with the snatch-and-grab informality of the lesser folk who ate at the tables below. " You want for nothing, it seems. Food and wine, heaven be praised, you have in plenty."

" Yes, Uncle," James agreed. But the wistfulness of his guest's tone made him feel ashamed as Junker Gerhard swallowed hastily, took a draught of wine, then crammed in a fresh mouthful as if he feared such a chance might not come his way again.

" Is it not splendid to be a King, who can do whatever he chooses, and favour those to whom he is well disposed? " The big Dane sighed gustily. " I have ever had a generous nature. It irks me sorely that I should be a poor man with little to bestow, whereas you, nephew, need not deny yourself what would have been my supreme joy."

James responded with anxious sympathy. " It is true," he agreed, " that the bestowal of gifts gives me great pleasure——"

" Aye, indeed," sighed Junker Gerhard. " So it would have given me——"

" You will allow me, Uncle, while you are in Scotland . . ." murmured James, flushing hotly, " to see that——"

" My dear nephew," said Junker Gerhard in a heroic tone, " believe me, poverty has taught me a few things. I will accept your generosity in the same spirit as, I believe, you would have accepted mine. . . ."

" My lord the King," said the Earl of Argyll, leaning forward to divert the course of the conversation as he became aware of its drift, " will it please you to listen to Blind Harry's songs after the boards have been removed? "

" It—er—will please me very well," James replied, when he had detached his attention from his uncle's troubles.

" There is also another fellow waiting outside whose tales are worth hearing," said Patrick Hepburn.

" We will listen to them both," said James, turning back to his guest. " You have wandering fellows like these in Denmark, Uncle? "

Junker Gerhard, speechless because he had taken advantage of the diversion to cram his mouth fuller than ever, nodded, chewing vigorously. " Denmark is the very home of such minstrels. But tell me, nephew," he mumbled, presently, glancing about him, " where are your brothers? Do they not appear at your Court? "

James frowned. " Sometimes. But it seems wise that they should remain oftener at home for the present."

Junker Gerhard nodded understandingly, and lowered his own voice till it was slightly less far-reaching: " There was some talk that your father thought to make the young Duke of Ross his heir instead of yourself. What was the truth of that? " he asked blandly.

James shrugged. " I do not know," he said.

" Would your brother now make cause against you? "

" I think not."

" And the youngest, John of Mar? "

James winced at the mention of the title to which his nine-year-old brother seemed to have so much less right than the young uncle whom he still remembered with a boy's sharp, irrational grief. " My brother John is only a little lad still."

" How does he promise? "

" He will be clerkly, I believe," James said. " He seems always to ail something so that he makes little progress in knightly matters. But he cons his books well enough."

" Takes after his father, eh? " said Junker Gerhard, belching gently. " It is as well that you are the eldest, for nothing goes right for a country with a clerk at the head of it. I have heard already of your knightly zeal. How is it with you in the sweeter arts? A fine lusty lad like yourself must already have caught the fancy of many fair ladies." He leant towards James, breathing rather heavily as he whispered: " Who is your present fancy, nephew? "

His roving eye surveyed the women seated near him with expert care, and his gusty whisper carried far and wide as he continued aimiably. " Which of the fair dames I see about us is your latest bedfellow? "

James blushed furiously, ducking his head in an attempt to hide his embarrassment, painfully aware of the ripple of amusement with which the inquiry had stirred the somnolence of the Court's after-dinner mood, so that the tall head-dresses of the ladies bobbed like a border of bright flowers.

" Why—none as yet—I——"

Junker Gerhard's bellow of laughter startled the pages at the serving-tables and made the grooms and maids at the lower end of the hall look up from their platters. He brought his big hand down on his nephew's shoulder in a companionable gesture which made James wince.

" Have no fear, nephew. That is something you will soon put to rights I have no doubt in the world. It wants but a beginning, then all goes as sweetly as birdsong on a summer morning. Or evening it might be. Eh? " he added knowingly, jabbing with an elbow towards James's ribs. " When I was a lad of less than your age the lady who was my paramour had already been brought to bed of a fine babe."

" My lord the King, the Chief Huntsman is waiting for instruction," interposed the Earl of Argyll. " Will it please you, to ride out for a day's sport in the morning? "

" It will please me very well," said James. " Uncle, you will ride with us, I hope."

" If you can find a horse to carry me," said Junker Gerhard with a roar of good-natured laughter. " I must own that I have tended to take my sport astride a pretty mare instead of a stallion, and in the bedchamber rather than the hunting-field of late years. I fancy my performance. . . ."

He winked and nodded, enjoying the laughter which greeted his sally, though James, who preferred his humour to be somewhat subtler, was relieved when the servants began to clear the

boards from their trestles in order that the evening's entertainment
might begin.

Junker Gerhard, however, quite unabashed, was cheerfully
informative, and, as the evening proceeded, showed himself
willing to offer the most explicit advice on all matters concerning
the blandishment of ladies, a sport at which, by his own account,
he was remarkably expert.

" I have never set all that much store, nephew, by your
hunting and hawking," he admitted. " Sorely tedious, to my
mind, such exercises are. Compare the pursuit of a woman. . . .
Ah, there alone, nephew, a man finds a quarry worthy of his
skill and subtlety, as the greatest poets and story-tellers have well
known. Hark to me, nephew. This, I believe, you may not have
heard. . . ."

He murmured and smiled, closing one eye in a meditative
wink, elucidating his story with gestures which explained a
number of things that had so far puzzled James, whose circumstances had set him somewhat apart from the cheerful company
of pages and esquires among whom such matters were freely
discussed.

To Junker Gerhard such ignorance represented an educational
deficiency which he was well qualified to adjust. He set himself,
therefore, the task of finding his nephew a suitable paramour
without delay. For if ever a lad had the sort of charm that
presently would set every woman at Court buzzing round him for
his favours, it was his young nephew, James. But there he went,
the silly innocent, eager for experience, his head stuffed with
romantic nonsense, up in the clouds one day and down in the
depths the next, tormenting himself with chains and penance for
the part he had played in his father's death, yet fretting for a
chance to enjoy his new authority so much that it would not be
long before he wrenched himself free of the leading rein that the
clumsy schemer, Angus, thought himself entitled to hold because
of some cock-and-bull nonsense about cats and bells.

Aye, aye, pretty soon, Junker Gerhard told himself, watching
the Scottish scene out of his small, shrewd, drink-hazed blue eyes,
James would make himself King of Scots indeed. Meanwhile,
his uncle was grateful to him, and sought to make some return

by offering to initiate him in the art of which he himself had a vast, and on the whole a reliable fund of knowledge. He had already made a start. But because theory was all very well, though not the crux of any matter, he decided to look about during the next few months, for a lady who would be a suitable object of James's attentions. As a connoisseur, Junker Gerhard went carefully about the business. She must not be too young, for James was fastidious enough to be distressed by the blunderings of mutual ignorance. Nor must she be too old, for he was an ardent lover of beauty. She must not be a fool, for his nephew was far too intelligent to fear a clever woman's rivalry. Nor must she be a schemer. James stood to lose too much if she set her mind on what was to be gained. Above all, she must have benevolence, for if he read the signs aright, James would have to do with many women during the course of his life, and it was essential that his first mating should work the need for a mother out of his system for good and all.

James was unaware that his uncle had given any such thought to the matter. He knew only that his advice on the subject of women was shrewd and unexpectedly kind. It was a comfort to reveal both his innocence and ardour to a man of the world whose own revelations made it clear that nothing James had to tell could ever shock him. But Junker Gerhard bided his time. Yule passed and the lean season of Lent. It was not till the Court had gathered again at Linlithgow for Easter that Junker Gerhard drew his nephew's attention to Mistress Boyd as she passed them on the swirl of a country dance in the great hall.

" What think you of the lass in the golden gown, nephew? She that is next us now."

James watched the strong, sweeping movements of the big, dark young woman and nodded thoughtfully, his head a little on one side, his long fingers stroking the firmly jutting chin on which, as yet, only the fairest down disappointingly showed.

" She looks . . . both kind and comely," he said at last.

" That was my thought, nephew," Junker Gerhard agreed. " And such qualities go less often together than might be supposed. Who may she be, I wonder? "

" I do not know," James admitted. " But I will find out."

While the fiddlers rested, the company settled down to listen to the harping and carping of Blind Harry, from the place reserved for him by the fire. The old man's voice quavered across an attentive silence, gaining strength it seemed, from the rapt attention of those who clustered about him, as they sat on the rushes at his feet, crowded the benches, perched on the trestle tables which had not yet been removed. But James, as he leant back in his high chair, his face shadowed from the flickering torchlight, scarcely heard him. He was looking anxiously for Mistress Boyd.

He found her easily enough, sitting on a bench with a number of other young people. Her face was lit by the torchlight which spluttered and wavered above the sconce braced against the wall before her. James could see that the blind minstrel's tale held her rapt. Her mouth softened. Tears filled her eyes. She clasped her hands. He could see her breasts rise and fall. Listening now himself, James shared her excitement, her delight and grief at the tragic tale. And then, in the silence which followed, she looked round and caught his eye as he leaned forward, emerging from the shadow of his chair.

She flushed. James smiled. And after the briefest hesitation, Mariot smiled back. Then Blind Harry began to sing again. This time the song was one they all knew, and the voices rose about him from the dimness as he gestured them to take part. James sang with them, and fancied he could hear Mariot's voice, deep and warm and strong, companioning his own. When Blind Harry was led away at last to refresh himself with a tankard of wine in the chimney-corner, James took advantage of the commotion made by those preparing for the dancing to make his way towards the young woman his uncle had admired. Under cover of the squawking of the fiddles tuning up in the gallery he said, with his usual directness: " Madam, I would be happy to have you as my partner. Shall we lead the dance? "

And Mariot, curtsying in a flurry which was not entirely assumed, answered in just the deep voice he had hoped: " You do me too much honour, my lord the King."

As he led her to the head of the line the music launched them into the exuberant country dance that was half a romp, the partners swinging and weaving, meeting and parting, swirling round, gowns and veils flying, to the high harsh music of the fiddles, the capricious light of the torches blown aslant by the wind of their passage, their heads bombarded by the painted bladders that Curry, the Court fool, had fastened to the thongs of a couple of hunting-whips and was brandishing with loud whoops. The bells on the points of his parti-coloured doublet and hose and mock coronet of scarlet and black, chimed their gay counterpoint to the lilting fiddles, but his long, sad, yellow face never changed its expression, though the sweat streaked his forehead as he leapt and gesticulated among the dancers, hooting and mocking as he was privileged to do.

" See there, my Sovereign Lord. You be a greater fule than poor Curry if ye think ye can swing sic' a sonsy armful frae the ground. . . ."

Laughing, James grasped Mariot round the waist after they had passed under the arch of arms raised high, took a deep breath and lifted her bodily off her feet so that she clung to him, shrieking as he swung her wide, while the nearest dancers scattered, throwing the lines askew.

" Ho, a Samson, a Samson on the throne of Scotland," yelled Curry, all his bells jangling as he turned a grave cartwheel and stood, feet astride and arms akimbo, applauding James's achievement without moving a muscle of his cynical, leathery face.

" I'll show you what such a Samson can do," James gasped, shaking his fist and laughing, as he swept Mariot down the centre and back again, to the steady rhythm of clapping hands. " Wait only till the dance be ended. . . ."

" Oh, no, my lord, mercy I pray, my lord," moaned Curry, prancing up and down with his hands protecting his bottom as if from an anticipated kick. " I do but my duty, as no doubt you will do yours when the world is abed and the lights are low. . . ."

Scarlet-eared, James was thankful that the next stage of the dance whirled him away from Mariot, though, as he led the line outwards he was further disconcerted by the sight of Junker Gerhard's gap-toothed grin and applauding hands. But when he met Mariot again and clasped her vigorous body, he fancied, as his hand strayed upward over her ribs, that he could feel the quickened beating of her heart. Suddenly abashed, though he guessed her to be smiling at him, he could not meet her eyes. He was aware of a tumult in his own body; he felt dizzy with desire, yet ashamed at the same time lest others should see and mock him. Then, as he swung her for the last time, and the music of the fiddlers sawed out the final chords, the crackle of applause was followed by an unexpected silence.

Heads were turning, those nearest the door midway down the long wall were rising, the heat of the crowded hall was pierced by a draught of cold air as if by a threatening sword. James, still holding Mariot by the hand, was suddenly alert at the sight of the armed men, mud-splashed and rain-soaked, who were talking in the entrance to the Earls of Argyll and Angus. The news they had brought was borne to him by a score of startled voices.

" Revolt . . . the north is in revolt. . . . Dumbarton is to be held against the King. . . ."

CHAPTER EIGHT

JAMES let Mariot's fingers slip from between his own as he stepped forward to hear for himself. And at his coming men and women drew back, their faces quenched and grave. Only Curry, the fool, standing gaunt and round-shouldered, his balloons bobbing gently at his feet, smiled for the first time, as if the relief of no longer being required to whip up the gaiety of the gathering was so exquisite that anxiety itself was welcome to a man for whom laughter was a weariness and folly mere stock-in-trade.

" What is your news? " James demanded as the group by the doorway drew back to receive him.

" My lord," said the Earl of Angus, " these men come from the north with news of insurrection in the name of our former King. It seems that Lady Forbes is displaying a bloodstained shirt which she claims to be your father's, as a banner to rally the discontented in Aberdeen."

" Ihmhm. In the absence of its Bishop," commented Argyll. " Elphinstone would never have countenanced such a thing. When he returns——"

" Since he is now at the English Court," Angus interrupted, " something must be done without him. Who else has joined this affair? "

The bearers of ill-tidings, with the gusto peculiar to their kind, had the names pat, and brought them out impressively, pausing to enjoy the consternation that each caused.

" The Earl Marischal . . ."

" Likely enough," said Argyll, shaking his head.

" Old Hearken and Take Heed was ever one for the old ways," said Angus.

" John, Earl of Lennox, and his son Mathew, the Master, are also with them. . . ."

" More's the pity."

" Huntly besides. . . ."

" What are we dallying for? " cried James, as the prospect of battle eclipsed the charms of Mistress Boyd. " Where are they to be found? If Dumbarton has been garrisoned against us, then, by heaven, let us ding it down about their ears! "

His ardour was as contagious as fire. The hall was at once in a hubbub as young men freed themselves from the detaining arms of the sweethearts who protested loudly at the prospect of their revels being spoilt, while James, dancing from foot to foot with impatience, shouted for his armour and his horse.

" Softly, softly, my lord the King," murmured the Earl of Argyll. " We will ding the walls of Dumbarton down indeed, but scarcely by pelting them with the stones that come first to hand. The artillery must be assembled from the Castle of Edinburgh. A team of oxen will be required to trundle the great gun, Mons. Men must go before them to level the road."

" Blessed saints, if we daunder so, these fellows will still be defying us at midsummer."

" My lord, we should daunder to less purpose if the great cannon sank in a bog," Angus pointed out.

" Then let those that have enough patience wait for the guns and those that have not set out with me."

" I will go with you, my lord the King," said Patrick Hepburn, Earl of Bothwell.

" And I," promised Lord Drummond.

" And I . . ."

" And I . . ."

The eager voices echoed.

Argyll smiled wryly. " Since so many make haste, others must go slowly," he said. " If it be your pleasure, I will remain with the guns."

Angus said nothing. The diversion was one he welcomed, for certain plans of his own, less concerned with Scotland's welfare, would be easier to carry out if James were occupied elsewhere.

Before his departure James took reluctant leave of his great-uncle, for Junker Gerhard had already announced his intention of leaving Scotland for the English Court. Spring made for easier journeying, he explained, for an old man who had come to set great store by his comforts. When James begged him to remain at least till his return from Dumbarton he slowly closed one blood-shot eye and laid a finger along his nose in his favourite gesture.

" In my circumstances, nephew, you would realise that it is often wiser to move on before the past follows closely enough to chafe one's heels."

" But you will return, Uncle? "

" I will, nephew," Junker Gerhard promised gladly.

For a little while, James was sad. But presently, as he splashed through the April weather, both Junker Gerhard and Mistress Boyd were forgotten. For the prospect of battle set his heart thundering as no woman had yet done.

Dumbarton held out, however, in spite of Argyll and the guns. And Lennox eluded James and his contingent, till he was re-luctantly obliged to return to Edinburgh for the next session of Parliament in June with the battle un-won, and to remain there to receive the ambassadors of their most Christian Majesties, King Ferdinand and Queen Isabella of Spain, who came bearing gifts, and dropping hints about an unspecified Spanish princess for whose sake, it was hoped, James would dismiss the thought of a closer alliance with France than would suit either England or Spain.

James received the present of the exquisitely wrought sword and dagger sent by their Spanish Majesties with real pleasure, for such weapons were the wonder of the world. He charmed the Spaniards, as he charmed most foreigners, not only by being able to speak their language, but by his evident interest in Spanish affairs. Though the prospect of the Spanish match was the airiest fabrication on the part of King Ferdinand, whose daughter was already pledged to Prince Arthur of England, the courtesies were so prolonged that it was autumn before James was free to rejoin his army, and jog off beside Lord Drummond towards Stirling in search of the Earl of Lennox.

They found him at last on Talla Muir, and James at once gave battle, shouting a view-hulloo as he led the charge. Lord Drummond, sweating with anxiety, scarcely dared watch that hurricane onslaught. If the King should come to any harm, heaven help those who should have governed him, he thought, pounding after the reckless boy who seemed to have forgotten that knights and men-at-arms could be more easily replaced than the King of Scots.

" My lord, in my place, you would have done as much," said James, as he returned, breathless and triumphant.

And Lord Drummond, whose kindred were not conspicuous for their meekness, could not with honesty deny it. He mopped his brow, shook his fist, and grinned, for the success of the royal forces had taken the heart out of the revolt. Bygones, after all, men began to say, were best let go by. As the days drew in the resistance began to fizzle out, though Dumbarton did not fall till the end of the year, so that James had no time for festivities at Yule.

But when Parliament assembled in the Tolbooth of Edinburgh in February the disaffected lords duly appeared before it to answer for their part in the affair. The Earl of Lennox, with his son, the Master, Lord Lyle and Lord Forbes, the Earl of Huntly and the Earl Marischal, were sentenced to death and forfeiture of lands and goods. But James granted their plea for mercy almost before it was made. He had enjoyed the excitement of the chase far too much to be anything but grateful to those who had provided it, and his only regret was that the excitement of the rebellion had so soon spent itself, for the monotony of official business was something to which he found it very hard to return.

" Mother of God, how I weary of the sight of so many columns of figures," he complained to the Lord High Treasurer. " I wish my uncle from Denmark had not left us for the English Court. He at least knew how to enjoy himself."

" He did indeed, my lord," Sir William Knollis observed dryly. " Such enjoyment is easier when taken at another's expense. The bill is high enough."

" Have we not paid it? " said James. " My uncle had five hundred pounds for his expenses in Scotland."

" My lord, so it is recorded in my accounts," said Sir William Knollis. " But it seems that Peter the Fowler, at whose house Junker Gerhard lodged, now requires a further hundred and eighty-six pounds, seven shillings. This, too, I have paid."

" Doubtless my uncle bestowed gifts," said James, seeking to be loyal to Junker Gerhard's kindly memory.

" Doubtless," said Sir William Knollis, adding dryly. " It is to be hoped that the King of England's Treasury can stand the demands which now seem likely to be made upon it, if our experience is any guide."

" King Henry," said James quickly, " can take good care of such matters, I believe." He smiled, at the thought. Outrageous spendthrift though he might be, Junker Gerhard had taught him many things which were not to be assessed in terms of shillings and pence. He had been wise, after his fashion. And he had been kind. " I shall miss him, for all he has cost us," James said sadly, for Junker Gerhard's going had left him short of counsellors, though he never lacked friends.

So he was glad when Bishop Elphinstone, back from the embassy to King Henry of England, came to talk informally of the visit on which he had already reported officially to the Council.

It had not, he admitted, been altogether an easy journey, for he had accompanied the Archbishops of St. Andrews and Glasgow and since the latter's elevation they had, it seemed,

squabbled over precedence till they were not on speaking terms.
"And the seventh King Henry, though he received us with all
courtesy, does not trust us," said Bishop Elphinstone.

"By all accounts, my lord Bishop," said James, "he trusts
nobody, in England or elsewhere."

Bishop Elphinstone sighed and nodded. "Yes, he had the
look of a man who sees the enemy lurking in every shadow, fears
the thorn guarding every flower." Then he smiled, fingering the
parcel under his cloak. "I hope my gift will give you pleasure.
I contrived to visit Caxton's printing press and bring back a
sample of his work," he explained, as he drew it forth. "This
folio was printed for the first time four years ago in Westminster.
He has called it *Le Morte d'Arthur*, though Sir Thomas Malory
treats therein of much else besides."

James took the book, ponderous between its boards, and turned
the thick, clumsily bound pages with delight, his voice awed as
he murmured stray phrases from Caxton's preface aloud.

"'Many noble and divers gentlemen of this realm of England
came and demanded me . . . why I have not made and printed
the noble history of the Holy Grail and of the most renowned
Christian king, Arthur, which ought most to be remembered
among us Englishmen before all other Christian kings. . . .'"

After a while he looked up, smiling. "My lord Bishop, I
thank you most warmly for a gift after my own heart."

Bishop Elphinstone nodded. "I thought it well might be.
Think only, my lord, of what treasures we might put in the hands
of Scottish students with such a printing press in our own
land. . . ."

But James's attention had returned to his new treasure. "'To
whom I answered that divers men hold opinion that there was
no such Arthur, and that all such books as been made of him be
but feigned and fables. . . .'"

The time was not yet ripe, reflected Bishop Elphinstone. He
would be mistaken to press upon James now an idea which would
flourish better if it sprang from his own mind later on. He rose,
therefore, and prepared to take his leave, for James, with chin
on fists and elbows spread wide on the table-top, seemed unlikely
to notice whether he went or stayed. And James, lost to all but

the world of Arthurian chivalry, saw himself, as Easter approached, riding with the worshipful knights from Camelot to Joyous Garde, where on the battlements of his cloud castle beckoned . . . Mariot. And so it was of Mariot that he thought continually, during Lent, when his mind should have been on other things. And in his impatience, he fancied that the sad season would never end.

A larger company than ever had been bidden to Linlithgow for Easter, so that the courtyard of the Palace echoed to the hubbub of arrivals, the shouting of orders, the laughter of men and maidens. As night fell, torches bobbed in all directions as lords and ladies were escorted to their quarters, horses led away to the stables, and servants staggered under the weight of the great chests in which the ladies' most gorgeous gowns were carefully bestowed between layers of linen and lavender.

James welcomed his younger brothers, who had come with their governors, Patrick Hepburn and Alexander Home. Though circumstances had made them little more than shadowy strangers, they were all the family he had left. But the younger boys retreated into shyness from which he sought to tease them in vain. They stood rigid, in their brave new clothes, smiling uneasily at their splendid brother, till James gave up the attempt, and passed on to other guests, enjoying himself in his gorgeous new outfit of blue, scarlet and black, girt with a magnificent gold belt suspending the sword and dagger which had been the gift of their Majesties of Spain. In the grey March weather the old walls and sad-coloured tapestries of the Palace were lapped by a flood of colour which transfigured Linlithgow into a summer garden, and great fires baked the last of winter's chill out of the old stones.

As the days passed James held himself back from seeking out Mariot, conscious of the delay he forced upon himself half as an agony and half the quintessence of joy. Once, he encountered her unexpectedly on the stairs, and while instinct clamoured that he should surprise her with a kiss, Sir Thomas Malory's tales reminded him of his duty as a gentle knight. He bowed, therefore, stepped back, and offered her his hand.

" Madam, permit me to assist you."

Mariot curtsied. She had not seen the King close for many months. A great lad he was now, though beardless yet. Had his fancy for her outlasted the winter, she wondered, half-abashed and half-amused by his shy formality, which was so different from the forthright advances of older men, murmuring, " I thank you, my lord the King," while she laid cool finger-tips on his palm.

As they stood so, for a moment Mariot was well aware that he had but to pull her towards him and she would have over-balanced into his arms. But James, taut with unfamiliar shyness, scarcely enclosed the hand that touched his palm. Presently Mariot herself stepped down with a little sigh, and a swirl of shouting dancers forced them apart again.

So the days passed. At table James raised his cup to her, at the dance he touched her finger-tips, and when the party subsided, breathless, on to the surrounding benches to watch the mummers for a change, he often contrived to be at her side. Yet, eager as he was, and hopeful from her smiling gentleness, that she was not unwilling to receive him, he held back, as if aware of a frontier from which, once crossed, he could never retrace his steps again.

His preoccupation with her seemed to enclose him in a dream, so that he viewed his surroundings as if he beheld the whole world in miniature, on the curving sides of a bubble of make-believe, exquisite and without flaw. But like a bubble, he guessed it to be so fragile that a touch would mar it into nothingness. So, worshipfully, he kept his distance, increasingly perplexed, as the festival drew near its close, between the tumult of his feelings and the barrier of his inexperience. Soon she would leave Linlithgow and return home. How could he endure it? Anxiety tormented him till, one evening, he sought out Patrick Hepburn, and found him most comfortably unconcerned.

" Leave it to me, my lord," he advised. " And I will see that the lady is conveyed to your bedchamber with discretion, while all others are dispatched elsewhere."

Yet, in spite of such assurance, James fancied himself parti-cularly pestered, that night, by the attentions of those who escorted him to his bedchamber, and would scarcely endure his dismissal. He dared not look his chamber grooms in the face for fear of seeing them grin. These fellows knew something was afoot, that he could swear. Even his page, fussing about with the candle-snuffers, seemed determined to dawdle half the night. James

could have beaten the boy for the diligence with which he replenished the fire and drew his bed curtains. And it was so
quiet, when he had at last bowed himself over the threshold, that
the cluck of the flames sounded like secret laughter. Somewhere
in the dim corner beyond the candles which stood on either side
of the pavilion-like posts and roof of the brocade-hung bed, he
could hear the scutter and scrabble of a mouse in the shadows.
He wondered whether Mariot would shriek at the thought of it.
And then he wondered, unbearably, whether she would refuse
the invitation Patrick must by now have discreetly conveyed. The
thought made him as angry as a child refused a treat on which it
had set its heart. And then, frustration changed to utter desolation, so that his loneliness seemed more than he could bear. He
ached with longing, if only for the touch of her hand, the sound
of her voice. Out of an anguish of vacancy, he stretched his arms
above his head and yawned.

She laughed softly from the shadows of the doorway, making
him start. " So weary, my lord? Shall I go away? "

But James, afraid that she might go indeed, flung his arms
about her as a child pinions his mother's skirts. And then,
suddenly, he was on his knees, with his cheek pressed to her soft
body, thrusting aside the silken draperies, searching for the sweet,
warm smoothness of the naked flesh that curved so softly below
his exploring lips. With a little shaken sigh she stooped over him,
her hands moving through his hair, her body pressing against
him till the urgency of his need for her escaped his control. He
rose and bore her across the chamber to fall with her upon the
wide, lavender-scented bed, and there battle with the unfamiliar
forces that struggled within him, an agony of sweetness and a
sweetness of agony so blended as to be indistinguishable, spiralling
upwards to a point of unendurable bliss at which peace broke
blindingly over him like the dayspring of the world.

Then he was aware again of her soft body beneath him, her
strong arms holding him, her voice murmuring reassurance as she
raised a hand to wipe the sweat from his face.

" There, my love . . . there. Sleep now. . . ."

Out of an infinite depth of weariness he reached up to kiss her
lips. He could feel his body leaving hers, lingeringly, reluctantly,

as if for that unimaginable instant of unity which was already no
more than a memory, the curse of carnal separation had been
remitted, so that they had become, like the angels in heaven, one
flesh. . . . But now each must return to the void of separation of
which he had scarcely been aware till, with the unearthly
experience of earthly union, his solitude had been revealed to him,
a solitude so sharpened by contrast as to represent utter desolation,
from which his flesh-entangled spirit must now seek for ever to
escape. Then exhaustion blurred the edge of his new awareness.
Moving a little, till his head lay between her breasts, he slept,
while Mariot lay awake in the warm darkness, restless because
his inexperienced ardour had unskilfully sought only its own
satisfaction, and yet awed by the pathos of his need. They had
told her that the King was still virgin, but she had not believed
it. Now, as he lay, relaxed and at peace beside her, she knew it
had been true.

CHAPTER NINE

SO, while James slept, Mariot lay wakeful: wondering what
would come of it all, and how soon James's fancy would fade.
She was without illusions as to the ultimate outcome. A few
months, a year or two, and the King would look for a younger
face, a body virgin as his own had been. Lads for ever turned
against their first love; the humiliation of remembered ignorance
irked them when they were ignorant no longer. It was natural;
when it came she would have no more complaint than a mother
left behind by the son with his way to make in the world.

Mariot was experienced, but her contacts had been brief
intimacies with men older than herself, men who had been gallant
and casual even in their passion, occasionally so brutalised by
drink that she had refused them with indignation. James was
different, she realised, as time went on. He had taken her as a
tempest uproots a sapling, without understanding what he had
done. But afterwards, his patronage would enhance her value,

and he would be unlikely to bid her farewell without a handsome souvenir of his affection.

Meanwhile he sought her out, during the last days of the festival, with a most innocent ardour, commanded her to his chamber at nightfall, and arranged for her to remain at Linlithgow when the guests began to disperse to their homes. That summer he grudged every necessity which took him away from her, returning to Linlithgow like a homing pigeon to its dovecote, from Stirling, Dundee and Perth. In October, duty called him to Edinburgh, for the Church had indignantly summoned the Master of Drummond and his men to stand trial before the Lords of the Council for murder and sacrilege. They had fired the Kirk of Monyvaird over the heads of the hostile Murrays who had taken refuge from them within it. But every time he left her with reluctance, still spoke wistfully of his longing to return.

"I shall soon be back. I hate all things that keep me from you."

"A King must attend to his country's affairs, that I well know," she assured him, smiling.

"You will await me? Here in Linlithgow?"

"I will await your return here, dear love."

She was so calm. James never knew how deeply he had touched her heart. Sometimes she seemed as remote from him as the stars, so that he had to reassure himself by taking possession of her body with such violence that she cried out, and he was immediately contrite, for cruelty, even in sex, was as alien to his nature as falsehood. He did not guess that such remoteness was the instinctive defence of a woman who knew her triumph to be brief, and was already looking beyond it to the humbler life she must resume.

In October James returned as usual to Linlithgow, troubled by the judgment which had condemned the Master of Drummond and a number of his followers to death, in spite of extenuating circumstances and the personal appeals from the young man's relations. The family's distress disturbed him, for Lord Drummond had seen him through his first campaign against Lennox. But against the clamour of sacrilege, there could be no redress. Though his youth and inexperience made him little more than a

pawn among the bishops, his consent to the death penalty had
concluded the trial.

But the burden of responsibility for a young man's death slid
from him with the news of responsibility of a very different sort.
For Mariot now knew beyond any doubt that she was carrying
his child. She had been uncertain of how James would receive
her news. A lad of his age might well turn from her as pregnancy
blurred her beauty. Fear of the consequences now following the
pleasure they had taken in each other might frighten him away.
She had not looked for the pride with which he received the
tribute to his manhood, the gentler care with which he tempered
his demands to her condition, nor his utter delight in the infant
daughter born to them soon after the New Year. She must be
called Catherine, James declared, since it was on the day dedicated
to the Virgin Martyr of Alexandria that he had first learned of her
existence. And Mariot, relieved by the unconcern with which he
acknowledged his daughter, realised with a sharper pang than
she had ever expected to feel, that his child was soon going to mean
more to James than her mother, however chivalrously he might
seek to conceal the fact.

She saw rather less of James that summer, for at Easter a plot
had been discovered, by which the Earl of Angus and his son, the
Earl of Buchan, and various lesser gentry, actually bound themselves to kidnap James, with his brother, the Duke of Ross, and
hand them over to King Henry of England. The go-between,
some thought, though it was not proven, had been John Ramsay,
the former Earl of Bothwell, who had escaped Lauder Bridge and
lost his earldom to Patrick Hepburn when James came to the
throne.

The news surprised James less than might have been expected.
He had never trusted Bell-the-Cat, and was more interested to
learn why the scheme had broken down.

" How did you discover it? " he asked Patrick Hepburn
admiringly.

" As one discovers these things." Patrick shrugged. " The
King of England has not learned that it is worse to bribe too little
than not to bribe at all. One of Angus's men sought to double
his profits."

H

"See that he loses them all."

"My lord, I will indeed," Patrick agreed.

"Where is Angus now?"

"It seems," said Patrick, grinning, "that he has gone into England, no doubt because it is safer to bell a cat and leave others to capture a King. I suggest, my lord, that we conceal our knowledge of the plot, so that he may return in due course to discover what has marred it. Once he is again in Scotland you may treat him as you will."

"That is well thought on, Patrick," said James, amused by the thought of returning to Mariot with the story of what he had escaped.

So nothing came of the plotters' plans, and matters in Scotland went on as if they had never been made. Bishop Elphinstone, with the Bishop of Glasgow, Patrick Hepburn, and an escort including a certain William Dunbar, a priest with the knack of versifying, left for France to treat of the prospects of a French marriage for James.

And so the Earl of Angus, returning to Scotland at midsummer, to discover what had befallen his schemes, was met by a herald as he crossed the Border, and commanded to ward himself in his castle of Tantallon, there to await the King's pleasure. Alarmed, Angus returned, as required, to Tantallon, but fortified it against all comers. Expecting James to take as harsh a vengeance as he himself would have done, he had no mind to be set swinging over his own battlements as he had set others swinging over Lauder Bridge.

"Summon the artillery from Edinburgh. I will command the siege of Tantallon myself," said James. "Sir Andrew Wood shall also lie off shore in *The Flower* in case Angus seeks to escape me by sea."

It was a pleasant, not too seriously intended change from the more sedentary aspects of government and James amused himself well enough, though owing to the inefficiency of the guns, which were both difficult to handle and inaccurate in operation, both Angus and his castle remained unscathed. When autumn came, and the embassy was due to return from France, the besiegers abandoned the enterprise, and James went on to make his

devotions at the shrine of St. Ninian in Galloway before riding
north to welcome Patrick home.

In due course the Council decreed that Angus should be
deprived of the Lordship of Liddesdale, which he had been willing
to hand over to King Henry of England in exchange for lands
south of the Border. This, with the key fortress of Hermitage,
would be safer in the hands of Patrick Hepburn, whose loyalty was
beyond question. As for the future of the Earl of Angus, that
would be decided when he had made his personal submission to
the King.

But James, having spent an interesting autumn, and blown off
his anger against Angus with the explosions of the old-fashioned
guns, forgot him in the startling report from Ireland that a young
man calling himself Richard, Duke of York, had laid claim to the
throne of England, declaring that he had escaped the tragedy in
the Tower through the superstitious terror of a servant. And his
story, it seemed, was being sponsored not only by the Earl of
Desmond but by King Charles of France, the Duchess of Burgundy,
even by the Emperor. In his excitement, James hurried with the
news to Mariot.

" If this be true," he insisted, " then King Henry VII has no
more right to the throne of England than you or I."

But Mariot, pregnant again, was both peevish and sceptical.

" *If* it be true," she retorted, " why have we not heard of this
Prince Richard long ago? "

" Surely because those in charge of him did not wish to risk
the life of so precious a child——"

" Or perhaps because ten years changes children so much
that those who knew the child might well think they recognised
the man," said Mariot shrewdly. " Do you believe the Earl of
Desmond's story? "

" I see no reason to doubt it," said James. " The Duchess of
Burgundy accepts him as Prince Richard, her nephew, the King
of France invites him to his Court as Duke of York. Both know
better than I——"

" And care for King Henry even less."

James rumpled up his tawny hair and glowered at her,

refusing to be deprived of his lost cause. " Women know nothing
of such things."

" They know something of the motives of other women," she
retorted. And James, unused to querulousness, frowned.

For what appeared to be the return of young Richard, Duke
of York, from among the dead, sounded a very trumpet challenge,
to which a knight from King Arthur's table must respond if he
meant to honour his oath to defend helpless innocence against
all the forces of greed and corruption that sought to possess the
world. James responded to it accordingly, hoping all things, and
believing all things of the young man who was described by those
who had seen him as a big, shy creature in his early twenties;
tongue-tied but handsome, and regally gracious enough to plead
in his own person for the redress of his family's wrongs.

The Earl of Angus, tired of seclusion in Tantallon, made his
submission before the year was out, accepting the loss of Liddesdale to Patrick Hepburn philosophically, and accepting from him
in its stead the equivalent lordship of Bothwell, well away from
the Borderline. He then proceeded, with all the charm he could
display when he chose, to work his way back into the royal
favour, by supporting the cause of the self-styled Duke of York
over which so many others shook their heads. It was enough, as
he had hoped, to win him a place on the Council, now about to
debate that very affair.

" To displace the usurper and restore the rightful King of
England to his throne is a most worthy enterprise. You may rely
on me, my lord," said Angus, blandly ignoring his own recent
dealings with that very usurper.

" You will say as much at the Council meeting? "

" Surely, my lord the King," said the Earl of Angus, for all
the world like a great sandy cat which might at any moment
begin to purr.

And so, ignoring raised eyebrows, he took his place among
his former colleagues and prepared to show by vigorous nods
and astute interpolations that in this matter, as in all others, the
King had his most loyal support.

" My lords," James challenged his advisers, " in my opinion
we must lend his Highness of York all assistance in our power."

They looked at him doubtfully, cleared their throats, and sighed, while James, fretting vainly against their disapproval, clenched his fists and wished to heaven that he had been five years older, able to thrust their dour caution aside and demand Scotland's support on his sole authority.

" Better have a sight of him first," said Chancellor Argyll, wearily. The anxieties of the last few years had taxed his strength and his voice was that of an old, sick man.

" My lord," demanded the Justiciar, " have any persons of undoubted probity and personal knowledge of the two young princes—both probity and knowledge are essential—sworn that the young man calling himself Richard, Duke of York and younger son of King Edward IV, is indeed that very Richard and none other? "

" Why surely," said James, in surprise. " Has not his aunt, the Duchess of Burgundy, who is his father's sister, recognised and received him as her kinsman? "

" Yet there must be a world of difference between the bairn she saw—it cannot be less than eight years gone by, and likely more—and the young man who comes to her calling himself her nephew," objected the Archbishop of St. Andrews.

" Surely she must have questioned him? It seems that he speaks of his family with absolute knowledge."

" Such knowledge can be acquired," the Archbishop pointed out. " To gain it would be the first concern of an impostor."

" To have it would also be the mark of a true man," said the Earl of Angus.

James brought his fists down on the table-top with such violence that the ink-horns and sand-trays leapt. " Aye, my lords, why must we set out with the conviction that what he says is false, and only admit its truth when it is thrust upon us? Can we not believe that he speaks the truth, until he is proved an impostor? "

" We could do that, indeed, my lord the King," boomed the Archbishop of St. Andrews, turning his shoulder on the Archbishop of Glasgow, " but it would, to my mind, be in the highest degree unwise."

" Why so, my lord Bishop? " flashed James.

"When you have lived as long in this wicked world as I have," said the Archbishop, with his unexpectedly high-pitched titter, "you will know that truth, alas, is the rarest commodity in it."

"Rare, and therefore the more precious. Why should the King of France and the Duchess of Burgundy not have discovered such a pearl?"

"My lord," murmured the Archbishop of Glasgow, "I have recently been to France, you will remember. And I welcome the French as our allies as much as any man. But I believe I understand their motives none the less. It may be that King Charles cares less for justice than for the chance of haling King Henry from his throne."

"I have as good reason to wish him gone," said James hotly. "Has he not conspired with my own subjects against me? Does that deprive me also of my sense of justice?"

"If you rid yourself of King Henry you might have to do with a worse successor," said the Bishop of Aberdeen. "At least he is a man of peace, and Scotland needs peace more than she has done since the first King Robert's victories if she is to be great once more. I have been to England, my lord. So like my lord of Glasgow, I speak of what I know."

"Perhaps, my lord the King," said Patrick Hepburn softly, "this is not a matter now to be settled in a jangle among ourselves. Fortune may give us a chance of seeing Prince Richard before the matter need go forward."

James sighed. "Let us hope it may."

But the year went on without much prospect of personal contact with the Yorkist pretender, as James's Councillors exasperatingly continued to describe him. Angus attended Parliament with diligence, biding his time and encouraging James with calculated partisanship. Throughout the summer of 1492 the diplomats were busy and ambassadors hurried to and fro. With the autumn King Henry was so far irritated out of his habitual wary pacifism as to threaten France with an invasion, and though peace was made a month later, the expulsion of ' him of York ' was a condition of the agreement at Étaples, and King Charles hastily abandoned his protégé to the Duchess of Burgundy, that fiery enthusiast for all forlorn hopes of the house of York.

"If he will but come to me, I can offer more practical assistance than her Grace of Burgundy," James fretted, as he paced Mariot's bechamber.

But Mariot, queasy and wretched, was even less sympathetic than before.

"Surely we have enough troubles of our own without undertaking to bear those of others?"

"Is it not my knightly duty to see wrong redressed and a rightful King set over the people of England?"

"It may be," said Mariot tartly, "that you will have work enough to ensure justice for your own." She heaved her clumsy body round so that she could lay her aching forehead against the cool stone of the wall. "Oh, my lord, talk to me no more of princes, I beg you. My head aches as if it were cloven in two."

"It may be that I had better leave you," said James, whose own superb health made him not only impatient but even afraid of sickness in others.

"My lord, to speak truth, I care not whether you go or stay," groaned Mariot, "so long as you speak no more."

He went, much affronted. There were too many other calls upon his time, he said huffily, for him to bide unwanted.

The Estates, preoccupied as usual with the question of James's marriage, voted a thousand pounds, just then, for the anticipated expenses of bringing home a Queen who had not yet been found. Patrick grinned broadly at James as this was agreed. But James, preoccupied with his inner uncertainties, was for once not amused, and the more thankful when the Estates turned to legislation which would oblige all coastal burghs to build fishing vessels of at least twenty tons and man them with the able-bodied, workless vagabonds who constituted such an irksome problem. He even smiled wryly at the vehemence with which the rival Archbishops of St. Andrews and Glasgow were urged to set aside their contentious wrangling and allow their respective spheres of influence to be determined, not by the Pope, but by the King.

Throughout the session the attendance of the Chancellor had been uncertain, for the Earl of Argyll was now a very sick man and his death early in May took few people by surprise, though the appointment of Archibald, Earl of Angus as his successor startled all but those who had watched his recent manœuvres to regain the favour of the King.

King Henry of England provided the next distraction, by proposing at the end of the month that the current truce might well be replaced by a more effective and perpetual peace. He also offered a noble English lady, Katherine, daughter of the Countess of Wiltshire, as James's bride. Both suggestions were unwelcome, in view of the French alliance, which neither James nor his Councillors were anxious to compromise, the Yorkist claim to the English throne, which James secretly favoured, and the Scottish reluctance to consider any lady less than a royal princess as a future Queen.

When Parliament rose, James set out for Dunstaffnage, where he received the submission of a number of the leaders in the Western Isles. This, his first important venture into personal diplomacy, was triumphantly successful, for he knew Gaelic and spoke to the proud chiefs as to the equals they believed themselves to be. But he was restless now that Mariot was again near her time, and soon after his return he set off almost at once on a pilgrimage to the shrine of St. Ninian at Whithorn, which had been recommended to him by his confessor as a very hopeful source of grace and consolation. And afterwards he rode northwards, visiting Aberdeen to confer with Bishop Elphinstone who had expressed the wish to lay before the King his plans for the city of Aberdeen.

So James, somewhat soothed and healthily weary after days of hard riding, sat in a window embrasure of the Bishop's Palace, sipping mulled wine and listening to the chime of the masons' hammers as they worked at the great tower of the Cathedral, begun by Bishop Leighton fifty years before, and only within sight of completion now.

" A third University," said Bishop Elphinstone, " is, I believe, of the greatest importance to the people of this remote part of Scotland, my lord. We are cut off from the rest of the kingdom by lofty mountains and by the arms of the sea, so that the clear light of learning does not reach our superstition-haunted shadows. It should not involve any great expense. I am a man of modest requirements. I believe the building of the College could be

financed from the savings in my episcopal income, which have
been considerable during the ten years I have held office."

" Indeed, my lord? " said James, astounded. From what he
had seen of the rival magnificence of such contentious prelates as
the Archbishops of St. Andrews and Glasgow, the savings from
their archepiscopal incomes would not have sufficed to put up a
pigsty.

" Oh, dear me, yes," said Bishop Elphinstone. " I have no
interest in the banquets and processions, the fine robes and
companies of men-at-arms with which I have sometimes been
urged to glorify my office. My office, as I have always answered,
is already glorious, and the glorification of the man who holds it
is sheer vanity. I live simply, both because I wish to put the
money to other uses and because I happen to prefer to live so,
my lord the King."

James nodded. " Indeed, so at times do I. And yet," he added,
with a certain wistfulness, " I must own that I also love splendour."

" You are a King," said the Bishop of Aberdeen. " Splendour
is expected of you. But concerning this project of mine. May I
speak more of it? "

" Please do, my lord."

" We would start from small beginnings," said the Bishop,
enthusiasm warming his precise, scholar's voice, " with perhaps a
score of students. We shall not make the mistake of an earlier
foundation which was launched without sufficient funds, so that
it ran into needless difficulties. I believe we could contrive the
building of a chapel, a residence and a number of class-rooms
from the funds at my disposal. I have my eye on a young Scot,
at present in Paris, who might be persuaded to return as our first
Principal. Hector Boece is his name. I must also find a Chancellor
and a Rector. The Principal, *ex officio*, would be our Theologian.
We will also need a Sub-Principal, a Humanist, a Civilist, a
Mediciner and eight priests for divine service. . . ."

The Bishop had forgotten him, James could tell, as he sat in
his high-backed chair, his thin, sensitively fingered hands placed
together, palm to palm, as if in prayer, his eyes remote so that he
seemed to look through the veils of the future at the vision which
he sought to draw down to earth. There was so much he desired

to do for his beloved city of Abredeen. A new choir for St.
Nicholas's Church, a bridge across the Dee . . . the College which
should kindle the lamp of learning in the far north where men
still groped in ignorant darkness for lack of learning to lighten it.
At last, he broke off with an apology.

" Forgive me. My tongue has carried me away indeed," he
said, with his sweet, sudden smile.

" You need no forgiveness, my lord," said James quietly. " I
will write to his Holiness for his authorisation of the new University without delay."

But he did not at once return south. Beyond the episcopal
city, across the Moray and the Cromarty Firths, between the sea
and the northern mountains, Bishop Elphinstone had said, lay the
shrine of St. Duthac, for centuries the refuge of the distracted, a
place revered by his great ancestor, King Robert the Bruce. And
James, whose devotion was always kindled by a quest with some
hardness in it, rode on into the wilderness. And there, companioned by the memory of the Bishop's serene spirit, he found,
for a time, complete peace.

A week later he rode south to learn, on reaching Edinburgh,
that Mariot had borne him a fine son.

CHAPTER TEN

HE was to be called Alexander, James decreed, delighted by
the tenacity with which the minute creature already seemed
to grasp at life. But he rode back from the christening with
Patrick Hepburn, in a disturbed state of mind. Just past his
twentieth birthday, he was already the father of two children,
by a commoner whom his Council would never permit him to
marry. But this knowledge troubled him less than the fact that
he accepted it with relief. Brought up in the illogical traditions
of chivalry, which in some ways venerated and in others so oddly
defied the commands of Holy Church, devotion to a paramour
was honoured as one of the duties of knighthood. He was dis-

nayed, therefore, that since the sheen of his first worship had been arnished by the ignoble squabbles of recent months, his feelings owards Mariot had undergone a considerable change.

"I can no longer offer her the homage a true knight should offer his lady," he said wretchedly. "I am ashamed. I thought such feelings as mine were immortal."

Patrick Hepburn chuckled, but not unkindly. "So many have thought before you and been also undeceived."

"She did not seek to deceive, I swear," said James unhappily.

"I did not say she did, my lord. The deception caught you both in the body's sweet brief madness. It is over. And yet it was splendid, was it not, for a while?"

James nodded. "But what shall I do now, Patrick? I must care for Mariot, and the children besides. The Council will never let me marry her——"

"But they will be glad enough for you to arrange that someone else shall," said the Earl of Bothwell. "As for the children——"

"I shall house them in Stirling if Mariot marries," said James with sudden decision. "My children shall be the step-bairns of no other man while I live."

Patrick raised his eyebrows. "It is not necessary that you should make a home for them in one of the royal residences, my lord. They could as well be cared for elsewhere."

"It may not be necessary, but it is what I wish to do," said James. "Now, as to the marriage——"

"That at least you may leave me to arrange," said the Earl of Bothwell.

Mariot's marriage to Sir John Mure of Rowallan received the blessing of the Church in the spring of 1494, and at Patrick Hepburn's suggestion James let it be known that once Mariot's marriage had been blessed with children, he would confer upon her husband some of the lands lost by the Boyds when they fell from favour in his father's time. It was a marriage of sufficient distinction, for the Mures of Rowallan, though not royal, were at least kin to royalty. Elizabeth Mure of Rowallan had married King Robert, grandson of the great Bruce, over a hundred years before, and her grandson had been the first King James. But though his presence would have surprised nobody, James did not

care to dance at the wedding of his former mistress. Instead he
set out once more for the Western Isles.

He visited that recalcitrant area three times during the
summer, since after his first visit Sir John Macdonald of Islay
defiantly hanged the newly-appointed governor of the fortress of
Dunaverty over his own battlements as James sailed for home,
and such contempt of the royal authority could scarcely go un-
avenged. But James, who cared more for the reconciliation of the
Islesmen than their punishment, left the disciplinary side of the
expedition in the hands of Alexander Gordon, Master of Huntly,
while he himself sought to win the confidence of the western chiefs.
Speaking their language, sharing many of their enthusiasms, he
knew how to value the allegiance of a people who would resist
compulsion with fury but reward with fanatical loyalty a King
who sought to understand as well as rule. So the chiefs who made
their submission at once received royal Charters for their lands.
At Tarbert James found King Robert's old Castle in a ruinous
state and had it put to rights, building a dockyard and planning
for the fishing industry as if something of his great ancestor's
vision of Scottish sea power had been wafted to him on the soft
western air out of Tir nan Og, the legendary home of his country's
heroes at the far end of the path the moon made on the clear
waters that lapped the dazzling sands.

He found time, too, to entertain the men who had offered
him their allegiance; fishing, hunting, sailing and dancing with
them with such evident enjoyment that the chiefs who would have
defied a Lowland army to their last breath gladly offered all their
resources to a King who came among them with open hands.

" My lord, you will always be your own best ambassador,"
said the Master of Huntly, as the royal party prepared to leave
the west. " You have achieved more with those proud fellows
than ever I did with my men-at-arms."

" I doubt if I would have achieved as much, Alexander," said
James frankly, " had you and your men-at-arms not been at my
back. But I enjoyed myself. It pleases me to encounter men in
their own mountains, talking of their problems while the quarry
we have brought down together is being quartered by the huntsmen, and the smoke from the fire which will roast it already hangs

weet on the air. It suits me better than sitting indoors listen-
ng to the droning of long-winded advocates." He sighed. "And
yet it is to them that I must return."

"Spare but the time to turn aside and hunt a while with us,
my lord," begged the Master of Lennox.

"I can promise you good sport if you will visit Castle Campbell," said the young Earl of Argyll.

"Archibald is new-fangled with that gaunt great place he
inherited last year," said the Master of Lennox, whose kinsman
by marriage Argyll was. "Yet if you will but listen to him, my
lord, we shall all have a few days more sport."

James willingly agreed. "I will visit you all," he declared.
"Mathew, we will stop at your father's house in passing, and go
on to see what you and your good lady, Archibald, have made of
Castle Gloom——"

"Castle Campbell, my lord, I beg you," Argyll protested,
while the others laughed. "My father did away with yon ill-
omened name years ago."

"I like it well," James maintained. "You shall not deprive
me of one of the dearest bogeys of my childhood."

"Whatever its name, my lord," said Mathew Stewart of
Darnley, Master of Huntly, "we shall all see that you are as well
entertained."

"We will talk of naught but hounds and horses and our
quarry," James said gaily. "I have done with women—for a
while."

"My lord," grinned the Master of Huntly, "a man who has
made that boast goes in graver danger than any other."

"Not I," said James. But those about him smiled. For a
while the present was fair enough. Both past and future fell back
from the pleasant September days when mountain and forest
glowed with the sunset colours of frost-touched oak and rowan,
beech, thorn, bracken and fading heather, and they rode through
the crisping rime of early mornings at the fairy summons of huntsmen's distant horns towards the grape-bloom veils which hid the
horizons beyond.

James was exuberantly happy. His journey to the Isles had
stimulated him with its chance to encounter men of different

backgrounds and conflicting ideas. Novelty fascinated him, the
fantastic delighted him. He was happy to spend the night in a
shepherd's bothy or a woodcutter's hut, to drink water and ea:
steaks of fresh-killed venison round the fire at which it had been
roasted on an improvised spit, for his delight in magnificence had
always been balanced by his appreciation of the opposite extreme.
He had begun to let his beard grow that spring, perhaps sub-
consciously desiring to assert his maturity on the rebound from
his subjection to Mariot. It suited him, for its golden, closely-
curling profusion gave him a sort of leonine splendour, of which
he was not entirely unaware, and his love of the chivalric tales
of Sir Thomas Malory made him quote from the adventures of
the knights at King Arthur's Court till his companions came
to talk of their present journeying in the flamboyant terms of the
knight errantry of an earlier age.

But Lord Drummond, who joined them in Perthshire,
presently outdid them all, as he entered into the spirit of James's
fantasy with all the enthusiasm youth could desire. Galloping
towards them at sunset through a forest glade, he proclaimed in
archaic language that a maiden had been kidnapped by a renegade knight, who, out of direst malice, had bound her to a great
tree in a solitary spot which a venomous dragon was reputed to
frequent. Since he himself, alone and unaided, could not defeat
both knight and dragon, he implored them most earnestly to
make haste. For if the maiden were exposed to these terrors after
nightfall, heaven alone knew what mischief might result.

James was delighted, but his more sceptical companions
grumbled that Lord Drummond's mummery had come between
them and their supper, while huntsmen and servants, unaccustomed to such crazy talk of dragons and maidens, looked
askance at their betters and then over their shoulders into the
gathering dusk. Dragons . . . surely such creatures belonged only
to the old tales that the minstrels told by high-piled fires at Yule?
Yet the tale did not sound so good out in the forest at nightfall,
as it had done within thick stone walls. What if Lord Drummond's
nonsense should by any chance prove true?

The maiden was true enough, at least, they presently discovered. Wearing a tattered gown, with her long hair flowing,

bound about the shoulders, waist and feet with cords to a great tree, she confronted them as they rode after Lord Drummond, lit by the gorgeous colours of the sunset. And behind her, silhouetted terrifyingly against the blazing sky, waited the sombre, gigantic figure of a knight in blackened armour upon a blacker horse. James was enthralled.

"Mother of heaven, I'll ride a course with him!" he shouted. "Send him my challenge, and watch him well for fear that while I am arming he may steal away."

But the black knight remained, unmoving as Stirling Rock, as James was hastily stripped and reclothed in the armour which had been banging gently in the paniers of a fat pack-pony. The royal challenge was conveyed in proper form, and boomingly accepted. Lord Drummond set his men to hack back the undergrowth and mark the course for the encounter, while James, as enthusiastic as if he had not been up at daybreak and ridden hard most of the day, settled himself in the saddle, couched his lance in readiness, peered ferociously through the bars of his visor, then at the marshal's signal, plunged forward at the dark figure which faced him at the far end of the improvised tourney ground. For an enthralling, immeasurable instant he saw the black knight loom, hideously large, before the point of his lance encountered violent resistance. His onslaught was briefly arrested, then the black bulk toppled backwards over his horse's rump, and James surged on. When he trotted back, his lance at rest, the black knight was still lying on his back, helpless as a gigantic beetle, waiting for his supporters to drag him to his feet.

"I will dismount," James yelled from within his helm. "Get him to his feet that I may hew his head from his shoulders."

But the black knight, when heaved upright, at once flopped forward to his knees, anxiously holding the hilt of his sword towards James, in token of surrender. Reluctantly James lowered his own blade, sighing as his esquires hurried forward to release him from his helm.

"If all evil-doers were as easily overthrown, it would be an idle world of knighthood," he said sadly. "My Lord Drummond, I pray you will have the maiden released, that I may greet her with fit courtesy. . . ."

But the maiden, it seemed, had already been released, for she now came forward, as the knight's head emerged from the blackened helm, and took him by the hand to greet James with a deep reverence. James gaped at the sight, for the head which emerged from the sombre gorget was fair and tousled, the face that of a mere boy.

" My son and daughter, my lord the King," explained Lord Drummond, " who would beg that if their mummery has pleased you, you will graciously restore the family to your favour and pass the night under our roof."

James frowned, slowly remembering the case against the Master of Drummond. He had been on the bench himself when the Lords of the Council tried it, and young Drummond had been executed at Stirling in spite of his family's appeal. The massacre had been a violent, wretched business, but he had not been happy over the decision, for though the Murrays had been butchered in the church where they had taken refuge, a Murray had fired the first arrow and killed one of the besiegers. So now he was glad enough to pardon the Master's kinsmen. Bygones were better as bygones, he said, and heard the words echo, lingeringly, in his mind, as he stepped forward to raise the former victim of the feigned black knight from her knees.

" I will come most gladly. Madam, I compliment you on your mummery," he said. " It was a pleasant diversion for the day's end. I hope you suffered no hurt, for though the dragon may have existed but in imagination, the cords which bound you, I perceive, were real enough."

Smiling, she looked down at the weals on her white wrists. " It is nothing, my lord," she said.

Afterwards, when they had eaten and the servants had retired, it was pleasant to gather round the fire piled high against the sharp frost of the autumn evening and listen to the lingering sweetness of the harper's songs. James was tired, at last, content to let the music drift through him without the effort of consciously listening to its wild beauty. Refusing formality, he chose a bench in the chimney-corner, clasping his hands round his knee, tilting his head back to blink at the smoke-blackened rafters from which the soft croodling of the pigeons roosting there drifted own to form a background to the harper's poignantly plucked hords.

Now and again he looked round the circle for the maiden and he black knight, but the light in the hall was dim and veiled with a blue haze of peat reek. Sometimes he thought he saw the dark-haired maiden in one part of the hall and sometimes in nother, but because sleep lay like lead on his eyelids he could not be sure.

Next morning he was up before his huntsmen, demanding his orse before the sleep-fuddled men had found their boots. If the port were good, James had planned to remain out till nightfall. But it so happened that his horse went lame, they lost their quarry n a chasm, one of the huntsmen hurt his arm in attempting to etrieve it, and a storm of rain turned the vivid country-side into a chilly quagmire from which even James was glad to extricate himself soon after midday. And then, with the perversity of northern weather, the storm passed, the sun shone, and James, who hated abandoning an enterprise, fretted because he had allowed himself to be daunted by the day's misfortunes. Wandering moodily out-of-doors, he caught a glimpse of what seemed a familiar figure, on the castle green, though most of the girl's dark hair was demurely hidden by a dark hood, and she bore a basket demurely on her arm. He caught up with her just as she turned into a woodland path.

" Madam," he said softly, " I trust you suffered no ill from our ordeal of yesterday? "

She turned abruptly, startled. He was amazed to see unexpected hostility in her eyes, and in the voice, singing sweet with a blurred edge to it that reminded him of the lavender-blue haze which lay between him and the distant mountains on such autumn days as this, when the spiders' webs gave nearer objects the shimmer and fantasy of a dream. But she said only:

" You are mistaken, sir, I fear," and would have turned away had not James moved too quickly, so that he stood across her path.

" Mistaken, Madam? Did you not share your brother's mummery? You were tied to a tree yonder in the glade, while

I

he, as a black knight, mounted guard against all comers. An
then, I——"

She gave him a ghost of a smile. " Sir, that was my elde
sister Sybilla and not I."

He looked at her closely. He could tell now that he had bee
mistaken. This girl was more beautiful. Also, her eyes were bot
angry and sad.

" What—what have I done amiss? " he stammered.

" Sir, I loved my brother," Margaret Drummond said.

There was something in the sorrow of the simple statemer
which made him hesitate to follow her as she walked away, an
his face was downcast as he returned to the great hall. He di
not see her again before he took his leave next morning. But h
took away with him the memory, less of the gratification of Lor
Drummond and his family at the removal of the royal displeasur
than the rebuff of the girl who had turned away from him into th
dripping, gold and scarlet autumn woods.

He came often upon the thought of her, unexpectedl
troubling, as he rode to Inverness for the northern justice eyres
It fretted him when he afterwards returned to Edinburgh to mee
his Council and arrange for the reception of the French embassy
which was daily expected. There was talk, as usual, of hi
marriage, and James agreed to remain in Edinburgh to receiv
the ambassadors, letting himself dream of such a bridal, as h
sometimes did nowadays. What would it be like, to hear the bell
ring and the people shout for the fairy-tale princess from Spain . .
or France . . . or Naples . . . or Savoy . . . who could tell? . .
riding up the High Street of Edinburgh on their King's saddle
bow?

He would not house her in the starkly chill apartments o
Edinburgh's Castle Rock. Instead he would build for his lady .
fair royal palace in the city below. The canons knew what the
were about when they chose the site of their Abbey of Holyrood
Why not build his palace in the shelter of the crags, within soun
of the Abbey's bells?

And then, as he rode without ceremony to Castle Campbel
for a few days' hunting, he saw Margaret Drummond again.
She was quite unaware of him as she returned from a searc

for blaeberries with the other maidens. A strand of hair had
escaped from her hood, and she pushed it casually back, laughter
enhancing the moonlight beauty he remembered. Stepping
quickly into the shadows of the gateway, James let her pass
unnoticing, then hurried in search of Argyll.

" Archibald, I need your help. Mistress Drummond must not
know me for the King."

Argyll's grin suggested that it was not long since James had
declared himself done with women. " I fear it has already got
about, my lord," he pointed out, " that your presence has
honoured Castle Campbell."

" Yes, yes, no doubt," James agreed. " But if you give it out
that I have taken some disorder which keeps me abed I will
change the fashion of my hair and habit. So at least I shall seem
a stranger for a time."

Argyll agreed, as ready as any other recently married man to
foster a romance. At supper that evening James's place at the
high table was empty. The story went round that he had caught
a fever from exposure to the foul air of the marshes when loosing
his hawk at a bittern, and been persuaded to keep to his bed.
The few members of the household who knew James by sight
were sworn to secrecy.

Later that evening, a quietly dressed young clerk drifted so
unobtrusively through the great hall between the groups of
dancers, that not a head turned as he approached the deep window
embrasure in which Margaret sat alone, looking out across the
superb arch of star-spattered sky towards the river below.

" Madam," said James quietly, " I am commanded by my
lord of Argyll to ask if you will not take a cup of wine against the
night's chill."

She answered absently: " I thank my lord, but I have felt
no chill as yet."

" Then you are sad, not cold, madam, I fear," said James.

She looked up then, startled. But the light was dim, and since
she had been told the King was abed, she did not question the
identity of the drably dressed young clerk with the beautiful voice.
The news of the King's arrival had indeed saddened her with
memories of her brother's trial and execution, so that she had

withdrawn from the familiar hubbub of dancers to struggle with the strange confusion of emotions which had been further complicated by the brief drama of her recent encounter with the King. But grieving could no more bring back the dead than anger revive them. Margaret was young and life was urgent within her. To her dismay she began to find that the image of her dead brother's face was blurring, changing. When he looked at her out of the past, it was with alien eyes. Twisting her hands together, she wished the King had never come to Castle Drummond in September, or that she had stayed at home now.

"Sad? It may be so," she agreed.

He sat down on the velvet cushion which masked the rough stone of the window-seat, drawing his knees up to his chin and clasping his hands round his ankles. "I, too, am sad at times," he said. "It comes down upon me like a helm that lacks a vizor, utterly darkening. A deeper darkness, too, than any you can know."

"How so?" she asked him sharply.

"Sorrow is dark, but guilt is darker," James said. He was not speaking for effect now, but quite simply, as if her presence had so rebuked his make-believe that he must now speak as truly as he knew.

Margaret looked at him in astonishment. "You do not seem," she said, "like one who can know guilt."

"And yet," said James tonelessly, "there are times when I feel more guilty than any man alive. I tell you . . ." He broke off with an abrupt gesture and slumped forward, his head in his hands.

"Yes, tell me, sir, if it will ease your heart."

"I did not give my father the love I owed him as a son," said James in a low, strained voice. "I believed what others told me against him. I deserted him at his time of greatest need. I brought about his death."

"You struck him down?" Margaret exclaimed.

James shook his head. "No. And had I known his danger I would have saved him. But because I did not, though I was a child and those who constrained me full-grown, I must hold myself ever guilty."

"What does your confessor bid you?" Margaret asked uneasily. For James had now lost all caution in his revelations, and an incredible suspicion of his identity had begun to stir in the depths of her mind.

"My confessor commands me to do penance," James said wearily. "And this I have done, making pilgrimage each year to the shrine of the blessed St. Duthac in the north and to St. Ninian's most gracious shrine in Galloway. I make gifts to every altar by the way, perpetual masses are sung at my command, and yet the memory irks me. Though I may be forgiven, I shall never forgive myself. This very year——"

"What then?"

James raised his head from his hands and looked forlornly up at her. "This I have never told another soul. Yet, I have the desire to tell you. If only in order that . . ."

She clasped and unclasped her hands in silence. But her eyes questioned him.

"If I tell you this, perhaps there are other things you will understand," James said abruptly. "It may be that you will know that for the wrong I do and the right I have left undone grief haunts me beyond any blame other can add."

"That I can well believe," she said slowly. For the moonlight had showed her the tears that filled his eyes.

"I have done penance, gone on pilgrimage, girt round my body an iron chain which I have sworn to wear till I die," James said. "Yet it is a fearful thing for a son to bring his father to his death. What will become of me at my own life's end?"

"My lord," said Margaret, impulsively, "surely we shall all find only one refuge whatever our deserts, and that the mercy of God."

He bowed his head. "You can say that. And yet—I perceive you know me?" he said softly.

"I know you," Margaret said.

Slowly he raised his head and looked at her. "This time," he said, "you will not turn away?"

Margaret looked at him for so long in silence that the beam of moonlight which had slid across the rushes and up the rough stone wall as they talked, now slipped over the edge of the crudely-carved mullion to leave them confronting each other darkly against the unfathomable blue of the night sky. Behind them the laughter of the dancers and the twitter of the violins might have belonged to the world of the living, while two fated creatures plighted their troth among the dead.

Then, with a sort of desperation, Margaret held out her hands.

" May our blessed Lord and His lady Mother deliver me from evil," she cried, " for I cannot turn away."

CHAPTER ELEVEN

JAMES rode away from Castle Campbell in wild spirits. Swearing and floundering in the mire the members of his escort watched his shrewdly spurred horse leaping the potholes of the winding track. James had seen Margaret again only at the point of departure, questioning her anxiously, as he held her hand over his heart. He would count its beats till he saw her again. Would the time seem as long to her? She had stood silent, but he had been satisfied, for her answer had been plain enough to one who looked deeply into her shadowed eyes.

From Inverness, wearied by the crackle of parchments, and the deliberations of the learned advocates, he rode on to preside again at Elgin, from Elgin to Banff, and from Banff at last to Aberdeen, thankful for the opportunity to enjoy the wit of Bishop Elphinstone and hear his latest plans for the new University. But their discussion was interrupted, to the Bishop's disappointment, by the ceremonious arrival of a young Frenchman bearing a letter which he could by no means bring himself to deliver till he had knelt, with every appearance of secrecy, and presented James with a white rose. A white rose, in November, in the north of Scotland; it could scarcely have been obtained on the spur of the moment, the Bishop reflected. But its significance was as evident as it was exasperating. Such a gift from her Grace, the Dowager Duchess of Burgundy, could only mean the last thing James ought to waste

ime with just then, thought Bishop Elphinstone, beating a tattoo
on the arms of his high-backed chair with impatient finger-tips
while James broke the seal and read the wheedling message from
the fiery lady who had been sister of the Yorkist King of England,
Edward IV.

"Forgive me, my lord Bishop," he murmured as he read.
"Your project has my warmest approval. But this—this is great
news. . . ."

"Indeed, my lord?" Bishop Elphinstone sighed.

"My lord Bishop, the Duchess writes to ask permission for
Prince Richard of York to visit Scotland. Nothing, I believe,
would please me more. Do you not agree, my lord, that we must
offer him every assistance in our power to right the monstrous
wrong done to the house of York?"

"Provided, my lord the King," said the Bishop dryly, "that
he is indeed a member of it."

"My lord, there seems to be no doubt. Has he not returned,
like Lazarus, from the death King Richard planned for him?"

"Do we indeed know that King Richard planned that death?"

"On what grounds do you say he did not?" cried James in
astonishment. "Did not King Henry himself proclaim his
guilt?"

"Not till King Richard was dead on Bosworth field, and
unable to answer the accusation of the man who stood to gain
most from it."

"But, my lord . . ."

Bishop Elphinstone smiled at the sight of James's startled face.
"If King Richard killed the lads why did not King Henry accuse
him of that among other things, when he first roused England
against him?"

James waved the letter impatiently. "My lord Bishop, if
Richard, Duke of York, is alive and plans to visit me, does it
matter which King failed to bring about his death?"

"I think it does, my lord," said the Bishop. "King Richard
might be careless enough to take for granted that his orders had
been carried out. But King Henry, I believe, would make so very
certain that he can be in no manner of doubt now."

"As to that, my lord," said James, "we shall see."

" You will permit him to visit Scotland? "

" I will indeed."

Bishop Elphinstone spread his hands protectively over the plans for the University which was his darling project, something which, on its completion, must make the name of King James glorious. It was distressing to think that the King, a young man of the highest intelligence and the deepest devotion to Holy Church, might be distracted from this noble opportunity by a trumpery project, a crazy escapade which was calculated to poison Scotland's relations with her great neighbour at a crucial point.

" Is your mind set on championing this claim, my lord? "

James nodded. " As set in its favour as you are set against it. Your opposition puzzles me, my lord Bishop. I did not think you would be swayed by the expediency of not irking King Henry overmuch."

" Shall we set Satan to cast out Satan? " asked the Bishop. " The more guilty King Henry is of the Yorkist princes' death, the more certain it is that this man is guilty of an imposture. Henry Tudor would not botch such a task, though Richard Plantaganet might."

" Will you reconsider that judgment when you have seen the Prince? "

" I will, my lord," said Elphinstone with a wry smile, " most gladly. If indeed I ever do. . . ."

There James had to leave the matter. But his enthusiasm for the venture was unshaken. Being what he was, his reply to the Dowager Duchess of Burgundy contained an even more cordial invitation for Prince Richard of York than he would have sent if Bishop Elphinstone had not attempted to shake his conviction. And of this, the Bishop was only too well aware, though he could not know that James, delighted by the prospect of knightly adventure, had broken his journey south to tell Margaret Drummond of it.

" What could be a fitter cause for knights to seek worship? Are we not bound by our vows to succour the weak and aid the dispossessed? We shall ride forth like the fellowship of King Arthur's Round Table. And you will give me your favour to bind about my helm, dear heart, so that my arm shall be the stronger because I am your knight."

He sat on a cushion at her feet in the small solar at Drummond Castle. A guitar lay across his knees, for he had been picking out by ear some of the melodies he had heard in the Western Isles. She smiled at him, because when he took her hand, her heart raced, and when he rose to his feet and drew her towards him till their bodies touched, the very resistant substance of her flesh seemed consumed by her longing to identify herself utterly with him. He held her so close that she could feel his body stir against her, urgent and imploring as his shaken voice. The everyday world drifted about them, unsubstantial as a cloud. Only his eyes lived as they smiled into hers, his lips on her lips, his imperious hands never still.

" Margaret . . ."

She could not answer. Her breathing choked her, her head dropped to his shoulder like a sun-wearied flower.

" Margaret, I shall conquer the world if I may bring it home to your feet. Tell me . . . tell me . . ."

" Tell you what, my dear lord? "

" That you love me indeed, and will have me for your knight? "

" Oh, my lord, you must know that I could not have borne what you have done to me . . . except for love. . . ."

His grasp about her tightened till she could say no more, and yet when he loosed her she drew him close again.

" You could not be dearer to me if you were the conqueror of all Christendom and the heathen lands beyond," she said softly.

" My sweetest lady, never would I have believed it possible," James said. He looked at her, held at arm's length, with half-closed eyes, his smile reaching her out of a dream, as he drew her to him again.

" Believed what, my lord? "

" That a woman could be friend as well as lover. You are my mirror of perfection, my pattern of beauty, for whom I will draw sword against all the world. Yet it means as much, perhaps more, that we can talk together, you and I."

" We have been talking together so long that my parents will wonder what has become of us," she said, struggling still to check them both. Her mother had worried at the sight of the King's devotion, saying sadly that she would sooner see her daughter a humbler man's wife, happy and secure, than a King's mistress, with his whims for her fate. But her father had disagreed. The King, he maintained, offered a greater destiny than any they could dream. But Margaret no longer cared for destiny. Only for the look in James's eyes, the worshipping urgency in his hands. . . .

Now and then remote sounds, half-heard, reminded her that the work of the household was going on as usual. She could hear the grindstone whir as the men sharpened their knives in the yard below. Sheep bleated as they were driven out to pasture, cows lowed from the byres, the maids started a new song as they sat at their spinning. Each familiar sound was like a thread which bound her to a world which was hers no longer. One by one the threads snapped as James talked on.

"I cannot bear to leave you here, where other lovers may find you. I shall grudge every look, each word you exchange with man, woman or child. You are mine. Are you not, my dearest heart?"

She laid her cheek against his. But she was silent.

"Are you? Are you?" he persisted.

Slowly she nodded, her face still hidden.

"Yes, James," she said softly.

"I shall take you with me," he declared.

"I——"

"I will make a home for you, see that you are cherished as you deserve. All Scotland shall know how utterly I worship and revere you——"

She laughed then, shakily. "James, this is crazy talk. What will the Council say?"

"It matters less, nowadays, than what I say, sweetheart. It is no affair of theirs. Let them arrange my marriage. I shall choose my love."

She went suddenly still in his arms. When he spoke of marriage, the ice of the fairy story seemed to pierce her heart. Cold and remote, she watched, as if from the summit of a mountain peak, all the comings and goings on the plain below. She and

James, though their bodies might still be close, now seemed in spirit far apart. Between each on a mountain peak, all the sorrow of the world, all its pain, seemed to run like rivers in spate, lapping the foothills in a tide of blood and fire. Nightmarishly she knew that she could only reach James by wading through these floods, that the river of fire must drown her as he was drowning in the river of blood. Frenzied with terror she tried to plunge forwards. But at the first movement, the whole fantasy dissolved, and she found herself looking into James's anxious face, within a hand's breadth of her own.

" Dear love, what ailed you? Blessed Jesus, you hung in my arms like one dead."

" It was nothing. No more than a waking dream."

She spoke lightly, though she was haunted by the irrational conviction that she had seen a fable of her fate. If she ventured now, there would be no return for her to the old ways. And the future lay before her, untrodden, without direction, so that she looked in vain for guidance, while the mysterious sixth sense of her race prickled her spine with dread.

" With me you need fear nothing. You will come with me? "

" I will do whatever you wish," she said at last. " Yet—I beg you to go warily."

But James only laughed as he kissed her. Enchanted by the idea of having her near him, he arranged with the Governor of Stirling Castle, Sir John Lundy, and his wife, that Margaret should visit them discreetly. He himself would spend with her every instant he could wring from the demands of the Council, the sessions of Parliament, the Courts of Justice, the administration of his royal estates, the construction of a new navy, the reconciliation of the rebellious elements in the Western Isles.

Never, snatched in fragments though it was, had there been such a summer since the world began. James was so happy that his delight spilled from him like sunshine, in a spray of small gracious gestures, as he tossed a joke and a coin to the beggar who pulled off his cap by the wayside, blew a kiss to the children who cheered him as he rode by, left half a rose-noble in the basket of the old crone who brought him wild strawberries, rewarded the page who hurried with news of Margaret's return from her devotions, the fiddler who played so sweetly beneath the window of their chamber, tossed spur money to the boys of the choir because he had disturbed their singing by clashing noisily to his place during Mass. He strolled with Margaret in the Castle garden, rode with her into the hills, walked by her side along the bank of the silver Forth, and told her excitedly of the Court's preparations for the visit of the Duke of York.

It was imperative, he maintained, that he and Margaret should have their wardrobes completely overhauled against his coming so that when the Court looked for leadership to the King and his lady, they should not look in vain.

" The King and his lady . . ." Margaret shook her head at him. " James, do you never fear that I may turn dizzy when you sweep me to such heights? "

" It matters less since you climb with my arm around you," James said, swiftly dropping the bundle of bright patterns of the silken stuffs which the merchants had brought, to kneel beside her.

" We may climb together," Margaret said in a suddenly shaken voice, " yet I—I must descend alone."

" Descend? Indeed you shall not——"

Margaret made a little gesture as if brushing his protest aside. " Do not spoil what we have by pretending that it must last for ever," she said. " Soon, as I well know, you must marry a royal lady of whom your Council approves——"

" In two years," James said fiercely, " I shall be twenty-five, free to revoke all decisions taken during my minority and make all others unadvised. I shall bear them the burden of a King. Am I to be denied the privilege of a scullion? May I not ask the woman I love to share my tasks as well as my delights? Is it too much? Would you rather companion a less burdened man? "

" You know I would not. Yet you know also, that such a future is not for me." Her voice broke, then recovered, remote in its sadness as the call of the whaup from the hills.

" Why not? "

" Your people would never permit it," she said quietly.

" I shall not ask their permission," James protested. " Did not the fourth King Edward of England marry Elizabeth Wood-

ville first and inform his Council afterwards? Why should I not
do the same? "

She caught her breath for an instant, as if at a mirage of
unbelievable delight. Then slowly her eyes closed, and she shook
her head. " Have not the envoys from King Henry of England
already offered you the hand of his daughter, the Princess
Margaret? "

" That six-year-old brat? " James exploded. He was up
again now, pacing the chamber with great strides, sending the
bundles of silks and satins flying before him, with impetuous
feet.

" That marriage," said Margaret, " which, above all others,
will bring peace and prosperity to Scotland after so many years
of poverty and war."

" King Henry may not long be able to make such an offer,"
said James, whirling round with his sudden, impish grin. " The
Prince of the royal house of York will soon have his kingdom
again."

" Do you believe that indeed, James? " Margaret asked.

James nodded. " I do. I must. Can you not see that it will
mean everything to us? And yet, in another way, it can make no
difference at all." He was on his knees beside her again, sub-
merging her doubts in a torrent of words. " You are my love
and my lady, my solace by night and my delight by day. At
the first sight of you my life broke into flower. Your beauty,
sweetheart, is so dear to me that against you all other women
seem like rooks and daws. How shall I put in your place
some foolish puppet whose only merit is the crown her father
wears? "

Margaret took his clasped hands and raised them to her lips.
" James, James, do not rage at me like the very lion on your
standard. My most darling lord, I beg that you will moderate
your wrath. You must not put Scotland's needs at despite for me.
I love you so much more dearly than any other soul on this sweet
earth that I will be happy to give you all you need, asking
nothing again except that for my sake you will make Scotland
glorious. If I but retain your love, how shall it irk me if you choose
another Queen? "

"Because I worship you," James whispered, "I would hav
all Scotland also offer you worship."

Laughing, Margaret took his face between her hands. "Dea
James, having your love alone I shall never miss the rest. Now
you have sworn your troth to me, I shall not care who boasts tha
she has been to your bed."

"My dear and only love," James protested, "I swear to yo
on the Evangels that I have no other desire than to see you crowne
my Queen. Let the Council wag their beards. I shall not car
Once I am of full age they must listen to me. I have listened t
them too long. Only two years, dear love. Only two years . .
two years . . ."

Two years. The words tolled like a passing bell, Margare
thought with a sudden shiver. But she forced herself to say
"Indeed, it is not long."

"Not long enough. Our happiness clamours for a lifetim
for eternity," said James in triumph.

She shook her head at him. "Let us forget the future for
while and take pleasure from what lies beneath our hands. Pic
up the patterns. What shall I wear to greet his Highness of York
The coif and wimple, alas, are now quite gone for good, like th
tall steeple head-dresses. I regret them less. They were to
troublesome in a high wind. But I loved the smooth freshness
the white stuff which framed the face so kindly."

"What need has your face of kindness?" James stooped t
kiss it. "Few can wear the new styles that bare neck and boso
and draw the hair back under the little Frenchified hoods as we
as you. And I am glad that men's foolish long-toed shoes hav
also been abandoned. I had never the patience to tie my toe-ti
to my garters. But touching the visit of the Prince: it seeme
to me that we might well pay him a pleasant compliment b
greeting him in blue and tawny, since these are the colours
York."

The prospective visit was, on the whole, popular, for many
Scotland's greatest men resented the persistence of the envoy
from England, Spain and Rome who were so anxious to weake
France by persuading James to join this league or that again
her. The Scottish nobles, therefore, were now willing enough

honour the Yorkist pretender, if only to show King Henry and his associates that, in the matter of alliances, Scotland would also do as she pleased.

James was delighted by the prospect. In the exultation of that blissful summer all things seemed possible, his own youth inexhaustible. The pinnacle of his happiness brushed the floor of heaven. He had but to reach upwards and pull down a handful of stars to decorate Margaret's new gowns. He swept from one enterprise to another at such a pace that the noblemen on escort duty were both dusty and disgruntled, while James, shouting for a fresh horse, was ready to set out again; for the Isles in a new sea coat and hood of finest tawny cloth from Rouen, lined with white lambskins; for his annual pilgrimage to Tain in a crimson and black riding-coat of velvet, with his minstrels jogging among the men-at-arms; to Leith to inspect his ships berthed there and discuss the laying down of new hulls with Sir Andrew Wood and the Bartons, that great seafaring family of a father and three sons, as earnestly as if he had no other interest in the world. And then to horse again, flinging himself off at St. Anthony's Chapel of the Crag as he rode by, for as long as it took him to cross himself and gabble an Ave and a Paternoster, spinning a silver unicorn to the old monk who shambled out too late to catch the coin, back on his horse and a hundred yards away before the bemused custodian had retrieved it from the dust.

The keepers of the wayside chapels knew that the King never passed them, however pressed, without checking his horse and bowing his head, seldom rode by without dismounting, usually stayed long enough to say a prayer, often to light a candle. They never knew when he was coming or how soon he would be gone, but a fury of hooves on the cobbles outside the wayside shrines of St. Mary of Whitekirk, Our Lady of Grace, St. John of Ayr, or Our Lady of the Heuch, to all of whom James showed special devotion, would bring the drowsy monks out at a run, for fear one of the hideously diseased or merely idle beggars who haunted such places should intercept the shower of gold.

A streak of genuine devotion to a dimly perceived vision of heavenly things ran through James's contradictory nature like a gold thread through a motley brocade. Not even the credulity and corruption of a Church which worshipped the bones of long-dead saints and believed prayer itself might be bought and sold, could tarnish that nostalgic intuition of eternal verities. Still sorrowing for his father's death, James prayed for Margaret as often as he prayed for himself.

But because, from each act of penance, performed with real grief and humility, his erratic nature rebounded violently towards an equivalent extreme of pride and joy, James returned from pilgrimage in October in a mood to welcome the arrival of the Yorkist pretender with as much display as one reigning King could show another. The Court was at Stirling, for James wished Margaret to have her share in the excitement of what promised to be as marvellous a tale as anything which had delighted Sir Thomas Malory. Might he not, like another King Arthur, lead his knights to the restitution of a great wrong? And Margaret, listening while he declaimed from Caxton's precious folio, smiled. But she also sighed.

" ' At the Court of King Arthur there came a young man bigly made, and he was richly beseen; and he desired to be made knight of the king, but his over-garment sat over-thwartly, how-beit it was rich cloth of gold. . . .' "

James looked up and laughed. " Shall it be so with the Duke of York as with the knight they mocked for wearing La Còte Male Taile, when he came to King Arthur and begged to be avenged? "

" If he comes from the Courts of France and Burgundy, he will surely be richly beseen," Margaret demurred.

James shook his head. " He has been long in the field. I understand from Desmond and Kildare that when he sought to land at Deal he was beaten off. Then he laid siege to Waterford. But it was too straitly guarded in the interest of Henry, the English usurper." He broke off. " Why do you laugh? "

She held out her hands in a swift gesture of compunction. " Forgive me, dearest heart. I love you dearly for that zeal for justice which blazes so fiercely that every shadow of doubt must be consumed. Already, as you wait to greet the man who has trailed his woes about Christendom, he is England's crowned King, and Henry in an outcast's grave."

James flushed, bit his lip, then grinned. " Mock me if you will, dear heart, but indeed, I know no other way. I must believe always and utterly in what I do, and if that offends you, it is of no avail. Indeed, my dearest, I shall never be otherwise."

Margaret ran forward suddenly into his arms. " Never, my sweet lord, could I endure it if you were."

CHAPTER TWELVE

THE " young man, bigly made," who declared himself to be Richard of York, arrived in Scotland in the sort of weather oftenest associated with November, an easterly haar that soaked every banner till it hung lifeless and beaded the beards of the knights and men-at-arms drawn up beneath the sagging blue and tawny decorations.

Trumpets sounded forlornly in the mist as his horse picked its way between the heaps of refuse outside Stirling's gate. The lepers waiting for alms hirpled forward on stumps and crutches, their petitions whistling between lips and noses so devoured that their faces seemed scarcely human. But the newcomer did not notice them, for he was too much occupied in commiserating himself for the trials he had endured to spare any attention for the trials with which others were afflicted. He was soaked to the skin, since he had refused to wear the armour, which had been made over for him in haste by a fellow who had taken no trouble to see that it fitted, so that it chafed him almost everywhere. He was weary too, weary of being bundled from one country to another, as his presence became inconvenient for its ruler. He had received the most cordial letters from the King of Scots, but no warning as to the prevailing climate in Scotland during November. Already he fancied that he had caught a rheum, for chills ran up his spine as fast as the rainwater, spilling from his collar, trickled down it. His face, handsome and pleasing when he smiled, looked leaden with discontent, for he was too wretched to care what impression he was making on the groups of townsfolk who scuttered out of

K

their hovels to peer and point as his cavalcade went by. He was saving all his dwindling stock of charm for the moment when he must greet his host. Meanwhile, he wished to high heaven that they would cease the clamour of trumpets with which the news of his arrival preceded him, since the distressful neighing sound was making his ears ring.

But when at last the preliminaries were over, and he had been escorted from the dismal courtyard to the great hall where, in a blaze of heraldic colour, King James awaited him, the prospect changed as completely as the prospect of seas and continents changes when a globe is spun. Warm again as the mulled wine coursed through him, he was comforted by a change of clothes and by the eager interest of King James, a splendid figure in his royal robes, who stepped down, impulsive hands outstretched, from the throne round which his expressionless nobles stood.

Soon his guest was sufficiently reassured to relax for a little the desperate vigilance of a man who might, at any moment, be confronted by a question that he could not answer, knowing as he floundered that the briefest hesitation would set suspicion leaping at him from his questioner's narrowed eyes. He took another draught from the goblet that James's cup-bearer presented on bended knee, and smiled broadly. But just then a few quiet words from someone standing unobtrusively at his elbow made apprehension catch him, like a hand at his throat, once more.

" And how does this weather compare with what you experienced in the Tower, my lord? " murmured Bishop Elphinstone.

" It—it is something similiar, my lord Bishop," the young man stammered. " Yet—after so many years——"

" Can you remember anything precisely, I wonder? "

" The cold——"

" Yes, indeed. Were you hungry besides? "

" Yes, I believe so. But when the bread was mouldy," said the young man recklessly, " we—we used to throw it to the birds."

" A natural diversion. What birds did you feed? "

" Sparrows . . . seagulls . . . pigeons . . ." The light hazel eyes glanced hither and thither, themselves like birds terrorised by a stooping hawk, under the persistence of the Bishop's steady gaze.

" No others? "

" Not . . . that I recall, my lord. . . ."

" H—m," said Bishop Elphinstone. " I had the jackdaws in mind."

Cornered, the young man visibly controlled the beginnings of panic. His eyes steadied. He returned look for look. " I saw none, my lord Bishop," he said.

" And how do you expect to find your sister, the Lady Elizabeth? Henry's Queen, at least, should know you, should she not? " persisted the Bishop of Aberdeen.

But at that moment the pealing silver trumpets summoned them to dine, and the swiftly lowered lids prevented the Bishop from deciding whether relief or merely anticipation had lit up the odd, light eyes.

Seated at the King's right hand, served, as James was, on bended knee, the Duchess of Burgundy's protégé revised his ideas about Scotland as he ate and drank and listened to James's plans for his entertainment.

" All Scotland's chivalry waits to do honour to Prince Richard of England," James assured him warmly. " I have planned tournaments at which you will not only witness the fairest jousting we can show, but have yourself a chance to enter the lists at your pleasure. I also trust that when I ride about the country, my lord Richard, you will give me the pleasure of your company. It may serve you well to see how another country is governed, since you are so soon to set about the task of governing your own."

His guest glanced sharply at him. He had already encountered suspicion and mockery, opposition and adulation in plenty, but now, for the first time, he was faced with a faith akin to that which moves mountains, that state of mind which all great artists know, who from the very inception of their task, see it also completed, glorious and whole. The young man had told his story so often that it had become something apart from himself, standing up, as it were, on its own merits, like brocade so rich that it scarcely needs the man within it to counterfeit him. Now, James's unquestioning belief achieved a sort of reconciliation within him. He and the story again seemed one.

"My lord James, I thank you," he said slowly. "But—in the matter of your plans for me—I fear that I shall be unable to sustain my rank as I should. Since . . . since . . ." He broke off, glancing down at his carefully darned hose, lifting his arm to exhibit the threadbare elbow of a doublet which had once been gorgeous, but always intended for a slighter man.

James laid a hand on his wrist. "My lord Richard, do not let such trifles vex you. Naturally your present resources are limited. Do me the honour to accept an allowance for your personal expenses, besides those of your household, for your clothes and armour, horses, and whatever you lack besides——"

"My lord, I am ashamed to rob you," the young man from Burgundy said with sincerity.

But James brushed his embarrassment aside. "You need not be. Nothing will give me greater pleasure than this chance to exchange the tedium of state affairs for the delight of riding forth to champion a dispossessed heir. Has your Highness read the tales of Sir Thomas Malory?"

"I have had little time for reading of late, my lord James."

"Likely enough," James agreed. "But tell me something of your childhood. How did you fare together, you and your brother, during that monstrous imprisonment? Was the attempt on your life unexpected, or had you both long gone in dread?"

But his guest had been sufficiently cross-questioned on the Tower of London. He drew the back of his hand across his eyes. "Will you forgive me, my lord? It is a painful memory——"

"It is I who should ask forgiveness," James said contritely, "for my boorish questioning. Let us talk of the future and think only of the past when the time comes to avenge it. I have summoned the nobility of Eastern Scotland to meet us here. Others await us at Perth, Falkland and Linlithgow. Word has also gone out for weapon-showing throughout the country, in order that we may support your case in arms, if the usurper is not to be dislodged by more peaceful means. There is also the question of a marriage alliance. Our two countries should be linked by a marriage between our ruling houses. My beautiful cousin Catherine, Huntly's daughter, would make a fair and gracious Queen and a worthy consort for you, royal cousin."

"Your Highness does me too much honour. . . ."

James waved the protest away. "All I offer is the chance to regain your own. Is that not so, Patrick? " he appealed to the Earl of Bothwell, confident that Patrick's enthusiasm, which his drearier colleagues called recklessness, would companion his own. As the Earl of Bothwell echoed his assurances to their guest, he himself turned to the Bishop of Aberdeen.

"Are you satisfied now, my lord? "

"Less satisfied than you will be to hear me say so," Bishop Elphinstone murmured, with a quizzical glance in the direction of the young man now smiling confidently on the Earl of Bothwell.

"And why not, my lord? "

The Bishop rummaged with some deliberation in the pouch that hung from his girdle and produced a coin. "From the offertory at Mass last Sabbath morning," he explained as he flicked it on to the board and listened thoughtfully to the dull sound which followed.

"Would you say, my lord, that such a coin merits the design stamped upon it? "

"I would not," said James, weighing the counterfeit on the palm of his hand.

"Why not? "

"It lacks the ring of truth, my lord Bishop. I trust you will clap someone in the stocks for it."

"I will, when I can find him. You have not as far to seek," said Bishop Elphinstone, with his little withdrawn smile.

Frowning, James turned away. His reverence for the good Bishop did not extend so far as to suffer his scepticism gladly. For, as he afterwards told Margaret, Prince Richard was all he himself had hoped. "He is handsome and well spoken. As is only natural, French is his chosen tongue, though he can make shift to understand those who speak Scots. I have great plans, sweetheart, plans which may help us too."

" Dear James, how can that be? "

" My Council seeks a marriage alliance with England. If the English King were to marry a lady near to the Scottish throne . . ."

Hope rushed to her cheeks in a bonfire of colour, then faded, leaving her paler than before.

" My lord, he is not yet King of England."

" Many people have taken fright, because they fear he will be," James assured her. " The Spanish ambassadors have had instructions from King Ferdinand to do everything in their power to see that I abandon Prince Richard's cause, bribing me if need be, with the offer of marriage to that Infanta who is already pledged to England. But King Ferdinand admits in his letter of instruction to his ambassadors that his offer is not to be taken seriously, since it cannot be fulfilled."

" How do you know these things, James? " Margaret asked, smiling at his air of mischievous satisfaction which made him look so young, for all the manhood of his closely curling beard.

" Because, dear heart, the letters from King Ferdinand had the misfortune to arrive before his ambassadors, and since the messengers did not suppose that I knew Spanish, they were not sufficiently careful to prevent me from reading them," James explained cheerfully. " His Holiness has also written. He wishes me to enter the league against France."

" What will you do, then? "

" Advise the Council that I will consider withdrawing my support from France and the Duke of York——"

" What? " Margaret's voice was sharp with unbelief.

" On consideration of a marriage between me and the Spanish Infanta," James went on calmly. " Since this is impossible, because she is already pledged to England, I need not fear the acceptance of my terms. But to return to Spain with them will keep Don Garcia busy. I have also requested the Archbishop of Glasgow to go with him. It will be a delicate mission after his own heart."

" But—if he should succeed? "

" He will not succeed, sweet love," said James. " But by the time his failure brings him back we shall have to do with King Richard IV of England."

Margaret laughed and laid her cheek against his. "Oh, my dearest lord, how it must hearten Prince Richard to hear you. For you speak of all his hopes with just such certainty as of to-morrow's dinner. Speak so to me, James, of the love between us. For sometimes . . . I am afraid . . . as if darkness were round me at high noon."

He took her with one fierce movement into his arms. "My love . . . my little love . . . do you not see how much a friendly King of England, allied with us by marriage, will help us? Why is my Council harping still on an English match for the Scottish King? To secure peace, the promise of prosperity. All these Prince Richard offers me in gratitude, at no such price. The same stroke that wins him his throne wins me my freedom from the need to marry any but you——"

"And so, because you wish for his success——"

"Because I need it," James said grimly, "I forbid myself to doubt. For doubt breeds fear, and fear in turn failure. Instead . . ." Laughing, he stooped over her, kissing the lids of her uncertain eyes.

His purpose of championing a new King for England trembled and grew, gorgeous as a soap-bubble, irridescent with all James's passionate imaginings, as the reflections float on a bubble's convex surface; distorted, exquisite, swimming with a rainbow's prodigality but tenuous as a waking dream.

In January, 1496, the marriage of the Lady Catherine Gordon, daughter of the Earl of Huntly, to Richard, Prince of England, was celebrated in Edinburgh. James presented the bridegroom with his spousing gown of white damask, and also bore the cost of providing him, his six servitors, two trumpeters and his armourer, with all they required for the tournament which followed, during which James, for once unlucky, was thrown and sprained his wrist.

In March, uneasily aware that temporal considerations had somewhat eclipsed his attention to his religious duties, James made a Lenten pilgrimage to the shrine of St. Duthac, but his fowlers, minstrels and men-at-arms went with him, and when he came south again to spend Easter at Stirling, he brought Margaret back from Castle Drummond, where she had been since Yule, elated because her parents had now agreed to place her under his protection. At Stirling, she was to have her own appartments, Sir John and Lady Lundy were to care for her, referring their expenditure to the Treasurer, against James's personal charge.

Stirling, in April, was already crammed with the retinues of the nobles who had come to meet Prince Richard of York, and in the great hall of the Castle itself it was scarcely possible to move for the number of young noblemen anxious to earn the King's favour by displaying their zeal for the chivalric cause of the English pretender. Angus towered among the brilliant assembly, cynically surveying the thrusting mob round the prospective ruler of England. Bishop Elphinstone, disassociating himself from an enterprise of which he could not approve, was not present, but the Earl of Buchan had come with his clerkly brother, Patrick Hepburn had brought the Duke of Ross, now a lanky lad of twenty, for whom James was anxious to obtain the office of Archbishop of St. Andrews, now vacant after the death of his father's favourite, Schevez.

Early in the year as it was, the heat in the crowded hall was overwhelming, for a fire still blazed on the broad hearth, and ladies delicately patted their moist foreheads while men more frankly mopped their faces with the lining of their elaborately slashed and hanging sleeves, as they forced their way about the hall, with shoulders and elbows encountering shoulders and elbows all the arduous way.

Later in the evening, when the festival was nearly over, Margaret laid a hand on James's arm. Bending towards her to listen, he was surprised by the fear in her voice.

" My lord, who is that man by the door? "

" There are a dozen, sweetheart."

" Only one in black, pale as a tallow candle, hatless. He is speaking now to my lord of Ross. . . ."

" To my brother? Oh, that is but John Ramsay. He escaped the halter at Lauder, long ago. They say he was distraught afterwards and hid himself in England for fear of sharing his friends' fate. He returned this year on my promise of pardon."

" I do not like him," Margaret whispered.

"No more do I. Yet my father did. And for his sake I shall let Ramsay bide. He forfeited the earldom of Bothwell that I gave to Patrick. Yet he has his knighthood, and I shall see he has other lands if he serves me well."

"I have been watching him," Margaret said. "He has been in talk with my lord of Buchan. Now he is saying something to my lord of Ross which has made him glance at you, half-fearful. Is he up to mischief, James? He leaves a trail of—of treachery behind him, falsely shining like a snail's track in the dust."

"My darling love," James teased her, "this is mere fancy. What mischief should Ramsay make? I have treated him well."

"Too well, perhaps."

"I doubt it. Let him be."

But Margaret continued to watch Sir John Ramsay as he made his way about the crowded hall. She might be fanciful, but she could swear that he spread alienation wherever he went; so subtly, with a word, a glance, a smile. James might be right when he maintained that such a creature was best ignored. She longed to believe him, in this as in other things. But something far-sighted and desperate within her still cried out against him, and went unheard.

Easter passed, and the lovely days of early summer, so precious to man and beast after the rigours of a wearily prolonged winter, drifted by as swiftly as the petals of hawthorn blossom borne down the peat-dark burns towards the rivers and the sea. Margaret was thankful to look round the great hall of Stirling and not see Ramsay whispering to some uneasily attentive listener in a corner. She would have been less comforted had she known that he was jogging southward along the orchard-bordered English lanes towards King Henry's Court.

In June, the Archbishop of Glasgow returned from Spain, vexed by the impossibility of pinning King Ferdinand down to any definite proposal. But he brought with him a new ambassador, Don Pedro d'Ayala, whose honest discomfort at his own unsatisfactory task of playing the Scottish King with further vague courtesies at once endeared him to James, who took him to see the ponderous artillery, headed by the great cannon, Mons, assembled on the ramparts of Edinburgh Castle, and introduced him with pride to the pretender to the English throne, whom d'Ayala obligingly greeted with all the deference due to a prince of the house of York. But there was, for all his courtesy, the definite suggestion of a twinkle in the Spaniard's extremely shrewd brown eyes.

So the brilliant soap-bubble which was James's project swelled as the summer went on. His guest, now the husband of one of Scotland's loveliest women, still aroused enthusiasm wherever he went. And the plans for the invasion went forward. In July, James, believing himself to be on the threshold of great events, made pilgrimage, first to St. Duthac, then to St. Ninian. And afterwards he came to bid Margaret farewell in such a state of exaltation that she trembled. In such moods men ran straight on to their enemies' spears, fought against insane odds, refused to see that further resistance meant sheer butchery.

" Have a care of him, I beg you," she whispered to Patrick Hepburn. " He goes forth like one possessed."

" Madam, it will not last. We have a sobering journey to the Border," the Earl of Bothwell said.

So James rode south across the regal purple of September moors, and Margaret, left behind, waited, remembering how James had ridden away, the iridescence of the bubble about him, so that sometimes it seemed like King James and sometimes like King Arthur who rode with the company of the knights of the Round Table to avenge a monstrous wrong.

It was during the second week of October that James returned, stalking into her chamber in a right royal rage. His boots and hose were mired, his cloak stained, his plumed hat draggled. As he flung his gloves on the floor Margaret cried aloud and ran to him, knowing that the bubble had burst, leaving him heartsick as a cheated child. As she kissed him she wept for what the failure might mean for them both. But something in her rejoiced, for since the fantasy had taken him he had too often seemed a stranger, and here at last was the James she knew again, bitterly chagrined and bedraggled but undoubtedly himself once more.

" My lord, where is Prince Richard? "

"Could I but lay hands on him, I would gladly wring his neck," said James. "He should be back by now, like the rest of us, a pack of curs with our tails between our legs."

"Oh, James, is his cause lost?"

"By his own folly," James said furiously. Rolling his sodden cloak into a bundle, he slung it across the chamber at the waiting page, who, half-hidden by a curtain, was hopefully alert. Kicking off his boots, he sped the boy's departure by hurling them after the cloak, while he himself padded damply about in his long hose, and his gloves slapped limply as wet fish against the stone of the spiral stair as he threw them after the rest.

Margaret sighed, then sank down on the cushioned bench by the hearth till James's first wrath should have spent itself, as she knew it would. In silence she watched him pacing about the chamber with hasty strides that sent the strewn herbs flying so that the aromatic dust of lavender and rosemary, thyme, bog myrtle and fennel rose about him till she smiled at her absurd fancy that his anger had set the very boards he trod on fire.

"I see no cause for mirth," James raged. "All my fair project lies in ruins because Prince Richard would sooner grumble at his misfortunes than take the chance to end them. Blessed Mother of God, never have I been so enraged!"

"That I can well believe," said Margaret. "But what befell?"

James shook his clenched fists high above his head, then let his arms fall limply to his sides. "Nothing!" he said forlornly. "Our hopes were all still-born. The muster was at Ellem Kirk, ten miles short of the Border. There the purpose of Richard, Duke of York, to claim the throne of England was proclaimed and safe conduct promised to all his subjects joining the army of liberation forthwith——"

"Well?"

"Not an Englishman stirred," James said. "Can you believe it? With their rightful King but a few miles away, prepared to deliver them from the oppression of a vile usurper, not a man from northern England sought the honour of being the first to kiss his hand!"

"It may be," Margaret said, "that Prince Richard would have fared better had he not been escorted by the Scots who have so long come to fire the thatch and pillage the store that when the Scots escort their own King the doors are barred against him besides."

"So said Prince Richard himself," James admitted gloomily. "When I wished to march on and force them to their allegiance, Prince Richard looked sickly at me and refused to go on. He was reluctant, forsooth, to shed more of his subjects' blood!"

"Had there been bloodshed, James?"

"The Borderers had fired a roof or two, maybe," James admitted, "in the urgency of their zeal. Perhaps they also drove off a few flocks and cracked the skulls of the husbandmen who sought to stop them."

"Scarcely the best way to further Prince Richard's cause."

"So also said Prince Richard," James agreed. "We exchanged such furious words that had it not been for our royal dignity we might have crossed swords besides. When I called him squeamish he called me a barbarian. And then he rode back across the Tweed at Coldstream, while I——"

"Let your men rage the more because of your disappointment?"

Turning away, James nodded. He thrust his thumbs through his broad belt, hunched his shoulders, and paced away from her, his head down, so that he saw neither her outstretched hands nor the loving kindness of her smile.

"Oh, James, James . . ."

Abruptly he whirled round, furious at the reproach he fancied.

"Do you not understand? If Prince Richard fails it matters less than that I fail also. More hangs on this rebuff of a soft fat fool who grumbles at wet weather and hard riding and must sleep on a feather bed instead of campaigning in the heather wrapped in his cloak. How could I make terms with such a King of England? You and I——"

"Dear heart, I know——"

"But it is not over yet," James said savagely. "If the great hulking oaf will not win his kingdom, by heaven above I will spit

his claim on my sword and cram it down English throats as the
old wives cram geese for Christmas."

"You will invade England without him?"

"As soon as I can collect another array."

"James," Margaret pleaded, "it may be that by playing for
such a high stake you will lose all. Will you not be content with
what we have?"

"I would sooner stake all and lose it than keep the little I
dared not risk."

"James . . ." Margaret began, then hesitated. She closed her
eyes, and her outstretched hands groped dazedly for support.

He was beside her on the instant.

"It is nothing amiss, dear heart," Margaret said. "Do not
leave me, James, yet awhile. I ask no more than that we should
be together while we may."

"Blessed saints," James cried, "with you in my arms, defeat
comes to mock me!"

"But, James, I seek no splendour. Only——"

"Nay, but I seek it for you. I would offer you the stars on a
golden platter could I reach up to pluck them down."

"Forget the stars and hold me close. . . ."

For a time he was indeed able to forget the collapse of his
Arthurian enterprise. Briefly comforted, he sat at her feet
till dark came down, weaving plans for the future which
should rise, phoenix-like, from the ashes of his hopes for Prince
Richard.

He brought Margaret from Stirling to Linlithgow at the end
of the month, then dismayed her by suddenly setting out for the
Border again. She had hoped that they would keep Yule and
New Year together. But he remained at Melrose. Lonely and
wretched, Margaret longed for her mother. The ladies James had
appointed to attend her were courteous enough when the King
was about. But in his absence they did not trouble to conceal
their conviction that her heydey was over. And so, towards the
end of March, when James came to see her before his annual
pilgrimage to Tain, she begged him to take her home. She was
dizzy and sick with pregnancy. But James was already making
plans again.

"Once our son is born you shall return to Stirling. When I come south I shall contrive to give courage to that great blubbery fellow. . . ." And afterwards he would take her in his arms, whispering encouragement. "We shall do great things." Sometimes he would say, "you and I together." But oftener: "the boy and I."

James could now scarcely bear to see the once-admired Prince Richard lounging sulkily about the Court, basking in what admiration he could still find, apparently unaware that his untimely retreat had dealt his cause a blow from which it was unlikely to recover. And yet, exasperated as he was, James obstinately refused to hand over the Yorkist claimant either to his former champion, Charles VIII of France, or to Henry VII. Though the man's flabbiness was irritating beyond measure, he was still his guest.

Junker Gerhard, somewhat subdued and ponderous nowadays, visited Scotland again that year. But he found James sadly apt to tighten the purse-strings, on account of his other expensive committments, so that his great-uncle could only shake his head over his loyalty to another guest, who was also engaged in out-staying his welcome.

"Chivalric obligations? Bah!" the old warrior said. "Why let a good-for-naught empty your coffers when you could refill them by handing him over to King Henry? Take the price Henry Tudor offers. That fellow York must have cost you the ransom of an Emperor."

James had just paid seven pounds to the skipper of *The Rose*, in which his great-uncle had come to Scotland, and seventy-six pounds to various Edinburgh merchants for expenses incurred since his arrival. But he was too depressed for this irony even to make him smile.

The matter was settled, as it happened, by the Yorkist pretender himself, who declared, just as James announced a muster on the Border, that he would make no further demands on the King of Scots. Gladly agreeing, James prepared to speed his departure. He provided a ship, handsomely equipped and victualled, manned by Andrew and Robert Barton, to take his disappointing guest, his wife and all their household, back to

Ireland. In the circumstances, the more ribald considered that
the Bartons' vessel, *The Cuckoo*, was well named. But at the same
time, with the perverse tenacity which had already so distressed
Margaret, James persisted in preparing yet another attempt to
convert the north of England to the Yorkist cause, though his
recent expenditure had left his resources so depleted that he had
to sell his own great gold chain and various pieces of jewellery in
order to pay the men hired to get the artillery on the move.

Don Pedro d'Ayala, too wise to argue with James, rode with
him to the Border, joined him at cards, listened with genuine
interest to his far-flung plans for Scotland, his contention that a
King should marry less from diplomacy than choice. He also
heard much of the personal government which James meant to
initiate when, in a year's time, he reached full majority. It was
indeed largely because of the patience with which he listened so
long that, after James had failed to crack the defence of Norham,
d'Ayala contrived to persuade him to retreat rather than to hurl
his ill-equipped forces against the Earl of Surrey. D'Ayala, who
loved Scotland, had no wish to see Border bickering develop into a
full-scale war, and was thankful when James agreed to mediation, if
Surrey withdrew again across the Border. By the end of September
James had signed a seven-years' truce, ordered ten trentals of
Masses at the shrine of St. Ninian for what he belatedly recognised
as a deliverance, with five trentals to Our Lady Kirk at Kyle and
five more to St. John Baptist at Ayr. In October he set off again,
this time to St. Duthac's shrine in the north, and afterwards the
northern eyres occupied him, with the usual respites for music,
hawking and the chase, until Yule.

He missed the cultured, kindly companionship of d'Ayala,
whom he had hoped to take with him to the north. For the
Spanish ambassador had been obliged to return home on instructions from King Ferdinand, who had been alarmed by the
reports d'Ayala sent back, in case his ambassador had become too
well disposed to Scottish interests. But soon afterwards, James
received two pieces of news which, though not actually associated,
made his head sing as it might have done if his helm had been
dented by two shrewd blows from the same sword.

For the man he had entertained so royally as Richard, Prince

of York, had been captured after landing in Cornwall, confessed
to being an impostor, under compulsion of torture, no doubt,
and been afterwards hanged at Tyburn. And Margaret Drummond, home again at Drummond Castle, had been safely
delivered—of a girl.

PART THREE

1498 - 1502

CHAPTER THIRTEEN

'HEAVEN be praised I was not born to be a clerk!' said James fervently. His quill screeched across the parchment before him in the signature which caught his character more faithfully than any portrait painter was ever to do. The first capital was trenchant as a bare sword, the A that followed secret as a slammed door, the impatience in him erased the monotony of the looping M into a mere line, his gaiety asserted itself in the whirling scrolls of the E and S; his passionate truth, his profound sense of obligation and reverence for his royal office were contrastingly solemn in the final R. From the abrupt termination of the last downward stroke, so typical of his suddenly changing moods, he tossed the quill towards his secretary, grinning at the man's efforts to catch it in mid-air.

" My lord, I fear there is more yet. . . ."

James, who had stretched his arms high above his head, let them fall in a gesture of humorous resignation. " Heaven grant me patience! How much remains? "

His secretary, fumbling nervously among the coiling parchments, discovered what he wanted and hurried back. " By this charter the Earl of Angus seeks to grant certain lands. . . ."

Archibald Bell-the-Cat detached himself from the group of noblemen who were standing about the presence chamber and lounged forward. James glanced curiously at him. The great, grizzled man had the indefinably foolish air of a lad at his first courting. It sat oddly on a man of fifty, with grown-up sons and daughters. Since it matched James's mood of the moment to plague someone, he looked with the more attention at the document now awaiting his confirmation.

" H—m, aye, my lord . . ." he murmured as he read, " this rings more like a ballad than a prosy charter. ' For the singular affection which I bear to Janet, daughter of Lord Kennedy. . . . I convey to her the lands of Braidwood and . . . ihmhm . . . ihmhm

163

. . . with the remainder to the heirs male procreated between herself and me. . . .' "

Glancing up, his eyes wide with mock solemnity, James did not miss the discomfort of the shifting feet, the bitten moustache, the irritable flicking sound with which Angus snapped thumb and finger of the hand which hung by his side.

" It is my fancy to make a gift. . . ."

" A generous gift, my lord. Did you not life-rent the same lady in the barony of Crawford Lindsay? . . ."

" I did," Angus rumbled, aware that a ripple of amusement was passing over the group behind him.

" Together with the lands of Dunsiar, Kettilscheles, the forest of Dye and Handaxwood——"

" Since these lands are mine to dispose of, subject only to your royal confirmation . . ." boomed Angus.

James raised his hand. " My lord, there is no fear that my confirmation will be withheld. I had no thought but to admire the lady. . . ."

" Indeed, my lord the King? Why so? "

" Because," James said blandly, " it would seem that she knows something of the art of belling him who once belled the cat to his advantage. Tell me, my lord, what is she like, this lady Janet, who has a fancy for owning so many Angus lands? "

Angus flushed to the margin of his greying beard and shook his head like a baited bear while James amused himself, not without malice, by poking fun at the man who had once had his fun at the expense of the bewildered boy that he himself had been. Angus, James remembered, had first made him King of Scots and afterwards tried to drive a bargain with the King of England to take his kingdom away. So the note of warning in his voice did not escape the attention of those listening to the sudden little drama. They drew closer, glanced at each other, then from Angus to the King.

But only James saw anger flare up in Angus's ice-blue eyes, and his own expression changed at the challenge, as explicitly as if he had tossed down a bludgeon and reached for his sword.

" My lord the King, I have no mind . . ." Angus began. Then he broke off, biting his lips. Even he lacked the temerity

o tell James in his present mood that he would be better occupied
with his own business. But James, knowing it very well, smiled
as men smile at the prospect of an encounter likely to relieve the
tedium of a life which had been of late made up of too much duty
and too little pleasure.

" You have no mind that I should be interested? " said James,
deliberately insufferable. " So I would suppose. But I must
confess to admiration of anyone capable of driving so hard a
bargain with you, my lord Archibald, who are not commonly
bested. It was her father, I fancy, who escorted me to the Isles
a month since. I shall inform him that it would please me to
see his daughter at Court. Meanwhile . . ."

The quill screeched again, the strong, impatient, gay and
authorative signature exploded across the page. Aromatic smoke
rose from melting wax, a taper glimmered, the royal seal splodged
down.

" I wish you joy, my lord," said James with an almost impish
grin.

In silence, Angus bowed. Without a smile he turned away.
But James sat looking after him, so thoughtful that his secretary,
scrabbling again among parchments, had produced the next
charter, and spread it in front of him before James noticed that
it was there. And even when the quill was in his hand, and his
secretary had indicated the place for his signature he still sat
without movement, his eyes speculative, a faint smile curling one
corner of his mouth. The chance of tormenting Angus, who had
taken so many such chances in the past, was too good to be
missed. He would invite himself as Kennedy's guest when he
next rode to Galloway.

For James was in a difficult mood that spring, as everyone
who had to deal with him was agreed. His visit to the Isles
had gone very differently from earlier expeditions. Severity had
now alienated many of the proud and independent people
whom his moderation had already done so much to win. Those
who knew James well were of the opinion that such a change of
policy merely underlined the fact that now, having reached the
age of twenty-five which freed him from his Council's leading-
strings, he meant to dictate his own terms and ask no man for

guidance. But had Margaret Drummond been present, instead of
slowly regaining her strength after the difficult birth of the little
daughter who had been christened Margaret Stewart, she would
have known that a deeper distress was driving him. For James
most often sought to make trouble with those about him in the
hope of forgetting his own.

Hints of this showed themselves as outbreaks of irritability at
any mention of the dramatic failure of the campaign to unseat
Henry VII from the throne of England. The rights and wrongs of
the recent drama were still argued furiously by the nobility of
Scotland, who, with half the chivalry of Europe, had been hood-
winked, it now seemed, by an impostor's impersonation of the
Duke of York. Most of the pretender's former champions in
Scotland, wise after the event, stoutly maintained with head-
shaking and protestations that they had never been deceived.
John Ramsay, back in Scotland again, after his latest visit to
King Henry, smiled to himself. But James was not amused by
such a turning of coats.

" The fellow had a shifty eye. I saw that at the first," maintained Lennox, as the Estates assembled in the Parliament Hall
a few days after James had signed Janet Kennedy's charter.

" I fancied there was something odd in his way with the
English tongue," said Argyll.

" He handled his weapons too clumsily for a gently born lad,"
said Lord Home.

" But if, as he told us," James broke in, " he was bundled out
of the Tower of London for dead, and shipped overseas as a
child, small wonder he forgot his own tongue. He never heard it.
He handled his weapons clumsily, aye, but what chance had he,
leading the life of a vagrant? Did he not lack the training both
of page and esquire? "

" But, my lord James," objected Patrick Hepburn, " King
Henry had his confession taken down by trusty clerks who swore
to its accuracy. The fellow admitted his real name to be Perkin
Warbeck. His parents are vouched for by King Charles VIII,
who would have sent them both to England had it pleased King
Henry to confront them with their son."

James swept such circumstantial evidence aside. " I admit

all that. What then? We know something of King Henry, my lords. He won his throne by violence. Some maintain it was by violence that he held it. Is that not so, my lord Bishop? " he appealed to the Bishop of Aberdeen, who, quietly seated in the background, had been listening to the discussion with interest.

" It is not proven, my lord the King."

" Nor is the imposture of Perkin Warbeck," said James. " The confession was wrung from him under duress. My lord, if no oath taken under duress is binding, surely no confession obtained by threat of torture is to be believed? "

" Holy Church herself relies on torture for the correction of obstinate heretics," pointed out the Earl of Argyll.

" Torture is a devil's weapon," said James furiously.

" We have no evidence that King Henry used it," Bishop Elphinstone pointed out.

" And the fellow's parentage was discovered by King Charles," Huntly added.

" King Charles," James retorted, " would discover a raven to be white as snow if it would keep King Henry's troops out of France for a single day."

" My lord James, you are hot in the defence of a man who served you ill enough," Earl Patrick said, grinning. " Why take so much pains over him? Rightly or wrongly, Henry hanged him, and that's the end."

" Just so. But why? Why did King Henry hang him if he was not afraid? " James said quickly. " Did he hang Lambert Simnel, whose imposture was laughable? No, he turned him loose and employed him as his scullion. If this fellow were Perkin indeed, he would have served as well for a laughing-stock as Lambert Simnel in the kitchen or the mews. But now stone dead hath no fellow, it seems. What if King Henry feared the truth too much to let him live? "

" My lord the King," said Bishop Elphinstone, " I pray you will not let your concern for truth blind you to what is best for Scotland. You have done all one man may to show your indignation. But to risk the welfare of your country for a cause that is not even our own would seem to press chivalry too far. The Earl of Surrey is a very formidable soldier——"

" My lord Bishop, so am I," James flashed back.

" I know it well," Bishop Elphinstone went calmly on. " But you are also a statesman. Your reign has already achieved much for Scotland. If our project prospers, yet another lamp of learning will be kindled in the north, justice ensured by binding the sons of the landed gentry to remain at school till they be fitted to administer the law to those they govern, shipbuilding renewed till all our dockyards ring to the wrights' hammers. Your seamen have driven all alien pirates from our shores. The most formidable chieftains of the Isles have made their submission——"

" A few only. The others still take advantage of my patience. I must change all that."

" If you challenge rebellion in the Isles, my lord, you have the more reason to avoid war with King Henry," said the Bishop. " No man welcomes a conflict on two fronts."

" That I cannot deny," said James, unexpectedly reasonable. " And since the chieftains are within my dominions and King Henry is not, the choice is simpler. The charters were granted to the chieftains during my minority. I shall revoke them, now that I am of age. Archibald, I look to you, as my lieutenant of the southern Isles, and to you, Alexander, lieutenant of the north, to see that my orders are carried out. You have my authority to evict the recalcitrant and feu the lands to new tenants of your choice."

Argyll and Huntly glanced questioningly at each other. They were under no delusion as to the consequences of such appointments. James's sudden departure from his former policy, the only fault of which was that it might seem too slow, was abrupt enough to suggest that he was now in a mood to welcome trouble for the sheer pleasure of overcoming it. So, if anybody had remembered, he had once jammed his heels against the flanks of his little pony, many years ago. It had been, then, to attract the attention of the kinsmen he loved. Now, it might well be to distract his own attention from disastrous loving. For the pretender from whom he had hoped so much had now failed him utterly, speaking, when compelled, perhaps the truth, perhaps only a terrorised babble of falsehood wrung out of him by the unbearable threat of subtle pain. No one, now, would ever be sure of truth or falsehood. But

this James knew, and the knowledge frenzied him; his own fairest
chance of personal happiness had expired with the pretender's last
choking gasp on Tyburn. Had he instead now been King Richard
IV of England besides. . . . how different so much else might
have been.

James brooded, pacing to and fro, his expression so forbidding
that his nobles left him alone, drifting into groups about Argyll and
Huntly, to discuss with approval or head-shakings the wisdom of
the new policy, as James forgot the Isles, in grieving for the lost
cause of the white rose. With Richard King in England, Scotland's
royal alliance already achieved and good relations ensured by his
marriage with Catherine Gordon, James himself would have been
free to marry whom he chose. Richard would have secured peace
and prosperity, returned Berwick, paid a princely sum for Scotland's assistance, guaranteed the Marches. Now . . .

Bishop Elphinstone fell into step beside him, seeking for some
way of consoling the savagely distressed young man. " My lord,"
the Bishop said gently, " is it not possible that you are putting too
high a value on the virtue of gratitude? "

" How so, my lord Bishop? " said James, startled to find that
Bishop Elphinstone had so accurately read his thoughts.

The Bishop sighed. " They say that nothing is more common
than the revulsion of men who have been heroically aided from
those who have aided them," he pointed out. " While I cannot
approve of the superstition which refuses to save a man from
drowning, I can well believe that it may be on the risk of a
stranglehold that it is based."

" Such a risk I would have taken gladly, my lord," James said.

Bishop Elphinstone frowned in some perplexity. James was
like a certain type of apple, a favourite of his, which matured to
perfection against the sunny southern wall of his palace in
Aberdeen. Given happiness enough, his gifts should develop into
splendour. Lacking it, the Bishop feared their very diversity might
bring disaster. And so, because he knew all about Margaret
Drummond, he also sighed. But he was unaware of the little
drama of the Angus charter, so he was not unduly concerned at
the sight of Lord Kennedy waiting for the chance of a word with
the King. He had nothing more urgent to discuss, it seemed, than

the merits of various hawks, which he hoped to show the King
when he broke his journey from Galloway at the Kennedy
mansion. So the Bishop wondered why the Earl of Angus
pausing just within earshot of the sportsmen's conference, glared
at them so. . . .

James visited the Isles again in August. But it was an unhappy
experience. Discontent had already begun to alienate the people
He rode, it seemed, through an uninhabited country-side, for the
boats lay idle on the beaches, the nets flapped untended between
the posts on which they had been spread out to dry. No children
ran to meet them, no old wives called down blessings from the
wayside. Doors were barred, windows shuttered, in the little
hamlets on the edge of the whispering tides on which the golden
seaweed rocked. Only the gulls gave them raucous greeting and
the seals barked from the sea-fretted bays.

" There will be trouble here presently," Huntly said.

" So it seems," James agreed. " Can you deal with it, you and
Archibald? "

Huntly laughed. " I believe so, my lord."

But James returned to Stirling to make preparations for his
usual pilgrimage to Whithorn in a troubled state of mind. He had
not seen Margaret since the news of the execution of the Yorkist
pretender, though he had been informed of her progress, sent gifts
to her child and the nurse, and life-rented Margaret in enough
property to provide for all their needs. But a perverse fury of
frustration had made him prefer to go hungry than be content
with half a loaf by way of consolation. Such friends as Patrick
Hepburn or Alexander Gordon were honestly unable to see why
Margaret Drummond should not remain his mistress. For such
relationships had been James's habit in the past, and he was helpless to explain why his feeling for Margaret was something for
which an unofficial relationship no longer sufficed. He could not
even understand it himself.

Ever since he had been initiated by Mariot into the sweet,
sharp, sudden satisfaction of a man's mating, he had craved it
from time to time as he had never craved either for food or wine.
He had taken it gladly where it was offered, offering passion in
exchange. But tenderness he had given only to Margaret, knowing

afterwards that without her he must go forlorn about the world. With such a woman as his Queen, the strongest strands in his nature would have been twisted together into an integrity which no circumstantial stress could break. Without her, the violence of his conflicting desires threatened to ravel them beyond disentangling, so that his greatest gifts might be used to bring about his own destruction. Blinded, like Samson, by misplaced trust in those secretly working against him, he might yet stand among his enemies between the pillars of a house in Gaza.

But first the extremity of his most bitter disappointment set him searching for distraction among his other responsibilities. Before setting out for Galloway, he commissioned Patrick Hepburn, as Master of his Household, to visit Mariot's home in the west, and make arrangements for Catherine and Alexander to be brought to Stirling. It was time he took charge of their future, as he had always meant to do. Whatever else he must deny them, they should at least be cherished as his first-born bairns.

While he waited for Patrick to return James could settle to nothing. The manuscripts of the astrologers and alchemists who so greatly influenced his father, had remained, dusty and neglected, during the years when James had too much on hand to find time for them. But now, restless and unhappy, he prowled about the royal apartments, peering into the old chests which stood against the walls of a chamber he seldom used because of its distressful memories. For it was behind the very arras that still mouldered on the damp wall that he had overheard the astrologer's fearful prophecy. The lid of another old chest creaked back, and James lifted out one of the ponderous volumes within, flicking his way through the elaborately beautified pages with their illuminated capitals and red and blue paragraph headings. Inattentive at first, then less casual, his attention was finally caught by the astonishing claims made by John of Rupescissa, on *The Consideration of the Fifth Essence*, that mysterious quinta essencia, the elixir which, as the philosophers maintained, prolongs youth and wards off even the corruption of death itself.

" *Deus est testis,*" the alchemist had written, " *quod nunc tibi tantum secretum revelabo quod paucis aut nullus adhoc fuit revelatum.*" The utilitarian Latin presented no difficulty to James, who took pride in being able to read it as easily as French or Spanish. "God is my witness," he translated, "that I shall now reveal to you so great a secret that it has hitherto been revealed to few or none and is the arcanum of all philosophers. Pulverise the mineral antimony until it is imperceptible to the touch and put it in the best distilled vinegar . . . pour on it more, over a slow fire . . . put all the vinegar into a still . . . you will see a stupendous miracle, because through the beak of the alembic you will see as it were a thousand particles of the blessed mineral descend in ruby drops like blood. . . ."

On the threshhold the Earl of Bothwell, just returned, paused. But James did not look up. The old alchemist's nostalgic longing for miraculously restored youth seemed to cry aloud to him from the spidery elaboration of black lettering on the yellowed page. " I declare by God's love that . . . never in nature was there a greater secret. For all men have toiled to sublimate the spirits of minerals and never had the fifth essence . . . it takes away pain from wounds . . . its virtue is incorruptible, miraculous and useful beyond measure. Forty days it needs to putrefy in dung in a sealed bottle and then it works marvels. . . ."

The children in the doorway peered, awestruck, round the Earl of Bothwell's thigh. Catherine, grave and tall, her faded blue gown thriftily mended, her straight fair hair braided and hanging to her waist, held the stocky small boy back as he struggled to wrench his hand free. Alexander was impatient. Why did he have to stand there while the Lord Bothwell watched a man in a plain russet gown?

" Where is the King, Sir, that I was promised to see? " he demanded, his clear, indignant voice breaking through the haze of speculation as a bell through a sea fog. " The excellence of the fire of the secret adept is so great . . ."

James swung round, closed the book, from which a cloud of dust shot up, then tossed it back into the chest. But Alexander, who had broken away from Catherine's anxious restraint, was already at his side, surveying the battered volumes with wide, reverent eyes, before the lid cracked down upon their mysteries.

" So books please you? " said James, searching instinctively for some spar to throw across the gulf which separated him from this unknown, freckled child, who was, so astoundingly, his own son.

" What is a book, Sir? " Alexander asked. He stood sturdily before the stranger, surveying him with as much interest as he was himself being surveyed, his fair head held at just such a questioning angle, swaying a little from heels to toes, as if like James, he was always impatient to be off and away, his eyes so like his father's that Patrick, watching them together, smiled, as he pushed the shyer Catherine gently forward.

" Have you not seen books where you come from? "

" No, Sir. I would know more of them."

James picked him up by the belt and slung him on to the table-top. " So you shall. But wait a while till I have greeted your sister. Are you weary with your journey, Catherine? "

" No, Sir, I thank you.' A smile passed over her face, elusive as moonshine half-obscured by clouds.

" Do not be afraid," said James gently. But as Catherine turned her questioning eyes on him he realised that reserve, not fear, had kept her so far silent, and with the knowledge came an understanding of the conversations she had half-heard, the sidelong glances, perhaps the hostile embarrassment of the stepfather irked by housing the King's bastards among his own bairns. " It will be different now," he promised, stricken afresh by the uncertainty of her wary smile.

Alexander, on the other hand, seemed unaffected either by fear or shyness. Kneeling on the table-top, he had already tipped up the ink-horn and sent the sand flying as he grabbed a parchment and a fistful of quills.

" With such materials men wrote books in the old days," James said. " Would you learn the way of it? "

" Yes, Sir. Will you show me now? "

James laughed. " Scribing is not to be learned in a day." Reaching up, he deftly tucked a quill behind one of Alexander's ears, while the little boy hunched his shoulders and giggled. " I will have you taught," he said. " Patrick, make arrangements for Catherine and Alexander to have their apartments here in the Castle. See that women are engaged to wait on them. And send

Master Paniter to me that I may make arrangements for their schooling, before I leave."

" Leave, my lord? "

" To-morrow I ride into Galloway," James said.

CHAPTER FOURTEEN

IN the royal stables the scene of furious activity was typical of the eve of one of the King's pilgrimages. Since the Master of the Stables had been given only a few hours' notice, the farriers' hammers rang far into the night and acrid smoke from scorched horn drifted from the stableyard as grooms hurried to and fro and esquires toiled by torchlight to furbish their masters' harness and weapons for the journey in the morning.

As usual, James's falconers accompanied him, with a selection of his favourite birds, hooded and leashed, the huntsmen and their servants with his swiftest hounds, while quiet nags were anxiously bespoken by the Italian minstrels. For the mischievous Curry was going too, and the foreigners had not forgiven him for the former occasion on which he contrived to slip burrs beneath their saddles so that the antics of their mounts flung them all here and there. Eight young nobles rode with the King as his personal bodyguard, others accompanied him from motives of devotion or diplomacy, and the enigmatic John Ramsay had his own reasons for keeping close to the King. These would require more mettlesome mounts, since James was apt to set so furious a pace that his followers were often hard put to keep within sight of him at all.

Sometimes, in the lighter mood of the journey homeward, it amused him to elude them all for hours, and then sweep past with a whoop of triumph, his cloak streaming like a banner, so that horses reared and hounds gave tongue as the whole cavalcade set off in pursuit. It was all very well for the lads, grumbled the older men. They loved such madcap rides. But those with wives and bairns to mourn them cared less for blinding about the hills

with dusk coming down and hiding in heaven knew what potholes
and peat-haggs. Even Curry, that privileged individual, who
habitually welcomed a few days in the saddle as a respite from the
buffoonery which was his livelihood was less enthusiastic than
usual. He had been suffering, recently, from piles.

" See that they dinna gie me yon nag wi' a back as broad as
a kitchen table," he grumbled to the Master of the Stables. " Or
I'll hae to attend the King wi' a cushion clasped to my posterior.
Yon's a joke that wears thin after a wee while. And so, mair's the
pity, does the cushion."

" How long will we be gone, think you, this time? " someone
asked.

Curry's long, lugubrious face seemed to grow even longer.
' I've dune all the speiring I daur. Since my wife's like to be
brocht to bed within the month, it would suit me weel to ken.
But he'd tell me naething for all my antics. He's awful camsteerie
he noo."

" Heaven save us, then," groaned an elderly man-at-arms,
' for dear kens what cantrips he'll be pleased to play once he's
made his offering. Gin I lacked faith in blessed Ninian, I'd be like
to regain it after I've ridden on pilgrimage ahint King James.
Absolution acts on him as if his sins were lead. Eh, I've seen him
come oot o' yon chapel looking fit to tread the air."

Curry nodded his heavy head. " Aye, that's so. But he seems
to kinda miss the weight, ye ken, so that he loses nae time in
getting himsel' reloaded."

" Tuts! " said the Master of the Stables. " Think shame on
yoursel', Curry. Have ye nae mair respect for the blessed relics
than to talk like yon? "

" Placed as I am," said Curry gloomily, " respect's no' a
marketable commodity. But I must away and see whit my lord
the King's after. Eh, but dear kens whaur we'll end up this time.
Kittle as he's been this while back, yon bairns that's come to the
Castle is the daftest notion yet."

To James, on the other hand, the presence of Catherine and
Alexander offered a perverse consolation. To them, at least, he
was able to offer the protection which was their right, as no merely
expedient act of expiation but a gesture inspired by genuine

affection. But the curiosity aroused by their arrival had irritated him, a favourite hawk had recently gone astray on the marshes near Stirling, he had overset the table with a sudden movement when playing chess, and lost his temper with his opponent when riding practice courses in the lists to the lee of the Castle rock. He had afterwards apologised handsomely for the lapse, but he was still ashamed, and thankful to be riding westward to seek the help of blessed Ninian against a horde of problems, even against himself. Tossing a fistful of coins to the fungoid growth of lepers about Stirling's gate, James set off at a pace which strung his company out along the dusty track for miles behind him. His bodyguard, young and well mounted, galloped hard on his heels while the pack ponies jogged, the sumpter-men cursed and the Italian minstrels wailed that their nags were about to bolt. Far to the rear, white as a miller from the clouds of dust that fell gently back to earth about him, Curry, with his cushion, bounced and swore.

James had always loved the west country, with its gentle roll of hills and the softly kissing air at such seasons as these, when the warmth of summer lingered though her zenith had long passed. Many of his favourite shrines were in the west, and in the mood of penitence which burdened him so heavily he did not fail to offer his devotion to Our Lady of Grace at Kyle, St. John Baptist at Ayr, St. Mary of Whitekirk, on the way to the greater shrine of St. Ninian, whose sanctity had heralded the dawn of Christendom when all Scotland still lay nameless and pagan beyond. So on his way westward, James ordered trentals of masses, gave alms to the assembled poor, and showed such reverence to every wayside saint that the less nimble of his followers were exhausted with scrambling on and off their horses to thump down yet again on their knees.

"It'll be a different tale by the morn's morning," Curry assured the weary Italians, as they trudged from the stables to the Guest House of the Priory in which they were to lodge at Whithorn. Shrugging their disbelief, they sighed so prodigiously that the irreligious Curry cackled, cutting a sudden caper which contrasted comically with the unchanging melancholy of his long, lean face.

Curry was not the only one to anticipate the King's change of mood. Quite a number of the local gentry were waiting, next day, for him to emerge from the Priory, duly shriven and ready to begin his homeward journey. And James, lighthearted as if the weight of the world had fallen from his shoulders, agreed at once to turn aside for a few days' sport.

" Then, my lord the King, may I instruct your followers to look for you this evening at my house? " asked Lord Kennedy promptly.

" You may, my lord," said James, gay as the freakish wind that swayed the tops of the trees which were already parti-coloured as the doublets of the men who rode beneath them, as summer's green was ousted by autumn's red and gold.

So the Italian minstrels, complacently led by Curry, and followed by the sumpter-men and pack-horses, laden with the royal linen and hangings, down pillows, feather beds and brocaded coverlets, spare doublets, hose, short gowns and long, cloaks, tippets and hats, set off for the Kennedy mansion. Behind again plodded the beasts bearing the portable organ and chapel furniture which made it possible for James to hear Mass wherever he might be benighted on pilgrimage, and the fluting calls of the hunting-horns grew fainter as the baggage train wound its way across the rough, scrubbily wooded hills where the trees seemed to crouch down for shelter against the prevailing west wind.

News of their coming had gone ahead of them, so that they were greeted by a scurry of excited servants, all on their mettle to show the King's men that the house of Kennedy would lodge him as handsomely as any in the land. In the doorway waited Lady Kennedy, a monumental dame who stood as high as her husband in her hose, keys chiming at her belt and narrowed eyes watchful as she checked the burdens of the men who staggered past her, barking hoarse instructions as abruptly as a seal on the rocks. Lady Kennedy neither rested herself nor allowed respite to her servants, and the news of the King's coming had put her on her mettle. Scouring, sweeping, polishing; hammering, hanging, pressing; shaking, strewing, kindling; baking, boiling, and roasting went on, upstairs or down, the livelong day.

Maids swept the stinking rushes from the floors of hall and

M

solar, coughing and sneezing, holding their noses at the putrid
stench of ancient bones forgotten by the hounds, and men stamped
in with armfuls of wood, fresh rushes and sweet herbs. The
mildewed hangings were torn down from their tenterhooks in the
great bedchamber; a fire kindled on the hearth; rosemary,
verbena and lavender scattered on the boards. The King's bed
linen and hangings were unpacked, his possessions set about ready
to his hand, a chamber nearby cleared and equipped with chapel
gear as his private oratory. No one knew at what moment the
King himself might appear, so at their lady's command men and
maids ran hither and thither, calling to each other for greater
haste, with coats kilted and sleeves rolled high, panting and
crimson-faced, hungrier for the delicious wafts of roasting meat
and newly-baked bread which tantalised them from the kitchen
below.

"Mother of God," drawled Janet Kennedy, as she strolled in
from the orchard, a half-eaten apple in her hand, "what a hurly
burly they are making. Is there ever to be an end to the noise?
My head aches at it."

"It is not every day that the King's Majesty so honours our
house," her mother reproved her."

"Heaven be thanked," said Janet. "We should die of such
exertions if they were often required."

"I cannot say you look anywhere near death," said Lady
Kennedy. Janet's dove-grey gown made her red hair blaze
and revealed much more of the perfect lines of neck and throat
and young, firm breasts than was usual in the remote country-side
where the muffled propriety of coif and wimple still traditionally
lingered. Her hair was smooth, her heart-shaped face, softly
flushed as a peach against a south wall, was undisturbed by any
trace of effort, while Lady Kennedy herself continually mopped
away the rivulets of sweat which dripped into her eyes.

"Are you not glad of that? It would be a sorry thing for our
lord the King to be greeted by the corpses of those who have died
for his entertainment," Janet said.

Lady Kennedy clucked impatiently at her daughter. At a loss
as she often was, when confronted with this child who might almost
have been a fairy changeling had not such beliefs been repudiated

by Holy Church, she found the scolding she drew breath for die away. Janet's mockery irked her, as always. Had it been possible, she would have said that her own child's strange green eyes had the power to send cold fingers of fear pattering down her spine. Janet was so unlike the others. She was unlike any child she had ever known, Lady Kennedy thought, resisting the panic-struck impulse to cross herself as she faced that indifferent green stare.

" Do not stand there as if you had neither hands to work nor feet to carry you," she commanded. " Go upstairs and see if all is in order for the King's Majesty."

What would she do, Lady Kennedy wondered, if her daughter defied her. She was a woman grown, too big to be beaten nowa-days, even supposing that one dared lay a finger on her while she stood there, staring. It was with relief that she saw that Janet, for once, proposed to do what she was told. Never, since she was a tiny thing, had her mother or her nurses known the child follow anything but her own inclination. When they thwarted her she would cry herself into such convulsions that they were obliged to yield for fear she would die. An odd, thrawn bairn, even her father called her. And though she would not own it, her mother sometimes imagined her to be something stranger, a creature who had come to terms with forces that walked unseen.

How was it possible to understand a child who shared none of the little joys and sorrows of childhood, but wandered through the world as if the people about her were shadows? Things pleased her more than people. In her teens she had often spent summer days and nights out on the hills, terrifying herd lads by appearing on the skyline with her long red hair streaming on the dawn wind, or lying for hours beside the peat-darkened water of the burns that careered down from the hills at the back of the homestead, her head a little on one side and her eyes half-closed, as if she were listening to the confidences of a friend.

But rich stuffs also pleased Janet. She loved gorgeous colours and fine embroidery, fur and velvet and satins which came from lands across the seas. She wanted to take them into her arms and hold them against her heart because their beauty intoxicated her more than the wine she seldom touched. She craved for beauty,

still more for power. Possessions gave power. The land wa
beautiful. She wanted to own land because then she would ow
both power and beauty. That was why she had gone to bed wit
Angus. He had promised her Braidwood and Crawford Lindsay
But they were only a beginning. Already people called her th
lady of Bothwell, because Angus had given her lands from th
Bothwell barony which he had from Hepburn in exchange for th
lost Lordship of Liddesdale. But she would demand more, muc
more, before submitting again to the frenzied embraces of a
elderly lover whose sons and daughters were older than herself.

Now, with the King coming, she had no particular plan i
mind as she turned and went slowly up the stairs. Certainly sh
did not care whether she was doing as she had been bidden
Already she had forgotten her mother's command as she drifte
towards the great bedchamber as silently as a wreath of mist. Sh
found it empty, for the Kennedy servants had done their work
replenished the fire, and withdrawn with the members of th
King's household to refresh themselves below stairs.

It amused Janet to see what a transformation had bee
wrought on the usually austere chamber. The King, like hersel
must love colour, she thought. For the great bed was hung wit
cloth of gold into which panels of crimson velvet had been em
broidered. The pane which lay across it matched them, and th
pillows were of azure satin, with a head-sheet of ivory white
Inquisitively, she moved about. The King's bath was ready
tented with scarlet stuff to hold off the draughts. Janet smiled
That was wise. For at this season of the year the draughts alread
flew about every chamber in the gaunt mansion like invisibl
darts.

They had laid out a change of clothes for the King: crimso
satin and black velvet for the doublet, a side gown of black line
with crimson, with long black hose and slippers of crimson velvet
A belt of gold lay beside the black velvet bonnet, with a prett
toy of a gold-hilted dagger, studded with so many jewels that sh
blinked as she turned it about in the firelight, buckled on the le
side. Beautiful, those jewels, themselves like tiny fires. She dre
the dagger from its sheath and held it to her face, laying the hil
against her cheek.

So James, bursting unexpectedly into the chamber Lord Kennedy had indicated from the stairhead, already half out of his soaked doublet, in too much haste to plunge into his bath to wait for his servants to be summoned, saw her standing there, her pose half-acquisitive and half-devout, as she turned her lips towards the dagger's hilt, almost bruising them against the cold hardness of finely-cut jewels. She was looking at him, he saw, above the bauble. Though he must have startled her, she had not moved, even drawn a sudden breath. Intrigued, James kicked the door shut, slid the bolt across it, and came towards her, mudstained and blood-daubed where a bramble had drawn its thorns across his cheek, his hair plastered to his forehead below the riding-hat he presently snatched off and spun into a corner.

He did not touch her, but he was not unaware of the subtlety of the gesture with which she emphasised every curve of her young body as she turned towards him. The candour of his glance stripped her as she stood, was received with equal candour as she held her ground.

" Madam," said James, " if your presence here be part of the hospitality offered, never was there a better host since time began."

" Alas, my lord, I came here but by chance," said Janet, though the boldness of her wide green eyes belied her words. As James ripped off his doublet and tossed it aside, she stepped forward.

" Sir, your shirt is as wet as if you had swum a river. If you keep it on you will catch your death." She spoke softly, but at the touch of her hands James started as if hot irons had branded him. " Come to the fire," she urged, triumphantly aware that he was shaking as her hands moved deftly about him. Though her first touch had seared, her finger-tips were cold as marble. With a sudden shout of laughter, James took her in his arms.

" A fine one you are, to talk of my catching my death. It seems I must warm us both," he said.

At the foot of the stairs, Lord Kennedy was explaining matters, as far as he was able, to his wife. " I tell you, the King is a law unto himself on these occasions. He has kicked the door of his bedchamber shut behind him and shot the bar across. What more would you have me do? "

" But we must see he has such things as he requires. Hot water
for his bath is waiting. The pages are in readiness to bear it from
the kitchens. Supper is all prepared and the tables set. You must
go up, my lord, and knock upon his door to ask if we may send
servants to wait on him."

" Indeed, madam, I will do nothing of the sort," said Lord
Kennedy roundly.

" Heaven save us, husband, why? "

" It is more than I would venture."

" Indeed? So we are to seem lacking in hospitality? After all
my toil, you will let the King suppose we have taken no care for
his comfort? He must need the refreshment of a hot bath and a
flagon of mulled wine after a day's hard riding."

Lord Kennedy shook his head. " The King drinks less than
any of his noblemen, and eats no more than an anchorite, I
verily believe."

" At least, husband, you will yourself wait on him and make
sure," fretted the hard-worked hostess, " that he has all that he
requires? "

" After he has kicked the chamber door shut and shot the bar
across it? " said Lord Kennedy, who had seen enough, before the
door closed, to be tolerably complacent. " When did you see
Janet last, my dear? "

The colour of Lady Kennedy's overheated face darkened still
further. " My lord—you do not mean——? "

" I mean only," said Lord Kennedy, " that you would do well
to be circumspect before starting a hue and cry to find her. Only
if she can be discovered elsewhere will I wait upon the King
outside his chamber door."

" Janet—that graceless child——"

" She is no child nowadays, madam," her husband reminded
her. " The gifts already bestowed by Angus have made her a
lady of means——"

" Angus! I have no wish to see her name coupled with his,
as you well know."

" Give thanks, then, for the coupling which may turn her
attention elsewhere. Drummond did well enough out of his
daughter's association with the King's majesty, did he not? "

" It may be so," said Lady Kennedy, distractedly, still shaken by the discovery that the daughter by whom she had been so often perplexed and angered, might, after her own fashion, have planned such a high destiny.

But Janet had planned less than followed a sort of blind prompting, which owed little to deliberate reasoning and much to the pulsation of her blood. So far, James understood. He, too, sought certain things, and with violence. That they were very different from those on which Janet had set her heart was not yet apparent. He only knew that violence leapt between them so fiercely that it seemed to fuse their bodies in an embrace from which he could not endure the thought of being parted, so that being parted, they came together again with an urgency stranger than anything either had ever known, uncaring what might come of it, withdrawn from every other consideration but the longing of the flesh for a union of which only spirit is capable, not knowing yet that for all the molten ardour of flesh on flesh their spirits must remain solitary, as the round earth's poles apart.

Meanwhile, the royal household passed the time in their several fashions. The escorting noblemen were well enough amused; for Lord Kennedy could offer hunting and hawking enough to keep them all occupied. The servants were glad to lounge about the kitchen quarters and flirt with the pretty maids who found so many excuses to leave their spinning for more interesting assignations that Lady Kennedy was furious. Curry went fishing, as befitted a philosopher, while the Italian minstrels, shivering in the clammy mists of the western autumn, huddled as near to the fire in the great hall as the claims of their betters permitted, drank themselves bilious with mulled wine, and sighed for home.

And then, one morning, all was bustle again, for the King was setting out to ride to Edinburgh, where Parliament was due to assemble in a week's time. He was, as Curry had predicted, in tremendous spirits, bestowing gifts to minstrels, huntsmen, servants and the crooked beggars who had clustered about the gateway ever since his presence in the Kennedy mansion had been known. He took leave of Lady Kennedy with a graciousness which quite flustered her, but her husband noticed, as he mounted his horse to ride with the King as far as the limit of his land, that James reined his own horse back before they left the courtyard, whipped off his bonnet, and blew a kiss towards an upper window. And when a half-blown rose fluttered down towards him, James caught it, raised it to his lips, and tucked it into his hat-band as gallantly as any lovesick lad.

"Maybe, madam, you will have fewer complaints to make of our daughter for a while," said Lord Kennedy that night.

"Pah, the King's fancy is easily caught by a pretty face, as all the world knows. He will have forgotten the girl before the leaves are green again."

"I doubt, my dear, if Janet will allow herself to be so easily forgotten," said Lord Kennedy.

But Janet had not yet made up her mind whether she wanted to be remembered. The cold-blooded, calculating streak in her which contrasted so oddly with her tumultuous response to physical desire, warned her that James's name had already been linked with that of at least two women, and though Mariot Boyd had done well enough out of it, and Margaret Drummond could probably have done better, the status of the King's latest mistress must inevitably be precarious, and her supremacy brief. Her father also mentioned, during the weeks that followed James's departure, that the Council were pressing him to agree to the English marriage. King Henry, it seemed, had not only made a firm offer to the Scottish King, but sent the necessary embassy to Rome to obtain the Pope's consent to a marriage within the prohibited degrees. And King Henry never spent money idly, as everyone knew.

As Janet saw the problem, therefore, she must make up her mind whether association with the King on what terms she could obtain offered better prospects than marriage with Angus, whose appetite had been sufficiently whetted, she fancied, for him to set the claims of his grown-up family aside for those of a young second wife. But was as much to be gained by becoming the wife of a middle-aged Earl as the mistress of a young King? Janet ordered a horse from her father's stables and set off to ride about her property while she pondered the alternatives. The English brat could not be more than eleven. If she chose James, she would

not at first have much to fear from his legal wife. But how did
the Drummond business stand?

Janet suddenly remembered the thoughtful way John Ramsay,
that undulating tallow dip of a man, had looked at her during
the recent royal visit, because she held the Bothwell lands that
had once been his, she supposed. He might be willing to oblige
her by finding out whether the Drummond affair still endured.
He was too often at the King's elbow not to know. But knowing
the truth, would he tell it? Almost everybody in Scotland, it
seemed, except the King, knew that Ramsay hated him, ever
since the day when the executioners at Lauder Bridge had spared
his life but taken his lands. Her father said that Ramsay went
whispering to King Henry every now and then, and that King
James must be demented to have him back. Janet switched her
horse to a faster pace as she tried to make up her mind what
such a man's report would be worth and what it would cost to
get it. Being of the same habit herself, she recognised in Ramsay
another who gave nothing away.

Patrick Hepburn found James more difficult to deal with than
usual that winter. For though he had forgotten his encounter
with Janet almost as soon as the withered rose petals fell from his
hat, he still shied crazily away from the English match. The
Council were at their wits' end. Every now and then they would
get him, as they thought to consider it, and then, after a period
of sepulchral gloom, he would suddenly break out into furious
objections and the persuasion was all to do once more.

There was no sense in it, even Patrick Hepburn had to admit.
If Margaret Drummond had ever made any demands on him, it
would have been easier to understand James's reluctance to bind
himself elsewhere. Patrick, who knew James better than most
people, was very sure that she had not. But he was also sure
that James had not forgotten her. People had said for some time
that James had secretly married Margaret. Patrick thought that
in that case James would have told him. But he still might marry
her, he believed, if they pushed him too hard to marry elsewhere.
So he urged the Council to let James alone till the news from
Rome made a decision imperative, while he himself undertook
to see, as far as possible, that James stayed away from Perthshire.

Early in the summer which followed his meeting with Janet, James again visited the Isles, with that attentive shadow, John Ramsay, at his heels, and found Argyll and Huntly having as hard a task to quench the Islemen's grievance as to dowse muir-burn in an east wind. On his return a Border incident at Norham almost led to the breaking off of diplomatic relations with England, and James took up the Scottish grievance with such indignation that only the patience of Bishop Fox of Durham stemmed the breach which James seemed anxious to widen rather than close. Patrick, shaking his head over him, thought he could guess what a deliverance the possibility had seemed.

Once again, as James moodily paced his privy chamber after he had received news of the settlement, Patrick ventured to suggest that he might marry to please the Council, and continue an unofficial relationship to please himself. Was not half a loaf, as they said, better . . .

"I had sooner have no bread, Patrick," James cried.

"But it is not as if you went fasting, my lord," Patrick Hepburn pointed out patiently. "I heard much of the beauty of the lady of Bothwell, and how pleasant you found her when you rode last autumn into Galloway."

"God forgive me for that, Patrick," said James, taking his head in his hands. "I never wish to see her again."

But he had reckoned without Janet. Nor had he realised how Angus's unexpected second marriage, to Keir's daughter, would affect the situation. Janet learned that she had tried Angus too high, and had been jilted in consequence, as she was struggling back to life after weeks of such critical illness that she neither knew nor cared if she would see another dawn. And the news of the Angus marriage acted on her like a draught of aqua-vitae. She had never been angrier in her life. Calling her women, sending a page full-pelt to the stables, she gave orders that those escorting her were to be ready to ride to Stirling within the hour.

And so James, pottering about the garden which was being laid for him in the Castle, was startled by the request for a private audience by " the lady of Bothwell " who had ridden with all haste on business which was his most vital concern.

Grumblingly at a loss, James dusted the earth from his hands,

and followed his secretary into the small presence chamber, to
stand there blinking, unable to see anything for the brightness of
the sunshine outside.

"Well, my lord . . ." said Janet coolly.

As sight came back to him James saw that Janet's eyes were
uncannily green between the shadow of her green riding-hood
and the brilliance of her hair. A bale of cloth, it seemed, lay
beside her on the window-sill.

"Why, Janet," said James uncertainly, as he felt her strange
quality draw him once more towards her as the moon draws the
responsive tide, "have you turned pedler? What merchandise
have you brought?"

Her laugh was as strange as ever, an octave of falling notes,
like the curlew's call. He remembered thinking that once before.

CHAPTER FIFTEEN

JAMES neither spoke nor moved as Janet's gesture revealed the
identity of the bundle on the window-seat. The drama had
been too obviously contrived. Stiff and unapproachable, he
surveyed the woman who had roused his senses perhaps more than
any other, and yet, paradoxically, touched his heart less than
most. Already he was framing the phrases which would promise
investigation, and imply his willingness to meet any obligations
should her claim prove justified. . . .

And then Janet, exhausted by the long journey she had taken
so soon after her rigorous confinement, the frustrated fury of her
resentment against Angus, the necessity of wheedling officials to
obtain an interview with the King alone, made the first spon-
taneous gesture James had seen from her that day. Putting up
one hand in the bewildered movement of one brushing aside
cobwebs, groping with the other as if in sudden darkness, she
swayed, murmured, and collapsed without grace, arms and legs
spread-eagled, at his feet.

Armoured as he had thought himself, within his mistrust of

the contrived, James was not proof against such a piteously natural collapse, for he was kind, and consternation overwhelmed him as he knelt beside her. Blessed Name of God—had she died at his feet? The child bundled on the broad window-seat set up a thin, persistent wail. If she were as lifeless as she seemed . . . James shouted frantically for his page. . . . He must send for a leech . . . a woman to quieten the child. . . .

Then Janet stirred. Thankfully, James stooped to raise her. Heaven be praised, at least her death did not lie to his charge. As he gathered her into his arms, she opened her eyes, so that he felt suddenly dizzy. The old enchantment swept over him. Though she lay without movement, her fingers trailing, he could have sworn that her hands were clasped behind his neck, drawing him down, drawing him close, till her lips parted beneath his. He had crushed her to him before he knew what he was about.

"James . . ." said Janet softly. "Oh, James . . . are you there? I have been so ill . . . so much afraid. . . ."

Reproaches would have been useless against him, demands merely antagonising. But such a confession of weakness in a woman he had known to be so strong, so sure in every urgent gesture, disarmed him utterly. He forgot everything except that she was sick and in need of consolation, that he, bound by his pledge of knighthood, was there to give it.

"Rest now," he bade her. "I will have women tend you. They will bring you wine."

She clung to him, then. "Do not leave me . . ." she begged. "I want only you, James. Hold me close . . . I am so cold . . . so cold . . ."

He could feel her shake as he folded her green cloak more closely and bore her across the room to the settle in the far corner out of the draught from the door. He held her against him till the warmth came back to her cold hands and the returning circulation drove the sickly pallor from her thin face with the enormous, dark-encircled green eyes in which his resolution seemed to drift, to drown. On the window-seat the child, unheeded, continued its high, forlorn complaint.

A couple of days later, the Earl of Bothwell, riding to Stirling ahead of the other members of the Council, arrived at the Castle

to bring James the news from England. His experienced eyes
surveyed the usual swirl of townsfolk and country people, men-at
arms in a variety of liveries, bare-legged Highlanders in their
saffron shirts, merchants and pedlers, knights, esquires and pages,
priests and vagabonds, who were passing in and out of the courtyard. But he fancied that he detected an air of excitement about
some of the groups which made the indifference of others more
conspicuous. Something, in fact, had happened of interest to the
gossip-lovers. Something, perhaps, of some significance, he
guessed, as he made out the dark figure of John Ramsay, drifting
from group to group, either to gain information or to give it.
Ramsay? He must have ridden with the devil's own spurs. For
surely he had been in Edinburgh when the envoys from England
arrived? The fellow made him uneasy. There never seemed to
be any accusation one could grasp and drag into the light of day.
Muttering to himself, Patrick Hepburn drove his horse through
the scattering crowd and sought a private audience with James.
It was easy, then, to guess what had caught Ramsay's fancy, so
that he was buzzing round Stirling Castle like a wasp round the
cook's finest sugar-castle for the King's table. If Ramsay were
paid by King Henry of England to watch his interests, he would
inevitably be anxious to discover what lay behind the arrival of
Mistress Kennedy. At such a time, an association with her was
the sheerest folly of all.

"My lord James," he grumbled, "surely you are aware that
the lady of Bothwell was handfasted to Angus before you set eyes
on her?"

"I know it well, Patrick. Was I not minded to amuse myself
by showing Bell-the-Cat that others had a way with kittens?
As to the infant——"

"Which, my lord, may just as well be his——"

"Have you seen it, Patrick?" said James ruefully.

"No."

"It will make you laugh. But I believe it will convince you.
It gave me a grue at first. To look at flesh and blood as into a
mirror."

"My lord, what do you intend to do now?" asked Patrick
abruptly.

James raised his eyebrows at him. " Why, what should I do? I have commanded that apartments be placed at the disposal of Mistress Kennedy."

" Here, in Stirling? "

" Where else? She is fit to go no further. To compel her to journey on would be to force her through death's door. You need not frown. I am enough of a physician to know sickness when I see it. She has exercised none of her wiles, I swear——"

" My lord James, a woman's subtlest enchantment is such weakness. It is like the feint by which a swordsman baffles the defence before the thrust which follows, when his enemy is off his guard."

" To have failed in kindness would have been monstrous," said James roundly.

" No doubt. But her presence at this time could scarcely have been more unfortunate. I have ridden ahead with the news from England——"

" And that is——"

" His Holiness has been pleased to grant King Henry the dispensation which is required before your marriage with the Princess Margaret can go forward."

James laughed suddenly. " How much, think you, did such a concession cost the King of England? "

" Less, perhaps," said Patrick, " than if his Holiness had not been anxious to assist King Henry to break our bond with France. Be that as it may, the Council is hard on my heels, and the English envoys with them. What is to come of Mistress Kennedy?"

" She shall bide," said James. " What have they to do with my care for a lady in distress? "

" Have you seen Ramsay? " said the Earl of Bothwell, pausing, as he prepared to take his leave, in the certainty that he could move James no further.

" Ramsay? No. Yes, I believe I did, not long since. He came to ask me something about the trees I ordered for the orchard. As you well know, I have given him charge of my privy purse. The apple trees were some he was to obtain for me in the south. Do not shake your head like a sick bear, Patrick. I know he runs with gossip to King Henry. But what of it? What is one paramour more or less when the bethrothal is not even agreed? Those things which are of first importance I take care Ramsay shall not know."

So Janet stayed on at Stirling as the King's honoured guest. John Ramsay, unobtrusively observant, took note of the fact, balancing its significance against the presence of the English envoys, the anxiety of the Scottish Council for James to make up his mind, the traditional Franco-Scottish alliance which King Henry's proposal sought to undermine, and the dramatic possibilities which the conflicting interests of his betters offered to a man obsessed by the searing purpose of revenge. John Ramsay in his thirties had withered rather than matured. Deprived of the warm current of life-giving affections, he was like a truss of budding foliage, wrenched from the main stem and carelessly cast aside, autumnal without ever knowing summer's glory. He had always been pale, but now the smooth oval of his beardless face was yellowish and shrunken, as if the passion of bitterness and revenge had jaundiced his very flesh. He had come back to Scotland with hatred as his informing purpose; feigning submission, watching the King gird Patrick Hepburn in full Parliament with the symbol of the earldom which had once been his.

For years he had planned to kill James. And yet he had not dared. He had taken all the preliminary steps, winning his confidence, accepting his pity, taking the appointments James offered as a surly dog is driven by hunger to beg for scraps. He knew very well that James had been warned against him, also that he had defied that warning. The knowledge shook him with the rage of a man who endures his enemy's kindness as helplessly as a goose is crammed for Martinmas. His failures had daunted but not checked him; it had been some consolation to assist King Henry to frustrate James's plans for the Yorkist pretender. He had enjoyed giving the English King the information which ensured that the north of England was so well garrisoned that its people dared not, even had they been willing, support the cause of York.

But such minor achievements merely whetted his desire to strike nearer the heart. The thought of assassination terrified him, for he had not the stuff of martyrs in him, and it was unlikely that the man who killed a much-loved King would escape the consequences alive. The King's food, his wine, were tasted before he touched them, as a matter of course. So that way, too, was blocked. What possibilities remained? A man like James, he fancied, might be made to suffer more subtly than by physical violence. An injury directed, not at the King himself, but at a creature dear enough to him could deal a less dangerous and more effective blow.

So the arrival of Janet Kennedy interested John Ramsay a great deal. Making himself useful in various ways, congratulating himself that James took his acceptance of his pardon at its face value, he was industrious after his fashion, biding his time. He took stock of Janet. She was in high favour, it seemed, lodging at Stirling throughout the Council's visit, kept discreetly out of sight, but refreshing James after the long, wearisome sessions with interludes of gaiety, so that his wild laughter could be heard out in the corridors along which John Ramsay padded, listening. The child and its nurse, too, were well cared for. Ramsay peered into the cradle sometimes, tossing the nurse a coin for the chance of seeing how much the little crumpled face with the fuzz of red-golden hair above it favoured the King. And yet, he could not say that the King's heart was surely in the keeping either of the lady of Bothwell or her child. He was as often in the company of Catherine and Alexander, the brats who were also lodged at Stirling now that their mother had been married off. Dissatisfied, Ramsay waited for the situation to clarify itself. If he were to strike, he must make sure that the wound would be mortal. The risk was too great to be taken in vain.

But the task of keeping watch on James taxed even Ramsay's malice, for there were times when the King seemed almost to have mastered the art of being in two places at once. He dispatched the Council with no definite answer, sent the English envoys back to King Henry with a series of courteously pettifogging questions with the evident object of delaying the outcome, and rode furiously about the country, regardless of weather or weariness. In the Isles the trouble produced by his change of policy was beginning to smoulder dangerously towards combustion point, now that the death of his complaisant pensioner, the disinherited Lord of the Isles, had focused the hopes of the Islesmen on his son

Donald Dhu, whose legitimacy was so hotly asserted by the Islesmen that he had been taken into custody by the wary Earl of
Argyll. In Aberdeen, James inspected the progress of the new
buildings for the University, met the prospective Principal,
Hector Boece, who had returned from Paris in August, and discussed with the Bishop the advisability of beginning tuition
without delay.

Business and pleasure took James from Aberdeen to Inverness,
from Inverness to Dundee. He hunted, attended sessions of the
local courts, ratified charters, and went on to Lanark, to Glasgow,
and to Perth, early in 1501, for the christening of the Earl of
Buchan's second son. By March he was back at Stirling, tramping
unexpectedly into Janet's chamber where she was trying a new
fashion of dressing her hair and humming to herself, well satisfied
by her reflection. She saw him immediately, yet watched him in
the glass for long enough to guess at his mood before turning
slowly round to greet him with a deep reverence so much at
variance with her intimately-mocking smile, that James could
accept either, according to his state of mind.

" My lord, I am thankful for your return," she said. " I have
gone in fear——"

" Of whom? " said James abruptly. But he did not yet offer
to take her in his arms. Janet's brows drew slightly together.
Where had he been? To Drummond by any chance? Jealousy
fretted her like a burr. She sidled up to James, letting her head
droop a little towards his shoulder in the way she had.

" Of—of Angus, my lord. He has threatened me."

" Threatened you? How has he dared? "

Janet smiled. Disabling in oneself, how useful jealousy could
be when aroused in others. " On account of the lands he bestowed
on me," she murmured. " He has sought to have me live nearer
him than I should be in Galloway——"

" What has your whereabouts to do with him? Is he not new
married? "

" Yes, indeed," Janet murmured. " So I thought."

" I will send him to the right about," fumed James. " And if
you are in need of lands, I have more to bestow than ever Angus
could."

N

Janet laid her hands against his chest, kneading his crimson
doublet with her finger-tips like a little cat. " My lord, you are
always generous," she murmured. " But what had you in mind? "
she went on swiftly. " A landless lad has but a bleak future, I
must own. A royal father's sons are to be looked for among the
nobility——"

" So you have said before," James pointed out with the wry
shrewdness that occasionally took her by surprise.

" Indeed, my lord? "

" Aye, many times. I have had it in mind, however, and
delayed only for perversity, maybe," he added with a crooked
smile. " The Earldom of Moray reverted to the Crown in——"

" James—oh, James, that would be a royal gift indeed. And
the lad bears your own name? "

James nodded. He was aware of being rushed. The vague
memory of the sheepish expression on the face of the Earl of
Angus, as he produced for ratification the charter making certain
lands over to Janet, teased him warningly. There was a gleam
in her eye now that he had not noticed before, her small, even
white teeth had closed on her lower lip as if to check an exclama-
tion. And yet, he might well be misjudging her. She was anticipating his recognition of their son rather than wheedling gifts
out of him for herself. He had a gift in mind for her too. If the
child was to have Moray, his mother could neither go landless nor
let him lack her care.

" I shall give you the Castle of Darnaway, Janet."

" Oh, James . . ." She was like a little cat again as she pressed
herself against him, her shining green eyes wide.

" In life-rent," he added.

" Oh." He could feel her delight tempered with uncertainty.
" Where is Darnaway, James? "

" On the Findhorn."

" So far away? "

" It is the traditional seat of the Earls of Moray."

" Ah, that is different. When shall we go? For you will take
me there? You will not bundle me into the wilds, bag and
baggage, like a dismissed——"

" We will go to Darnaway together, when all is set in order

for you," James promised. Then, teasingly, he added: " but that will not be yet a while."

" Oh, James, why not? You do not know how weary I become of the great affairs which keep you from me, working so long and so late with those sad-faced Councillors who shake their heads at every pleasure you snatch from the dreary round of duties. When shall we ride together into the mountains to see our new home? For that is how I shall always think of it, James, whatever you put on the charter. Your home and mine . . ."

James stooped at last and kissed her on the lips.

He had not forgotten Angus's arrogant interest in Janet's movements, though he did not immediately find the opportunity to show his disapproval. But towards the end of April, when he was making his way back up the west coast from the shrine of St. Ninian, he unexpectedly encountered Angus in Glasgow. James had stopped to dine with the Bishop before riding on to Stirling, and Angus, who, it seemed, was planning to take up residence in Bute with his new wife, had come to confer with the Bishop on matters connected with his tenancy. Seated some distance away from James at the Bishop's table, he painstakingly refrained from looking in his direction till James's indignation was sufficiently inflamed for him to send a page, once the boards were drawn, with a summons for the Earl to wait upon him in the chamber which Bishop Blackadder had set apart for the royal business. And Angus kept him waiting for just long enough to bring an impatient man's temper to boiling point, so that James whirled round on him as he entered the room.

" Does it seem likely, my lord, that I have all day to wait upon your convenience? "

" I have but newly received your summons, my lord the King," said Angus heavily. As he and James faced each other, the hostility James had felt over ten years ago, as a boy in his teens, then so much at the older man's mercy, flared up again now that the balance had swung the other way. But their positions were not yet quite reversed. Angus was still formidable enough to be reckoned with, though James was not inclined to let prudence deter him.

" My lord, it has come to my notice that you have sought to

restrict the movements of a lady in whose welfare I have some concern."

"Indeed, my lord the King?" rumbled Angus belligerently.

"I refer to Mistress Janet Kennedy, sometimes known as the lady of Bothwell."

"So I supposed," Angus said. The words were plain and his tone offensive. James coloured angrily at both.

"By what right have you presumed to take such a step?" he demanded.

"The right was given by the protection I extended to her, my lord the King, before the matter was any affair of yours," said Angus curtly. "In proof of it I offer the very charter which received your approval some time past."

"Such gifts confer no rights whatever, my lord, over her person," said James. "And furthermore this is something you can scarcely have desired. Your own marriage last year was not to her."

"My right over her person, my lord," said Angus furiously, "is as great as yours, and of the same order. Therefore, since she came first under my protection, I claim the prior——"

"My lord Angus, no man shall speak so to me and escape correction," said James. "You will place yourself in ward at the Castle of Dumbarton and there await my pleasure."

The two men glared at each other for a moment during which it seemed possible to James, even to the horror-struck officials who had unobtrusively edged within earshot as the voices rose, that Angus would strike him, and so end the argument with the fall of a sword on a traitor's block. And then, after a struggle for self-control which shook him from head to foot, Angus swung round and tramped from the room, the clash of his spurs on the flags vibrant with the resentment he must otherwise conceal.

The next day James rode eastwards, at his usual headlong pace, fretting while a fresh horse was saddled, covering a hundred miles through difficult, hilly country in two days, arriving at Stirling, mired, sweating and in high spirits, to seek Janet out as soon as he had bathed and changed his clothes.

"My lord," she greeted him, "you are as gaudy as a victor

in the lists. What courses have you won since I last set eyes on you? "

" I shall not say," James retorted. " We have better things to do, you and I, than to gossip together. Have I near foundered half a dozen good horses to enjoy no more than a sisterly kiss? "

" How much more do you seek? " mocked Janet, holding out her arms.

The charter for Darnaway was prepared by the end of the month, and James brought it to her on the first of June. Janet scanned it carefully, her narrow eyebrows arching towards the line of her bright hair, her mouth twisted into a grimace as she read.

" What ails you? It is yours fast enough now," James said, stooping to read over her shoulder.

Janet's slim forefinger followed along the lines. " Listen, James . . .' from my cordial love for Janet Kennedy, lady of Bothwell, daughter of John, Lord Kennedy, grant her in life-rent, as long as she remains without husband or other man. . . . Without husband or . . .' Must you add that? "

" Because I am fond, I need not also be a fool," James pointed out, grinning. And John Ramsay, who had happened to be near enough to the open door to hear what was going on between them, frowned and passed on.

" I do not understand you," she said sharply.

James twisted a curl on the back of her neck between finger and thumb. " Let us say that having seen one man's folly enrich you, my love, for the benefit of another, I am not minded to do the same. Since the land is mine, you shall enjoy it only as long as the enjoyment is mutual——"

She was on her feet, her sudden temper flaring, her strong fingers wrenching at the tough parchment. " It is an insult. I will tear this thing in pieces and throw the fragments at your feet."

James folded his arms and watched her with a broad grin. " Tear it if you can. But you will get no other," he said blandly. " Think first. Then think again."

Janet desisted abruptly. " You—you are both untrusting and . . . unkind."

"Oh, no," James said. "Not unkind."

For a moment he was astonished to see that her expression, as she glared at him, was not unlike that of Angus at the climax of their recent encounter in the Bishop's Palace in Glasgow. Then Janet recovered herself, held out her arms, and smiled.

"Forgive me, my lord. Indeed, I meant nothing of what I said. I am too deeply beholden to you for your great goodness to me, and to our beloved son. His future is now assured, James. When I think of what you have given him: the lands and earldom of Moray, with the burgh fermes and customs of Elgin and Forres, the office of Sheriff of Forres . . . the lands and lordship of Abernethy. . . . Oh, James, how soon shall we go there together to see what is his—and mine? "

"Soon," James said. "Soon . . ."

But time passed, and he did not arrange the visit to Darnaway, though he sent experts with instructions to put in hand all necessary repairs against his coming. Janet, in Stirling, had never known him so restless. He seemed like a man stretched visibly on the racking distress of an agonising uncertainty, from which, at intervals, he sought to distract himself in a bewildering variety of ways. Sometimes he sought her, imperious and demanding, again and again. Sometimes she did not see him for weeks, sometimes for days and nights at a stretch, he scarcely left her. He hunted that autumn on Benmore and at Strathfillan with as much zest as he made his retreat with the Friars Observants in the forest of Glenartney, emerging to hunt again, to ride to Perth and Dunfermline, to inspect the progress of the building at Aberdeen and take counsel with Bishop Elphinstone. Piqued as she was by his absences, Janet did not think that he sought out other women. She was more resentful of his affectionate care for Catherine and Alexander, children of a woman he seemed to have forgotten. Yet they had their own rooms, instructors and servants at Stirling as if they had been his legitimate son and daughter. Janet wondered about them now and then, as her thoughts needled to and fro, seeking sometimes her own blatant advantage, and sometimes disguising the pursuit, even from herself, with the name of her son. Would James one day marry her off too, and add Moray to the royal nursery? She smiled ironically at the thought. If he chose to treat all his sons as kindly as Alexander, he would soon have quite a family under his care. Was there not also, somewhere, the brat that Margaret Drummond had borne him? And others, no doubt, besides, Janet thought indifferently. They did not matter.

But Margaret Drummond, Janet guessed, without quite knowing why, was the one woman whose rivalry she need fear. For Janet was close enough to James to be aware that she did not even in his moods of utmost passion, possess him wholly. She caught a look, sometimes, in his eyes, when he was unaware of being watched, of such heartsick longing that jealousy at once seared her pleasure in him like a lightning flash. She did not know his inmost thoughts. Of that she was well aware. James, who could be the most candid of men, sometimes shied away from inquiry like an unbroken colt from whip and rein. About certain things he would never speak. Of the fetter he wore in daily penance she had only the occasional evidence of the chafed skin above his hip-bones where a band might have rubbed him sore at the end of a twenty-mile ride. She had offered him salve once, but he had refused her so abruptly that she had not ventured again.

One evening in late September he did not return when he was expected, and Janet, inexplicably restless, strolled out into the garden he had had made with such care and expense, high among the buildings on Stirling Castle's rock, so that its small space offered the solace of close-shorn grass, fragrant flowers and herbs to those weary of the harsh protection of stone walls. Because of its contrasting pleasance she preferred it before the great new garden he had recently spent so much money in stocking with fruit trees on the plain below. Anybody could make a garden in a fertile valley. Only James would have earth carried, basket by basket, to make a garden on a barren crag. If she loved James— she was never sure if she really loved anybody, except of course, the child—if she loved James, it would be because he did that sort of thing, she thought, as she strolled towards the parapet from which she might perhaps see him, heralded in the distance by a towering cloud of dust. But the country-side below the great rock lay peaceful in the evening light which turned the links of

Forth from silver to gold. She stood there, thoughtful, till a slight
noise behind her made her turn, smiling, her hands already half-
outstretched. But it was John Ramsay, looking as disconcerted
as herself.

"I—I had thought to find the King in your company," he
explained lamely.

"It is not often you do not know where to find him, Sir
John," said Janet. Forgetting that she had once thought they
might come to terms, she did not trouble to hide the contempt she
felt. She could understand hatred as readily as devotion, better
perhaps, indeed. But she had no use for the one which mas-
queraded as the other. And she was too shrewd not to recognise
such a masquerade now.

"No," agreed John Ramsay in his lifeless voice. "It is not
often I do not know. Perhaps you can advise me where he may
be found?"

"I cannot," Janet said.

"And would not, if you could?"

"And would not," Janet agreed, then suddenly added:
"without knowing more of why you seek him."

Ramsay looked at her with the blank, direct stare that
makes some eyes more secret than others which hide their
thoughts behind lowered lids. "Surely, madam, my duties in
connection with the King's disbursements from his petty
purse——"

"Need neither bring you keeking round cradles nor listening
behind doors," she told him roundly. "Whether the King by
making his devotions with the good friars, or attending to other
interests at Castle Drummond——"

She gasped at the words as if she would have caught them
back. They had escaped her before she was aware, released on
an impulse of jealousy near akin to the anger Ramsay had roused
in her, rather than from any thought of doing James harm. But
Ramsay had not missed their significance. He was watching her
between narrowed lids, his eagerness imperfectly masked by the
casual tone in which he drawled:

"So you—think he goes there?"

"I think nothing," Janet snapped, annoyed both with herself and him.

He laughed, a dry crackle that suggested phlegm rather than mirth. And at that moment she was aware of James behind him, arrested in mid-stride, his cloak still flying out with the speed of his arrival, then falling about his tensed limbs as slowly, she fancied, as a pall is lowered on a bier. For her keen perception, abnormally heightened by her recent indignation, seemed to present the two men moving with fantastic deliberation, like the puppets sometimes shown at Court on Twelfth Night. From James's face, as the folds of his cloak fell, the smile took as long to fade as the sun at his back to sink behind the horizon hills. With the same nightmare slowness Janet saw him turn on John Ramsay a stare so piercingly deliberate that it seemed to probe his inmost purpose, then turn the same inquiry on her. The strangeness of it all made Janet feel sick. Unaware that she had taken a step backwards, she was yet to remember the oddly terrifying little scene in the Castle garden whenever she smelt lavender. Its sharp fragrance was all about her from the carefully tended bushes she had crushed.

And yet all James said as he held out his hands to her was: "We shall have rain. The sunsetting is too yellowish for fine weather." But, though Ramsay had disappeared, shadow-like, James did not kiss her. Instead, he stooped and straightened the bruised stems of flattened, grey-green foliage. "A pity. They were just taking root," she heard him say. But when he straightened up, it was neither to reproach her nor to inquire what she had been about. Instead, he gripped her arms above the elbows with sudden excitement, though she could feel the weariness in him the instant his hands touched her. Vitality seemed to flow from her till she was drained of it as his dark-circled eyes blazed at her with the wildness of a man drunk. But not with wine, Janet thought. She laid her palms on his chest, pushing him away to see him better.

"James," she whispered, "what is it? What has gone amiss?"

He laughed, then. But though he spoke, it was not to answer her.

"Where is your household gear?"

"Why—here and there, James," she said bemusedly, unprepared for the sudden demand.

"Have it dispatched, then. I will see it is collected in Edinburgh. I will install you as mistress of Darnaway, madam, before the leaves are down."

CHAPTER SIXTEEN

THEY rode coastwise to the north, sometimes passing through woods in which the golden defiance of frost-tinged chestnut and lime was mocked by the sombre constancy of fir and pine, but oftener along paths which lay bleakly between bare hills and the sea, so that the sand blown off the dunes gritted against their teeth and drifted into the folds of their clothing. Janet had arranged for the nurse who had care of Moray to mind him at Stirling till she should summon them. She was anxious to have James to herself for a while. His devotion to his children might be praiseworthy enough, but Janet did not fancy being ousted from her place in James's affections by her own child. As usual, they were escorted by a mixed retinue of every sort of entertainer, though Janet complained loudly that she would rather have had a few stout fellows with her coffers of gear. Only a man would have chosen to take his fiddlers with him and leave all her changes of clothing to follow with the baggage train.

"Had you attempted to lift the coffers which contain your finery, madam," James mocked her, "you would have understood why I had it borne by sumpter beasts. It would have broken the back of any others, I swear."

Janet pouted, switching petulantly at her horse as they jogged. "I had not thought you would show me less care than your beasts of burden. If we encounter a storm, I may be chilled to death, since I have only the mantle that is about me now."

"If your mantle is soaked, I shall buy you another," James promised.

"I shall hold you to that," Janet said.

At Arbroath, which they reached in a deluge, James was better han his word. While they rested at the Guest House in an inxious flurry of monks bearing hot possets for the travellers and extra logs for the fire, James sent for a merchant and bought two mantles instead of one.

How like him that was, Janet thought, as they rode on towards Montrose. Better than his word, provided he was following his fancy; but worse, much worse if he felt himself coerced. When she came first to Stirling, her journey had seemed vain. But once he had taken her and the child under his protection, she had been showered with gifts which ranged from Darnaway itself to the skeins of sewing silk she needed to finish her embroidery. Only James, improvident in all things, would have parted her from her luggage, which included at least three mantles, and ridden with her through a downpour, so that he had to buy her another. And then, to buy her, not one mantle, but two. . . .

And yet James was no fond fool. If he suspected he was not receiving the value he demanded—less in effects than in affection —he would be angered at once. She could deal with that, of course. It was less easy to deal with the dark moods which had come upon him oftener of late. At first he had been able to throw off the brooding gloom; later she had been able to free him. But during the last few weeks she had not been so sure. Was her skill waning? Or was it something else? Someone else? She wished she had not been so curt with John Ramsay. Now, even if he did follow James to Drummond Castle, it was probable that she would never know where he had been. Certainly she would never demean herself to ask.

But James seemed, for a time, cheered by the diversion of the journey. Once again he was a delightful companion; attentive, informative and gay. But it was a new experience to ride by his side and see the people come running to cheer him, to watch James doffing his bonnet, bowing, waving to the children, blowing kisses here and there, tossing a coin to an old fiddler who limped by the roadside, sawing out a threadbare melody. James . . . and his lady . . . She amused herself by pretending that they rode together as King and Queen of Scots, her mouth twisting

as she reflected that though the men escorting them referred as a
matter of course to " the King and the lady " the country people
probably used a briefer and more descriptive term.

At Stonehaven James stopped to make his offering at the
Church of Our Lady. At Aberdeen they admired the progress of
Elphinstone's new College, at Inverness they were storm-stayed
by weather for long enough for Janet to beat James soundly at the
cards and listen to the laird of Balnagowan's harper. But her foot
was tapping as she wondered how long it would take James to
make his devotions at St. Duthac's shrine in Tain. The whole
enterprise seemed unreasonably prolonged. Would they never
come to Darnaway?

She hid her impatience however, and accompanied him duti-
fully on the last stage of his pilgrimage, laid her offering beside
his, reflecting thankfully that now James had placated his
conscience by making gifts to the friars of Inverness, to five
separate altars at Tain, to the priests of the Chanonry of Ross, of
Forres, Elgin and Kingussie, he would be ready to enjoy worldlier
pleasures again.

Her endurance was tried high as James prolonged his devotions, lit candles, kissed relics, bespoke Masses, and listened to
elevating conversation from the shrine's custodians. Janet was a
natural sceptic, too shrewd not to be aware of the commercial
aspect of the penances and pilgrimages prescribed by confessors.
Her own beliefs were so well smoored down under layers of self-
interest and common sense that even she seldom penetrated to
where they lay hid, a kernel of time-shrivelled, ancient fetishes
and taboos wrapped about with a houselling cloth of Christian
terminology.

A temperament such as that of James, swinging from an
extreme of emotional piety to an equally violent extreme of
physical desire was something of a mystery to her. But she told
herself philosophically that it might well be no more than two
sides of the same coin, and when they left Tain at last, she was as
gay as he. For James, shriven and absolved, was now ready to
match his recent spiritual indulgences with others of a more
pleasing sort. And they were riding together towards Darnaway,
which was not only to become her son's home and the home of his

sons after him, but was already hers, her very own, on conditions which were not even irksome—at least, not yet.

But when she came in sight of Darnaway, splendidly set among autumnal woods, between mountain and river, she checked her horse with a cry. " Oh, James. It—it is scarcely more than a rickle of stones. Is this all you have in mind for me? " Her voice was as forlorn as that of a cheated child.

Laughing, James put an arm about her shoulders, as he reined his stallion alongside her palfrey. " But I told you as much before we set out. That was why I sent the wrights on ahead of us. They have made the roof sound, and the floors. The rest we shall order together, you and I."

She looked up at him sidelong. Could he be mocking her? She was never quite certain of James. Just when she felt most confident, when he had seemed most deeply enchanted, he would shake himself free from her detaining arms, or in the midst of laughter turn suddenly grave, his eyes blank, as if they no longer saw her there before him, but something—someone—nearer than she, though a hundred miles away.

That evening, as they sat at supper before the great fire which had already done much to drive the chill from the hall that had stood so long desolate, she was suddenly aware that James was watching her. Janet enjoyed her food. It gave her pleasure to feel her strong white teeth bite fiercely into the drumstick of one of the fowls which had been roasted on the spit before them. For the rich aroma had made her so much hungrier that she could scarcely wait for all the basting and turning, the carving and serving to be done and the food set before her at last.

" Well, my lord? " Her voice was sharp, for she was weary, and all James's promises of repairs could not quite ease her disappointment. There were great dark patches on the rough plaster of the chamber walls where the rain had seeped in. Bats and birds had roosted in the rafters and spattered the flags with their droppings. The wind skirled through cracked panes and set broken shutters clacking upstairs and down. " It seems I have the better appetite. You have scarcely touched either food or wine."

" That matters less, my sweet, since you are enjoying both."

There it was again, the comment that could be taken both
ways, meaning either that her comfort was all he cared for, or that
he was amused by her greed.

"Would you rather I fasted and let the good food waste?"
she snapped, keeping her voice low, so that only he would hear,
and the servants standing back among the chilly shadows suppose
her to be speaking of more intimate things. But James spoilt it
all by answering her so clearly that she blushed.

"No, indeed, it would distress me to think you had denied
yourself so much pleasure."

"It would please me the more if you ate as a man should
after a hard day's riding," she said. "James, what ails you? I
beg you, dismiss the servants, so that we may be alone together.
We have ridden so long in splendour, and been stared at by the
way till I feel like a freak at a fair."

He smiled, but told the servants to put the sweetmeats before
the lady, and seek their own supper at the far end of the hall.
Janet stretched out her hand to him, but it was so long before
he took it that she was shaken out of her petulance by new
anxiety.

"You have had something on your mind this long while. I
have known it, though you said nothing. Surely it cannot be
your sins. Have you not rid yourself of them all, thanks to blessed
St. Duthac?"

"No, it is not a sin," James said slowly. "At least—if it is—
I know not what more to do. I have held out against it as long
as I may, and yet its expediency defeats me——"

"The expediency of what, dear heart?" Janet demanded,
her spirits rising as she spoke. For expediency could surely have
nothing to do with Margaret Drummond. And Margaret
Drummond was the only creature that she feared. Instinct still
told her that for all the fervour of their mating James had never
completely abandoned himself to her. There was something
lacking, something withheld. And the same avidity that he had
noted as she ate, with which she acquired land, clothes, furs,
jewels, taking pleasure like a little animal in her growing hoard,
drove her to seek what she still lacked—knowing not what it was
—only that its importance came from being denied. But now, as

she burrowed towards the source of his trouble, she began to feel she might have been mistaken. If it was but some expediency that troubled him, it was easily dealt with. Expediency was something which never troubled Janet at all.

James sat with one elbow on the board and his chin on his hand, staring at the flames. With a swift gesture, Janet left her place, drew forward a low stool and seated herself at his feet, folded her arms across his knees, and looked up into his face.

" Tell me," she wheedled, as he still sat silent.

James did not look at her. But at last he spoke.

" Before I left Stirling," he said heavily, " I bid the Earl of Bothwell accompany the Archbishop of Glasgow and the Bishop of Moray to the Court of King Henry and there treat with him on my behalf."

" On some grave matter, I take it? " said Janet, puzzled still.

James nodded. " They are to draw up a treaty for the marriage of the Lady Margaret Tudor and myself. The Earl of Bothwell " —he paused, then forced himself to continue—" is to stand sponsor for me at the bethrothal ceremony in the Palace of Richmond as soon as the terms have been agreed."

Janet drew in a quick, short breath. So it had happened, as she had known it must. Her first thought was that she had been none too soon in getting her charter: her second that he had only granted it because it was better she should be out of the way. James would not have her at Stirling, with the plans for the wedding fast going forward. In either case, Darnaway was hers, but ruinous, and the time during which she could count on James's indulgence of her extravagance shorter than she had supposed. She laughed softly.

" So, my lord, Darnaway is to be mine only while I remain unmarried. What would you say if I made you free of my bed but while you too remained single? "

" Though the Lady Margaret of England is but a child of twelve," said James curtly, " it is not seemly that my name should be coupled with others while my marriage with her is agreed."

" Even though our marriage lacks the name, but nothing else? Or do I charm you no longer? That I would not once have thought." She smiled up at him, her face in shadow, but the firelight haloing the hair which was brighter than his own, her hands reaching up to encircle his waist, the weight of her slight body lying across his knees.

James stooped to raise her. "You need not think so now," he whispered. "Forget the future. These few days are ours."

And they were pleasant, for Janet could be excellent company when she liked. James enjoyed his hunting parties by day, the cards, dice and supper by the fire as dusk came down, the delights of the present shutting out the future's insistent demands, as a heavy curtain excludes the chilly probing fingers of an east wind and a grey dawn.

Now and then Janet tried to interest him in the most urgent repairs, but James only laughed and told her that the place was hers. She must get it set to rights. He never seemed to mind, she thought fretfully, whether he were in a hovel or a mansion, provided the company was to his liking. He was as attentive to her as she could have wished, but he was also charming to the bevy of maidens from Forres who sang to him in the rain, casually friendly to the huntsmen who showed them such excellent sport and the man who brought him Alexander Gordon's present of a fine grey horse, to the local gentry who came to pay their duty to the King and the mother of their future lord.

But Janet's quick eyes made less of the folk who tramped in and out of the castle than the mud they left behind them, so that the heather and bent strewn on the flags must be changed more often than she could get men to cut it. She fretted over every crumbling wall and leaking gutter, each patch of damp, cracked pane or missing hinge. When James had gone, she would have it all seen to. She had authority to draw on the rents of her son's earldom, and these, thriftily managed, should be enough, Janet thought, after going through the contents of her charter-chest with such concentration that she was not aware that James had returned from his inspection of the stables to stand in the doorway, laughing.

"You have rubbed dust from these old parchments all over your face, and there is a spider's web in your hair," he mocked her.

"You should be pleased, James, that I take care of my

possessions, since they are your gift," Janet retorted. " I have
been working out the rents to make sure they will cover the
repairs we must order at Darnaway. You do not understand,
James."

James swung her to her feet and kissed the dust off her nose.
" Nor, I swear, do you. This is no fit study for a woman. Leave
it to the clerks."

" But I understand it very well," she said, twisting herself free.
" Better than many clerks who make a pretty living out of their
lord's folly. Are you not grateful, James, that I should see your
son is not defrauded? "

" Grateful indeed, and so will he be also, when he cares for
more than the way to his mouth," James laughed. " But come
down, now, and see the hawk a fellow has just brought me. . . ."

Yes, it would be easier to get down to business when James
had gone, Janet thought, as she stuffed the papers back into the
charter chest and followed him. So she was not altogether sorry
when he announced, early in December, that he could stay no
longer, though she clung to him at parting as if she guessed that
between them nothing would ever be quite the same again.

James sent her a present of Rhine wine from Aberdeen. He
also chose her a beautiful salt cellar of silver gilt for her table,
and dispatched it with a gracious message, which made it clear,
he hoped, as he rode southwards, that it was a parting gift. He
fancied that he knew Janet, by now, too well to doubt that she
was in search of the best terms she could get. She gave good value,
too, after her fashion. He could not grudge her anything she had
gained from his own rash impulse to best old Archibald Bell-the-
Cat, though it had involved him in a handsomer tangle than he
had bargained for. Well, it was as good as over now. He hoped
Janet had the sense to see that for herself. If not, he must make
it clear. James sighed; he hated the necessity for disagreeable
explanations.

So he sent Janet a Christmas gift of fur slippers and snug
anklets with a note advising her not to leave her warm hearth in
the winter weather, and set about keeping Yule in Edinburgh for
the last time as a single man, diverted by the usual horde of
guisards, minstrels and fantastically dressed blackamoors, but

o

most of all by an acrobatic rope-dancer, who cut his capers high among the smoke-blackened rafters of the hall. For James's attention was most surely caught when danger emphasised a performer's skill.

Early in the New Year he left Edinburgh for Stirling, with John Ramsay among the company, conscientiously alert in the interests of the King of England, doggedly pursuing his personal plan of retribution, weighing against each other the evidences of James's deepest affections, still seeking the most vulnerable spot, awaiting the chance to strike. Childless himself, John Ramsay was too astute to discount entirely the possibilities of paternal affection, though Catherine was insignificant, and Alexander might well be no more than a load on his father's conscience. Or else he might mean as much to James as Ramsay sometimes fancied. He could not be sure.

Young Alexander greeted James gladly, for the King's coming meant the relaxation of the most irksome rules and the possibility of unexpected diversion. Anything might happen, from violent explosions in the laboratory where the King sometimes allowed him to watch vile-smelling, strange experiments, to spurts of blood and yells of anguish from the servants paid to endure the King's 'prentice hand at blood-letting. One morning they had set out, in a scurry of hastily saddled horses and swearing grooms, to search for monsters in the hills. Another time they had taken a trip in one of Sir Andrew Wood's ships to see the infants whom James had sent to the Bass Rock in the custody of a dumb nurse.

" I had hoped that when they first spoke it would be the language used in Eden," James explained to Alexander.

" But they do not speak at all, my lord," Alexander pointed out.

" Not yet," James admitted sadly.

It was exciting to speculate on what diversion the King would devise next. But on this occasion the visit, which began well, with a tooth extraction for which James paid the victim handsomely, and the unexpected escape of a basketful of frogs, intended for the laboratory, among the ladies, was afterwards disappointing. James was preoccupied, and Master Paniter shook his head over Alexander's future.

"I fear my lord," he said reluctantly, "that the lad has not the makings of a knight."

"How so?" James was indignant. "Any son of mine——"

"My lord, he is near-sighted. Have you not noticed how he peers and frowns?"

"I took it but as a sign of greater interest," said James. "Are you sure?"

"Quite sure, my lord. I tested his eyes myself."

James sighed. "I had set my heart on it. He has both courage and zeal. Heaven save us, what a misfortune that he should not also have the eyes. What shall we make of him, Paniter?"

Patrick Paniter pursed his lips and scratched his shaven pate. "He is clerkly enough, my lord, and the Church offers as fine a career as any. Your own brother now holds St. Andrews."

He paused, and James stood silent. Both knew that the health of the Duke of Ross had been failing, ever since he reached manhood, till the small flame of his life now guttered like a rushlight in a gale. By the time Alexander was grown . . .

"Tutor him, then, as a clerk," James said.

He was dismayed, but not overwhelmed. John Ramsay, who had contrived to be in attendance, noted his kindness to the lad who had been so obviously fearful that the King might be angry. But he also noticed that James seemed distracted even while he comforted Alexander, as if his mind were set all the time on graver matters than the choice between the careers open to a lad of nine.

The return, next day, of the Earl of Bothwell, and James's haste to see him, offered an obvious explanation. For James summoned Bothwell into his privy chamber without giving him time to dine. Ramsay, with the rest of those in attendance, had to content himself with noting the King's anxiety and Bothwell's air of mingled weariness and triumph, before the closing door left those outside it to their speculations.

"Well, Patrick, is it done?"

"It is, my lord. You are betrothed."

"Heaven help us both. How did she seem?"

"A plain child," said the Earl of Bothwell frankly, "who has

been so well drilled that it is not easy to say what manner o
maiden she may be. But reticence is no fault in a great lady."

"No," said James, adding jerkily: "tell me more, Patrick
How did it befall?"

Patrick Hepburn swung his knee over one end of the heav
table and turned towards James, who had flung himself down i
the high-backed chair at the far end, and was restlessly pricking
a pattern on the table top with the point of the dagger which
their Spanish Majesties had given him over ten years ago.

"We were well enough entertained," he said judicially
"since King Henry has always been more noted for thrift than
for hospitality. But I have seldom shivered more in our northern
winter than in the Palace of Richmond. The damp seemed to
trickle along my bones. The King scarcely marked it, but I
thought the Queen sore ailing. Both received us graciously, but
young Prince Henry was in such a passion that he would not greet
us at all. They say that when he received the news of his sister's
bethrothal he flung himself on the floor of his chamber, raging
and striking the boards with his clenched fists."

"Strange. What ill will has he to Scotland?"

"I know of none, my lord. It may be that he is angered by
the thought that his sister will become Queen of Scots while he
is still a child in his father's kingdom. It may be that he wished
her married to someone other than yourself. I cannot tell."

"It matters little," said James impatiently. "Tell me of the
betrothal."

"I stood there, my lord, before them all," said the Earl of
Bothwell, "the King and Queen, the Lords Spiritual and
Temporal of England, the Orator of His Holiness the Pope, the
Ambassadors of Spain and Venice a glorious assembly of lords
and ladies in their finest array, and Prince Henry, standing apart,
fists clenched and chin thrust out, squat and square already,
though he is no more than a lad. His pale small eyes glared at
me as I repeated the words my lord of Glasgow read. My lord,
I liked their ring.

"'I, Patrick, Earl of Bothwell, Procurator of the right
excellent, right high and mighty, Prince James by the Grace of
God King of Scotland, my sovereign Lord, having sufficient

authority, power, and commandment to contract matrimony in the name and for my said Sovereign Lord, with thee, Margaret. . . .' "

" What else did you note? " said James sharply.

" The audience was in the Queen's chamber, because she was too ailing to leave it," Patrick said. " And though the Archbishops of Canterbury and York were present, it was the Earl of Surrey who introduced the matter at debate."

James smiled wryly. " Him we have already encountered. Did the Princess speak? "

" Aye, in answer to the Archbishop of Glasgow," said Patrick. " He asked her as kindly and tenderly, it seemed, as if she had been his own child, whether she were content, without compulsion and of her own free will, to entertain the proposal that I made."

" And how did she reply? "

" She looked up, pale and unsmiling. Then she said: ' if it please the King, and my lady my Mother the Queen.' "

James sighed, and jabbed with his dagger at the board.

" Take heart, my lord," said the Earl of Bothwell. " I do not doubt she would have spoken more warmly if she had not been told what she must say."

" I hope so indeed," said James heavily. Then he rose, stretched his arms above his head, and let the dagger fall, so that its point entered the wood and stuck there, quivering. " Oh, Patrick, how strange it seems. Strange, and far off, and cold. This is no bridal such as the poets sing."

Patrick Hepburn frowned. " My lord, I pray you to remember that this is a matter in which you have had no experience."

" No experience? You would say I know nothing of love? "

" My lord," said Bothwell earnestly, " I believe that by using that word you dig a pitfall in which, if you be not wary, we shall all be engulfed. We have to deal now less with love, that sweet and homely joy which men and women of all estates may know, than with a high and mighty contract of marriage made between princes alone."

James nodded. But he did not speak. His face was bleak as the winter fields.

"Surely," said Bothwell, "this you have always known."

"Aye," James agreed, "but such knowledge has been like the tally that is chalked up against a man on an alehouse door, forgotten pleasantly enough till the day of reckoning comes. And then——"

"And then, my lord?"

"He must pay. Or his credit is gone for ever," said James. But his voice was harsh as an east wind.

CHAPTER SEVENTEEN

JAMES roved distractedly about the royal apartments, long after Patrick had taken his leave. Ambition, worldly wisdom, Scotland's best interests, all supported the English marriage, as Patrick had painstakingly pointed out. Agreeing, James had been at a loss to understand how brain and will could consent, while some subtler faculty still cried aloud against the intolerable burden of expediency. In such a mood, the news brought by an usher that the lady of Bothwell had arrived and sought immediate audience touched off the smoulder of frustration into a sudden, bright rage. Had he not buried his dead past? How dared Janet bear it, unsummoned, from its grave?

As she entered, he scarcely looked at her. But as soon as the usher had left them he turned on her all the bewildered fury which Patrick's report of his successful diplomacy had ungratefully aroused.

"Janet," he said abruptly, "why have you come?"

His tone startled her by its harshness. Turning from the fire before which she was trying to bake the leaden chill out of her limbs, she looked at him in silence, assessing his state of mind, quickly considering her best response. For once she was disconcerted. She had thought he would be pleased to see her. Too late she blamed herself for over-confidence. It would have been wiser to have begged the hospitality of a friend's house, changed her mired clothes and dressed her hair instead of appearing before him just as she had stepped from her sweating horse in the courtyard below.

James was staring at her now. She fancied he was noticing every strayed strand of bright hair, each daub of mud and bramble-torn rent on her dark green riding-dress. The thought stung her vanity into an equally sharp retort.

"Indeed, my lord, is there any reason why I should not come?"

"Yes," James said.

She shied away from the reproof, plunging unwisely into the reproaches which, had she been less weary, she would never have allowed to escape.

"That is a strange thing to hear from you, my lord," she said, "when I remember what has been between us two. Did I not leave home and kindred for your protection? Can you now forbid me to seek it?"

"Are you in need?" said James.

"Need?" she blazed at him suddenly. "Am I but one of the beggars that hirple about the shrines you load with gold and silver, as if the saints in heaven were hucksters whose prayers are to be knocked down to the highest bidder? Need? Do you count need in terms of your purse and mine? Can you not understand that a woman may welcome consolation more than the chime of a coin?"

"I understand," said James. "But it surprises me. I thought when I left Darnaway, that you were consoling yourself very well. It gave you as much pleasure, I could see, to set the workmen hammering and heaving, sawing and plastering and glazing and carving, as it had ever done to keep me company."

"You thought yourself well quit of me," said Janet, viciously wrenching at the catch of her sodden cloak and kicking her feet free of its clammy folds as she paced about the small room, unaware that its panelled walls threw back the sound of voices which an arras would have stifled, so that those in the presence chamber beyond caught their tenor, though they missed the words, raising speculative eyebrows at each other as they lounged, picking their teeth or kicking their heels, drumming with finger-tips on the small leaded panes against which the winter rain still lashed.

John Ramsay, moving nearer, thoughtfully frowned. What he now heard suggested that the King's devotion to Mistress Kennedy need scarcely any longer be reckoned with. But one never could tell. Quarrels did not always estrange. Until this altercation had run its course it would not be safe to decide whether the lady of Bothwell had clawed her way back into the King's favour or scratched him sorely enough to be cast aside by the scruff of the neck. Ramsay pursed his lips as he listened. Merciful saints, what did the King see in such a wildcat? And yet, she had courage, he had to admit. Few men, with the King in a towering rage, would venture to stand up and give even better than they got.

" Quit of you? " James was saying. " That is an odd fashion in which to describe my gifts. An earldom for the child, Darnaway for yourself——"

" On such terms as would irk a harlot."

" Only a harlot need find them irksome. Are you not content to be mistress of your son's home and rule it for his comfort? "

" Content? " said Janet shrilly. " Did you think I would be content, James, in that great desolate place at the back of beyond, with no company but the servants and the rats, and no music but the soughing of the wind and the drumming of the rain? Content? You cared little for contenting me. You wished me out of the way——"

" I can listen to this no longer," James said. " You must go——"

" I'll go when I've said what I came to say, and not before," stormed Janet. " Aye, strike me if you will. I have no fear of violence, James. I have known it often enough. Yes, you have hurt me for your pleasure. It makes little odds to me if your fists clench and your eyes glare. When you are angry you are like the man I knew in Galloway. Remember? The night you first took me—in the great guest-chamber with the gold and scarlet hangings making the place so fine that I marvelled at the luxury a King enjoyed even on pilgrimage. Because you are angry you will remember——"

"I am angry no longer," James said.

With dismay she saw it was true. For some reason her reminder of the wild delight she had given him had had the opposite effect from what she had hoped. Instead of inflaming him further, till anger slid insensibly into the kindred frenzy of desire which she knew so well, it had extinguished the blaze utterly, leaving only a blackened waste of arid indifference against which she was helpless. It was so unexpected that she panicked like a fighter whose weapons have been struck away. Yet because she was never one to submit to defeat she hurled herself on disaster as a disarmed man hurls himself in despair at his opponent's throat.

"You are not angry because you no longer care what becomes of me," she said. "You find me a castle in that northern desolation, you take me there and wheedle me to stay, then you go, leaving me——"

"You very well know that I could not stay," James said. "A King cannot set the country's affairs aside because a woman demands it."

"Can he not? That depends, perhaps, on who makes the demand," Janet said wildly. "Oh, I know very well, James, that I was only useful for a while to ease the ache for a woman's body which you could not slake elsewhere. It will be different now that Margaret Drummond has recovered her health, will it not?"

For a delighted instant she thought once again that he would have struck her. But he checked himself in mid-stride, his hand arrested as if by sudden palsy, his eyes defenceless for an instant, before the lids fell, so that she saw there such pain that she was goaded to taunt him again, recklessly aware that with each taunt she was destroying her own hold on him, and not caring, as long as she hurt him enough.

"You thought I did not know of the messengers that bore fruit and comfits and trinkets to Drummond while she lay sick, and brought you news of her puling girl-child. You used me, yes, used me, James, chivalrous knight as you are, to staunch the longing that you could not bear. And now, because she is better, you have done——"

"I have done with many things, Janet," said James tonelessly.

" I have this day received news of the betrothal in which my lord
of Bothwell stood proxy for me before the King and Queen of
England."

Janet set her hands on her hips. With her feet apart and her
draggled gown twisted about her ankles, she looked a fine lady
no longer, but a kitchen wench in a screaming rage.

" So you are to be married. That's what a man says, often
enough, when he seeks to cast off a mistress. It's an old tale. But
I'll be bound it is not a tale you've told Margaret Drummond."

" Mention her name again," said James in a voice as mono-
tonous as the sound of the rain falling on the flags of the courtyard
outside, " and I will have my grooms bundle you out of Stirling,
once and for all."

" Her name, her name! " shrieked Janet. " You mumble it as
slaveringly as the priests mumble over the relics that keep them
in comfort all their lives. Her name, her blessed, holy name——"

James walked past her without turning his head. She shrank
back, one arm thrown up, anticipating in terror and delight, the
blow that would send her reeling, the fury with which he would
lift her to her feet, the tumult which would change to caresses. . . .

But he passed her as if she had not been there. Wrenching at
the latch, he swung the door back and was gone. The men idling
about the presence chamber peered curiously at her, till she
slammed the door shut to give herself time. But John Ramsay
neither peered, nor winked, nor nudged his neighbours. Near
enough to hear Janet, at least in the last furious moments when
she had been too distraught to control her voice, he now stared
after James, instead. And when he rose to follow him, ostensibly
to inquire whether he could be of service, there was a new gleam
in his eye, and a brisker purpose in his tread.

James became aware at last that someone was speaking to
him.

" Eh? What's that? Oh, it's you, Ramsay. Yes . . ." He
ran his fingers through his hair. " You can tell Mistress Kennedy
that I will send a man to see her safe to Darnaway. It is not
fitting she should ride alone."

Ramsay's lip curled as he bowed over the King's instructions.
Most men would have cared little whether a cast-off mistress

crawled north on her hands and knees after such a scene as he
had just overheard. Perhaps they had not seen the end of
Mistress Kennedy even yet.

"Command Quintin Focart. He is a man of sense."

"It shall be done," murmured Ramsay. "And you, my
lord——"

"Send a page to the stables. Have them saddle the grey and
summon the fowlers. Half a dozen lads may come besides to run
ahead and start the quarry——"

"In this rain, my lord?" Ramsay ventured to murmur. He
had no mind to ride forth himself, yet he dared not let the King,
in his present mood, go unaccompanied. Heaven alone knew
where he might ride. To Drummond, as like as not. And after
what Janet Kennedy had said he must know. He must know. . . .

"It lightens already," said James, without looking at the sky.

But he did not ride to Drummond that day. Nor indeed, for
many weeks. As Janet had guessed, in the near-clairvoyant state
of acute jealousy, the thought of Margaret was seldom far from
his mind. But he was sorry for his anger against Janet. What had
befallen was not her fault, but his. He sent a messenger to
Darnaway with his greeting and the latest news from the Isles.
She should not brood, up there in the north, of his unkindness.
Then his thoughts swung back against to Margaret. Her illness
had been one of the strange, indefinable complaints which took
its own slow course. But it was, it seemed, over now at last.

Over now . . . over now . . . over now . . .

The words thudded out in his horse's hoofbeats on the turf
that was greening again as the spring began. Many other things
must also be over now, he reminded himself, as he sought perpetual occupation for body and mind. He rode furiously about
the country, from Council meeting to hunting forest, from Stirling
to Edinburgh, inspecting the building work at Holyrood, then
back to Stirling again, making a retreat with the Friars Observants,
then galloping back to Edinburgh through a thunderstorm to
transact business at Leith. Over now . . . over now . . . over now . . .
Ramsay, cursing and sweating, toiled far behind the devilish
stallion that only James dared ride.

Easter passed and May came in with gentle weather that set

the lambs leaping and the catkins swinging. James rode from Edinburgh to Queensferry to inspect the ships which were being equipped, under the orders of Sir Andrew Wood, to assist his kinsman, the King of Denmark, against the Swedes. He listened, questioned, praised all that Sir Andrew showed him, dined on board and enjoyed his meal. When he stared blankly or answered at random Sir Andrew only chuckled. The King was as distracted as any other man soon to be married.

In June James commanded the Court's return to Stirling. As they rode, the men in the hayfields straightened their backs to snatch off their bonnets and wave, recognising James easily. For no one in Scotland rode as crazily as the King. Only a few children, gathering flowers by the wayside, were near enough to see his face and wonder who went by looking so stern and sad.

" Over now . . . over now . . . over now . . ."

The rhythm beaten out by the hooves of his galloping horse seemed to pound on his naked heart. Here he and Margaret had ridden together, there was the tree to which he had tethered her horse when she asked to be helped down to rest in the shade. The very branch he had twisted back towards the trunk because it caught her hair still mocked him with a spider's thread of memory. There they had gathered flowers that he had laughingly twisted into a crown and knelt to lay on her head as she sat by the river's bank. She had looked up at him, then, so strangely that he had shivered in the warmth of the noonday sun. And the memories through which he now rode were so vivid that the present seemed no more than a veil behind which another order of reality lived and moved.

Even Alexander thought James sadly absent-minded that summer. When Master Paniter brought the boy to report the progress of his education to his father, Alexander could see that he was not listening at all. He just nodded and went striding about. And before they had made their obeisance, he was gone. When they looked out of the window, there he was in the court-yard below, already setting off at a gallop with the men of his personal bodyguard hopping and swearing on the cobbles, as they tried to compel their excited horses to stand still for long enough to mount them.

On the fourteenth of the month James rode cross-country to Dumbarton, for Patrick Hepburn, as Captain of the Castle, was dissatisfied with its defences in face of the uneasy state of the west. The party was bogged, lost and benighted, and a local shepherd had to be roused from his bed to guide them back. On the twentieth he rode to Leith, told his escort to wait there while he went by boat to the island of Inchkeith, where the hawks were being schooled by Hannay and two other falconers. But from Inchkeith he unexpectedly ordered the boatmen to row on to Kinghorn on the far side of the firth. The longing against which he had been fighting ever since his return to Stirling had suddenly overcome his resistance at last. At Leith his escort waited in vain for him to return to them, for at Kinghorn James had called for a horse, tossed the contents of his purse to the vigilant beggars who had collected by the waterside, and set off alone for Falkland. There he paused only long enough to change horses before pounding on.

On the far side of the Forth an agitated company were now aware that James had eluded them, for the boatmen, returning to Leith, innocently admitted that they had rowed the King to Kinghorn. At Kinghorn, a baffling crowd pointed six ways at once. But John Ramsay wasted no time in argument. He had been expecting something of this sort to happen for some time. While the rest of his companions shouted at each other, he slipped unobtrusively away, commandeered a horse in the King's name, and rode straight for Castle Drummond.

James had been living so much in the past that the evidence of time's passage jolted him like an unexpected step at the top of a stair. The turret chamber in which Margaret sat at her embroidery was as he remembered it. But the child who now bore her name and his was singing to herself as she played on the floor at her mother's feet, turning to stare in dismay at the strange man who stood so silent, while her mother rose, unsmiling, to stand before him, her hands limp at her sides. They dared not move, thought the child, herself suddenly afraid. At her whimpering wail a nurse came running, to be struck agape by the sight of the King.

"Do not be afraid. I shall not bite you," James said, thank-

ful for the chance of laughter. " Is she to take the child? " he
asked Margaret, adding to the nurse as she nodded: " But you
will bring her back before I go? "

" My lord, I will," the nurse whispered. Then she gathered
up the little girl and fled. James and Margaret were alone again
as they had not been since their child was born, the years of
separation flowing between them like a swift stream which no
mere words could bridge. In silence still, James knelt, and in
silence Margaret stooped over him to lay her cheek against his
hair.

" I knew, always, that you would return," she said at last.

James took her hands and kissed their palms. But still he did
not speak, and Margaret could feel him tremble.

" My dearest lord . . ."

James looked up, startled. " You can still call me so? "

" Why should I not? "

" After all that has passed? "

" My sweet love," Margaret said, " shall we not remember
instead the happiness between us? "

" That," said James, " I have never forgotten."

" No more have I."

Letting her hands fall, he stood up and began to pace to and
fro. " You know something of what has gone into these last
years? "

She nodded, delicately ironic. " My lord, throughout my
illness, someone always contrived to hearten me with ill news, as
is the custom of those in attendance on the sick. ' My lord the
King has done this . . . my lord has done that. He is gone into
Galloway . . . to the house of my lord Kennedy. . . . ' "

" So you know that? "

" Yes, James."

" And yet . . ."

" How long ago did I tell you that while you loved me still
I should not care who boasted she had been to your bed? "

" Yet there is more."

" I know it."

" Other women——"

" Yes."

" I am betrothed to the Princess of England——"

" That too, I knew."

" Margaret! " He swung round to face her. " Margaret, while I am with you I know the rest of the world for shadows. In you, with you alone I touch reality and truth. You are the tall candle without which the altar is in darkness. I cannot be bereft of you again."

She shook her head slowly. " This is wild talk, James."

" What other talk will serve? There is so little time. Already they are spinning the silken thread of the rope that will bind me to the Tudors. But the noose is not yet tight. I can still throw it off, Margaret. I can still go free——"

" What is freedom, James, that you have it not already? "

James threw his arms wide, wheeled round, strode back to her, his vehement gestures setting the very hangings astir. " Freedom for me is the right to choose who shall companion me on the throne of Scotland. Shall every kitchen lad who takes a drab to share his hovel claim that right before the King? I am weary to death of so much wrangling and huckstering. Mother of God, I might as well be chaffering with a greasy Jew from the darkest ghetto in Christendom as treating with the King of England. Would you believe that King Henry wishes me to assure him, before appointing twenty-five English attendants for the Princess, that their salaries will surely be paid by me? "

Margaret smiled at his outraged face. " But, dear heart, this is well known regarding King Henry——"

" His meanness is not all," James interrupted. " He has asked me to pay the salaries of his daughter's English attendants, and that I will do, while I remain their master. But he has also asked me to abandon our ancient alliance with the King of France. And that, by heaven, I will not."

" Indeed, I should hope not," said Margaret.

" We have to watch him," James said, " as we would watch a merchant caught giving short weight. Every letter must be scanned, every document searched for the meaning it hides as well as the words it bears. This affair has trailed on for years, till I am heartsick. It is not in my power to weigh and consider

and haggle and demur. Let them say aye or nay and take my
hand on it and make an end."

" I know it well. And for that forthrightness I love you,"
Margaret said.

He swung round to take her by the shoulders. " Let us finish
it all."

She stared. " James, what can you mean? "

He flung his arms wide as the magnitude of the opportunity
offered him lifted his heart. To him, who had been unfaithful,
not once, but twice and again, came this chance of staking everything on his faith not only in Margaret, but in himself, and his
ability to believe that their destinies were linked not merely while
his fickle fancy dictated, but so long as they both should live.
For this, he was all at once ready to defy not only King Henry,
but his own advisers, even Bishop Elphinstone whom he revered,
the expectant nobility, and the common people, whose romantic
hearts were set on the Thistle and Rose match with which the
poet Dunbar, back from visiting London as a clerk in the train
of the Scottish ambassadors, had so caught their fancy.

" Finish this huckstering folly," he cried. " Tell the King of
England to offer his daughter elsewhere. Toss the quibbling
lawyers' screeds on the nearest bonfire——"

" James! Are you crazed? "

"Less crazed than I shall be if this affair goes forward. Listen
to me, Margaret," James said earnestly. " What companionship,
what solace can I have from a child of twelve, or give her in my
turn? You know me, I believe, better than any other soul. You
know when to check and when to cheer me. You let me talk,
knowing that when I have talked foolishly there is more chance
that I will act with wisdom. Do not shake your head, sweeting.
It is the truth. You are the quiet counterpoise that swings my
violence true. How often have I seen the leeches weigh this
compound and that till each holds the other poised? It is so with
us."

" Yes, it is so with us," she said softly. " But that does not
mean you must make a Queen of me, James. Did I not once
warn you that I had no head for heights? Come to me when you
will, leave me when you must. It will be better so."

" It will not be enough," said James urgently. " With you
my side I shall be such a King as I can be with no other. My
ve, my darling, I beg you, command you, entreat you, im-
ore you . . ." He knelt, his head flung back, his poised, taut
gure so urgent in its entreaty that she covered her face with her
inds. For very love of him she might well yield to his demand.
et as he spoke, she was appalled.

" You cannot refuse me. I know it." It was a shout of
iumph.

" Do not press me further now, I implore you," she whispered.
Give me time to pray, to think, to strengthen myself before I
iswer. You have taken me so utterly unawares——"

" That is true enough," he admitted.

" Give me time, James . . ."

" If you desire it. But I shall return——"

" Indeed——"

" And soon. For if I am to oppose the King of England, my
irpose must be known forthwith. Saints in heaven, what would
give to see the old miser's face when they bring him word
' it."

" But, James——"

" Say no more now, sweeting," James commanded as he
ssed her silent. " I will return to Falkland, where no doubt the
entlemen of my household are plaguing the good Abbot of
indores to know what has become of me." He grinned at her
iddenly. " It gives me such pleasure to outwit the good fellows
ho seek to protect me——"

" Such a whim is scarcely sufficient reason to oppose the King
f England——"

" For such opposition," said James, suddenly grave again, " I
ave the best reasons in the world. Now, dear heart, I will go.
ext time I come it will be to learn that you will agree to the
arriage which sets me free from Tudor huckstering. Once
e are married, sweetheart, I shall be at peace with all the
orld."

" It might well be that you were at war with England,"
Iargaret said uneasily.

But James laughed as he shook his head. " King Henry could

P

hardly own his daughter so ill-favoured that he had to go to wa
to save her from being jilted. No, he would not dare! "

She caught his gaiety as they went down the narrow spira
of the staircase together, so that they came out into the sunshin
laughing, hand in hand. Dear James, thought Margaret, as h
vitality tingled up her arm from the hard pressure of his finger,
how wistfully he had spoken of peace of mind. Was there anyor
less likely to possess such a grace in all the world?

" From Falkland," James was saying, " I must return t
Stirling. And from Stirling . . ."

" James," said Margaret suddenly, " did you not say you ha
ridden here alone? "

James, already reaching for the reins the groom held ou
turned swiftly.

" Yes, indeed, so I believe. But, sweetheart, why——"

" It is no matter," Margaret said, passing her hand across he
eyes. " I fancied that I saw—someone slip into the shadow c
the archway——"

" Where, sweetheart? I see no one."

" I thought it was——" Margaret began, then checked her
self. " It was but my fancy. God speed you, dearest lord. An
come again. For now——"

He took her hands and kissed them, smiling. " Yes? "

" I think that if you did not, I should die."

" I shall return," James said.

He rode to Falkland in a state of wild happiness which wa
scarcely dashed by the arrival, next day, of the Bishop of Moray
one of the negotiators of the English marriage, obviously prepare
to bring up the question which James, just then, wished least t
hear. For he would presently be ready to loose off a bombar
which would set the whole hobnobbing huddle of long-winde
bletherskites running all ways at once with their hands over thei
ears. All except Patrick. Patrick would laugh as well as scolc
James fancied. Meanwhile, he must distract the Bishop'
attention. He did not wish to spoil his explosion by lighting th
match too soon.

" How do you, my lord Bishop? " he said heartily, as h
entered the presence chamber unperceived and clapped th

startled Bishop on the shoulder. " This is too fine a day to be indoors. Will you take my challenge to a game of bowls? "

The afternoon sun was warm. James stripped off his doublet and played in his shirt-sleeves, till their lengthening shadows stalked far ahead of them. The wagtails flirted their long tails as they scurried across the smooth grass, the gnats gathered in viciously droning clouds. Pausing to mop his face, James watched with only vague concern the arrival of a servant in the Drummond livery. Even when the man flung himself from his horse, and left the beast untethered while he ran to them, James was unprepared by any premonition for what the man kneeling at his feet, and fumbling his bonnet between his fingers, could not say. And then at last, an inkling of it caught him by the throat, so that he too was speechless. Only the Bishop of Moray, trundling up to them, broke the spell, with a sharp command.

" Speak, fellow. His Highness has more to do than stand idle while you regain the use of your tongue."

" Your Highness . . ." the man gasped. " I have been sent to inform you——"

" Well, continue," said the Bishop irritably.

" That the—the Lady Margaret and her sisters ate some poisonous thing this morning when they broke their fast. Your Highness, the physicians could do nothing. By noon all three were dead."

PART FOUR

1502-1513

CHAPTER EIGHTEEN

IT was June again, June, 1503. The " right high, right mighty and right excellent and most Christian Prince, Henry by the Grace of God, King of England and of France, Lord of Ireland, seventh of his name," as the heralds proclaimed him, had left his Manor of Richmond to see his daughter set out on her long journey north. The lean, wary-eyed man, who sagged, it seemed, under too many superlatives, said farewell with unexpected emotion to the petulant little girl who clung to him and wept, while motherly ladies-in-waiting sighed and dabbed their eyes, horses stamped and bridle-bells rang as the procession waited, between two solid banks of gaping, pointing citizens, in the street below.

" Her be coming now. . . ."

" No, 'tis naught. . . ."

" 'Tis she. Riding a fair palfrey, with the Earl of Surrey and his lady conveying her. Law bless us, see but the satins and silks of all the gentlefolk that throng about her. . . ."

" Yonder rides Sir Davy Owen ahead . . ."

" My lord of Derby, that's Constable . . ."

" The Marquis of Dorset rides yonder . . ."

" My lord of Kent, look there . . ."

" See her footmen strutting in single file beside her. For all the world like geese going to water, be'an't they now? "

" Look yonder at the silken litter slung between two horses. That's for her to rest between the towns when she need no longer be seen by the folk as she goes by."

" There rides Sir Thomas Worteley, that's Master of the Horse to her. . . ."

" Ah, here come the heralds. . . ."

" And Lords and Ladies, Lords and Ladies, Lords and Ladies . . ." chanted a small boy astride his father's shoulders, as the brilliant, apparently endless stream of riders in their gay

clothes paced past with plumes nodding, jewels glinting, bridle
jangling, in the midsummer sunshine, while the cheers of the
crowd lining the roadside, scrambling up the banks, even climb
ing the trees, kept pace with the procession in a deep roll of
sound, bright-tipped with children's cries.

So the great folk rode, taking the ancient way from London
to the north, chattering or silent, glum or gay, paying more
attention to each other than to the little girl who made scant
response to the attempts of the Bishop of Moray to tell her about
the country of which she was now Queen. Presently the Bishop
who did not much care for children, also fell silent, and wondered
instead how her waiting bridegroom's welcome would stand the
scrutiny of such shrewd statesmen as the Earl of Surrey, now
jogging impatiently at the head of the long procession.

From James the Bishop's thoughts went back to that other
day in June, just over a year ago now, when his game of bowls
had been so violently disrupted by the man from Drummond who
set the wagtails fluttering as he burst upon them with his out
rageous news. The King had received it with such incoherent
rage and grief that the Bishop of Moray, who had never been
tempted from the prospect of advancement to the highest possible
position in the Church by any of the warmer-hearted sins, had
been amazed. He was aware of James's attachment to Margaret
Drummond. But he had also known of other attachments, and
concluded that none could therefore have gone deep. His
Highness would, no doubt, have got over it by now.

It was at least to be hoped so. He had been like a crazed
creature that day, the Bishop remembered, sending his messengers
galloping not only to Drummond but to Bothwell to discover the
whereabouts of Mistress Kennedy, pacing to and fro till they
returned with the news that Mistress Kennedy had indeed come
south to the property given her by the Earl of Angus, but had
been bedfast at the time of the tragedy at Drummond, since
she had but newly given birth to a child after being long in
labour.

" She bid us assure you, my lord, that she would come as soon
as she might set foot to ground," his messengers added.

But James only looked at them as if they spoke a strange

tongue, and when at last he answered, it was as if he could scarcely control his own.

" It . . . does not matter . . . now," he said thickly.

As the monstrous suspicion subsided, he began to torture himself on the merciless wheel of speculation. Had he done anything, left anything undone which might have brought that agonising death on Margaret and her sisters? Wisps of Court gossip drifted constantly about him, and as the days passed he began to catch their meaning.

" Taken with cramps and vomitings . . ."

" Poison? What else? "

" Shellfish at midsummer? Maybe . . ."

" They say King Henry was well served . . ."

" By whom? "

" Who knows? Scotland is full of his creatures, nowadays. . . ."

" Others say . . ."

" You heard of the Kennedy affair? "

" They quarrelled . . . she and the King. . . ."

" Mistress Kennedy? . . . I'd never put it past her. . . ."

" Who stood to gain more? "

" Why, King Henry surely did. With the royal marriage contracted for. . . ."

James turned for consolation to his unsuspecting children. Catherine and Alexander at least knew nothing of the recent tragedy, and were not watching him covertly, like all the others, to see how sorely he was stricken by Margaret's death. Presently James began to take Alexander about with him, delighting Master Paniter with his decision to make the boy Archdeacon of St. Andrews, as a first step in his clerical career.

It was on his return to Stirling with Alexander, who had made his first public appearance with his father at St. Giles, that James entered his private apartments to encounter with stupefaction, across the disorder of open coffers, the bold smile of Janet Kennedy.

" My lord," she said hastily, " I am come here at your command."

James turned to Alexander. " Go to Master Paniter now." Alexander went, glowering resentfully over his shoulder, as

Janet began to babble against the inimical silence which even she found hard to bear.

"It was to tell you that I was carrying the child I came to Stirling at Candlemas. But you were angry, and I said naught. So now, when you sent for me——"

"Sent for you?" said James tonelessly.

"Yes, indeed, when our child was born. I came as soon as I could. I have been ill, James. I bear my children hard."

"I am sorry," said James.

She blundered on. "James, I did not do it. I know what they are saying of me. They have shouted after me in the dark. A crowd broke my windows at Bothwell. They have threatened to stone me. James, I am not a timid woman, but I have gone in fear of my life. I did not do it, James." Her voice broke on a high note of terror. "By heaven above I swear——"

She broke off at sight of James's stony face.

"Do not speak of it," he said.

"I will not," she promised. "But I implore you, James, let me stay."

"Why?"

"Why? For so many reasons. Because you are sad. Because I am afraid of the voices in the dark and the threats they whisper. I will care for Moray and the baby with the rest. It cannot be for long, that I well know, but I will serve you gladly while I may——"

"Stay if you wish," said James in his dead voice.

So Janet stayed. But James did not. Within a few days of Janet's arrival, with her children and their nurses, James had set off again for Whithorn, on his autumn pilgrimage. Alexander rode with him, delighted to be again chosen as the King's companion. They went by Glasgow and Paisley, stopping a few days at Ayr, where James roused himself sufficiently to buy Alexander a tippet of taffeta, suddenly realising that, in the midst of a crowd which had put on their best clothes to greet the King, the King's son, intolerably, seemed shabby.

Alexander, peacocking in his new clothes, made James smile spontaneously for the first time in months.

"Fine clothes become you well, my lad."

"Indeed, sir, I think so too," said Alexander frankly, squinting over his shoulder in an attempt to see down his own back.

James laughed outright, to the relief of all who heard him, for his blank-eyed, ghastly pallor had made them fear for the health, even the reason of the King whose friendly informality had made him so much loved.

"You are not subtle enough for a churchman, Alexander," he said. "They will teach you in due course that there are many other ways of using your tongue than to say merely what you mean."

"Are all churchmen subtle, my lord?" wondered Alexander.

"No." James thought of Bishop Elphinstone and sighed. The Bishop had expressed himself most explicitly, for instance, in favour of the English match. Well, now the good Bishop would have his heart's desire, James thought, for Margaret's death had removed all reason for seeking to avoid the alliance which all his advisers regarded as a triumph of diplomacy. Margaret's death. . . . James found himself confronting that enigmatic tragedy once again, as if the lesser distractions to which he had now begun to yield only had the power to decoy him a little way from it before twisting back on themselves to confront him with it once more, wondering as he had done a thousand times, and fruitlessly, how it had come about.

Had the food the three sisters ate that midsummer morning been indeed corrupted by the heat, as some of his leeches, perhaps anxious to comfort him a little, said? How could it have been man's deliberate work when no man—or woman—had known he was about to ride to Drummond? He had not known it himself. And while he did not seek Margaret out, while it still seemed that he had wearied of her—as he had wearied, God forgive him, of others—surely it was worth no one's while to take that innocent life. Then how——? And why——?

With a violent effort, James wrenched his thoughts from that wheel of torment, compelling himself to smile again, his hand on his son's shoulder.

"What did you say, lad? I fear my thoughts were elsewhere."

"You looked," said Alexander bluntly, "as if you wished you were dead."

James sighed. "It may be that I did."

Alexander's frank face crumpled with concern. "Oh, no."

"Would you grieve, then?"

"I would wish to die with you, my lord," said Alexander simply. "Wherever it might be."

"We shall offer you a better future than that," James said, touched in spite of himself, by such homage, and believing that he spoke the truth.

Janet was still at Stirling when they returned, and on the best of terms, it seemed, with all concerned, from the Captain of the Castle to the little nursemaids who fetched and carried for the royal children. James discovered a diverse noisy company in the great chamber. Young Lord Lyle, the ward of the Abbot of Dunfermline, Lord High Treasurer, who now shared a tutor with Alexander, was pulling the Earl of Moray, rising three, along by the feet, while Catherine, disregarding the commotion, hummed to herself as she rocked the cradle in which Janet's baby lay. Janet herself, equally oblivious of the hubbub, was inspecting with concentrated attention half a dozen bolts of scarlet velvet and various trimmings appropriate to a doublet for young Moray, which an obsequious merchant had laid out for her inspection. Unabashed by his raised eyebrows, she greeted James boldly enough.

"Welcome, my lord. We have spoken of you many times. The bairns have wearied for your return, for until I promised you would take them to see the strange things in the laboratory I have had no peace. So indeed I trust you will."

"My lord," Alexander burst out, glaring at the red-haired, shrill-voiced lady he so much disliked, "if the lesser bairns come, they will overset everything. It is different for me. I am the eldest, saving only Catherine, who is but a girl."

"True, Alexander," said James, pinching his son's ear. "We will take them all to see the hawks instead. You hear that, bairns?"

They clamoured round him.

"Will you take us now?"

" Not now," said James. " But soon . . ."

Janet, while James was occupied with the children, took the opportunity of completing her purchase. " I will have an ell of the scarlet, half an ell of the velvet for the sleeves, and bordering as required," she said. " Bring me next time Holland cloth sufficient for six pairs of sheets, fustian enough for as many blankets, and patterns of Rissilis black, with matching velvet and damask for lining the cloak I require, besides French brown for the bairns' winter mantles."

" Madam, you shall have everything to-morrow," the merchant promised, bowing to the lady who was giving the order, though his eyes swivelled round to see if she had been overheard by the King.

" Then gather your gear together and be gone," said Janet tartly. It piqued her to discover that she interested James less than his children. If he meant to be rid of her, she had better equip herself while the chance remained. It would not, by the look of things, be so easy to charge all she needed to the King's account next year. She glanced at James, sitting on a low stool by the fire with the children jostling round him to hear if he had brought any strange beasts home from his travels or any comfits in his pouch. Children liked James, and well they might, thought Janet crossly. He might weary of their mothers, but he took trouble enough with the bairns. He'd scarcely given her a look yet, but he'd taken Moray on his knee already and was jogging him up and down to a gay rhyme that soon had the shy little boy shrieking with delight.

Mollified by Moray's pleasure, Janet picked up the embroidery she never had the patience to sit over long and watched James as he played with the children who were so uncannily like and yet unlike showing the traces of other strains in a pair of dark eyes, a tip-tilted nose, echoing his colouring with their fair or red-gold hair.

But when he looked up at her presently, over Moray's head, she saw that sadness and bewilderment shadowed his eyes yet.

" You're wearied with riding, my lord."

" No," said James. " I'm never wearied."

" But the laughter's gone from you," Janet said, as the

children, stuffing sweetmeats into their cheeks, drifted back to their games. " This'll never do, my lord, for a man that's to be married by this time next year."

" I shall contrive laughter enough to please them," James said harshly.

And indeed, many of those who saw James at a distance after his return from Whithorn thought that his pilgrimage had healed him of his grief for Margaret Drummond. But some who knew him better were less certain. He had revived, indeed, but strangely. His voice had changed, a wild note cracked his laughter, there was sometimes a dead blankness in his eyes that were at other times overbright, so that here and there the more superstitious remembered the tales of wandering spirits that could drain a man's soul from his body through eye or ear, insinuating themselves in its place to enjoy the solace of carnal passions from which they had been long outcast, keening for their lost humanity on the north wind. Whispering such tales, the superstitious would cross themselves and look at James sidelong. Would a man in his right senses let Mistress Kennedy bide at Stirling, with the bairns he set such store by, knowing what was said?

But James had never cared much for what people said. And to be made to laugh again, however wildly, was something which earned her his gratitude. He gave orders for the priests who sang Margaret Drummond's masses in Dunblane to send their charges quarterly to the Lord High Treasurer. And he let Janet Kennedy remain.

He himself, as he warned her, would not be at Stirling much. There was a great deal of business to put through with the Council, and he wished personally to see what progress was being made by the builders on the royal palaces of Falkland, Linlithgow, and his new project at Holyrood. In November, the southern justice ayres would take him to Jedburgh and Melrose.

" You'll be back at Stirling, though, for Yule? "

" No," said James.

" Well, since I'm needed to order things at Bothwell," said Janet sharply, " I might as well be doing it as skelping other women's bairns."

" Just as well," James agreed.

"Alexander will weary for you," she said.

"Not while he can watch the apothecaries seeking the Fifth Essence or the Philosophers' Stone," said James. "Master John Damien that came from France a year back has promised to work wonders if I can but supply him with what he requires."

"With gold, no doubt, which he will multiply?"

James nodded. "It would be useful, you must own, you that I once called greedy as a gipsy," he added, with a bleak smile.

Janet lifted her head from the pile of account books which she kept so meticulously; one for Bothwell, one for Darnaway, a third for her personal gear, and spoke with sincerity. "Oh, James, greedy I may be, but it vexes me to see others' greed deceive you. I know nothing of leechcraft or alchemy, but at least I know the smell of a rogue when it is quite so strong at my nose."

"The quest for the Fifth Essence is a very proper exercise pursued by the most learned Abbots and Priors with the sanction of Holy Church. Or at least without her open censure," James corrected himself.

"The quest for gold is one they share with the rest of us," Janet said, as she queried an entry made in her steward's illegible hand. "Here's this old fool thinking I'll let pass anything I can't read. And Master Damien persuading you that if you give him gold he can make it breed. Never in this world, James. Keep the gold in your pouch and leave breeding to lusty folk like you and me."

James laughed, as she had hoped, and let the matter drop. He also announced his intention of jousting again, which pleased her. During October he took part in the tournament at Stirling which she and the children, screaming with excitement, watched from the Castle walls, while the nursemaids picked the little boys off the parapet as fast as they scrambled back, and Janet's hand flew to her lips as she watched the puppet figure that was James hurtle at another puppet, far below. Now that James was jousting again, he might be said to be coming back to life indeed.

She had achieved much in the way of reconciliation. But she could not win him completely, it seemed. He announced, on leaving for the Border, his intention of spending Yule as the guest of the Abbot of Arbroath. And Janet, snapping her fingers in the way that had come to her lately when annoyed, went on with her preparations for her journey to Bothwell early in December. She was not going empty handed. For James, undeterred by his Treasurer's sighs, had commanded him to present Mistress Kennedy with a hundred French crowns on the day she left Stirling, and Janet herself had listed such a quantity of household gear that it took several wagons to convey it. Cloaked and hooded for departure, she checked over each item as it was loaded by the King's men.

"A great pot . . . a quart stoup . . . a pint stoup likewise . . . a kettle, three small pots . . . four pans . . . two ticks of feather beds . . . forty ells of white material for blankets . . . four candlesticks . . . four cushions, sewed and lined . . . sixty ells of cloth for sheets. . . . Take that foolish grin off your face, man," she told the Captain of the Castle. "Shall I not plenish my house without your grinning at my thrift? A fine outcry there'd be if you were sent home without your wages. . . ."

Moray was to stay at Stirling with the other children and their nurses, by James's command, but the new baby was sickly and Janet was to keep it with her for a while. She waved goodbye to her young son as he stood by the window to watch her ride away. She was not a fond mother, as she knew well enough. James was far fonder of his bairns for all his crazy ways of getting them, Janet told herself as she rode westward. Had she not seen him sit up half the night when Alexander was howling with toothache, and have the leech out of his bed because Catherine had a pain? Later, spending Yule in lonely state at Bothwell, she wondered how James's devotions were proceeding at Arbroath, and wished she could get him out of her mind, since she had now so little place in his.

But she had done her work sufficiently well for James to be determined at least to seem gay. The English envoys, in whose presence he had ratified the marriage contract in Glasgow Cathedral on the 10th of December, spent Yule with him at Arbroath, and James set the good monks in a twitter by importing a horde of trumpeters, luters, harpers and jesters, commanded the attendance of the local nobility, and scandalised those unprepared to find extravagance associated with piety by losing nearly a hundred pounds at cards over the festival.

Spring came tardily in 1503, first bringing news of the death of the Queen of England who would in a few months have become James's mother-in-law, and then that of his younger brother, John, Earl of Mar. The news of Mar's death brought James back from Whithorn for the funeral, though he took the opportunity to call on the way at Bothwell to see how Janet was faring, on a sudden impulse which surprised them both. With characteristic curiosity, James analysed, as he might have analysed a mixture bubbling in one of John Damien's retorts, the difficulty he found in keeping away from Janet. Lust was still one ingredient in her attraction, undoubtedly, but not the only one. He needed help if he were to laugh nowadays. There was an enchantment about Janet; in spite of all her blatant greed for other people's possessions and careful economy with her own; yes, in spite of a string of faults as long as the tale of the goods she had charged against him before she left Stirling. Their blatancy tickled his fancy. He always preferred an honest rogue to a subtle hypocrite. But, whatever the cause, James had to admit that it was hard, even impossible, to live on in a world which death seemed to be emptying of every creature he loved, and think of seeing her for the last time.

Janet was so frankly delighted by his arrival at Bothwell that he was a little comforted, against his will. She knew well how to provide for a fastidious man who was not to be satisfied with gross meals. Her cook had produced a subtler dinner than many he had eaten at his own table, Frenchified, with wine, sauces and savouries, served by candlelight with fiddlers playing behind the scenes. James asked to be taken to the kitchens before he left, praising the servants' work in his informal way, with golden crown pieces for the steward, the cook, the porter and the first fiddler. But he was silent as he turned to Janet in the doorway. It was she who spoke first.

"I doubt this must be farewell, my lord. In a few weeks that procession I've heard so much of will be leaving Richmond to bring our new Queen home."

"I shall be journeying north in the autumn," James said, as if he had not heard her. And yet there was a sort of desperation in his voice.

"Indeed, my lord?" said Janet, unsmiling. "So shall I."

As he left Bothwell, James turned his attention at last to preparing for his marriage which must not be less gorgeous because the bridegroom would so much rather have died. And so, as the royal procession wound its way north through the sultry weather of July, Scotland, at James's command, prepared to receive her Queen in splendour, while the Bishop of Moray mopped his face and frowned because the perpetual noise was giving him a headache. What with the trumpets blown by those who announced the Queen's approach, the furious sawing of the fiddles which greeted her at every town, the yells of the excited crowds and the perpetual flicker of brilliant banners, he was almost exhausted, and the Queen herself, poor child, looked as if she might be going to be sick. Unresponsive though she had shown herself, the Bishop spared enough time from his own troubles to consider what a strange homecoming it would be for her. The King she was presently to marry had at least one daughter almost of an age with his bride, and the Bishop himself, just before he left Scotland, had seen yet another little girl come to take her place in the royal nursery, her hand lost in that of her stout nurse, uncertain bewilderment in her very wide grey eyes. The Bishop of Moray needed no one to give a name to Margaret Drummond's six-year-old daughter. The incident had exasperated him, for after seeing the child, the King had shut the door of his privy chamber against all other comers, and done no more business that day. It was to be hoped that by now he had regained his composure, thought the Bishop, as his headache grew worse.

The towns on the great north road slipped past like the beads of a rosary, as the chanting priests came out to meet the new Scottish Queen, bearing their sacred relics in procession, giving her their great crosses to kiss. At Grantham, Newark, Tuxford, Doncaster, York, the citizens hung their brightest tapestries from windows and balconies, while all the banners of the local nobility flickered overhead. At each boundary the Sheriff of the County she was leaving entrusted the Queen to the Sheriff of the next, so that the banner on which the arms of Scotland were quartered with those of England, the red rose of Lancaster and the crowned portcullis of Henry VII, moved constantly forward, borne by men in the green and white Tudor livery, against the shimmer of changing devices displayed by the retainers of the noblemen through whose domains she passed.

The Queen herself, and all her lords and ladies, were even more gorgeous, in cloth of gold and silver, all shades of satin, velvet and brocade, furred, even in high summer, with ermine and vair, their jewels outshining the burnished steel and burning gold of helm and sword-hilt, so that to the Bishop's bilious eyes the whole spectacle seemed to quiver in the blinding light. Groaning, he prepared to endure the greeting of the yelling citizens, prancing horses, chanting monks and pompous officials of yet another loyal town.

What the Queen thought of it all, the Bishop had not the remotest idea. He watched the small figure in crimson and cloth of gold making the same gracious gestures yet again, her round face quite expressionless, with its obstinate mouth and undistinguished nose, the close-set eyes from which the plucked eyebrows had removed all trace of character. As she turned this way and that to greet still more officials, more important clergy, she might have been a cleverly fashioned doll instead of a human being, the Bishop thought, so that he questioned her as they left York, for the very reassurance of hearing her speak.

" Madam, the country must seem very different in these parts from the lush fields of Richmond."

Her lips trembled a little, as she looked fearfully at the fells and dales about her. " It is, my lord Bishop," she said politely, in a voice as flat as any of the gold plates on which the Archbishop of York's delicacies had been served. But having spoken, she continued. " Is it much farther still, my lord? "

" No, the greater part of the journey is behind us now," the Bishop told her. " From Durham we pass by the New Castle, thence to Morpeth, Alnwick, and Berwick. Thereafter we shall enter Scotland——"

" And see my lord, King James? "

"Yes, indeed. He is most ardently awaiting you," said the Bishop, hoping to heaven that this might now be true, as the great company, newly swelled by the Earl of Northumberland and all the local nobility in their finest array, surged towards Berwick and the Border at last.

The Queen had taken to her litter again. Berwick was a haze of sound: the thunder of the Castle guns rivalled by the peacock screeching of every sort of trumpet; the twanging, sawing and pounding of musical instruments, the full-throated chanting of tonsured choirs. She was scarcely aware of being borne into Scotland, curled up in her litter like an exhausted kitten, undisturbed by the roaring guns of the Castle at Dunbar.

In Edinburgh James, in his long hose, ruffled white shirt and riding-boots, was struggling into a jacket of crimson velvet, bordered with cloth of gold, while a group of his friends put aside the attendants and laughingly waited on him themselves. But James scarcely noticed that he was taking his cloak from the Earl of Argyll, and his cap from the Earl of Lennox, while his sword was girt about him by the Earl of Huntly, instead of by his usual chamber groom.

"It is to be hoped that all is in order for the state entry into Edinburgh," he said irritably, "since I cannot both meet the Queen at Newbattle and remain behind to make sure."

"All will be in order, my lord, depend upon it," said Argyll, with the soothing superiority of an already married man.

"There are to be pageants enough, and all the decorations heart can desire," said James, unable to stop talking from sheer nervousness. "The people must wear their best. Heaven be praised Hamilton has brought the fleet safe back from Denmark. He and St. Andrews are my nearest kinsmen now. I have given away enough cloth of gold and velvet and satin and taffeta to clothe an army. The Treasurer will complain bitterly. But I cannot help it. I must give all I can. . . ."

All indeed . . . with the one thing lacking that he could not give, because he seemed to have no love to give anyone any more. James crammed his cap on his head and clattered off down the stairs with Argyll, Huntly and Lennox behind him, to ride as fast across country as he ever rode against an opponent in the

ists. Meanwhile, a sedater company, headed by his brother,
Archbishop of St. Andrews, with young Alexander as Archdeacon
in attendance, and scores of escorting churchmen, nobles and
gentlemen, ambled in a more leisurely fashion to the meeting
place.

The Queen and her escort had already arrived at Newbattle
as the drawbridge rang hollow under the hooves of James's
galloping horse. At least the haste for which his grave counsellors
constantly took him to task was becoming in a lover, he thought
ironically as he was led forthwith to the Queen's chamber. News
of his arrival had gone before him. So, in so far as was possible,
she was prepared. But James was not. She stood in the doorway,
a slight, gorgeous, round-eyed figure, blank-faced with apprehension, not so tall as his daughter Catherine. They stared at each
other, mutually shocked beyond speech or movement, till the
rigid discipline of a lifetime's ceremonial came to their rescue, as
if the pause that seemed to hang between them for a twelve-
month, had been merely long enough for them to catch their
breath. Only someone who knew James well would have guessed
that the courteous phrases with which he greeted the Queen and
her company rang hollow as an empty vault, or known with
what relief he turned to greet the veteran Surrey. At least, as
soldiers, they had something in common. And as they talked
together, James felt himself revive.

It was over at last. Escorted by Surrey, James clashed
towards the stone spiral of the stairs. But as the first turn brought
him round to face the closing chamber door again, he saw the
little girl who had ridden so stolidly up the whole length of
England fling herself in a storm of tears into the arms of a lady-
in-waiting. And her cry from the far side of the limit of endurance
haunted him strangely as he rode away.

" But—but he—he is an old man with a great red beard! It
chafed my cheek. And why did he show my lord Surrey so
much more favour than me? "

CHAPTER NINETEEN

AS the sunset faded behind the horizon hills the first flames leapt from the faggots piled high on the Castle rock. From Holyrood another bonfire sprang into life, from Arthur's Seat a third. Then another, and another, till the city seemed a web of cloth of gold stitched on black velvet to those watching from the Castle walls, with the pale sword of the Forth beyond. In the streets the citizens danced round the fires till they dropped asleep on doorsteps, exhausted with running and shouting and striving to catch in their cupped hands the wine from the fountains which sent a glorious crimson spray high into the air, bespattering faces and gowns as it floated down again.

It was nearly over, all the jangle of bells and roaring of cannon, the braying of trumpets and sawing of fiddles. Next day it would be back to the bench and the loom and the plough and the field, but so long as the bonfires held back the darkness it was still holiday for those who could fight the drooping lids from their weary eyes. And after that, memories gorgeous enough to deck the rest of their threadbare days. The day before his marriage the King had ridden up the West Bow and down the High Street of Edinburgh with the Queen behind him, his great bay horse all trapped in cloth of gold, the leather of saddle and bridle silvered and deeply fringed with threads of gold. He had worn a jacket of cloth of gold with a fur-trimmed doublet of royal purple. His hose had been scarlet, his spurs and stirrups gilt, his velvet bonnet, his collar, his belt and dagger, all encrusted with great jewels. The splendour of it, and something in the look of him, had made the old wives weep, without knowing why. A gentleman usher had borne the great sword before him, sheathed in purple velvet. The Queen's little hands, clasped round his waist, could scarcely be seen for gems, and her slight figure was eclipsed by a gown of cloth of gold.

Racing through gardens and orchards, scaling walls and toiling up the wynds, the people of Edinburgh followed the royal company from point to point gaping at the pavilions where the Knight and his Paramour begged the King's permission to ride a course against the Defender who had wronged them, saw the keys of the city presented to the Queen by an Angel who descended from a window high in a wooden wall from which beamed a legion of the heavenly host sponsored by the Parish of St. Giles, while the choir shouted a Te Deum from behind the barrier. Surging on, they witnessed the tableau of the Judgment of Paris, delighted when the golden apple, which should have gone to Venus, was snatched by Mercury for the Queen. Justice, Prudence and Temperance, richly robed, displayed themselves above the newly carpentered archway through which the royal company passed, the King sweeping off his bonnet in honour of the tableaux showing the salutation of Gabriel, and the marriage of Joseph and Mary. Then, as they neared the end of their journey, the procession disappeared from the crowd's sight at the entrance to James's new Palace of Holyroodhouse.

But next morning, long before the ceremony in the Abbey was due to begin, the same crowds were waiting, and every glimpse of those concerned was reported by the fortunate from their vantage points to the others packed below.

" Yon's the Archbishop of York. . . . Ahint him comes the Bishop of Durham. I ken his device. . . ."

" Tuts, gie's oor ain folk, can ye no'? "

" Aye, here they come. Lord Hamilton, that's close kin to the King. . . . Eh, but he's braw. Did ye hear that his gown was the King's gift? Gold-flowered damask, I've heard tell. Here's my lord St. Andrews, that's the King's brither. Lord save us, he looks an awful sick man. Yon wee lad that's by his oxter, he's the King's bairn, ye ken. Archdeacon, nae less, ihmhm. My lord of Glasgow . . . my lord of Aberdeen . . . they'll be awa' to seek the King's Grace, I'd think. . . ."

" Here he comes. . . ." The crowd roared as James, a figure from a fairy tale in white and crimson and gold, appeared, walking steadily between the Archbishops, a black velvet bonnet on his bright hair, looking neither to right nor left, his face pale and set within the russet of his beard. The shouting died a little then, for heads were turning, necks craning to see the stranger. "She's nae mair than a bairn," someone cried, as the small figure of the Queen, also in white and gold and crimson, appeared, her hands held by the Earl of Surrey and the Archbishop of York, her train borne by the Countess of Surrey, also in cloth of gold.

Afterwards came the lords and ladies of both nations in a surge of crimson and purple, green and blue and silver, gold and black; velvets and satins and furs and jewels; the officers of arms in their gorgeous coats, hurrying esquires and strutting pages who ignored the shouts and whistles of the holiday crowd that slowly fell silent as the singing within the Abbey mingled with the crying of the seagulls, cruising overhead between the Forth and the Nor' Loch. Sweating and squabbling as the day became hotter, they waited outside Holyroodhouse. For the coronation ceremony was to be followed by dinner in the new palace and every man was alert as the heralds emerged at last to cry:

"*Largesse . . . largesse . . . largesse . . .*

"*To the high and mighty Princess Margaret, by the Grace of God, Queen of Scotland, and first Daughter engendered by the very high and mighty Prince Henry the Seventh, by that selfsame Grace, King of England. . . .*"

Then the trumpets clamoured and the sun struck blinding gleams from the golden crowns flung high in the air, the crowd seemed to grow in stature as a forest of hands reached up, then was dwarfed as hundreds grovelled. The day wore on. And from the open windows of the Palace came the sound of fiddles and glimpses of the great folk passing to and fro in the dance, the crackle of clapped hands. And when it was dark . . . the fires.

Alexander had not enjoyed it as much as he had hoped. His father had told him he must be happy because it was a very splendid marriage.

"Will you be happy?" Alexander had asked bluntly.

But his father had not seemed to hear. And his uncle of St. Andrews had looked sick all the time and leant on him hard. Alexander had promised his father to give his careful duty to the pale young man who sagged, coughing, under his gorgeous cope, shivering constantly, in spite of the heat, the Archbishop of Glasgow took the Service. But he envied the pages bustling importantly to and fro between the Palace and the Abbey. He longed so much to see and hear but could not, while he trailed along beside his uncle, in the vestments they had remade for him, his hands meekly pressed together, palm to palm, his eyes squinting down at his finger-tips.

But to-morrow it would be different, Alexander promised himself. For he had only undertaken to attend his uncle throughout the coronation ceremony. To-morrow there was to be jousting, his father was to dub forty new knights in honour of the Queen, and girdle three new earls. His half-cousin James, Lord Hamilton, was to be made Earl of Arran, with two others besides, and their largesse would be cried before the whole company.

And so, when night came, Alexander thankfully stripped off his heavy robes and dossed down with a rowdy party of pages on mattresses dragged into the great chamber as soon as it had been vacated by the yawning company. He was determined to keep out of his father's way for fear new duties were laid upon him. But next morning, as he chased his bedfellows about the passages, before the great folk were about, his attention was caught by the sound of laughter from the Queen's apartments, within which people were scurrying to and fro, demanding basins and ewers of hot water, damask towels, and shears. When curiosity got the better of caution, Alexander slid through the doorway on the heels of one of the chamber grooms. What he saw appalled him. His father was seated on a stool with a great towel round his neck and the clippings of his beard scattered all round him, while the Countess of Surrey, also girt with towels, was slapping lather on his cheeks, and the Earl, lean and unsmiling, offered his lady the razor in place of the shears. Nearby the young Queen, surrounded by her gratified ladies, was clapping her hands and jumping up and down.

Alexander stood motionless, unable to believe in a sight as dreadful as the shearing of Samson, till, as the pale oval of James's estranged face emerged from the white froth and Lady Surrey stood back to survey her triumph, he could bear it no more, but turned with a choked cry, and fled, out of the Queen's chamber, out of the Palace, running like a crazy thing towards the stables, his stammering commands to the grooms so incomprehensible that he ran to the saddle-racks and heaved down what he wanted himself, slapping the saddle across the back of the nearest palfrey so suddenly that the little beast reared and all but broke its halter. Sobbing and panting, Alexander buckled the girths, snatched the bridle from the stable lad and threw himself across its back like a sack of meal. Scrabbling for the stirrups as his legs swung down, he jabbed his spurless heels at its flanks and turned its head towards Stirling, which at least was home.

In the Queen's chamber the babble of laughter and crackle of clapped hands had drowned his outcry. Lady Surrey gently dabbed James's chin, which the drastic treatment had reddened, then dropped him a curtsy as she turned to the Queen, now checked between capers, staring at the doorway through which Alexander had disappeared.

" Who was that boy? " she demanded, her voice both scared and shrill.

" Madam," her ladies chorused, " we saw none."

" He glared at me," said the Queen, pouting.

" Oh, madam . . ."

" Surely not——"

" Consider instead the fair face of the King. . . ."

The Queen giggled again. Alexander was forgotten as James came forward, looking so different that the child who had wept for fear of him could scarcely credit the evidence of her eyes.

" Madam, try for yourself the smoothness of his cheek. . . ."

" Oh, madam, not with your hand alone. . . ."

Coyly, the Queen leant forward to kiss the smooth face now on a level with her own, as James knelt, laughing as he had assured Janet that he would laugh, to please the child who was now his Queen, at Lady Surrey, at her enigmatic husband, still watching in the background, his arms folded, his thin lips just curled into an indulgent smile.

" Madam," said James, " we must persuade the lady to accept a barber's fee. Does it not seem to you that it is well deserved? "

" Yes, oh yes, indeed," she whispered, her head on one side, her ring-loaded hands clasped before her.

"How do I look?" he teased.

"Why, sir, most beautiful."

Still kneeling, James bowed to Lady Surrey, one hand laid across his smooth chin and the other on his heart in such elegant clowning that the Queen squealed with delight. "Madam, name your barber's fee."

"So they were right after all," the Queen's high voice proclaimed, "who told me I should find pleasant fooling in Scotland."

"Sir," said Lady Surrey, "you must not talk of fees till you have seen the work." Clapping her hands, she cried: "A glass! Find me a glass, then, idlers!"

In a soft scurry of laughter and compliments the glass was brought and held before him. James looked at his own face as if at the portrait of a stranger, and as quickly looked away. For the blank eyes mocked the laughing mouth, the vigour of the chin that had not been bared since his first love-making belied the soft curves of the cheeks' high bones. He did not care to guess at the conflict these things implied. In the last resort, the priests said, a man's defences were built up from within. He alone could permit or deny access to the man those eyes revealed, whom that mouth hid. As he turned to the Queen, his smile now mocked them all.

"Madam, it is for you to say. Most humbly we await your Majesty's judgment."

Giggling, her knuckles to her lips, she watched him slyly as she pondered. "Sir," she said at last, "since you have been barbered for love of me, and I shall be fifteen years old next birthday, let my lady of Surrey receive fifteen ells of whatsoever stuff she shall choose. . . ."

"She shall have fifteen ells of cloth of gold," said James, amused to note their amazement, determined to show these foreigners that he was not mean because he ruled a poor country. But Lady Surrey's protestations still contrasted with the enigmatic reserve of her husband, whose part in the performance, as far as James could see, had merely been to produce the razor, which his lady now daintily returned. So James was glad to take the opportunity, offered by a small flurry over the Queen's choice of mantles, to lead his guest towards the window embrasure, where they might talk in peace.

"I hope, my lord of Surrey," he said, "that our country makes a better impression on this visit than on your earlier one?"

"I have thought less of the country, sir," said the Earl of Surrey, "but enjoyed the more cordial welcome offered by its King." He smiled. "If I remember rightly, my lord, you were anxious only to spit me on your lance-point when I crossed the Border last."

"And would again," said James gaily, "should you come in arms against us."

"Quite so," agreed the Earl of Surrey.

What a comfort it was, James thought, to talk to a soldier whose tongue was as sharp as his sword. The honeyed nonsense of the last hour had quite turned his stomach. Surrey, with his leathery old campaigner's face, cross-hatched with scars and wrinkles, was almost as good company as one of his own comrades-in-arms. Chuckling, James recalled the campaign of nearly ten years ago, wondered what would have befallen them all ten years hence. Surrey's eyes narrowed as he too looked ahead.

"Artillery, I believe," he said, "will presently change the face of warfare."

"It may be. But I would still rather commend my cause to the valour of the men I led. . . ."

"I place less faith in men than in their weapons, my lord," said Surrey in his creaking, broken-winded voice. "The bravest men, ill-armed and unwisely led, will be butchered by a disciplined force with better weapons. . . ."

"Now that," said James, "I deny . . ."

"But consider only . . ."

"I am prepared to prove my contention in the field. . . ."

"All that," said Surrey warningly, "is surely over now, my lord."

"Yes," James said regretfully. "So indeed it is."

A fretful voice behind them made both men swing round. The conference among the ladies was over and the Queen was bored.

"My lords," she complained, "I have been dressed to ride

out with you this long while. I have put on my gayest gown and my most splendid mantle. I did not think I should have to command your attention before you told me how fine it seemed."

Such reproaches became more frequent, James found, as the days passed. The Queen would romp with him wildly while it pleased her, then, for no particular reason, show a surprisingly vicious temper, so that James was as startled as if a pretty kitten had bitten him. She was, he discovered, keenly aware of her importance, instantly jealous when he tried to talk to anyone in her presence, and at times most genuinely homesick, so that she wept for loneliness as Catherine or Alexander might have wept over the loss of a pet dog.

James found the odd association, which it was as yet unthinkable to consider marriage in anything but name, quite bewildering in its ambiguity. He had been possessed, many times, by the fierce loves of the flesh, rung once by the agonised yearning of the spirit. Now, for the first time, he was pestered by pity for a creature who irritated him with her shallow worldliness almost as much as she distressed him by her forlorn youth. But just when he had been most moved by compunction towards a better understanding, he would be irritated by her complacence all over again.

There was evidence, too, that she was of her father's disposition. Though the final instalment of her dowry had not yet been paid, she showed the greatest determination to inspect the dower lands which James had made over to her. In particular, prompted perhaps by her ladies, who had discovered which properties were of the greatest significance, she announced her intention of visiting both Linlithgow and Stirling, as soon as the Archbishop of York and the Earl and Countess of Surrey and the other guests from England had received their parting presents and left for home.

" I pray you to indulge her in that whim, my lord," murmured Lady Surrey, as preparations were made for departure, " since she must needs be sorrowful to lose so many friends, notwithstanding her joy in her husband's loving kindness."

" I had thought it might be unwise to expose the Queen to the rigours of travel so late in the year," James said uneasily.

" On the contrary, my lord, if I may be so bold," urged Lady

Surrey, " nothing, I believe, will distract and cheer the Queen so perfectly as a change of locality. She is all agog to see the castles and palaces of which she has heard so much."

James looked at her thoughtfully. He wondered just what Lady Surrey, not to mention the Queen, had heard. But he sent messengers to Stirling forthwith, whose arrival caused a considerable commotion, as the nurses and children whose rooms in the Castle would presently be required were warned that they must exchange them for lodgings elsewhere. This confirmation of recent rumours shocked Alexander, who questioned Master Paniter in dismay.

" I heard the servants saying as they packed our gear that the King would have no care for his bastards now that he had brought his Queen home. Sir, is that so? "

" I believe not," said Master Paniter, though he had also been flurried by the sudden order to bundle and go. " The King has plans for you all still. You, Alexander, are soon to study at St. Andrews. Moray and young Lyle will go with you. The girls are to submit to their governesses till they are of an age to marry. Your future, I promise you, is still assured——"

" Then why have we been hurried out of the Castle for that cod-eyed wench? " demanded Alexander. " The Castle was our home——"

" To speak so of the Queen is folly which could lead to your death," said his tutor sternly. " Never let me hear you do so again, even behind closed doors, even to me."

" I meant no harm," said Alexander sadly. " But it is true."

" Then keep the truth to yourself unless you wish to see only Stirling Castle's dungeons. St. Andrews is a fair city. We shall do very well there, in the care of your gentle uncle."

" He is sick. I expect he will die," mourned Alexander. " And I liked going to the King's laboratory in Stirling, to see what strange potions Master John was brewing. He let me watch him mix the materials for the distilling of the *quinta essencia*. Sir, some of his brews had the strangest stench imaginable."

" That I can well believe," said Master Paniter dryly. " I am not sorry that you will not be able to visit the laboratory for a while. Master John, to my mind, is one of the most plausible scoundrels that ever brought discredit on holy orders. Abbot of Tongland, indeed! The fellow has but caught the King's fancy with his nimble tongue, while I, who have toiled for as many years in his service as——"

Alexander flung his arms about his tutor in furious championship. " Master Paniter, I swear that when I am a great churchman, I shall see that you are appointed to the richest benefice I can obtain for you. I will speak for you to my father——"

" You are a good lad, Alexander," said his tutor, mollified. " I believe that you mean truly to do as you say."

" But indeed, I always do, Master Paniter," said Alexander.

As a married man, James found his journeyings newly formidable. His personal possessions, in the old days, might have loaded one pack-horse, and the conveyance of hangings, and bedding, silver plate, hawks, horses and hounds, from one royal residence to another had been part of the day's work for his household servants. But now, before every departure, he was half-deaved by the high-pitched hysteria of a score of comfort-loving women in danger of being parted from the innumerable possessions without which life, apparently, was not to be endured.

The first intimation of the changed state of affairs was brought by Master James Doig, a trusted household official of some years' standing now appointed Keeper of the Queen's Wardrobe, in a state of such agitation that he could scarcely wait for an audience until James had dealt with the day's quota of state affairs.

" My lord the King, I must ask ye to relieve me frae my position," he blurted out as soon as James had nodded permission for him to speak. " For by all the Saints above us, the work ye've gi'en me is mair than any man can thole."

James, raising astonished eyebrows, indicated a stool on the far side of the table at which he still sat among the parchments his secretary had not yet had time to clear away. " Sit down, man, and tell me what's amiss, then we'll see better how to mend it."

But Master Doig was in too distracted a state to do anything but pace the chamber, agitating his arms like windmill sails as his grievances exploded from him.

" Foreigners! I cannot be doing with them. Nothing's to their mind. The weather's cold, the fires smoke, the servants are impident. This one must have her gear washed, yon one's displeased with the browster that redds up her gowns. To-day, sir, believe it or not, they're fair ready to scairt each other or claw my een oot for fear some of the great kists yonder will be left behind when we pass to Linlithgow. The Queen's Grace sits there, quiet as a bonny wee mouse in a gaggle of geese, that thinks mair of fissing at each other than of their duty to attend her. And as for me "—Master Doig drew himself up to his full height, and slapped his broad chest with his fist—" they scold me, my lord, as if I were a scullion, each one demanding that I shall ensure the carriage of her gear whatever's left behind."

James contrived to hide a smile behind his clasped hands. then he pushed his chair back and rose. " It seems that you need reinforcements, man. I will come at once."

They took their departure at last, and reached Linlithgow in due course, but after more trouble and expense than James had ever supposed likely to attend the conveyance of a number of ladies' possessions a few miles this way or that. Eighteen carts lurched and lumbered along the uneven tracks as they bore the Queen's ladies' precious luggage from Holyrood to Linlithgow. But twenty carts, ten days later, were required to take a mysteriously increased quantity of possessions from Linlithgow to Stirling, at a cost of thirty-six pounds. The clamour of the Queen's household, where Master Doig's black-browed disapproval of such feminine fancies provoked the English ladies to even shriller protestations, made James's ears dirl. By the middle of October it had become more than he could endure without respite, and though the Queen pouted and sniffed at the idea of being even briefly forsaken, she could scarcely protest at the pious purpose of a thanksgiving pilgrimage to the shrine of St. Duthac in Tain.

" What orders have you against your departure, my lord? " asked the Master of the Stables.

" Have them saddle my fastest horse."

" And for your suite, my lord? "

" I shall ride alone," said James.

He went headlong, feeling the fret and frustration from the niggling preoccupations of a horde of strangers blown far away as he covered the miles, while the equinoctial gale flicked the golden leaves from the swaying branches of the wayside trees, to swirl high above him in the piercingly blue sky. He reached Elgin unheralded, to the astonishment of the reverend Fathers, whose porter came running to hale them from Compline with the news that the King himself was at the gate. Too weary even to eat, James flung himself down in his clothes, woke demanding a fresh horse and was off to Tain in the morning, as if he were himself kin to the south-west wind rather than a mortal creature of flesh and blood.

He heard Mass, made his offering, and began his journey southwards. The fret had gone from him now, replaced by a great weariness, as much of the spirit as of the flesh. Since the solitary madcap journey had been unpremeditated, he could still look for a little respite from the attention of his loyal subjects, few of whom knew where he was. Almost without thinking he turned his dun nag's head towards Darnaway. As he rode, he noted the uneven beats of its hooves with a flicker of satisfaction. He would have to stay now. The beast had gone lame.

Janet was scolding the steward in the stableyard when James rode up. Her voice, which could be so subtle, had an edge to it like the frost that could take the skin off a man's face up here in the north. She was wrapped in an old cloak and her nose was peaked. James sat still on his horse, in two minds whether to turn and ride away. He had come to Darnaway for comfort, not for scolding. Of that, it seemed, he was likely to have enough at home.

Then she turned and saw him. Her hands flew to her mouth as if to check a cry, and as her hood fell back her bright hair blazed against the granite grey. She came towards him on tiptoe, walking delicately between the puddles of the cobbled yard in heavy boots that were spurred like a man's. Glancing over her shoulder to make sure that the steward had hirpled off to rouse the household, she stood beside his horse, staring up, her wide green eyes, swimming unexpectedly with tears, level with his knee.

"Have they changed you so?" she said in a toneless voice, then, with a little grimace of distress, she laid her cheek against his thigh.

R

James had forgotten that she had not yet seen him beardless. He rubbed his chin with his thumb and laughed. " Not so much as you'd think, Janet. Let me get down. Here's your fellow coming for the horse." He swung himself to the cobbles and turned to the groom. " Tend him. He's lame. If he does not mend I shall leave him and take another."

" Yes, my lord," mumbled the groom, trying not to stare at the changed face that he would not have known for the King's.

" Come then, for you must be sorely in need of both food and rest," Janet said.

It was strange to see her so decorous, so remote. Food and wine were set before him by the fire that burned all the year round on the hearth in the great hall, since even high summer could not bake the chill out of the granite walls. While the servants bustled about them, she—she of all people, who never cared what folk thought—made careful conversation. And when they were gone, it seemed, at first as if she were going to be more careful still.

" How is Moray, James? I have had no word these many weeks. It is not surprising. Still—I am his mother——"

" He is by now at St. Andrews. Master Paniter is tutoring him with Alexander."

" So our crazy household at Stirling is broken up? " she sighed. " I am sorry. What has come to the others that I used to skelp as hard as my own bairn? "

" They are being cared for," James said, frowning.

" I am sure of that," Janet said quickly. " You are a kind father, James. A good mother, alas, I shall never be. Like the birds, I am more ready to push them from the nest. Later you must see our bairn that I still have with me. She lies asleep upstairs. But first, tell me of other things. I will build this wall of words no higher between us. Married you are and married you will remain. Do you not know me better than to think I seek to grip you like a falcon that will not loose her prey? We can still companion each other well enough, surely? "

" That is my hope," said James. He was not sure why he had come to Darnaway. Perhaps because the child in the cradle upstairs was the only one of his household in Stirling unaccounted for, one way or another, now. Perhaps because he wanted to make it clear to Janet that while she chose to remain at Darnaway, he saw no reason why he should not come to her. It would be different if she insisted on playing a more dangerous game. He did not wish her, for instance, to persuade him to Bothwell again. The choice, as he would presently make clear, was hers. But his was a subtler need, less for her body than for her laughter. He had been surrounded by humourless formality so long that he ached for foolishness. Yet with Janet in this mood of painful rectitude, it seemed as if he might seek in vain.

As if she had divined his thought, Janet gave herself a little shake, perhaps to rid herself of too much propriety, then leant forward, elbows on knees and chin propped on one palm, the fingers of the other hand outstetched to the blazing logs.

" And now, James, tell me of lighter things," she said.

" Lighter things . . ." James stared, too, for a moment into the flames. Then the glowing embers and the charred fragments seemed to shape themselves into the outraged features of Master James Doig, the Queen's most touchily dignified servitor, as he complained of the difficulties of dealing with the mountainous luggage of the Queen's English ladies. And suddenly he was telling Janet of the eighteen carts which had creaked towards Linlithgow with their precious chests of satins and velvets, the twenty carts which had groaned under a greater load, the shriek ing consternation of the ladies when one of the carts capsized, and all the chests fell out, one bursting open so that the hawthorn bushes by the wayside were festooned with hoods and tippets till they looked for all the world like a bothy at St. Giles' Fair. . . .

Because he had so long forced himself to laughter, the laughter which now came unbidden was sweeter than he had ever dreamed. James rocked in his chair, beating his hands on his knees, the tears pouring down his shaven cheeks, while Janet opposite him held her aching sides and gasped.

" Oh, James . . . I have not laughed so for over a twelve-month. . . ."

" I never thought to laugh so again," said James.

CHAPTER TWENTY

" THE poet Dunbar to whom you allow the pension of an honest servitor, has been mocking his betters again, my lord," complained Master James Doig.

Grinning, James turned from the casement, through which he was watching a kestrel hover over Arthur's Seat, and held out his hand for the document which Master Doig was surveying with the corners of his mouth turned down. " He has a waspish tongue, as Master Damien knows to his cost. Let's hear what he has against you."

" He has been reading it aloud, I have no doubt," grumbled Master Doig, " to the sots who companion him in every alehouse of Edinburgh, and all because I sent him to the right about when he came begging to me for cast-off doublets. He writes most scurrilously."

" Let me read it for myself, man," said James.

With the greatest reluctance, Master Doig was persuaded at last to part with the broadsheet, from which James, in delight, presently began to declaim.

" ' The Wardrober of Venus' bower,' aha, Jamie, that's you indeed—' To gif a doublet is as dour . . .' Were you so? Think shame of yourself! "

" I did but ask him what became of the last he had from us," said Master Doig, self-righteously.

James shook his head at him. " Why ask him that, when you know the answer as well as I do? Parted with it for a stoup of ale, what else? Well, he's paid you out for speiring. Listen to this:

' *When that I shaw to him your markis,*
He turns to me again and barkis,
As he were worrying a hog;
Madam, ye have a dangerous Dog! ' "

"The very bairns run barking behind me when I walk up the High Street," Master Doig complained. But James, beating the rhythm with hand and foot, read on.

> "'*He is ower muckle to be your messan,*
> *Madam, I red you get a less ane,*
> *His gang gars all your chambers schog;*
> *Madam, ye have a dangerous Dog.*'

That's a close thrust, Jamie. Lap-dog, indeed, and ponderous enough to set the floors quaking! Man, it's worth a cartload of doublets. Give him a couple of mine and tell him to copy that poem out a dozen times that I may have it by me when I weary of compliments and courtesies. And look less dour about it," he added, clapping the affronted official on the back. "Do you not know that Dunbar is as lazy as all the rest of the rhymers? Make him write it out a dozen times and he'll take care not to offend again. Take it to him with the doublets and my command that next time his money runs out he's to submit his petition in rhyme."

"As you will, my lord," said Master Doig glumly.

James sighed. How often he had wished during the last two years that a sense of humour could be engrafted as easily as the strains of apple trees he had been introducing into his new orchards at Stirling. In the old days the Court had been a merry place. What had come over people that they had grown such a monstrous sense of their own importance? Even Master Doig, bringing another broadsheet to James next evening, as he watched the dancers in the great hall, seemed only slightly mollified by it. "This I received from Dunbar at noon. Pah, it still reeks of the ale he has spilt on it."

"And none the worse, if ale sets his wits to work," said James. "Ah, who called poets thankless? Hark how he changes his tune:

> '*O gracious princess, good and fair,*
> *Do well to James your wardrober;*

> *Whose faithful brother most friend I am:*
> *He is na Dog; he is a Lam . . .'"*

Chuckling, James was less aware of the jigging, gorgeously
dressed dancers moving between him and the hangings of
crimson and purple velvet, than of the roaring stench of the dimly-
lit alehouse in which the poet was probably at that moment
sitting, huddled in his shoddy cassock, his tonsured head, with its
eagle's beak and shrewd little laughter-creased eyes, laboriously
bent over another precious parchment across which his goose-
quill shrieked, gouts flying as he jabbed impatiently at the
ink-horn, glancing at the empty mutchkin by his elbow with a
sigh.

James had his family's easy ways with the common people,
and had often amused himself by eluding the vigilance of his
nobles to see for himself how they fared. The high-nosed ladies
who had come north with his English Queen never got used to
his lack of ceremony, grumbling that he took as much trouble to
thank an old wife for a frame of her new season's honey or a
pound of butter as to acknowledge the magnificent gifts of a
reigning king.

So now he was unaware that they were waiting for him to
dance, as he chuckled over the sly jingle, while Master Doig
stood beside him, making convulsive efforts to appear gratified
by the fooling which had taken the King's fancy.

> " ' *Your Highness can nocht get a meter*
> *To keep your wardrobe, nor discreter*
> *To rule your robes and dress the same:*
> *He is na Dog; he is a Lam . . .'"*

" I shall show this to the Queen," said James. " It will make
her smile."

" Will it, my lord? "

James looked thoughtfully at Master Doig, then back at the
grimy broadsheet, marked with the imprint of greasy finger-tips,
and reeking, undeniably, of the ale spilt over it. " Perhaps,
indeed, it will not," he agreed.

It was difficult to know what would amuse the child to whom he had been nominally married for over two years now, two years during which her vigilant ladies had guarded her from any closer contact with her husband than a chaste kiss, given and received in full view of them all. She lived at his Court in a delicately perfumed, gently warmed world of her own which James might visit but from which, after a discreet interlude of make-believe courtship which he found as irritating as it was pathetic, he was excluded in a whirl of thistledown protestations of her Highness's fatigue and the lateness of the hour.

With a crooked smile he handed the broadsheet back to Master Doig. " You are right, I believe. But keep it safe, man. I doubt not that in time to come folk will mind you the better for Master Dunbar's rhymes."

" Indeed, your Highness," said Master Doig piously, " I would be sorry to think they had no better cause for minding me than the sorry jingling of such a reprobate as you renegade friar. I have already bespoken a very handsome memorial in granite."

" Ah, as to that," said James, turning away with one of his mercurial changes from gaiety to sadness, " who can tell, Jamie, what will crumble and what will bide? "

Master Doig, somewhat huffily, withdrew, holding the soiled parchment between finger and thumb at a safe distance from his neat dark clothes, and James's thoughts returned unwillingly to Janet, who would have enjoyed the whimsy as he had done. He had been angered with her of late. She had been, in public, so correct, so decorously understanding when they met at Darnaway two months after the royal wedding. He had been amazed at the change in her. She herself had pointed out that the marriage must impose a certain discretion on them both which they had never troubled to display before. But the change, it seemed, had not gone deep. Nor had it lasted long. She was as exigent, as provocative, now, as she had ever been. Darnaway was a fine residence, and because it had been his gift she might have had the grace to be satisfied with it. It was insulting as well as inconvenient that she should have taken to spending so much of her time at the Castle of Bothwell, which had been the gift of another man. He had made it quite clear that he would prefer her to remain at Darnaway.

But last spring, a mere six months after so many promises of good behaviour, she had not only taken up residence at Bothwell but sent a message to him at Stirling to say that she was sick, a hint which he had parried by sending Master Shaw to prescribe and report. On the leech's return, with the news that he found the lady to be suffering less from the rheum which was keeping her abed than from a sorry state of low spirits, he had sent her a box of the latest confections from France, with a guarded message of good wishes for her recovery. When the shocked messenger brought back the news that the lady had thrown the confections out of the window, he had laughed. It seemed she was mending. But he had written coldly to say that if she wished to see him, it must be at Darnaway.

The necessity for severity was distasteful. And Janet, he guessed, might well defy him. He frowned as he watched the stately movements of the pavane which had followed a romping country dance. What then? The thought of any more emotional upheavals was more than he could abide.

He had got no further with his deliberations, next morning, when a page brought him the news that the Earl of Bothwell was without, and would welcome the chance of showing him something of the game of golf which had taken up so much of so many people's time that the Council had forbidden it for fear they neglected their archery.

"I cannot imagine why any man should prefer it," James said, after they had plodded across the sheep-cropped turf at the back of his new palace of Holyroodhouse for long enough to take the place of the new sport. "I find it mighty tedious, Patrick."

"Indeed, I thought you well might," Patrick Hepburn agreed. "But you must give it a fair trial, my lord, not condemn it out of hand. It is a rare, peaceable occupation for an idle hour."

James shook his head as he watched his companion address his ball and wondered at his liking for so slow a sport. Patrick had aged lately. It was possible to believe that he was over fifty now that his hair was grizzled at the temples. And his face had a yellowish pallor, strange in a man who had spent so much of his life out of doors.

"Why, Patrick, it is a most tedious performance. It might be tolerable, maybe, if it were played on horseback," James grumbled "But there is too much walking in it for me, as it is. Why chase the ball as well as hit it? Dogs or bairns could be trained to bring it back and wagers laid on the distance it travelled to enliven the sorry affair."

"Yet, as matters stand, it offers a pleasant method of exchanging confidential information and being certain it is not overheard," said Patrick Hepburn.

"What news have you for me, Patrick?"

"Mistress Kennedy is again at Bothwell."

James topped his ball and watched it trickle slowly away. "Against my express wish?"

"My lord, it seems so."

James frowned. "She may well say that her presence there is required for the administration of her property." Then, more sharply: "Or is Angus, think you, seeking to take up with her again?"

Patrick Hepburn shook his head. "I do not know. I have heard he is conveying his lands to his sons, reserving only the life-rent, so that he may be the more carefree in his old age."

"Heaven save us, Patrick, that sounds unlike the old fox. It is love or piety that has so changed him?"

"Neither, maybe. But Mistress Kennedy may have come to Bothwell to safeguard her rights. Do they not say that possession is nine points of the law?"

"If I thought there was more to it——"

"Whether or not, my lord," said Patrick bluntly, "might you not be glad to see less of the lady? As things are now?"

"I might," said James. "Yet it is hard to say such a thing —to shut an old friend out of doors——"

"Surely, my lord, we all know Mistress Kennedy for a——"

"I wonder," said James slowly, "whether any of us know her. Her faults are for all to see. It may be that her virtues lie hid. I will not see her at Bothwell on any account, still less if she comes there for Angus. Yet since the place is his gift, it presents a pretty problem."

"One way with problems is to set another man to solve them," said Patrick Hepburn, dryly reminding himself that something over twelve years ago he had said much the same thing.

"Janet is not easy for any man to manage. Whom have you in mind?"

The laughter creases deepened round Patrick's shadowed eyes.

"John Ramsay," he said, grinning.

James swung at his neglected ball, missed, and stood staring sombrely. "*Ramsay?* Why?"

"Let us say . . ." Patrick hesitated, seemed about to add something, glanced sidelong at James, then changed his mind. Perhaps the joke was too grim for the King to share. Plenty of people associated Janet with the death of Margaret Drummond. He had yet to meet another who thought of John Ramsay. Had it occurred to James? He could not tell. "Ramsay has owed you a grudge this long while for the Earl's belt you stripped off him to gird about my waist," he said. "And Mistress Kennedy holds fast to the Castle of Darnaway yet makes many journeys elsewhere. Marry them off and much, if not all, is set to rights."

"Patrick, you should have been a bishop," James said wryly.

"Heaven forfend. But you will think of it?"

"I will," James promised.

But though he did not forget, he pushed Patrick's suggestion to the back of his mind for consideration later. Meanwhile, riding to St. Andrews, he enjoyed a day with Alexander and young Moray, laughing to see that they were growing out of all their clothes, while Catherine demurely mended them. At Dunfermline he discussed with the Abbot what dowry should go with his eldest daughter when her marriage presently came in question, decided that little Margaret, at seven, was old enough to leave her nurse and begin the education of a great lady. The others might bide where they were, but he would bring Margaret's daughter to Edinburgh so that she might be under his own eye. Hearing this, the good Abbot shook his head and sighed. But James ignored him.

"She shall have her own apartments in the Castle," said James, "and be under the care of the Captain and his lady, who shall choose her servants and see her gowned as befits a King's daughter."

"If the Queen should hear that the little Lady Margaret is in Edinburgh, sir," ventured the Abbot, "she might take it much amiss."

"The Queen," said James confidently, "is no more than a child herself. She knows nothing of my earlier obligations. Yet I am determined to honour them."

In silence, the Abbot bowed.

Soon afterwards James was recalled to St. Andrews by the sudden death of his brother, the Archbishop, for whom he sincerely grieved. The estrangement caused by their father's attempt to disinherit James in favour of his gentle brother had not long survived the tragedy at Sauchieburn. But the Archbishop's death, while Alexander was still too young to step into the place which his father had in mind for him, created a difficulty. James only hoped he might be able to prevail on the Pope to agree to Alexander's nominal appointment. . . .

"Should you indicate, my lord, that such a favour would incline you to view His Holiness's invitation to join the alliance against France more kindly," murmured Master Paniter, "I believe such a favour might be more readily granted——"

"No one shall persuade me to abandon the alliance with France," James declared.

"But surely, my lord, it is not necessary, at this stage, to say so?"

James grinned. "Who supposes churchmen to be as harmless as doves?"

"Only those who remember that we were also commanded to be wise as serpents. Have you other letters for me to write, my lord?"

"I have indeed, Master Paniter," said James. "If half those who have asked for our advice were ever prepared to take it, I believe we should by now have set the world to rights."

His correspondence was now, in fact, increasing steadily, as Scotland's position in Europe improved, and her ruler became

someone whose favour was sought, not only by the smaller nations
threatened by their neighbours, such as Guelderland and
Denmark, but by the great powers who sought to swing the
balance in their favour. So James wrote industriously to the
Duke of Gueldres, the King of Denmark, the merchants of Lubeck
the Lieutenant-Governors of Flanders, Holland and Brabant,
offering assistance, arbitration, friendship and advice, as well as
to King Louis XII of France, the Emperor Maximilian, King
Philip of Castile, his father-in-law, King Henry, and the energetic
Pope Julius, assuring France of his loyalty, England of his
affection, the Pope of his humble duty, and promising his good
offices to all concerned, in a torrent of letters which kept both
Master Paniter and his personal secretary, Master John Murray,
now laird of Blackbarony, constantly occupied. It was, perhaps
the one period of his life when James was in danger of becoming
smug, and if complacence threatens a soul more mortally than
disaster, it was, perhaps, fortunate that it did not last long.

From St. Andrews James rode to Largo, to confer with Sir
Andrew Wood and the Bartons, on the progress of his new ships
the *Margaret*, built in honour of the Queen, and the *Great Michael*
which was expected to be the wonder of the world.

Sir Andrew, ageing now, and somewhat hard of hearing
accepted James's friendly gestures with reserve. For he had not
altogether forgotten the occasion during the year after his
coronation, when James had given his kinsman, Arran, command
of the fleet which was to sail to help Huntly and Argyll with their
campaign in the Western Isles. But James, who hated hidden
grievances, brought the matter up at once.

" The Earl of Arran did well enough in command of the fleet
that sailed westward last year, did he not, Sir Andrew? "

" Aye, my lord."

" He is a most gallant knight. What is more, he is my heir
till the Queen shall bear me a better. So it is fitting that he
should learn to take command."

" Yes, my lord. Provided that his learning is not too dearly
bought for Scotland," said Sir Andrew, whose opinion of the Earl
of Arran as one of the most preposterous young popinjays who
ever ordered his betters about was only too evident.

James gave it up. The old sailor was not to be browbeaten, for which he liked him no less. But because he knew that the old man was still hurt it was a relief to return to Stirling to see what progress Master John Damien had made with his mysterious tasks. Here, at least, he fancied himself safe from the demands of king-ship.

But one afternoon, in the late spring of 1505, it was when James was contentedly watching the subtle mixture in a glass retort stir and bubble over a fire of charcoal, while Master Damien, in a far corner, pounded various substances to powder before weighing each on the scales, that both were startled out of the depths of concentration by the precipitate arrival of a scared page.

" I ask your Highness's pardon," the boy stammered, his eyes goggling at the strange sights and stenches about him, " but the Queen's ladies have commanded me to beseech you to come to her chamber——"

" Now, of all times," James grumbled to himself, peering at the lambent mixture, as he stripped off the old gloves he had been using to protect his hands. " I will return as soon as may be. Will you watch in my place, Master John? "

" I will, my lord," said the Abbot of Tongland.

James reached the Queen's chamber to find the Queen hysterical, and her ladies in a flutter of agitation. They surged round him, sobbing, protesting, accusing in high, distracted voices.

" Oh, my lord, your poor lady . . ."

" The Queen, Sir, is distraught. . . ."

" Your Highness, it is too much. . . ."

" How can it be endured? . . ."

" My lord, I pray you to listen. . . ."

James clapped his hands as if to silence the clamour of children. " How can I listen if you all speak at once? "

" Sir, the Queen wishes . . ."

" My lord, the Queen is . . ."

" Your Highness, I can best tell you. . . ."

James stepped to the door and wrenched it open.

" Leave us, ladies," he commanded, in a tone which did not

consider the possibility of disobedience. They hovered, hesitated, then swept unwillingly past him on a wave of protest which he stonily ignored. The Queen, checked in mid-wail by the abrupt departure of her sympathisers, stared at James out of tear-blurred eyes, sniffing and gulping, with all her splendour spoilt. But now, for perhaps the first time since she had come to Scotland, James saw her as a personality in her own right, and realised with a shock that she was already seventeen.

"Madam, I beg you will permit . . ." he said, drawing his own kerchief from his neck. But she jerked her head away.

"Do not touch me, Sir," she said. Taking a deep breath, she began to speak in a high, tremulous voice, shaken occasionally with sobs. "I have been most shamefully ill-used, Sir. Your bastards receive more honour, more affection, than ever you have shown to me. One child who bears your name—without the right to it—is to be an Archbishop. Another is given an earldom. A third mocks me from the very Castle of Edinburgh with her attendants and fine clothes. And you have permitted a lady, Sir, of no reputation, to call herself mistress of the royal castle of Darnaway. Sir, it is an outrage. My father will not endure it."

James, smiling as he bowed before her fury, knelt to raise her hand to his lips. But she snatched it away.

"I am weary to death of your elegant courtesies," she cried shrilly. "I—how can you suppose, my lord, that I am unaware of their hollowness?" Clenching her small fists, she shook them in his face, "I am no pink and white angel from the top of one of your master cook's sugar confections. I am flesh and blood, Sir. I am a woman grown."

"Indeed, I perceive that to be true," James said. And his voice was both surprised and grave. "But calm yourself, madam. All that is over now."

As he spoke, he realised, with an odd, bleak certainty, that it was the truth. He must break Janet's influence, now that the Queen had become aware of it, or be prepared to face more trouble then Janet had any right to cause.

Next week he rode north to be Janet's guest for the last time at Darnaway. But he did not, as usual, ride alone. He had commanded John Ramsay to attend him, among others, and sent a messenger with a letter which not only warned Mistress Kennedy of Ramsay's presence, but gave a hint of what James had in mind.

Janet received them with the pride of a gambler showing a brave face after a lost game. There was gallantry in her poise as she greeted the royal party at the top of the steps, torchlight flaring behind her in the autumn dusk, her head high and her words wary, because everywhere, as they both knew, inquisitive eyes, eager ears, twitching noses anticipated an interesting scene. But both James and Janet were at least one in their determination to make as little of the matter as if it had no more importance than the change of partners at the bidding of the fiddlers' music in the dance.

"Madam, you know Sir John, I think?"

"I believe I do, my lord."

"It is my hope that you will come to know him better."

"So, Sir, I have been given to understand."

Their words were frosty as the star-hung night from which they took refuge in the smokily lit hall. Rubbing numbed fingers, stamping booted feet till the spurs rang on the flags, the party gathered round the high-piled fire while Janet clapped her hands to bring servants with mulled wine. James watched her with immense, unwilling admiration.

"The wind has a searing edge," he said confusedly. "I believe it will snow."

"Yes, indeed, my lord," Janet answered him in the same cool, indifferent voice, "I believe that it well may."

CHAPTER TWENTY-ONE

NEXT day James rode southwards, but John Ramsay remained at Darnaway. It was all, James thought, like part of a bad dream that had recurred at intervals, many times before. Could he, deliberately, and with set purpose, have cut the bond between himself and Janet? All his life he had acted on the instinct to take a knife to attachments as soon as they threatened to become fetters. Long ago, as a green lad aware of no more than life's new splendour, he had said farewell to Mariot. Patrick had had a hand in that. Odd that he should have had a hand in the break with Janet too. Mariot had wept. But Janet had not.

James puzzled his way towards understanding of what had been in Janet's mind as she received them the night before. She had accepted his ultimatum with such pride that he could not tell whether it irked her. Was it true what they said about Angus? Or were Ramsay's lands, his fine house in the Canongate, a surer consolation? Janet was the hardest bargainer he knew, and it was not, by such standards, too bad an exchange for her. She might well have weighed his own changed circumstances and decided there was little more to be looked for in that quarter. Strange, to be aware of all that and yet be hurt by the thought that he and Janet would not laugh together again. Ramsay would be close-fisted, of course. But James rather thought he could count on Janet to get her own way. She had an aptitude for that, he reminded himself, still half-lightsome and half-stricken by what he had done.

He went, on his return to Stirling, first to the laboratory, commanding those about the great gateway to say nothing of his return, so that he might obliterate the memory of his last sight of Janet in the doorway at Darnaway before going to see the Queen. It was disconcerting, therefore, to see Alexander, crimson-faced and girt with a leather apron, blowing up the fire below the great cauldron which Master Damien was laboriously stirring, oblivious of a stench so awful that even Alexander was attempting to hold his nose with one hand while he manipulated the bellows with the other. James frowned. This was no time for the boy to forsake his studies at St. Andrews. The Queen was not in a mood to endure Alexander's presence. It was, of course, his own fault. He had been too casual. How could he expect Alexander now to be aware that he was unwelcome?

Alexander, quite evidently, was aware of nothing of the sort. He greeted his father exuberantly. " Oh, my lord, how glad I am to see you. Did you know that Master Damien has been studying how a man may fly? "

"I did not," James said, abstractedly. "He was mocking you, I believe."

"No, my lord," said the astrologer blandly. "I have had the project in mind for some time. I am at work on the construction of wings, pinioned with eagle's feathers. . . ."

"Which are to be obtained only in the north," broke in Alexander. "My lord, will you not commission Dandie Doule and Robert Hannay, when they next go in search of hawks, to bring all the eagle's feathers here that they can?"

James nodded. "You may ask them, if Master Damien so wishes. . . ." Perhaps Alexander had better continue his studies elsewhere. He would send him to Paris, or one of the Italian universities.

"I will seek out Dandie Doule myself," said Alexander, "and say it is at your command. My lord, Master Damien says that the secret lies in the cunning construction of the wings and their bracing from the shoulders so that the air flows under them. A man may soar like a very eagle, it seems. It is but necessary to infuse the subtle spirit of the bird into the wings that lift the man. In this cauldron is fish glue——"

"So I supposed," said James dryly.

"To fasten the feathers to a skeleton such as that of the bird . . ."

"It may be that we shall not obtain sufficient feathers," demurred the Abbot of Tongland, now retreating before the alarming possibility that his random fancy might actually be required to take shape.

"Have no fear, Master John. I shall see that eagle's feathers by the sackful are sent down from the mountains," said Alexander. "I will bespeak them from every falconer in the royal service——"

"Put yourself to no such trouble. . . ."

"It would be worth any trouble, Master Damien, to see such a wonder," said James, interested in spite of himself, as he always was at the prospect of marvels. "Every facility shall be given you. What else will you require?"

"I will study the question, my lord, and let you have a note of such things as will be needed," said John Damien uneasily.

"And I will make sure that my lord the King will provide

s

them. Also that the falconers when they go north, have not the chance to forget," said Alexander.

But the look which the Abbot of Tongland gave him did not suggest that he was as pleased by this assurance as Alexander could have wished.

" The fire is waning," he grumbled. " If you cannot keep it blown up, I doubt we shall see no thanks for our labour. . . ."

" I will blow harder," Alexander promised, seizing the bellows again. " But in this matter of the eagle's feathers, I take it that the pinions must be taken from full-grown birds. . . ."

James brought his hand down on his son's shoulder. " Leave the rest to Master Damien. You shall ride with me to St. Andrews——"

" Oh, my lord——"

" I wish to talk of your further schooling with Master Paniter," said James in the tone which Alexander recognised as inexorable.

When James returned from St. Andrews alone it was with a sense of further deprivation. Master Paniter had admitted the wisdom of sending Alexander abroad. The teaching of Master Erasmus, at Padua, it seemed, was very highly thought of. James left him to make the necessary inquiries and rode back to Stirling, to be saddened yet more by the news that Curry, his gentle melancholy fool, had died in Edinburgh of the pestilence. But, though James mourned him, there was more talk at Court of Sir John Ramsay's marriage to Mistress Kennedy. And about that James had nothing to say. But presently he was overwhelmed by one of the darkest moods for years. The months seemed to echo into emptiness, like stones dropped down a well. He felt as if he had endured a lifetime's weariness when the long days came again.

During the summer of 1507 Bishop Elphinstone came to discuss the possibility of setting up a printing press in Edinburgh. James, welcoming the Bishop with real pleasure, was the more interested in the scheme he proposed because of the opportunity it offered for the Bishop's great compilation, the *Aberdeen Breviary*, to take the place of the Sarum version which had been used in Scotland so long.

" These men, my lord Bishop, are competent to print such a work? " James inquired.

" Oh, yes," said Bishop Elphinstone. " Chapman and Miller, who seek your royal licence, are skilled printers, who will make possible for Scotland all that Caxton has achieved at Westminster. The priests need no longer complain that they lack service books, nor the poets that their works perish with the parchment they are scrawled on."

" It shall be done, my lord," said James. " Get them to work first on your breviary and I will have them next try their skill on the poems of Master Dunbar. I like his impudence. The rascal shows neither fear nor favour."

The Bishop smiled as he rose to take his leave. " So you would hold the balance between sacred and profane? Well, so be it, my lord. May others do as much. It may be that we tap a spring of clear water when we set these men to work. But heaven knows what pollution it may encounter, or what storms swell it to fury on its way to the sea."

Who could tell, indeed, James wondered when the Bishop had gone. He pushed aside the official documents and picked up the latest broadsheet which Master John Murray now laid out for his attention.

" So the old reprobate has remembered my command to petition me in rhyme next time he lacks his pension."

" Doggerel, I fear, my lord," said Master John.

" Doggerel it may be, but he wheedles cunningly enough. Hark at this:

" ' *I am an auld horse, as ye knaw,*
Great Court Horse puttis me frae the straw,
To fang the fog by firth and fald,
Sir, let it never in town be tald,
That I should be ane Youllis yald.
I was never dautit in to stabell
My lyfe has been so miserabell
My hide to offer I am abell . . .'

Alas, poor fellow——" James tossed the *Petition of the Grey Horse*

across the table. " See this ballad is delivered to the Abbot of
Dunfermline, Master John, with a note to pay Dunbar's pension
forthwith."

" I will, my lord. And—er——"

" Aye, man? Out with it. Do not sit there mumbling. I have
a score of matters on my mind."

" My lord, the Treasurer was enquiring—is it your pleasure
that the priests should still continue to sing—for the Lady
Margaret Drummond in Dunblane? "

James sat silent, drawing stillness about him, it seemed, as
closely as the winding-sheet had once lapped his love. His face
was expressionless as granite, so that Master John Murray,
waiting, felt his own heart constrict with another man's pain.

" Yes," said James at last. In a toneless voice he added:
" That item is to be passed for payment—without question—as
long as I shall live."

" I will inform my Lord Treasurer, sir," said Master John
Murray gently. It was true, then, what people said. The King
had never got over it. He had often wondered, knowing how wild
his Highness had once been, and still was, they whispered. But
he had never dared to mention the matter till he received the
Lord Treasurer's direct command. " Is there anything further,
my lord? "

" Not to-day, John. Wait, send a page to ask the Queen's
Grace how she does, and say that I hope to walk in the garden
with her presently, if that should be her wish."

" I will, my lord."

Humming softly, Master John went to look for the Queen.
Himself a married man, comfortably established in the house in
the High Street of Edinburgh that had come from Lord Home,
doing well enough with the royal appointment and the office of
Depute Clerk Register, his interest in the Queen's first pregnancy
was the keener for the fact that his own wife, Isobel, was also
expecting a child, and near to the Queen's own time, if the talk
of early spring was anything to go by.

Isobel scolded him, sometimes, for leaving her alone, while
he rode after the King from Edinburgh to Stirling, from Stirling
to Linlithgow, and back to Holyrood again. If the King could

never bide in the bit, Isobel would say, for longer than it took
the smith to shoe a horse or a priest to mumble a Paternoster,
other people need not also forget that they had homes to enjoy.
But John ducked his head obstinately at her on these occasions.
" The King is what he is," he maintained. " And while heaven
grants me strength I'll not be far behind him."

James put his household more severely to the test than ever
that autumn, for he seemed too restless to remain more than a
few days, sometimes a few hours, in one place. At Whithorn
again, he donated a silver-gilt reliquary to the shrine of his
favourite saint, then returned up the west to inspect the work
being done on the manor house which the Earl of Lennox was
having remodelled for his second wife, Elizabeth, young daughter
of the Earl of Arran.

" How does it seem to you, my lord? "

" Well enough, Mathew, well enough," said James. " But
too far out of the world for me."

" You've changed," said Lennox. " Time was when you liked
nothing more than to be off to the wilds."

" I'm getting old, Mathew. And old folk need to have life
about them. Can you have me ferried across the Clyde to
Dumbarton, think you? "

" We'd be honoured if you'd bide——"

" I thank you, but I have too much on hand for idling,
more's the pity."

From Dumbarton, James called in at the Comptroller's new
residence at Craigbernard. There, too, no one could persuade
him to remain. Back to Edinburgh he went, leaving almost at
once for Stirling, Balquidder, and afterwards Strathfillan for a
day's hunting. But he would only accept one night's lodging from
the Earl of Argyll. Then on again, on again, on again, his horse's
hooves pounding out the miles by sandy track or gravel road, up
the steep tracks, between the passes, to Kingussie, Inverness,
Beauly, and Tain. There for a little while quiet came back to
him. He spent two days at the shrine. Then on again, by Ding-
wall to Inverness, forcing himself to Darnaway to see how the
servants were caring for his son's property. Strange it was, more
than strange to see the place again, with memories of Janet

everywhere, and to wonder, as he sat over the meal that was so
quiet without her gift of setting them all laughing, where she
was now.

The marriage with Ramsay hadn't lasted. She was back with
Angus again, they said. No fool like an old fool, James told
himself angrily. Angus again. So that old score wasn't yet settled.
Angus had not crossed his path for years, keeping to his earth in
Rothesay, the old fox, and letting his sons work their way back
into his favour. George and William now held nearly all the
Angus lands. The old man had only retained the life-rent of
what he fancied. James wondered why. Well, whether Janet was
with Angus or not, Darnaway was hers no longer. To-morrow
he'd walk the estate with his bailiff, and set them cutting down
timber, for the men working in the shipyards needed all they
could get.

Before he left for the south he climbed the turret stair and
worried over the little girl whom Janet had left behind, with her
nurse, and never a second thought, it seemed. She was well cared
for, but she coughed, drooping like a frosted plant. James, himself
something of a physician, sat with her thin wrist in his firm grasp
and wished the old days at Stirling back again, refusing to face
the thought that the forlorn little creature might die.

The days had drawn in again by the time he returned to
Edinburgh. He spent all the time he could spare with the Queen,
that winter, for she was both fretful and frightened as she grew
heavier, and had to give up dancing and hunting on the midwife's
advice. The Court spent Christmas and New Year at Holyroodhouse, there was some fine jousting in January, and James paid a
brief visit to Dumbarton early in February, to see how the shipbuilding there was progressing. Afterwards he hurried back to
Edinburgh to wait for news of the Queen, busying himself in
preparing the lists of those to be invited to the christening in such
good time that, through a clerk's blunder, the Earl of Arran,
whose position as James's heir would be so drastically affected,
actually received his summons before the child was born. But
on the 21st of February, a breathless lady-in-waiting, first with
the news, was rewarded with an exuberant embrace, a hundred
French crowns and a silver-gilt cup which James snatched from

the nearest dresser to pledge his son's health. A dance was held at Holyroodhouse in honour of the occasion, and the over-anticipated christening of the infant Prince took place two days after his birth.

But James's attention was soon diverted from the clamour of rejoicing by anxiety for the Queen's health. Her confinement had been a prolonged one, and had left her, it seemed, almost lifeless. James received the physician's reports with real terror. Could it be that heaven meant to exact retribution for his wild loving from his innocent wife? The burden of guilt which had alternately weighed him down and provoked him to further excesses since boyhood, came on him with redoubled sorrow now, driving him in frantic penitence to make his usual pilgrimage to Whithorn on foot, to the consternation of those expected to accompany him, who could scarcely hope to ride while the King walked, and were only slightly relieved when James reluctantly consented to modify his first intention to go barefoot.

Always happier in action, James at least enjoyed his journey. At thirty-five, he was perfectly capable of tramping twenty or thirty miles a day, and only allowed himself a break when he wore his shoes through and had to have them re-soled by a wayside cobbler who was almost too overcome by the honour conferred on him to handle his tools. The plight of his stouter companions caused him amusement, but obtained them no mercy. Limping and cursing, some fell by the wayside, while others un-obtrusively begged lifts behind other wayfarers' saddles. But the King made the entire journey, by way of Crawford, Newton-Stewart, Wigtown, Dumfries and Lochmaben, on foot and within the fortnight. Returning to Holyroodhouse, weathered, leaner and full of confidence in the saint whose intercession he had im-plored, he found the Queen not only recovered, but in a most unwontedly meek frame of mind, ready to listen to all his ad-ventures, even to agree to make a pilgrimage of thanksgiving with him as soon as her doctors would allow.

Her gratitude for his care of her touched him. While she was still too thankful for the bliss of recovery to be either petulant or peevish, her unaccustomed simplicity went to his heart. King and Queen of Scots were closer than they had ever been before, perhaps closer than they were ever to be again, during the days when James, awed by the apparent intervention of St. Ninian, watched over his wife and believed in heaven's forgiveness.

Patrick Hepburn, meanwhile, had been deputed to greet the special envoys from His Holiness on their arrival at the Border, assisted by various lords and gentlemen, among them Sir John Ramsay. James was sorry for the fellow, who looked bleaker than ever. Was that because Janet had left him? Though it had nothing to do with him any more, James felt suddenly furious at the thought of her back with Angus again.

The Pope's envoys, splendidly escorted, bore the greetings of Pope Julius, together with the magnificent sword and purple cap of maintenance which His Holiness conferred annually on one of the princes of Christendom with the title of Protector of the Christian religion. James received these tokens of favour with suitable meekness, but considerable reserve. Both he and every-one else present at the impressive ceremony in the chapel of Holyroodhouse were well aware that the appropriate response would be an immediate offer of allegiance to the League sponsored by Pope Julius against France. But this, as he had repeatedly told the Papal ambassadors, he was not prepared to do. He therefore asked the envoys to convey his gratitude and humble duty to the Holy Father, blandly admired the beautiful weapon with the figures of Peter and Paul and the name of the august donor in gold letters, the dolphins and acorns of the guard, the *repoussé* work of the scabbard. But though he sent the envoys on their way with a magnificent present, bidding them farewell with most aggravating good humour, he offered, on the other hand, no concession whatever.

After Easter James was engrossed by the preparations for a most gorgeous and expensive tournament to be held in Edinburgh, but his pleasure in it was marred by the news brought by Adam Hepburn, the Earl of Bothwell's eldest son, that because his father had fallen sick he must wait on the King in his stead.

"Never have I known him take to his bed unless he was so sore stricken that he could not stand," said James in distress.

"The leeches say, my lord, it is a fever from an old wound."

"I must presently set off with the Queen to give thanks for

her recovery to St. Ninian. I will also make an offering for your
father and expect better news thereafter. Tell him I have never
known St. Ninian fail."

"I will, my lord," said young Adam Hepburn.

But this time St. Ninian was less successful. First the Earl of
Bothwell was reported better but then it seemed he was worse,
till in September the news was grave enough to set James riding
furiously towards Hailes Castle on the great skewbald stallion
which so few men dared handle, let alone ride.

He found the Earl of Bothwell propped up among pillows in
the monumental oaken bed, its posts carved with every sort of
Biblical monster, including a goatish similitude of the devil,
popularly supposed to discourage the attentions of the original,
which his first wife, Joanna, had brought with her on their
marriage. In spite of young Adam's warning, James caught his
breath at the change in the friend whose towering presence had
sheltered him as a lad and companioned him as a man. Now, he
lay back on his pillows, inert as a felled tree, his chest heaving with
every breath, his nose pinched between gaunt cheeks, his mouth
agape for air.

"Why, Patrick, this is a sorry sight. I should have been here
long since, had I but known——"

"Time enough, time enough," the sick man said, turning his
head on the pillows to summon his son. "Wine, Adam, for the
King.... And—and throw the shutter wide ... I ... cannot ...
breath...."

"I will, sir." The young man hurried out.

"You should not trouble," said James.

"Nay ... but I'll be glad of it too," said Patrick, with the
ghost of his old smile. "My voice creaks these days like an
unoiled door. Tell me how things are ... since I've been here.
Is the ... Queen well?"

"Yes," said James, absently. Could St. Ninian who had
healed the Queen be ready to let Patrick die?

"And the ... Prince?"

"He cries too much, it seems to me," said James, as Adam
returned, bearing a great silver-gilt drinking-cup, and knelt to
present it first to James.

"Tell me what I have missed . . ." whispered the Earl of Bothwell. "Adam says Alexander . . . has gone to further his studies in Padua."

"It seemed best," said James briefly. "Next year I shall send Moray after him."

Patrick nodded.

"He was to have gone sooner," James said, "but he begged to be allowed to remain till Master Damien had made good his boast that he would gird himself with wings and fly from Stirling's walls."

The sick man beckoned his son to hold the wine again to his lips. "That I am sorry . . . I did not see. Did he make such a venture indeed?"

"He could not avoid it, once he had claimed such skill. Alexander gave him no peace, till he stood on the Castle walls, high above the crowd below."

"He . . . stepped off——?"

"Or was pushed," said James. "I should not care to say which. He seemed from far below to hover, I must own, for long enough to say a Paternoster. Then, as the crowd roared, he crumpled, flapped his wings, and fell."

"Killed . . . was he?"

James shook his head. "Because he fell into the midden he did no more than break his leg."

Patrick Hepburn wheezed appreciation. "What . . . then?"

James grinned. "He railed at those who ran to pick him up because they had given him hen's feathers and stolen the eagle's feathers he had meant to use. For the hen, desiring the dunghill, brought him low, where the eagle would have borne him through the skies."

Patrick Hepburn's grey face creased. "Eh, the old tod . . ." A fit of coughing shook him as he tried to laugh. "The . . . old . . . tod. . . . He'd have an answer ready . . . for the very porter at hell's. . . . yett . . ."

James laughed with him. "He owes the hen something, though. Had he fallen elsewhere he must have broken his neck. Dunbar had the alehouses roaring with the song he made of it, curse the fellow. I would stop his pension for his impudence could

I ever keep from laughter at his wit. The Abbot's back at his furnace and little the worse."

Bothwell's chuckle was as dry as the crackle of autumnal leaves underfoot. " Tell . . . me more," he whispered. " I weary, lying here . . . for news of it all."

" The great tournament went well," said James. " A splendid sight. Arran fought the French knight they call the Chevalier Blanc, who jousts as if he had been daubed in whitewash. Yet Arran sent him sprawling. I had the fancy, Patrick, as I watched, to mock him and his peerless lady by reversing all things next year and riding myself, black-armoured, to defend a lady as black as one of the Moor lassies that wait on my daughter Margaret in the Castle."

Young Adam Hepburn, standing shyly by the side of his father's bed, grinned delightedly, but the sick man shook his head. " Madcap notions still. . . . Will nothing sober you, my lord? " He turned laboriously towards his son. " Offer . . . the King another . . . draught. Then leave us . . ." As the door closed he murmured: " How does the little lady Margaret? Is she . . . beautiful as her mother was? "

James shook his head. " That she will never be," he said slowly. " But she is a sweet and gentle child. Too young for marriage yet, but already I have it in mind. Catherine I must dower first. I thought of Morton——"

" My first wife . . . was of that family. . . ."

They were silent for a while. Bothwell seemed rigid on his pillows, arms outstretched, fingers flexed on the counterpane as he fought for breath.

" I've wearied you," James said.

Patrick Hepburn slowly moved his head to and fro. With his eyes closed his lips formed round the monosyllable he had not breath enough to expel. As James leant forward and laid his hand over the restless fingers, the sick man's eyes opened, astonishingly blue in the pallor of his face.

" I doubt . . . you'll be needing . . . another Lord High . . . Admiral."

" You became Lord High Admiral when I became King," James said vehemently. " We both took office for life."

" Eh, but, that's . . . just my . . . meaning, lad. . . ." said Patrick
Hepburn. The lids fell again over the tired eyes. The breath
hissed between his lips. He was asleep, as James crept out
of the chamber, to make his way sombrely down the stairs and
bid the family farewell. A fortnight later, Adam, Earl of Bothwell, came to Holyrood to inform the King that his father was
dead.

James received the news with real grief, still shocked, as he
was, by the fact which his recent visit had brought home to him,
that Patrick had unobtrusively become an old man. As he sat
listening to the new Earl's halting description of the final scene
at Hailes, James kept hearing Patrick's whispered warning:
" You'll be needing another Lord High Admiral. . . ."

True enough. Who should it be? Arran would have been
his first choice, as Sir Andrew Wood had guessed. But Arran
was not available. He had been detained with his brother as they
returned from France by King Henry of England, who refused to
let them go free until they had sworn to persuade James to
abandon the French alliance and observe perpetual peace with
England instead.

" They defied him, most properly," James told the Queen,
who with the Bishop of Moray, was trying to persuade James
to avoid a quarrel with King Henry at all costs. " How can
your father ask it? He knows we are pledged not to oppose
France."

But the Queen, who was pregnant again and peevish, merely
tossed her head. " That you can scarcely expect me to know.
Why not do as he says? Then we can have James and Patrick
home for the festival."

" Because," James repeated, forcing patience on himself, " I
have undertaken to enter into no obligations against France."

" But, my lord," objected the Queen, " did you not say King
Louis was annoyed because you had not yet renewed the alliance?
Are you not free, then, to do what my father wishes? "

" King Louis," explained James, " wishes me to be friendly
only with France. King Henry wishes me to bind myself to
England. If I do what your father wishes he will believe himself
free to make war on France. If I join France, Louis will invade

Italy. So I shall serve the peace of Europe best by reassuring neither."

"He who seeks to hold the balance between rivals for power, my lord," put in the Bishop of Moray, "often finds himself abandoned by both."

James ran his hands through his thick hair in a distracted gesture. "So you, too, would seek to make me abandon my old allies?"

The Bishop of Moray shook his head. He was too diplomatic to anger James by a direct answer. "I ask you only, my lord, to consider the expediency of listening to your father-in-law, for the sake of the health of the Queen's Grace, and the satisfaction of His Holiness."

"I will not be bribed, even by His Holiness——"

"James!" The Queen covered her ears. "To speak so is sinful——"

"Nor under threat of the detention of my subjects," said James defiantly.

The Bishop of Moray cleared his throat. "Since it seems that King Henry may propose a personal meeting, my lord, had we not better defer further discussion until we learn more?"

"I will agree to nothing till my kinsmen are released," said James. "But if they are still prisoners at Yule we will seek to make merry without them. King Louis is also sending an ambassador. And I shall welcome the Sieur d'Aubigny, that peerless knight, a great deal more gladly than the English Dr. West."

There the matter remained. But Yule was not merry, for the baby Prince sickened over the festival. His wan flicker of life dwindled in the bitter days of January, till, just a year after the exuberant celebration of his birth, he died, and Scottish bitterness increased as King Henry still refused to release Arran, who had become once more James's heir. For during the summer which followed the Queen's second child died within a few days of her birth.

The sand of European politics shifted again that year. Pope Julius, changing his tactics, now joined France and the Emperor and persuaded Spain to ally herself with them against England.

But James, who had steadily refused to abandon France to isolation, also refused to see England isolated in her turn. He believed that the members of the new League of Cambrai would hesitate to attack England while King Henry had his support.

Scotland might be only a small country. But she was united under a King who had not only made himself loved, but spent the last ten years in building up a formidable navy, manned by such famous sailors as Sir Andrew Wood and the Bartons. James was fairly sure that while he refused to join any aggressive alliance, Henry VII would be much too cautious to take the first step which would bring Scotland into the field against him. This belief proved correct. But unfortunately King Henry considered it necessary to continue to hold James's heir as a sort of hostage. He had not forgotten the Warbeck affair.

In the spring James welcomed the great French knight, Sir Bernard Stuart d'Aubigny, only to be grieved by his unexpected death while the tournament arranged to welcome him was actually in progress. James, as planned, had perversely appeared as the Black Knight, in defence of the honour of the gorgeously dressed Black Lady about whom Dunbar wrote one of his more candid poems.

And then, once more, the pattern shifted. In April, 1509, King Henry died. James brought the news hesitantly to the Queen, afraid that it might have an adverse effect on her condition, since she was pregnant again. But it was never possible to predict what effect anything would have on Margaret Tudor. Almost in the instant of murmuring the appropriate prayer for her father's soul, she looked up at James with wide, excited eyes.

" My lord, I remember now. My father promised to leave me all my mother's jewels! "

CHAPTER TWENTY-TWO

THE canons of Holyrood paced from the cloister to the Abbey for their devotions, two by two, hoods hiding all but their nose-tips, hands clasped within their wide sleeves, eyes lowered beads chiming softly in time with their measured steps. From the morning sunshine they passed into the timeless shadow of the Abbey, greeted by the subtle waft of incense and a great surge of music from the organ-loft. Following the precise routine which varied with the festivals as the movement of the earth indicates the seasons of the years, the men whose lives were sheltered by their celibacy as by the great grey wing of the Abbey stones, knelt in their appointed places and the service began.

Like a broad river it proceeded, sonorous repetition breaking in waves of sound against the walls which three centuries had mellowed, their gravity rebuking the blatant newness of the King's adjacent Palace as a war-scarred veteran's steadfastness rebukes, for the discerning, the brash defiance of an elegant page.

" *Credo* . . ."

The rest was lost in a roar so sudden and so shattering that the chanting brethren fancied the Day of Judgment had overtaken them unawares. Some flung themselves on their knees, others made for the shelter of the splendid tombs commemorating former patrons, others tripped on the chancel steps or over the skirts of their habits as they fled. But a few held their ground, turning to each other with head shakings and frowns. One old canon, too hard of hearing to be able to make head or tail of the uproar, prodded his neighbour, his voice querulous among the rolling echoes.

" Have the brethren turned Gadarene swine? "

Outside the Abbey, startled pigeons clattered out of the dove-cots, runaway hooves drummed on the cobbles, shutters slammed back from the Palace windows. Within, the old canon cupped his hand behind his ear to catch the reply bawled by his neighbour.

" It is but the King, shooting a greater gun than ever in the Close."

The old man sighed. " Can no one persuade him to loose his infernal engines elsewhere? " he demanded peevishly. The scattered ranks of worshippers began to re-form, the organ emitted a series of uncertain squawks, as the shaken nerves of the organist were brought under control, and the service proceeded, gathering its former momentum by degrees.

In the bright morning outside James stood with a still-smoking length of tow in his hand, blinking and laughing, while Hans, the master gunner who had brought his craft to Scotland from the Low Countries, still clutched the sleeve by which he had dragged his patron out of danger.

" I ask your Grace's pardon, but dot is not wise, what you do," he explained. " To stand wis the nose as near ze touch-hole as if you smelt ze pretty flowers, zat is to smell trouble instead. *Gott sie dank*, I haf time to pull you avay! Phoo . . ." The good man let out a sigh of relief and knuckled the acrid fragments from the explosion out of his eyes.

" You are right, Hans," said James penitently. " It was so great a moment that I forgot. These guns of yours are better than any we have yet had in Scotland. I shall have a foundry installed at the Castle up yonder. We shall need guns by the score for the *Great Michael*; she shall be the most dreadful man-of-war afloat. I shall have such guns mounted also on the *Margaret* and the *James* and as many of the rest as can support the shock of such a broadside."

" I shall be very happy, sir," said the little Flemish gunner whose craft had pocked his goblin face with charcoal, and seared his bare arms from the flash, while his eyes were sunk like currants in pastry by long exposure to the glare of the furnaces from which the molten metal poured. " I am proud, sir, to bring to Scotland what skill I haf in the new warfare zat changes ze world."

" I wonder," said James, as much to himself as to the bandy-legged little man beside him, " how much change it will bring after all? "

" It vill make you ze greatest King of all Christendom for sure," said Hans. " If only you will take ze chance. So many hate it all. Ze horses bolt, ze knights are stricken down wizzout ze chance to strike——"

" I like that no more than they," said James. " Wrongly used, the great guns may yet mar all. At sea, they are best, though they serve well enough to batter down castle walls. Held in reserve, they may change the course of a battle. But chivalry must still challenge chivalry, knights ride against each other in fair combat——"

" Ach, sir," the little Flemish gunner blurted out, " so do not ze ozzers say. To win, yes, but how, they care not, nowadays. Chivalry? Bah, it is finished, I hear them say. Indeed, yes."

" It shall not be finished while I live," said James. " This shooting is but a new pastime. The fleet shall have guns. They will mar nothing there. At sea, knights cannot fight as if they were in the lists. But the great battle must still be fought by the mounted knights, with the guns used as the archers used to be."

" As you say, sir," Hans capitulated. But he sighed.

" Now as to this new hand culverin," said James, " I have a fancy to use it for sport as well as for warfare. But it is too heavy to be raised without support. When I took it to the mountains to stalk a deer, I lost the quarry because the boy that bore it went sprawling. Make me a lighter weapon, Hans, that needs less gear to go with it. A man laden with a great bag for gunpowder and as heavy a belt for pellets, with the culverin itself and the rest to set it on, is weary by the time he has dragged it all uphill, and longs for the days when he had to bear no more than his bow and a score of arrows."

" I shall see to that, sir," said Hans.

" I fared better in the rowing boats from which we shot at the fowls in the Forth," said James. " But I shall need another powder horn to replace the one lost overboard. And see that a keg of gunpowder is delivered to Holyroodhouse. But it had best be bestowed in the cloisters. The Queen has no fancy for it indoors."

" Her Highness, she is a wise lady, sir," grinned Hans.

" Ladies do not care for firearms," James admitted rather sadly as he went indoors. He liked to share his enthusiasms, and his growing collection of culverins was definitely unpopular, not only with the Queen and her household, but also with all but the youngest of his friends.

In his privy chamber, Master Paniter and Master John Murray both awaited him, one at either end of the long table piled with charters and petitions, accounts for the planks and cables, the tar, poles, chains and other gear supplied to the ship-wrights for the *Great Michael*, which James always liked to inspect before passing for payment; samples of sailcloth and hemp, a set of hawk's bells and an old glove; oddments which his secretaries

T

preserved with care among the official documents, knowing that in spite of his unfailing delight in all that was new and splendid, James had also a great fidelity to his oldest possessions, so that to throw out even the most battered object of his affection was the surest way to provoke him to demand it, haling everyone from his duties till the Palace was in an uproar.

"Is there word from Alexander?" James demanded.

Master Paniter sighed. "No, my lord."

"The boy never writes," said James.

Master Paniter cleared his throat to give himself time to formulate a reassuring phrase. "You will remember, my lord, that he explained some months since that his letters so constantly miscarried that he had come to think it not worth the time taken from his studies to write more."

James grinned. "Were I a lad with so many other occupations that the task of letter-writing was beyond me I doubt if I should have been able to find a better excuse."

"Yet he does study, my lord," said Master Paniter, hastening to the defence of his pupil. "Have we not the report of Master Erasmus, who finds him a lad of excellent understanding and most brilliant promise?"

"That is so," James agreed. "And at least it will not be long before he need write letters no longer. You are satisfied with your position in St. Andrews, for which Alexander begged so hard, I take it?"

"Yes, my lord. Having had the misfortune to arouse the disapproval of Bishop Elphinstone, I was glad to leave Aberdeen."

"I have seldom known the good Bishop angered against a man of mine," James said in a puzzled way.

"Bishop Elphinstone is getting on in years, my lord," said Paniter somewhat smugly. "His judgment—it may be . . ." His vaguely deprecatory gestures indicated that only the simultaneous failure of all his faculties could make the Bishop of Aberdeen unwilling to have Patrick Paniter as his archdeacon.

James let it pass. The passionate rivalry for preferment to the higher ecclesiastical offices was such a commonplace that it did not even shock him. "He approaches his eightieth year, I understand," murmured Master Paniter. "So it is only natural that

his ideas should be—somewhat definite—shall we say? I shall
be very happy to serve under my lord St. Andrews on his return."

" His return. Ah, yes . . ." James allowed his attention to be
diverted from the possible failure of the venerable Bishop's
faculties to a more immediate prospect. " What arrangements are
being made? I left them to you, Master Paniter, I believe? "

" I have a note here from a merchant now returned from
Padua where he saw my lord St. Andrews. He intends, it seems,
to return through Flanders, accompanied by Patrick Hume,
laird of Fastcastle. It is most probable that they will cross to
Leith."

" Then I will await him in Edinburgh," said James. " Is
there anything further? "

Master John Murray, who had left his place at the rising
hubbub of voices from the ante-room to see who were hoping for
an interview with the King, now returned. " My lord of Moray,
newly back from England, is without."

" And glad I am to hear it," said James. " Be good enough
to request his lordship to come in without delay."

But the Bishop of Moray, had returned from England in no
amiable mood. Complacently convinced that his good offices at
the time of the Queen's journey to Scotland would not be forgotten, he had journeyed south to convey James's congratulations
to King Henry VIII on his recent accession, as well as the personal
request of the Queen, his sister, for the dispatch of the jewels
which her father had promised. But his reception had been unexpectedly casual, and the memory of his interview with the
young King of England still rankled as he followed Master
Murray into the presence of the King of Scots.

" I am delighted to see you, my lord," said James, " I have
lacked my astute counsellor too long. From all accounts, the
new King of England is well disposed towards us. While you were
journeying, we received his formal ratification of the pact made
with his father. Arran is to be released forthwith, and he sends
us a gracious greeting."

The Bishop of Moray raised his eyebrows. " When I said that
I had been honoured by your commission to receive the jewels
left to the Queen's Grace by her father, the late King Henry—

God rest his soul—the present King of England laughed in my face," he said grimly.

"What?" James was incredulous. "His embassy reported him as so friendly, so gracious. . . ."

"So they would wish him to be, as any man of sense must. I formed a very different impression of the Eighth King Henry."

James began to scribble idly on the parchment before him with a spoiled quill, drawing little pictures of the strange animals from overseas which he kept for his amusement. "What impression did you form, my lord?" he murmured.

The Bishop of Moray's cold eyes narrowed. He was a proud man, whose personal ambition had been whetted rather than slaked by his rise from the position of a mere clerk to one within sight of the highest office in the Scottish Church. Now that the death of the Archbishop of Glasgow had removed one of the King's trusted counsellors, and old age must surely soon dispose of Bishop Elphinstone, who had been even more influential, he had high hopes of his own future. A less zealous financier than the Bishop of Caithness, he was more avid for power, and his recent rebuff had now disposed him to swing all his influence, which had formerly been in favour of the English alliance, against England and towards France. So he spoke with nicely calculated malice, but in sufficiently moderate terms not to risk a reaction. He never made the mistake of underrating those he served any more than those who opposed him.

"The young King Henry," he said at last, "is as ambitious as his father, but without his patience. He is lavish, but also greedy as a child which snatches the sweetmeats from the table without waiting for his elders to be served. He is quick to anger and rash in judgment. He has charm, wit, and gaiety. And he is an excellent horseman. I saw him joust——"

"How did he fare in the lists? I wish we might have the chance of an encounter," said James quickly.

"My lord," said the Bishop, "it seemed to me that he would not hesitate. He is so eager for glory that already he is choosing his allies."

"And his enemies?"

"That is in little doubt, my lord, I fear. Can any young

English King, straining like a warhorse against the curb of reason, fail to dream of adding other laurels to those of Creçy, Poitiers, and Agincourt? "

" We must hinder that," said James gravely. " You, my lord, who have seen King Henry for yourself, shall lead an embassy to His Holiness imploring him to command the nations of Christendom to keep the peace."

" Most gladly, my lord," said the Bishop of Moray. He was more than willing to make a diplomatic journey to Rome.

But the return of Alexander presently took priority of all other considerations. For James received news of his son's departure from Padua soon after the Bishop's return to Scotland, then of his arrival in Flanders. But the exact time of his homecoming depended on so many uncertain factors that it inevitably took James by surprise. He was again in conference with the Bishop of Moray when Master Paniter's arrival, in a state of considerable excitement, brought James to his feet, sending parchments scattering as he glimpsed a tall young man over his secretary's shoulder.

" Alexander! I had no news of your landing. You come as unheralded as the blessed angels. Why, how changed you are. . . ."

" Yet, my lord, how much the same." Alexander knelt to kiss his father's hand with the grace of a practised courtier. At seventeen, he seemed at first sight to have so little in common with the stocky boy who had left Scotland in *The Treasurer* that James was conscious of unexpected loss. This was a young man to whom he would presently be devoted. But he had been devoted, too, to the mischievous boy who had brought Master Damien sackfuls of eagles' feathers and rolled on the ground with mirth at the sight of the draggled figure which the spectators had dragged from Stirling Castle's dunghill.

" Can you forgive me for the letters that went astray? " Alexander asked. " I swear, sir, I wrote them. But those I entrusted with their delivery . . ."

James laughed. " Now I know that you are indeed the same." Linking his arm with that of the son who was now as tall as himself, he drew him to the long settle where they could talk in comfort.

" I have been young, lad, myself, not so long ago. Tell me
how you fared in Padua. . . ."

The Bishop of Moray, forgotten by both father and son,
surveyed them coldly. Young Alexander, as the nominal Archbishop of St. Andrews, stood between him and the highest, most
coveted position in the Scottish Church. There was, as far as he
could tell, nothing he could do about it. And yet, the wheel of
fortune, according to the poets, turned as the fickle goddess willed.
A touch of her hand transformed the whole scene for those who,
like himself, knew how to watch the movements of her wheel,
perhaps even to give it just a touch—with a whisper, an appropriate gift—to set it going in the right direction.

James was delighted with Alexander. His zest for life matched
his own. All business was at a standstill. The Bishop of Moray,
scarcely noticed, took his leave, and the secretaries were dismissed
so that James might listen to Alexander's description of life in an
Italian University, with its furious feuds and incessant intrigues,
the roaring gaiety and sober learning that clashed and blended
with the singing, stinking beauty of a medieval Italian city under
the burning blue southern sky.

" They would rather rejoice than eat, I believe," said
Alexander. " They stage great singing spectacles in the streets
of saints' days——"

" We must have such musicians in Scotland," James said.
" I have already foreigners in my service."

" Aye, that I know. Lombards, Flemings, and Frenchmen
besides. Leith was a babel of tongues when I landed, and the
coast is a spider's web of poles and ropes surrounding new hulls.
Are we to have the greatest navy in Christendom? I have seen
nothing like it."

" I will take you to see it now," said James, delighted by the
idea. " You will find that we have not kicked our heels since you
left Scotland. Besides the docks at the Pool of Erth I have caused
a new haven to be constructed on the seashore hard by the
Chapel of St. Nicholas to the north of the town of Leith. Here
the greatest ship ever built in Scotland is on the stocks. I have sent
to Flanders for guns, to France for rigging, to Norway and
Denmark as well as our own forests for wood. Copper and tin are

bespoken for the foundry at the Castle. That also you must see. . . ."

"My lord," said Alexander, "against whom do you think to make war?"

"Against none," said James. "That is to say, unless war is forced upon me. But he that shakes the sword often has the less need to use it."

"Perhaps, my lord," said Alexander dubiously.

"Let the fame of our fleet get about and we shall be able to assist our friends and defy all our enemies in Christendom," said James. "I have set myself to build a score of great three-masters such as the *Margaret* and the *James*, and the new vessel still on the stocks. These shall carry cannon to affright the world. I will show you my culverins. I have half a dozen elegant pieces. They rig me up canvas targets to riddle with pellets on the lawns behind the Palace. You shall have a culverin," said James.

"My lord," said Alexander, responding to his father's enthusiasm with the memory of an earlier craze, "how fares Master Damien, these days?"

"He still seeks the fifth essence," said James. "And if the potions he gives me from time to time are any indication, he may not be altogether wasting his time. After drinking his distillation, I have certainly felt a new man."

"So Master Dunbar claimed to feel in the alehouse," murmured Alexander.

"This is no mere drunken delusion."

"Yet, as I remember, it is aqua-vitae that Master John distils——"

"Till all its vulgar associations with the flesh are lost," James protested, "and it ministers to the spirit within, restoring it to its first youth, prolonging life, warding off death itself. . . ."

"So I believe some say," murmured Alexander, who seemed to have caught a certain scepticism from his master Erasmus. "And what of the earthier enterprise of making gold?"

"Master Damien has not so far succeeded in producing it in any quantity," James admitted. "It may be, as he maintains, that he has not been provided in the first instance with enough." He glanced sharply at Alexander. "Why do you smile?"

" At such a nimble excuse, my lord."

" Come," said James, " I will take you to see the foundry where they cast the guns."

Alexander was relieved to find that the work done by the melters and shipwrights now interested his father more than the doubtful labours of Master Damien. And James was delighted with the son whose former promise had been so marvellously fulfilled. Intelligent he had always been, and his affectionate nature, after all, neither distance nor diversity of experience could change. It was vexing only that he could not name Alexander his heir, for the new baby, who had been named Arthur, out of courtesy to his English uncle, died within a few months of Alexander's return, so that once again, with fresh clouds gathering in the sphere of international diplomacy, James was without a legitimate son. He showed Alexander all the favour he might, even making him Chancellor of Scotland in 1510, and indicated his genuine desire for peace by sending the Bishop of Moray to plead with the Pope not to force James into opposition by joining the Emperor and the King of Spain against King Louis of France.

As far as the Bishop of Moray was concerned, the result was not altogether unsatisfactory. He failed to impress Pope Julius, but he ingratiated himself with King Louis, and associated himself successfully with the ambitious young man who bore his dead father's title as Duke of Albany, and was now watching the Scottish situation, from a safe distance, in France. But Pope Julius proceeded with his intention of forming a so-called Holy League, the members of which were himself, the rulers of Spain and Venice, and the Emperor. Finally, he withdrew the title of "most Christian King" from King Louis, and dangled it before young King Henry of England, who needed no further inducement to join the formidable alliance again of France. Only one thing now held Henry from fulfilling the request of his Spanish father-in-law. James had refused to be cajoled into abandoning his traditional ally, and all the reports reaching Henry from Scotland extolled her fleet, her artillery, her country's unity in devotion to her King, till even Henry hesitated from attacking France until he could be sure Scotland would not attack him.

As the tension increased, James speeded up the work on the

Great Michael, gave Arran again charge of the fleet, entrusted his cousin Albany in France with a conciliatory mission to the Emperor, received envoys from the Pope and the Kings of England, France and Spain, and hoped that time, which had recently broken so many alliances, would set the members of the Holy League quarrelling among themselves. His pilgrimages were intermittent these days, for there was little time to spare from the demands of his own counsellors and the foreign ambassadors who glared at each other in the ante-chamber and tried to elbow each other aside. The Queen was pregnant again, sick and out of sorts, so that her grudge against her brother constantly fretted her mind.

" James, is it not monstrous that my brother will not give me the jewels my father left me? "

" It is monstrous indeed," James agreed. Her white, peaked face stirred him to compunction. He was gentle with her as she clung to him.

" James, make Harry give up my jewels. . . ."

" I will do all I can, my love. I have spoken plainly to the English ambassador."

" But the jewels have not come."

" Not yet."

" Then you must do more. . . ."

News came that Andrew Barton had been set on by Sir Thomas Howard, the English Lord High Admiral, and one of the sons of the Earl of Surrey, in his ship, *The Lion*, and killed in the subsequent action. An English Warden was murdered by a Scottish family on the Marches in revenge for the murder of their father by three Englishmen. French ships were boarded by English sailors off the coast of Scotland. English ships, in their turn, were plundered by Scots. As 1512 began the international situation was rising to the boil. If but a few sticks were thrust under the pot it would boil over. James was well aware of it as he rode to Newhaven for supper aboard the *Great Michael*, now afloat in her full splendour, equipped to carry thirty-five great guns and three hundred lesser ones, manned by a hundred and twenty gunners, a crew of three hundred seamen and a thousand men-at-arms, with the King's royal standard and the great blue and white banner of St. Andrew cracking in the snell wind.

At Stirling they were casting more great guns. At Edinburgh Castle the foundry was working night and day. James returned to Edinburgh to receive three rival ambassadors, sent the Spaniard away with his reiterated refusal to join the Holy League, warned the Englishman that nothing would persuade him to break with France, and reassured De La Motte, by consenting at last to a treaty by which Scotland and France bound themselves to come to each other's defence if either should be attacked by England, and to undertake not to make a separate peace in any war which ensued. While the treaty was being prepared in Edinburgh James first learned that the Queen had borne him a son at Linlithgow, then that King Henry had ordered Surrey to call the North of England to arms. So the Queen's household, rejoicing over the birth of a prince whose grip on life seemed stauncher than that of his brothers, presently became aware of the cold threat of war as they might have felt, sitting round a cheerful hearth, a sudden draught from an opening door.

" My jewels . . . I want my jewels. . . ." The Queen's high, fretful voice seemed always in James's ears.

Angus was back at Court again, after his years of seclusion; greyer, graver, and warier than he had been. He shook his head over the frantic talk, the crescendo of preparation, and the gathering possibility of war. Experience had saddened and embittered him. His new marriage had been childless, and though he gave out that he had returned from Rothesay to order his affairs, James had heard enough of his new association with Janet to fancy, with furious resentment, that he detected triumph in the Earl's cold eyes.

A number of Scottish leaders were now beginning to consider war inevitable. Arran's imprisonment, King Henry's hostility to France, the bonds of tradition, all made them welcome the Treaty of Edinburgh, by which James bound himself to come to the help of King Louis, if he were attacked by England. King Henry's sortie against Navarre was, most people now believed, a rehearsal for a full-scale war. And so, with her word pledged, Scotland's course was at least clear. Up and down the country men began to furbish their weapons, to gather and drill retainers, and leave with their womenfolk instructions for the management of their affairs against their victorious return.

James had worked for peace because peace was necessary to Scotland. He knew it was still necessary in 1513. But events likely to precipitate him into war were now gathering the momentum of a landslide. In February, Pope Julius died, and Leo, one of the Medici, succeeded him. In March Henry VIII sent his envoy, Dr. West, to try to influence James. Dr. West also took the opportunity of seeing the Queen.

With James, he failed completely, though James was ready to offer any concession within reason if Henry would keep the peace with France. But since this was just what Henry had determined not to do, such a condition produced a deadlock which West did all in his power to break. James wanted peace with England? Yes, undoubtedly. But not at the cost of a breach with France. West threatened him with the disapproval of the new Pope. James retorted that even His Holiness should not keep him from the course dictated by his conscience. If his dearest brother, King Henry, would forgo his war with France, he would have no more loyal and loving friend than the King of Scots. But if war with France was inevitable, King Henry must be prepared to encounter Scotland too. All West could obtain was James's promise that he would not invade England without a formal declaration of war.

But when James sought out the Queen after West had taken his leave of her, she was almost speechless with distress, and her ladies surrounded him with sniffs, and shudders, and tears, their consternation breaking out at last in a series of panic-struck wails.

" What will befall us? "

" Sweet heaven . . ."

" Blessed saints . . ."

" Mother of God, what will become of us all? "

Running to James in terror, the Queen hid her face on his sleeve.

" Oh, my lord, my lord . . . I am afraid. . . ."

" Why, love, what ails you? " James put his arm round her, gentling her as he might have gentled a scared horse or a shivering hound. Leading her to a window-seat, out of earshot of the whispering, peering ladies, he took her hands and smiled. " Now tell me, why are you so afraid? "

" Dr. West dined with me, as you know . . ."

" Had I known that he would distress you, I would have forbidden it."

" Oh, my lord, I would you had. Yet at least—it gives me a chance to plead with you."

" Which is what he wished."

" It may be . . . but I must warn you—against Harry. You do not know him, and I do. Oh, my lord, he is terrible when he is crossed. As a child he would kill any animal that offended him, or strike his head against the wall if he were forbidden. He will never yield . . . I tell you . . . he will trample down whoever hinders him. He will never yield. Never . . . never . . . never . . ."

" Madam," said James, " no more will I."

CHAPTER TWENTY-THREE

THE blur of Flodden Edge loomed through the driving rain as the great army which had mustered so bravely on Edinburgh's Boroughmuir endured the sodden sequel of a wet September in Northumberland. All summer the diplomats had hurried to and fro. Some, such as Dr. West of England and de la Motte of France, had served their country's interests to the utmost of their power; others had been more self-seeking. With the Bishop of Moray, for instance, Scotland's future was a less anxious consideration than the rival possibilities offered by French gratitude and Papal favour; the solid value of the bishopric of Bourges must be set against the tantalising tassels of a shadowy Cardinal's hat. Deciding finally for the former, since King Louis was less likely to be able to evade his obligations than Pope Leo, the Bishop of Moray accepted the offer of Bourges and spent 1513 in France. It was, on the whole, likely to be safer than Scotland, since, if

James were victorious, all would be well. But if he were defeated, as the Bishop well knew, he would not care to return home alive.

In May James had sent Lord Drummond to King Henry with a letter requesting him to agree to a truce for just one year, in the hope that such a breathing-space might give the princes of Christendom time enough to resolve their differences sufficiently to ally themselves, as His Holiness hoped, against the graver menace of the Turk. But Henry, as his sister had warned James, was not one to endure opposition. And James had further stung his vanity by referring to King Louis as " the most Christian King," a title which Pope Julius had since conferred on Henry himself. Further, there was the change from Pope Julius to Pope Leo, which, as far as James was concerned, was from bad to worse. For Pope Julius had once had high hopes of James, but Pope Leo, getting his information from prejudiced English sources, considered his determination to defend France against the wolf-pack of the Papal allies evidence of an incorrigible disposition. And so James, who had, whatever his other faults, been a devoted son of Holy Church all his life, was excommunicated forthwith.

But Henry, in a halo of Papal approval, sailed with his fleet for France on the 30th of June, and as the first wave of invasion broke on Picardy, de la Motte returned to Scotland with a personal message from the French Queen. Anne of Brittany sent James a turquoise ring, imploring him, as her knight, to lead his army but three paces into England for her sake. When the news of the invasion of France reached him, James summoned his Council and demanded their support for war. But since he had promised Henry that he would not invade England without warning, Lyon King of Arms was warned to hold himself in readiness to convey the news of his intentions to the English King in France.

At the same time, Arran was instructed to support the Scottish invasion of England by bringing all the force of James's cherished navy to the assistance of France. It was the first of the few but fatal blunders which were to plunge Scotland into the dark. Until that point, James, genuinely averse from war against his brother-in-law, had contrived at least to maintain the appearance of patience, only to come to the end of it just before the crisis which was to make the most urgent demands of all. And the folly of entrusting Arran with the command of the fleet was evident before the Scottish army set off for the Border.

For Arran, commanded to set sail for France, incomprehensibly led the fleet towards Ireland instead, with the idea, perhaps, of creating another diversion by besieging Carrickfergus, but afterwards returned to Ayr with the loot. James, enraged by such disobedience, sent at last for old Sir Andrew Wood. But before Sir Andrew could reach Ayr, Arran had set sail again for an unknown destination. The fleet which had been James's pride and charge for the last ten years disappeared into the mists from which it never emerged.

So, at the end of August, James rode south as furiously as if he hoped so to outdistance the jangled echoes of a summer which had held nothing but disappointment, stupidity and ill omens. His only comfort was the loyalty of the great army which had answered his summons to the war which they had not sought, and now streamed behind him over Soutra Edge; as the Earl of Surrey's force also approached the Border from the south. Highlanders and Islanders were led by their chiefs; earls and barons brought their contingents; knights and burghers, bishops and abbots, clerks and artisans, pikemen from the Borders and archers from Lothian rode or trudged southwards. And behind them rolled the new artillery, commanded by James's master gunner, Robert Borthwick; each great gun drawn by its team of oxen and followed by the carts loaded with shot and powder, spades and mattocks for the mending of the roads, smiths' tools, even a crane for mounting the guns at the journey's end.

James had set out in such haste that even his standards and spare armour had to be galloped after him. But he could not outdistance the memories of the months which had seen the wreck of his last hopes of peace. The Queen's voice seemed still in his ears.

" My jewels . . . they were my father's legacy . . ." And afterwards, her frightened face, her querulous, desperate voice: " Oh, my lord, my lord, you do not know what Harry is like. He will never yield. . . ."

It was harder to remember his last sight of Bishop Elphinstone

at the Council Meeting held before the Army left for the Border.
The old man had toiled south from Aberdeen to make a last
appeal, to stand alone before the assembly now bent on the
English war. And they had shouted him down till his voice
broke, exhausted by the effort to be heard.

"My lord the King, I implore your Highness to think well
before you launch us into this disastrous war against King
Henry. . . ."

"No. . . ."

"Sit down. . . ."

"We are bound by our pledged word. . . ."

"Would you have us seem afraid? . . ."

"My lord the King, if we are defeated now, all the work of
your great reign will be undone. . . ."

"Defeated? Who talks of defeat? "

"Do not listen to him. . . ."

"He is but a crazed old man. . . ."

The tears had run down the Bishop's thin, colourless face. He
had raised his arms as if entreating Heaven to still the hubbub
about him, so that he might speak on. His lips had moved, but
no words could be heard for the noise of men beating on the table,
pounding with their feet, mocking him. Among them a few had
sat silent. Angus had been one. James's own son, Alexander, tense,
with clenched fists, another. The Bishop of Caithness pursed his
lips, as if making a precise calculation. Errol, the Constable,
looked grave. The Bishop of Dunblane shook his head and
sighed. . . . But they were outnumbered. Excitement set the
others shouting as a gale fans a blaze in the heather. Huntly,
Argyll, Montrose, Crawford, Lennox, Glencairn, Adam Hepburn,
rose with swords rasping from their scabbards. Bishop Elphinstone let his arms fall, and stood for a moment, looking at James
in helpless sorrow. Then, turning unsteadily, he shuffled from
the chamber, groping for the doorway like a man in darkness.
The moment when he stumbled, before his servants could reach
him, and did not seem to care whether he rose or not, was one
James could not forget, however fast he rode.

And that strange business at Linlithgow after the Council
meeting, troubled him, too. Who had been the stranger in the

blue gown who had accosted him in St. Michael's Kirk as he sat with the Queen and his household at his devotions? Lindsay and the Marischal maintained that when they tried to lay hands on him he vanished away. A good excuse, no doubt, for having been so slow-witted. Some crazed fellow, it must have been. There were always plenty about at times like these. " Sir King, my mother hath sent me . . ." What use was that, when no one knew either who he or his mother might be?

Who had suggested it might be a piece of play-acting devised by the Queen's English household, even by the Queen herself? Had they searched behind the choir stalls? They might have caught a glimpse of that blue gown, James had maintained, at the time. But now, as he rode through the rain, he found himself wondering. The great King David, patron of so many Scottish abbeys, had been the son of the sainted Margaret. . . . Malcolm Canmore's Queen.

But he had not listened either to saint or play-actor. How could he break his oath to defend France if England attacked her? The Pope would have granted him absolution, James knew, had he chosen to ask for it. But in anticipation of just such an offer, he and King Louis had undertaken that neither party should accept Papal absolution for betrayal of the other. James had done, he believed, everything possible to prevent a conflict with his young brother-in-law. But once Henry had been flattered and cajoled into taking part in the dismemberment of France, nothing could turn him. And nothing remained for James to do but honour, at whatever cost, his bond with the French King.

Before the end of August he had crossed the Border into Northumberland at the head of his army. The subsequent capture of Norham, Etal and Ford had been heartening, but without ultimate significance. James knew that he had yet to reckon with the Earl of Surrey, now approaching, for the third time, at a crisis in his life.

Confident still, incapable of believing himself outmatched, James sat his horse on Branxton Edge as a dreary, dripping dawn broke on the 9th of September, watching his men move from their overnight camp near Ford to take up their new positions. Smoke from the bothies fired by the Highlanders drifted below him. The

desolate heave of foothills rose between him and the Border, out-
topped on the far side of Tweed by the Scottish hills which his
army now faced. For the English outflanking movement had
made the first Scottish position, on Flodden Edge to the southward, useless. As Surrey's force, ignoring them, approached the
Border on the eastern side of the sinister, deep-flowing Till,
James had been obliged to keep pace with it on the western bank
or, by remaining, leave the way to Scotland open. To enter
Scotland had not, James maintained, been Surrey's intention
when he sent James his challenge, on the 4th, to a pitched battle
which would settle the issue there and then. For English supplies
were short, and Surrey did not care for the sort of guerrilla warfare
at which the Scots traditionally excelled.

Surrey, James argued, had counted that his challenge would
decoy the Scots down from their " position like a fortress " on
Flodden Edge, to meet him on the level plain to the south. But
when James had refused to be drawn, Surrey had wasted no time
in argument. Instead, he wheeled away, marching north along
the eastern bank of Till as it ran to join the Tweed at the Border.
The ford across Tweed was at Coldstream, to the west of Till, but
by crossing the Till at Twizel Bridge, near where it ran into
Tweed, Surrey could then either deploy between the Scots and
Scotland, or cross the Tweed itself, now that the outflanking of
the Scottish army had left Scotland defenceless.

So it had been at once obvious that the Scots must match
Surrey's northward march. And this they did, keeping pace with
him on the western bank of Till. But what would Surrey do next?
An anxious council of war had debated the question in the
Scottish camp the evening before. James still had no doubt.
" Surrey," he maintained, " has issued his challenge to meet us
by to-morrow at noon in a pitched battle. I have accepted it. He
will not fail." James fancied he knew the man, though it was
ten years now since their encounter among the bells and bonfires
of rejoicing Edinburgh. It was hard enough to think of that
friendly companion as his mortal enemy, but quite impossible to
believe that he would break his knightly word. Circumstances
might change, but men did not. It was unthinkable that Surrey
should issue a challenge and then sneak away.

"I do not like it," Angus rumbled. "First he seeks to persuade us to leave Flodden Edge in weather that makes a bog of every valley. Then he retreats from his own challenge. I advise you, my lord, to retreat likewise, and get to Scotland before him, if indeed we may."

The dour words, the dismal dusk, the personal rivalry and bitterness that the last news of Janet had set smarting afresh, the burden of responsibility which his final decision laid upon him, combined to provoke James beyond restraint. He whirled as furiously on Archibald Bell-the-Cat as he had done once before.

"My lord Angus, if you fear the issue of this conflict, I need ask nothing further of you. You are free to leave those who value their lives less highly and go home."

Angus stood his ground, like an old warhorse whose flanks have been too often galled to feel at once the shrewdness of another blow. In silence the divisional commanders looked from the old Earl to the King. Some knew and others guessed that more than a brief flare of temper had provoked James's outburst. All wondered what would come of it. Angus had been a fiery rebel once. But the former blaze had died to ashes now. When he spoke at last his voice was toneless, so that no one could tell whether his decision came from pride or—fear, as James had said.

"I thank you. I will go." Angus bowed stiffly, collected his helm and sword, and paused. "Yet so that you may be sure of the loyalty of my house I will instruct my sons to keep the Douglas forces on the field."

"So be it." James turned his back. "My lords, let us take it that Surrey will not fail us. His purpose is but to choose a fairer field. Ours is therefore to outwit him. My decision is to take up on Branxton Edge the position we held on Flodden, save only that since the enemy has swung round us we shall face home again." He paused, and when he spoke once more, his voice had lost its formality. Laying his hand on one man's arm, gripping another's shoulder for an instant, his smile, his warmth, drew them all closer. In that hour of destiny, they were less his subjects than his friends.

"Huntly with your Highlanders, Home with the Border contingent, you shall lead the vanguard up to Branxton Edge.

When we face Surrey's force, you shall hold the left flank, while I command the centre. Errol, Crawford, and Montrose, you shall fight with me at the heart of the battle. My lords of the Church, whose presence we rely on to hearten us rather than to dismay our enemies, I pray you to keep to the rear. . . ." He bowed to the Bishop of the Isles, the Abbots of Inchaffray and Kilwinning, the Dean of Glasgow and his own son, the Archbishop of St. Andrews. But such an idea was too much for Alexander to endure.

"My lord the King," he burst out, "it may be that I will not serve as well as a knight when jousting is in question, but I have here a mace, and a pretty notion of using it. I pray only that you will permit me to fight by your side."

Pride and joy lit James's face as he smiled at the son with whom he had always felt a special bond. "Aye, Alexander, fight by my side if you will. And you, Adam," he told Patrick's son, who stood quietly behind his elders, "bring your men also to hold the centre. Mathew "—he turned to the Earl of Lennox —" I can count on you and Archibald to hold the right wing fast. As to the artillery, Master Borthwick, mount your guns on the forward slope——"

"Surely, my lord the King, you wish me to command the bridges over Till and see that no man crosses alive? "

"If my lord of Surrey seeks to cross you must not hinder him. He has a tryst to keep, my friend."

"But, my lord, this is war, not tourney."

James checked him brusquely. "I believe that my lord of Surrey seeks to keep his tryst. If so he must meet with neither let nor hindrance. Shall I cut the challenger to pieces before he makes his challenge good? "

"He has already showed scant chivalry, sir, in decoying you from your position of strength."

"Then let us shame him," said James. "Since we refused to meet him on the plain, he has forced us to follow him northwards. But Branxton is as fair a height as Flodden Edge. Let us await him with patience. He will come."

But Master Borthwick, knowing little of chivalric tradition, cared less. To his mind the ford across Tweed lay so conveniently that once Surrey crossed the Till at Twizel he would be demented to miss the chance of invading Scotland unmolested, while its defenders, hopelessly outflanked, awaited him in Northumberland, trusting to some tarradiddle of a knightly challenge.

"My lord . . . my lord . . ." Borthwick babbled despairingly, "I swear that at such a time as this my lord of Surrey will think less of knighthood than of victory. If I destroy the bridges he cannot slip past us into Scotland——"

"No," said James. "And there's an end. I have told Surrey I shall await him on the ninth, at noon."

The day wore on dismally. Rain sluiced the sullen surge of hills, shutting the two great armies into a drenching isolation through which as they groped for each other, filtered the occasional complaint of a sheep or a peewit's forlorn cry. Eerily silent, the Till ran between its banks, raindrops hissing on its surface or plopping off the sad trees that overhung its banks. The Scottish army was early on the move, for James's conviction that Surrey meant to face them yet made him more anxious that his force should reach Branxton Edge and wheel into position at once for fear of being caught by their enemies while still strung out in line of march.

Lord Home, Scotland's Chamberlain, commanded the vanguard of Scottish Borderers, a contingent mounted on their wiry hill ponies, swift-moving and accustomed to the country. With him went the men of Eskdale and Liddesdale, Teviot and Ettrick, magnificent wildcat plundering fighters; the Douglas contingent, led by George Douglas, Master of Angus, and his brother William, as their father had promised before he left James's headquarters to cross the Border at Coldstream ford. Behind them, on foot, came Huntly and his Highlanders, then the first of the central division under Crawford and Montrose, then James himself, with his personal bodyguard and all the rest of the central contingent. Alexander, in steel bonnet and plate armour, was at his side, the other churchmen, armoured like knights, behind, followed by Adam Hepburn and the contingent from Hailes. Behind again, surging fearsomely through the smoke of their smouldering bothies, came the rest of the Highlanders and the men of the Isles under their chieftains, disdaining armour for their round targes and fearful swords, striding barefoot, commanded over all by Lennox and Argyll.

They made slow progress as they neared the Edge, for the ground was so spongy that marching men slithered, horses floundered and the oxen could hardly move the guns. But the advance guard had reached the far end of Branxton Edge, as far as they could tell, by noon, and as they wheeled into position, the main body struggled after them, so that Sir Thomas Howard, leading the English vanguard along the track from Twizel Bridge, which he had crossed as the Scots began the ascent in order to block their homeward road to Coldstream, found himself confronted by the entire Scottish force. With the English vanguard alone he dared not risk an encounter, but sent an urgent message to his father, the Earl of Surrey, at the head of the main body which should by now be crossing Twizel Bridge, waiting in the next trough of rolling ground till Surrey should have come to his aid.

The Scots, too, waited while the Highland rearguard joined the main body, completing the change from column of march into four divisions in line abreast. Dismounting, the knights sent most of the heavy horses to the rear, for the state of the ground made them useless, then closed up into the formation which Bruce had made glorious at Bannockburn, ranging their eighteen-foot spears against the enemy which now faced them, banners displayed and weapons at readiness, each force massed on the crest of a slight rise, with a shallow dip between.

It rained steadily as the Scottish guns were dragged into position. Then, at last, James ordered them to fire. But the powder was damp, the gun teams disgruntled, and Master Borthwick, affronted at not being allowed to use his chance before, now failed to take the range of the enemy gun emplacements with sufficient care, so that his fire was ineffective. The clumsy missiles fell short, injuring only their own men. But the enemy guns, finding the range, sent their great iron cannon-balls crashing into the Scottish batteries, killing Master Borthwick and some of his men, as Home sent his Borderers into action. Their nimble ponies, which could gallop where more heavily laden cavalry must be mired, charged the English right wing and bore it triumphantly backwards, yelling with triumph as the Englishmen broke and fled between the baggage wagons, round which the Borderers swarmed. As far as they were concerned, the battle was now over. Nothing their leaders could do would rally them to reinforce the main body. If they spared a thought from the plunder which was the traditional objective of all conquest, it must have been to suppose that the main body had also borne its opponents down.

But here the struggle was desperate. Kicking off their shoes to grip the slimy turf, the Scots advanced down the slope in close formation, confidently presenting the enemy with a wall of spears. At Bannockburn, such tactics had been triumphant. It was otherwise now. For down the opposing slope the main body of their enemies advanced to meet them, armed with eight-foot bills, the terrible partisans which experience had evolved to beat the hedgehog of spears. The English bill combined a spear-point with an axe-head which could be swung against the shafts of the Scottish spears, shearing their heads like ears of wheat, leaving the Scots with headless staves, as useless as the straw. Tossing them aside, the Scots drew swords and struggled on; slipping, falling, hurling themselves against the relentless surge of the harvesting English bill. Locked in a murderous grapple they neither flinched nor broke, as the thunderous assault on steel cap and plumed helm, leather jack and plate of proof, sent the echoes rolling to the horizon hills.

On the right Lennox and Argyll's men charged, yelling, into a deadly hail of fire from the archers of the English left, and dropped, lightly armed as they were, in swathes. First Lennox, then Argyll went down, and their avenging followers surged over their bodies, only to fall in their scores, their hundreds, as the deadly fire withered them like frost. Then, drawing their swords, the English completed the destruction with a charge which took them through the scattered remnants of the bewildered Highlanders to the summit of Branxton Edge. There, still under control, they re-formed and prepared to throw their decisive weight into the central battle which still hung in the balance below.

As the sullen autumn afternoon waned towards evening, there was no Scottish panic, even when the magnitude of the disaster began to be apparent. As the leaders, fighting with their men, went down, the survivors closed the gaps, too breathless to shout, their defiance evident only in the fearful endurance of their blows the hissing intake of their breath sounding above the groans of stricken men, the English bills crashing against shield or helm in one continuous thunder-roll. Errol, Scotland's Constable, swinging a great sword, had his helm struck from his head, and the next swing of the Yorkshireman's bill split his skull. James, dismounted like the rest, flailed his way towards the banner of the Earl of Surrey, which swayed elusively beyond the barrier of bloodstained armour and swirling bills. In this most desperate hour he was gay again, as his lifetime's burden of trouble and sorrow fell from him, and the sheer sacrificial valour with which he now offered his life was permitted, it seemed, both to heal and shrive. As he struck, he rallied those about him, laughing between gasps.

"Well ... smitten, my lord Bishop. You handle your weapon as well as ... ever you swung censer. There ... and there ... and ... there ..." His blows were deadly, his stance as light as if he were once more in the lists. Thrusting at the whites of a knight's eyes through his visor bars, swinging his sword to send a man crashing, jabbing it between the joints of plate armour, he carved his way towards Surrey, while Crawford, Athol, and Morton sought to cover his desperate assault. Master John Murray, who had exchanged his quills and parchments for sword and steel cap, seemed to see, in an anguish of love, the sunlit kitchen where his wife stood smiling. Then, with blood gushing from his mouth, he fell. De la Motte, the French Ambassador, carving his way through the hubbub round the Scottish King, thanked heaven at least that because all James's personal bodyguard wore the royal device that day, the English could not know which blow struck at Scotland's heart. Then he, too, sagged, gasping, into the blood-churned mud, dying for France in the Scottish battle that he had helped to bring about.

And still the rain beat down; on muddy, trampled banners, battered helms, and reeling men. Little by little it darkened. And still the massacred Scottish centre stood, till Adam Hepburn, forcing his way after the King, felt the first shock of the English left wing, re-formed after the defeat of the Scottish right, strike them in the rear. Yelling to his men to face about, he fought on, sickeningly aware that they were now surrounded. Then Huntly fell, trying to break the stranglehold, and Adam after him, with Morton, husband of James's daughter, Catherine.

But James was unaware of the new danger. His sole objective still eluded him, eerie as a marshlight at dusk. Faint now with loss of blood from an arrow wound in the charge which had scarcely seemed to matter at the time, he thrashed on, his arms leaden, his breathing anguished, towards Surrey's banner, scarcely visible now in the gloom. His sword was a load beyond his strength. Blood blinded him. He never saw the fierce gesture of the man before him as he swung his bill high. Once more . . . With his remaining strength, James lunged and thrust. The English bill crashed down. A great blaze filled his world, as Alexander, stepping across his father's body, swung his mace like a crazed creature, his helm dented and useless as he jerked it off. Mud and blood sprayed upwards, plastering the tears on his face as he, too, fell.

Dusk changed to darkness. But the remnants of the Scottish central division were still unbroken, in the midst of men so weary that they could scarcely stand. The hail of blows slackened at last, as the exhausted attackers drew back, unable to tell their enemies from their friends. Little groups staggered away into the darkness, dropped where they stood, or dragged themselves painfully along on hands and knees. The Scots who still lived drew long, anguished breaths, leaning on their swords till they could gather strength enough also to creep away.

It was not till morning that Surrey realised the magnitude either of his victory or the price the Scots had claimed. For his own great force had suffered so severely that he dared not cross the Border to follow the remnants of the Scottish army home.

CHAPTER TWENTY-FOUR

" *Kyrie eleison . . . Christe eleison . . .*"

IN Dunblane Cathedral the voices of the choristers lingered on the still air and the candle-flames raised lambent finger-tips of intercession for Margaret Drummond, who had been the King's love.

" Lord, have mercy . . ."

Up and down Scotland bells tolled and old men hirpled after their weapons, women slammed cottage doors and snatched up their children as the news of Flodden swept past them on the weeping wind. Along the Cheviots bale fires blazed as the men of the Border division which had suffered least prepared to defend the frontier from the expected attack which did not come.

In Edinburgh the Town Council sternly exhorted the folk huddled about the Mercat Cross: ". . . forasmeikle as there is a great rumour lately risen, touching our Sovereign Lord and his army, of which we understand there is no verity as yet, wherefore we charge strictly and command, in our said Sovereign Lord the King's name, and in that of the Presidents for the Provost and Bailies within this burgh, that all manner of persons, neighbours within the same, have ready their arms of defence and weapons for war, and appear therewith before the said Presidents at the tolling of the common bell. . . . And we also charge that all women, and especially vagabonds, that they pass to their labours, and be not seen upon the street clamouring and crying under the pain of banishing their persons without favour; and that the other women of better sort pass to the Kirk and pray. . . ."

" *Kyrie eleison . . . Christe eleison . . .*"

On the battlefield the victors were busy; piling the weapons, searching for valuables, counting the dead. From the terrible shambles they brought the bodies of Alexander, Archbishop of St. Andrews, the Bishop of the Isles, the Abbots of Kilwinning and Inchaffray; twelve earls, fourteen lords, with over ten thousand others, gentle and simple, besides. The king himself, they believed, lay with them, and they disputed long over half a dozen terribly disfigured bodies, all bearing shreds of the royal device. But whether the body they took to embalm and convey southwards was that of James, no man, then or later, ever certainly knew.

In the Palace of Linlithgow Master Doig was doing his best to calm the frantic inquiries of the ladies who clamoured about him, sobbing and clasping their hands as they speculated on the bereavement of their sweet Queen. Every now and then they glanced over their shoulders to where she sat, weeping, yet listening to the incoherent consolation offered by Sir Archibald Douglas, the splendidly handsome grandson of the Earl of Angus who, like herself, was in his twenty-fifth year, and had been kept by other duties from the field of Flodden. Genuinely shocked as he was by the disaster, young Archibald could not quite keep from thinking that with his father's death the broad Border lands in Douglasdale, Jedburgh Forest, and elsewhere, were now his. Presently his grandfather's death was to make him Earl of Angus, and before another year had passed he was to marry the Queen.

" Alas, he was ever the kinder and better to me with every day that passed," she sighed. " And—and now I shall . . . never . . . have my jewels. . . ."

From every belfry in Aberdeen bells were tolling, tolling. Bishop Elphinstone sat in his high-backed chair, motionless, almost lifeless, it seemed, as he had sat ever since they brought him the news. Though he had known, in the way that those whose life is not lived merely in terms of time and space sometimes know things, that the conflict he had done everything in his power to prevent would bring some such tragedy, the knowledge could not even blunt the edge of the blow he seemed to have received, full on the heart. James . . . the lad he had guided, worked with, loved . . . dead with the chiefs of almost every great family in the kingdom and ten thousand of his people of every degree. . . . It was a cataclysm to sear the brain, so that the heart's agony was unmitigated by any satisfaction at having cried aloud against the course of action that led to it, and gone unheard.

The Bishop stirred at last, rising with the unco-ordinated,

fluttering movements of a very old man. As his secretary hurried forward, the grey lips seemed to move.

"I ask your pardon, my lord Bishop. I did not quite . . ."

But the Bishop shook his head. He had not known that he had spoken the words of long-dead King Saul aloud as he mourned for the young man who had been as dear as Absalom.

"Help me to my oratory," he said.

"*Kyrie eleison . . . Christe eleison . . .*"

Out across Scotland the bells bore the sorrow of the nation to every castle and mansion, street and wynd, farmplace, cottage and bothy, from the Border to the Isles. But while they mourned, they made ready. Everywhere defences were strengthened, blades ground to a keener edge. On the outskirts of Edinburgh old men and boys toiled to lay the stones that the women bore in their aprons to the Flodden Wall that was rising round the unprotected suburbs. And as they worked, they heartened each other, after the manner of folk, with the forlorn hope that some mistake had been made, that their King might perhaps still live.

"I've heard tell they never clapped eyes on the King's body. . . . Not for sure . . ."

"Mebbe he's no' deid. . . ."

"Mebbe . . ."

"Never a word of yon iron belt round the body of him they took awa'."

"It's no him, then. He aye wore it. Ma sister's man heard it frae Master Doig himsel'."

"They say folk hae seen him. . . ."

"Aye, crossing Tweed. . . ."

"He's been seen in Kelso. . . ."

"Na, he's gone on pilgrimage to the Holy Land, like he said. . . ."

"He'll come back. . . ."

"Come back . . ."

"Come back again. . . ."

". . . Back again . . ."

In the Cathedral of Dunblane the candle-flames' lambent finger-tips seemed to plead not only for Margaret Drummond but for James, who had been so vainglorious and so foolish, yet so dearly loved. And not only for James, but for all those others whom so many women mourned, up and down Scotland, who lay, as he perhaps lay also, in an unmarked grave. James, who had loved splendour and beauty, had had but little of either at the end. But the voices of his people gathered up his love and his kindliness, his laughter and zest, his delight in the children he had cared for at Stirling, his pleasure in strange beasts from across the seas, in great fierce horses and gracious ships, murmuring his requiem as they laid them before the everlasting mercy:

" He praised my strawberries. . . ."

" He thanked me for my butter. . . ."

" I was but a bairn that he took by the hand. . . ."

" He listened to my songs. . . ."

" I was an auld, dune wife. He kissed me. . . ."

" Heaven bless your Highness. . . ."

And the voices of the choristers, rising heavenwards, seemed to float on the still air.

" *Kyrie eleison* . . ."

THE END

Some Books Consulted

ACCOUNTS OF LORD HIGH TREASURER OF SCOTLAND.
Vol. I., 1473-1498; Vol. II, 1500-1504; Vol. III, 1506-1507;
Vol. IV, 1507-1513.

HISTORY OF MAGIC AND EXPERIMENTAL SCIENCE. Lynn
Thorndike. Vols. III and IV. Columbia University Press.

THE HERMETIC MUSEUM. Vols. I and II. Ed. A. E. Waite
Elliot.

LETTERS AND PAPERS OF RICHARD III AND HENRY VII.
2 Vols. Ed. James Gairdner. Longmans Green Ltd.

COLLECTANEA. Leyland. Vol. IV. Benjamin White in Fleet
Street. 1774.

MATERIALS TOWARDS A HISTORY OF WITCHCRAFT. H.
C. Lea. Ed. A. C. Howland. University of Pennsylvania Press.

LIVES OF THE BISHOPS OF ABERDEEN AND MURTHLAC.
Hector Boece. Aberdeen.

THE WORKS OF SIR THOMAS MALORY (based on Winchester
MS. discovered 1934). Ed. by E. Vinaver. Oxford Clarendon
Press.

LE MORTE D'ARTHUR. Ed. A. W. Pollard. Cape and Medici
Soc.

SCOTTISH LITERATURE TO 1714. Agnes Mure Mackenzie.
Maclehose.

THE RISE OF THE STEWARTS. Agnes Mure Mackenzie.
Maclehose.

THE POEMS OF WILLIAM DUNBAR. Ed. W. Mckay Mackenzie. Porpoise Press.

THE EDINBURGH BOOK OF SCOTTISH VERSE. Ed. Mac-
Neile Dixon   Pub. Meiklejohn & Holden.

THE BATTLE OF FLODDEN. Lieut.-Col. the Hon. Fitzwilliam
Elliot. Pub. Andrew Elliot.

THE MURRAYS OF ELIBANK. Lieut.-Col. the Hon. Arthur C.
Murray. Pub. Douglas & Foulis.

LIFE OF JAMES IV. I. A. Taylor. Hutchinson.

THE DAYS OF JAMES IV. Ed. G. Gregory Smith.

WITCHCRAFT. Charles Williams. Faber & Faber.

STUDIES IN THE HISTORY AND DEVELOPMENT OF THE
UNIVERSITY OF ABERDEEN. Ed. P. J. Anderson, M.A.,
LL.B.

THE DOUGLAS BOOK. 4 vols. Ed. Wm. Fraser.

HISTORY OF SCOTLAND. Patrick Fraser Tytler. Tait. Vol. IV.

EARLY TRAVELLERS IN SCOTLAND. Hume Brown.